"'THERE SHE IS, YONDER,' HE ANSWERED."—Page 5.
Frontispiece.

THE COPSFORD MYSTERY

OR

IS HE THE MAN?

THE COPSFORD MYSTERY

OR

IS HE THE MAN?

BY

W. CLARK RUSSELL

Author of "An Ocean Free Lance," "The Wreck of the Grosvenor,"
"The Convict Ship," etc., etc.

ILLUSTRATIONS BY A. BURNHAM SHUTE AND OTHERS

G R O S S E T & D U N L A P
PUBLISHERS : : NEW YORK

INTRODUCTORY

HOW MR. CLARK RUSSELL WRITES

In the first place Clark Russell writes what he knows, and only what he knows. He has himself been a sailor. In order to write about the sea, a man must have gone to sea as a sailor, for a ship is a very perilous thing to touch. Dana conclusively proves this in his "Two Years Before the Mast," which Clark Russell claims as the only real sea-book in the language, in the sense of being written out of sure suffering and bitter experience. But then it is no romance. It is difficult enough to sail a real ship, but to sail "a painted ship upon a painted ocean," to manœuvre a full-rigged vessel on paper, this indeed takes some doing. But Mr. Clark Russell has done it, is always doing it; indeed, he is the only novelist of the sea, who, since the death of Dana, strictly confines himself to doing business in deep waters. Upon the wall of the bedroom which I occupied while upon a visit to him a few weeks ago there hangs a discharge note, one of a primitive sort bearing date 1859. It is the discharge note that young Russell received when he left the *Duncan Dunbar*, and the only one of his discharge notes he has preserved. In this paper is distinctly stated that his "character for ability in whatever capacity" was "very good." Here then is official testimony to his knowledge of the duties of a seaman's life, and consequently to his ability to write accurately upon what he knows from actual experience.

In person he is a slight, middle-sized man, with a keen,

pleasant, sailor-like face, great frankness of manner, and a capacity for clean-cut, forcible expression which I have never heard excelled—the result possibly of between six and seven years of hard seafaring experience, a man of admirable spirit and inexhaustible store of anecdote. Forced by rheumatism to keep much upon his sofa, he dictates all his novels, finding indeed that he can work better so than if he were to pen them with his own hand. "I close my eyes, I realize intensely the whole scene, I see it as in a magic-lantern, I can dramatize the whole thing," said he to me when I questioned him upon his method of work. "My mind," continued he, "is full of memories of the sea; I close my eyes and they crowd thick upon me ready for transference to paper and thus I can vividly render a scene upon a ship's deck. The sunlight slipping to and fro between the shadows, a flash of sunset off the wet oil-skins of the sailors, with a mountain of white water roaring in thunder off the bow. There is a group on deck, hard-featured, weather-beaten, gnarled old faces and figures; their actions, their very words, the expression of each man's face rises to my memory as I sit here and dictate the story."

But it is not only memory with Clark Russell. He never puts pen to paper till all is carefully planned and mapped out. "The play is finished," Racine used to say before ever a word was written of it. And so with this novelist of the sea. Experienced as I am in the methods of writers upon every kind of subject,—novelists, scientists, dramatists, theologians, journalists, politicians—yet I know of none who go so systematically, I may say so interestingly, to work as Mr. Clark Russell. Each thrilling story is first placed in skeleton within the pages of a large note-book, just as a conscientious artist draws the naked figure and then clothes it in the garb of the period he has chosen.

There is first a general plot of the story, the dates of which are most accurately thought out; then come the *dramatis personæ*, the name of the vessel, the number and the names of the crew, the passengers, with their general characteristics limned out. "I generally choose some one I have observed with attention, who acts as a lay figure right through, and so I do not lose his personality," explained Mr. Clark Russell, as "for instance, 'Sir Mortimer Otway, bald, bright red face, sixty.' I know a man who exactly answers to this description. 'Captain Burke, pointed beard, sharp, bright,' and so on with the whole *personnel*. With regard to dialogue I find a difficulty in creating a verisimilitude for my sailors. I cannot make them swear, and a sailor, I am sorry to say, is nothing if he doesn't swear. They *must* swear, so I have tried to invent a few harmless phrases, such as these which I have jotted down," and Mr. Russell showed me as he spoke the following list of vigorous declamations: "CALLING NAMES.—You faggot! You hound of hounds! It's bruisily cold! By the great anchor! Woundy glad!"

Then the ship itself; it is not only exactly described—its tonnage, its cargo, its berthing, but there are numerous sketches of it which place it before Mr. Russell's eyes exactly as he imagines it, and so he is enabled to pace the deck, to go below, to dine with the captain aft, to go for-'ard to the men's mess, almost as though he were actually on board the ship itself. There are in addition references to well-known books of travel in which well-authenticated incidents are recorded, to official journals, to anything in fact that may be of use to him in the writing of what many an untravelled critic regards as an impossible occurrence, and which nevertheless has actually taken place. Here, for instance, are some notes I came across: "Sun and moon shining at once, January (Wilkes, 1,242)." "A horrible creature drags a man under water off the island." "Horrible valley of death strewn with skeletons." "Remarkable instance of a cotton-loaded ship from New York full of fire and yet arriving home." To these and a score of like passages from a voluminous nautical literature the references are appended.

"In the cruise of the *Beagle* it is told that an old seaman

grew misanthropic and lived alone in a cave in the Gala·
pagos. He was taken away by force by an old shipmate,
a whaler. Good idea to describe what passed in conversa·
tion between the two men, etc."

And again, no *locale* is ever imaginary in Mr. Clark Russell's books. "Even in writing of the most minute island,"
he said to me, "I always have an Admiralty chart of that
island at my side so that I may be exact in my bearings,
soundings, and the rest of it. I have only once imagined
an island, and that was in 'The Golden Hope.'" No situation in which he places his ships or his crews, dreadful
and unimaginable as some of them appear to the humdrum
stop-at-home, is ever an impossible one. For instance, in
his story, "List, ye Landsman," the notion that a ship could
be found in a cave with her masts telescoped so as to hold
her upright on her keel, the mast-head pressing against the
roof, has been ridiculed, but he found such a situation for
a ship in the *Nautical Magazine* for 1878. "The doomed
ship began to drag. As they drifted in they saw before
them a monster cavern into which slowly but surely they
were driven by the force of the westerly gale before which
they had been so recently speeding. At first there was
room for their mastheads to rise and fall with the swell clear
of the roof of the cavern, but gradually the roof became
lower, the masts came in contact with it, and were driven
through the bottom."

"Nelson never wrote a truer thing," explained Mr. Clark
Russell, showing me at the same time an imaginary sketch
of the incident which he had made in his note-book for his
own guidance, than "that at sea nothing is impossible and
nothing is improbable. Do you remember how in the 'Ocean
Tragedy,' I describe a vessel, long sunk, thrown up by a sub-
marine earthquake, upon which the skeletons of people are
discovered in the very attitude they were in when the vessel
sank? A few days ago (May 20th) I received the enclosed
cutting from a gentleman living at Ottawa, Canada." That
cutting was from a paper dated March, 1893. This slip Mr.

Clark Russell placed in my hand, and it ran, in effect, as follows: "There was a violent upheaval of the sea, about two miles distant from the Faroe Islands where the *Elsa Andersen* rode at anchor. When the alarm caused by this sudden sea had subsided, there was seen about a mile off a wreck which had not been there before the upheaval of the bottom of the sea. A boat-load of sailors was therefore despatched at once to this vessel, a green and ancient hulk, in the cabin of which, when the water had been all pumped out, were discovered three skeletons, two of them being men and the other a woman, this last being a person of gigantic build, and in life of nearly seven feet in height. About the neck of one of the male skeletons was a chain of gold, to which was attached a silver crucifix." Mr. Clark Russell is always fascinated by the weird and the beautiful in combination. "Imagine," said he, as he lay back in his chair, "a schooner sunk with all sail set, and several bodies on board under the hatches. You look over your ship's side, and you see this beautiful and yet dreadful image, perfect in the translucent water, with all its suggestion of the sleeping dead—death indeed giving all significance to the object you are looking at—and how beautiful are the prismatic hues of the fish gleaming between the masts! I have sometimes thought of writing a story based on De Quincey's idea —a visit to the submerged city Savannah La Mer, and how strange would be the walking through those silent streets, clothed of course in the necessary apparatus!"

"And may I ask you, Mr. Russell," said I a little later on, "what led you to the writing of your different stories?"

"I hardly know," he slowly replied. 'John Houldsworth' was the first sea book I ever wrote. I used to chat a great deal with an old fellow on the pier-head at Ramsgate, and the idea struck me how well I might ransack my own memories of the sea, and especially how useful it might be if I could place before the public something of the hardships, the privations, the perils of the merchant sailor. No one knows or cares about him. It was much the same with 'The

Wreck of the Grosvenor.' I saw a ship's company brought ashore once, and charged with mutiny. They proved conclusively that they had been very shamefully treated in the matter of food, nevertheless they were sentenced to various terms of imprisonment. And so," he added with a smile, "I wrecked the *Grosvenor*. The idea of 'The Sea Queen' I gained from an account I once read of the wife of a captain who took the wheel and steered the ship while the people were all down with fever, and her husband worked in the engine-room. It struck me as being one of those splendid instances of obscure heroism of which the sea is so often witness.

"My notion in writing 'The Phantom Ship' was to see if I couldn't prove that the 'Phantom Ship' so called was a material fabric worked by a crew answering to W. B. Scott's lines—

> "There was obstruction in their looks, not death,
> But an obstruction of the vivid soul:
> They lived, yet lived not.'

"Now that struck me as being very fine, very suggestive. Marryat in his 'Phantom Ship' makes the accursed structure intangible in one chapter—an essence, a cloud which passes through a vessel without hurting her; while in the next chapter she is solid enough to receive a visit from Vanderdecken's son, and in the end this absurd compound of the material and the visionary goes to pieces with a mighty crash of parting timbers. Poor Marryat missed the point of this beautiful legend. He was more at home with old Chucks the bo's'n than with the impious Dutchman.

"I have recently written 'The Convict Ship' and 'The Emigrant Ship,' and now my friend General Patrick Maxwell, the well-known translator of Schiller, has suggested to me a most interesting idea—that I should write 'The Slave Ship,' and so make the series complete. With regard to my 'Convict Ship' I must tell you a most curious coincidence. I had been maturing the story for six months, and collecting material, and indeed I had already written the first chapter, when I received a letter one morning from Mr. W. S. Gilbert, with whom I am not so fortunate as to be personally acquainted. He wrote asking me why I didn't turn my attention to 'The Convict Ship,' and suggesting that the sole difficulty would lie in the direction of a heroine. It was a very curious coincidence indeed." A naval officer at Mr. Clark Russell's table told how he was junior lieutenant aboard H. M. S. *Medea* when she brought the Koh-i-noor to England. The stone was placed in charge of two military officers, each of whom wore a key of the casket round his neck. The casket was hidden in the vessel. No man saving the two military officers knew where it was. Upon this he based his story entitled, "The Major's Commission."

"You go in very much for descriptive detail," said I. "I sometimes wonder how far such minutiæ is appreciated by the uninitiated public." "Ah," replied my host, "that is impossible to say. A man must have been at sea to appreciate all the little delicate shades and lights which go to the making of a perfect picture. Everything counts in the description; nothing is common or unclean for the sea novelist; the smallest touch of nature gives life to the picture. Take for instance a dead calm and the vessel rolling slowly; the burnished sea pale blue under a white-hot sky sloping into the dim distance, with a long-drawn swell running out in the stagnant recesses like a sigh with a response aloft in a drowsy beat of canvas. Then the image of the ship underneath, the inverted picture trembling into the depths, leaking off the ship, as it were, in colors, with your own face looking full up at you out of the wet blue back of a shark. But only a connoisseur can really appreciate all these delicacies—the occasional kick of the wheel, the rattle of the steering gear, the moaning gurgle under the stern— then a sort of slumbering atmosphere fore and aft, the clank of the spun-yarn winch in the languid air, the smell of paint arises hot, the jibboom seems to revolve like a cork·

screw into space. These and the like niceties are witnessed by the sea-artist, but are not appreciated, however finely finished, by the land-going reader, simply because they are utterly unintelligible. And then again there is the ma- nœuvring of a ship upon the water. The difficulty in writing about the sea does not consist in mere descriptions of clouds and waves, and sunsets; it is a far greater difficulty to sail the ship itself upon paper. Take for instance a ship which is going along under all plain sail, wind on her quarter. It comes on black to windward, with an ugly look in the run of the seas. Now comes the question of shortening canvas. What sail will a landsman who only knows the sea from a beach-combing point of view take in? How would he begin? What sheet, what halyard, will he start first? I might begin by hauling down the flying jib, and clewing up the main-royal, but would not that be wrong? Why of course it would, while your fore and mizzen-royals are still set. But it is all these details in which a sea-novelist must be perfect." An incident strikingly similar to some of those he so graphically relates in his stories once befell Mr. Clark Russell himself. It might easily have become a tragedy. Many years ago, when serving on board the old *Hugomont*, he was seated at supper one evening with the third and fourth mate in the starboard division of the deck-house, the port being occupied by the apprentices. It was a dead calm in the Indian Ocean, and the vessel was bound for Calcutta. Clark Russell, then a mere lad of fifteen years, happened to make some remark which elicited a scowling look from the third mate. Shortly afterward the fourth mate went on deck. In a moment the third mate sprang to his feet, closed the door, took off his belt and seized the boy by his throat. "Now," he said, "you young brute, I'll do for you." "He ran me backward," said Mr. Clark Russell, as he told me the story, "but did not strike me, and I fell on my back, which I thought would break under the strain, beneath a shelf on which were kept knives, forks, plates, etc. The burly fellow dropping his belt reached for a

black-handled table-knife, with which he menaced me. I
saw that he was insane, and I felt that my sole chance lay
in keeping perfectly motionless and silent. After a few
minutes he rose, threw the knife on to the floor, and walked
out, talking to himself, and I immediately went to Thomas,
the chief officer—a brother, by-the-bye," added Mr. Clark
Russell, "of Ap Thomas, the Queen's harpist. I wonder
if he could tell me where his brother is—as good a chap as
ever walked—and reported the circumstance to him. Well,
to cut a long story short, he was locked up in the cuddy,
and I can see him now as I gazed through the brass-barred
window, secured to his bunk and watched by two powerful
seamen. He got better before we reached Calcutta, but it
was a precious close shave for my life, I can tell you."

In speaking of style Mr. Clark Russell informed me that
he dislikes to recur to his earlier works, as he encounters so
much that needs revision and condensation. The only piece
of writing that ever gives him any satisfaction is the ac-
companying passage, which he was good enough to read to
me from a proof he was correcting of his new novel, "The
Emigrant Ship," now running in *The People*.

"When the Spanish vessel had diminished into a small
square of faint crimson light right astern, with the dark sea
ridging between and the line of the horizon faint and doubtful as mist in the west where the sky was barred with
streaks, like gashes of rusty blood-red light, the dark scud
out of the south pouring through the dying radiance like so
much smoke, the weight went out of the wind on a sudden,
in a dead drop, and aloft the collapsed and startled sails beat
out the thunder of twenty small guns, while in that strange
pause the briskness left the surge, and it ran softly, with a
sulky lift of the sea to right and left that made one think
of a sullen pout of preparation for a whipping."

It is descriptions such as these that have opened the eyes
of Englishmen to the wonder and the beauty of the sea.
Few there are whose joy in a sea voyage is not enhanced
tenfold by the memory of one of these beautiful works of

Clark Russell's. It is no less a critic than Sir Edwin Arnold who advises the reading upon a long voyage of "one of the noble sea-poems of Mr. Clark Russell—of which he has given so many and such admirable examples to his time— and while you hang over his perfect pages of manly adventure and maritime romance, you shall have the great sea interpreted to you by one of the very few who know its mysteries and its majesties; you shall enjoy the subtlest of all intellectual delights—that is to say, the translation of Nature into a living universe by the magic of genius; and you shall be gratefully aware that England, to whom the ocean belongs, has found a Marryat of the Red Ensign in these latter days to keep up in all our hearts the love which we must never lose for the 'Great Green Mother.' "

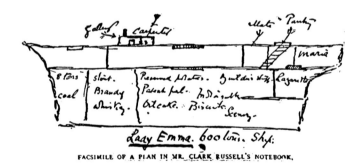

FACSIMILE OF A PLAN IN MR. CLARK RUSSELL'S NOTEBOOK.

LIST OF ILLUSTRATIONS

THE COPSFORD MYSTERY

Part One

THE COLONEL'S STORY

I

NOT to diminish the apparent improbability of this narrative, but to prove my own veracity in my relation of the share I took in it, I have called upon one of the actors to furnish me with her own experiences of what she saw and did. By her respectable testimony, if I do not persuade others, I may at least convince myself that the past, to which I recur, is not the distempered dream which, since I became old and infirm, I have been often disposed to consider it.

For the misfortunes that befell me and my child I have myself only to blame. I was guilty of two deplorable errors, both arising from a want of moral strength and courage. But the very sensibility which was at the root of the misfortunes I have had to lament, should supply a sufficient guarantee that my sufferings have abundantly expiated my irremediable mistakes.

Let this brief avowal suffice.

In the summer of the year 18—, my daughter Phœbe having recovered from a slight indisposition, I was advised by Dr. Redcliff to remove her for a few weeks to the seaside; and chose Broadstairs, in those days a town little troubled by visitors. I hired some rooms in the Albion Hotel, and

1

had soon the gratification of witnessing a great improvement in my daughter's health. She regained her old looks, her old vivacity of spirits, and within a fortnight of our arrival was strong enough to take an oar in a boat. Rowing soon became her favorite pastime, and she grew before long so expert at the oars as to be able to row a boat by herself. I mention this trivial matter to prepare the way for the circumstance I shall presently relate.

Phœbe was then twenty years old: in many respects resembling her mother, whom I had lost by death but three years before. She was dark, with a small, handsome, decided face; her hair was black and abundant, and she wore it with much grace, anticipating a later fashion: that is, in plaited coils, a mode that admirably suited the Greek cast of her features. Her nose was straight, her eyebrows narrow but very black, and so arched as to give her face, in repose, a prevailing expression of pretty surprise. Her mouth was small, the under-lip full, her complexion color less, but delicate and healthy; her forehead low and square, and her chin and throat beautiful in their outlines. Her height was above the middle stature; but she wore her dresses long, and suggested a more commanding presence when she walked than she possessed. Her character we shall gather as we progress.

Broadstairs fits the white cliff on which it stands with a snug air of design, and from the sea satisfies the eye with an aspect of rough and sober completeness. The rude, well-tarred pier, stumpy and solid, with the transparent breakers rattling the shingle under the creviced flooring, is a finishing detail of which the omission would leave a blank in the salt sentiment of the place. A simplicity strangely primitive and strictly maritime seems somehow to keep the town fresh as the breezes which sweep through its little ancient archway and rattle the windows of the cheery Frigate Inn; and this characteristic defies the eliminating magic of the trowel, for the sense of it is as strong to-day as it was years ago; when much overgrown matter had no being, and the delightful traditions of the smugglers—the dark nights, the subtle lugger, the mystified coast guard—lay all unencumbered to tax-hating imaginations by the bricks and mortar which now vex, and in some measure defy, them.

Phœbe did ample justice to the place by taking the best pleasure it offered. My faith was pinned to the dry land. The sands brought me to as close an acquaintance with the sea as I cared about; and there, hard by the cliff, I would sit, book in hand, a pocket-telescope by my side, idly speculating on the missions of the ships that went and came, or watching the little children paddling, bare-legged, in the sea, while Phœbe rowed herself from point to point in a boat, alone, feathering her oars like any young waterman, and often exciting the comments of loungers who, like myself, could find no easier diversion than staring.

One morning I was at the end of the little pier, sheltered from the sun by an awning. The sea was glassy, and crept, as softly as the touch of a blind man's fingers, up and down the beach, and around the projecting rocks near the pier. Great clouds, glorious to behold, white as wool with an edging of silver, and darkening their extremities to the richest cream-color when they drew away from the sun, hung over the polished deep. The sunshine made the little bay that gapes before the town festive with light, spangling the dry white sand near the cliffs, and deepening the hue of the brown-ribbed shore over which the water had washed, and giving relief to the spots of color lent to the scene by the apparel of the women and children on the beach by the vivid brightening of the chalk cliffs.

Phœbe was rowing as usual in one of the wherries belonging to the place. She had gone some distance in an easterly direction and was now returning with a fair tide. She passed the pier at a distance of a hundred yards, and it was a sight worthy of any man's admiration to remark the wonderfully graceful inclination of her form, her finely modelled bust, as she brought her firm, small white hands up to it. The keen stem of the wherry chipped the blue water into a spout of foam, and the oars flashed.

The great, stooping clouds overhead, the background of many-shadowed water, speckled with white sails, and this near boat, with its faultless figure of a girl impelling it for-

ward, made a picture worth converting into a **permanent**
memory.

"What a charming woman! How admirably she rows!
Pray, sir, can you tell me who she is?" exclaimed a voice
at my side.

I turned and saw a young man staring at the boat through
a field-glass.

"She is my daughter," I answered.

"I really beg your pardon," he said, covering his embarrassment with a well-bred bow and a pleasant smile. "I
trust you will consider my question as a piece of mental admiration unconsciously expressed aloud rather than as a
direct interrogatory."

"Then," said I, "I must esteem myself the more flattered.
My daughter certainly does use her oars dexterously, but I
wish she would take a boatman with her when she goes on
the water."

"I think she would act wisely in doing so. You will
allow me to repeat my apology for my heedless question."

He raised his hat and walked away. He could have done
no more nor less. What intrusion there was had been on
his side; he had acted properly in withdrawing, and his perception of fitness pleased me, and, I thought, showed him
a gentleman. By such small circumstances are we prejudiced in life. I met him again in the afternoon, when I
was with Phœbe. He took no notice of either of us; but I
watched him with a friendly eye, and when, my memory
having been freshened by the sight of him, I had mentioned
the incident of the morning to my daughter, I noticed that
she looked in the direction where he had come to a stand by
the rail upon the cliff, and turned her eyes askant upon me
with a half-smile of gratification in them.

A few days after this, I was seated at the window of my
sitting-room in the hotel, killing the hour before dinner
with a novel. The afternoon was very sultry; few persons
were to be seen; the sun poured upon the chalk, and filled
the air to a height of some feet with a haze, through which
objects were magnified and distorted, as though watched
through a medium of steam. Phœbe as usual was rowing,

but the hotel stood back, and the pier and the sea about it were hidden from me by the cliffs.

Interested as I was by my book, I was presently sensible of a gathering and ominous stillness in the air, coupled with an increase of heat, of which the effect upon the skin was to make it clammy. Overhead, and on either side of me, the sky was blue, though with a livid rather than an azure tint upon it. A distant grumbling like the rolling of a heavy van despatched me to the parade, to view the gathering storm, which I knew could not be very far off. It was stretched right behind the hotel from north to south—a long, scowling bank of cloud, straight as a line, as though ruled off upon the sky, and black as midnight, with the sun's rays upon it.

Where was Phœbe? I ran to the edge of the cliff, but could see no boat. I thence concluded that she had landed, and walked quickly toward the pier, thinking I should meet her. I asked two boatmen, one of whom was looking through a glass in the direction of the sea, if my daughter had come ashore.

"There she is yonder," he answered.

I shaded my eyes with my hand, but my sight being bad could see nothing.

"Where? where?" I exclaimed, hurriedly.

He gave me the glass and, levelling it at the spot he indicated, I saw, but very imperfectly, two boats, one about a quarter of a mile from the other; but I could not make out either of their occupants.

"Good heavens!" I cried, "do you mean to say my daughter is in one of those boats alone?"

"Ay," answered one of the men, "that's her."

"But what is she doing out there? Can't she see the storm brewing yonder?" I exclaimed.

"She's been carried away by the tide. I knew that 'ud happen one o' these fine days," observed the man who had handed me the glass. "Me and my mate has been waitin' to see her signal for help, and until she gives us a sign I for one won't go arter her. I had enough of trying to save visitors' lives last year."

He laughed knowingly, and the other man said, " A gent
and his wife was carried out by the tide last year, and arter
Bill there had towed 'em in, blowed if the gent didn't offer
to row him for a wager."

Just then came a sullen moan of thunder.

" For God's sake," I cried, half-wild with excitement and
indignation at the coolness of the rascals, " jump into a boat
and bring her in at once.   I'll give you what you like—only
lose no time; the storm will be on us in ten minutes."

" We'll tow her in for ten shillings," said one of them.

" You shall have it; off with you at once!" I exclaimed,
stamping my foot.

The promise transformed them.   They had whipped off
their coats, scrambled into a boat, and were rowing like
madmen ere I could have counted twenty.   I watched them
with great agitation, vowing never again to suffer Phœbe
to enter a boat alone, until they dwindled out of reach of my
sight.   Meanwhile the storm, instead of gathering overhead,
arched itself toward the east; some thunder-charged clouds
rolled out of it, and brought up a breeze, gentle at first, but
gaining strength at every puff.   The storm gathered in the
direction of Deal over the sea, and when the southern horizon was black with it, it broke.   I could see the zig-zag
lightning flashing upon the water, and hear the booming of
the thunder as it swept with a clear intonation along the
sheer surface of the sea.   The water bubbled and leaped
under the pressure of the wind; the atmosphere cooled, and
the boats about the pier bobbed up and down with quick,
sousing plashes.   The wind blew right off the land, but,
fortunately, grew steady, after having increased to what
sailors would call a fresh breeze.

For a long three-quarters of an hour I kept my eyes fixed
upon the point of the water whence I expected the boats to
emerge, and then I saw them.   Very slowly they advanced;
a strong tide and a strong wind and a jumping sea were
against them.   Not until they were within half a mile of
the pier could I clearly discern them, and then I observed
that there were three boats, and that the first boat, which
towed the others, contained four rowers.   These rowers

were my daughter, the boatmen, and a stranger, whose face, until the boats were within a stone's throw of the pier, I could not see; but on his looking around, presently, I recognized in him the person who had addressed me on the pier a few days before.

By this time the storm had entirely cleared away in the east, but had left behind it many clouds of long attenuated shapes, which chased the sky with torn limbs, and here and there poured a quick shower of rain upon the sea. The hindermost wherry, as the boats hauled alongside, shipped enough water on a sudden to log her and set the oars afloat. My daughter called a cheery greeting to me, but I had been made peevish by anxiety and suspense, and returned no answer, merely posting myself at the head of the steps up which she presently came.

"I hope," I exclaimed warmly, pulling out a half-sovereign and handing it to the man who had helped her up the steps, "you have received a lesson that will put an end to your going on the water alone. You have frightened me out of my wits."

"I am very sorry, papa," she answered, and if she had felt any fear all trace of it was gone. Her face was flushed with the exertion of rowing, and her eyes sparkled like the water where the sunshine shone on it. "I'll take care to profit by the lesson. I mistook the tide and rowed out, thinking that by the time I was tired the current would bring me back. Will you thank the gentleman," she whispered, motioning with her head toward the boat where the young fellow was standing while he put on his coat, "for coming to my assistance? I really *might* have been lost but for him."

"Why," I exclaimed, "I thought he had been in the same pickle, and had got the men I sent to you to tow him in."

He was now coming up the steps, and Phœbe could enter into no further explanations, so I stepped up to him and extending my hand said, "My daughter tells me you rowed to her help, seeing the plight she was in. Allow me to thank you cordially for your service."

"Indeed, I am only too happy to have been of use to her,"

he answered, taking my proffered hand. "I saw that if she drifted out much further she would soon need help, if she did not actually want it then; so I jumped into a boat and rowed out to her. These wherries are rather too heavy for a lady to row against a current."

"They are indeed," exclaimed Phœbe, speaking with a heightened color and a bright smile. "My courage was failing me fast, and I can't describe the joy I felt when I saw your boat coming toward me."

"To think," I cried, turning angrily toward the boatmen who were baling out the wherry, "that those rascals should require a bribe of ten shillings to save a human life!"

"We couldn't have done without them," said the stranger. "It was as much as the four of us could do to reach the land, and this lady pulled as strong an oar as any of us."

He here raised his hat and was going, but I exclaimed, "I have not half expressed to you the gratitude I feel. We are returning to dinner, and your company will give us great pleasure."

He thanked me in a hesitating manner, glanced at Phœbe, and accepted my invitation. I gave him my card and took his, on which I read the name Mr. Saville Ransome, and then we walked in the direction of the hotel.

I was naturally profuse in my thanks, for I really considered he had acted with great consideration and courage in hastening to Phœbe's assistance, and his pleasant evasion of the topic pleased me as an illustration of modesty. He mentioned that he was in lodgings in the High Street, and that he had been in Broadstairs since the previous Wednesday, and that he purposed stopping another month in the town. He said that he was very fond of travelling.

"I sometimes," he exclaimed, laughing and addressing Phœbe, "terrify my mother by quitting her house without saying a word. She is, perhaps, used to this habit now. I relish unexpected things, and one of my whims is to act in such a manner as to prove myself ignorant of my own motives. After all, Miss Kilmain, novelty is the salt of life. To make up one's mind to do a thing is to extract all the pleasure of achievement out of it."

"That must depend," said I, smiling at the oddness of the remark, "on the thing you mean to do."

"If you act as you say, then you are governed by impulse," said Phœbe.

"And so I am."

"To judge by the illustration you have given us just now of the quality of your impulses, you have every reason to be proud of their control," said I.

We had now reached the hotel, and I led the way upstairs. The dinner was over-cooked, of course. It was half-past six, and we were to have dined at half-past five. However, I had recovered my temper by this time, and found nothing to be aggrieved with in the fault that was entirely of our own contriving. The danger Phœbe had escaped, instead of silencing and making her reflective, as perhaps, it should have done, had raised her spirits, while the presence of Mr. Ransome gave a peculiar lightness and grace to her words and laughter, and imbued her with enough of self-consciousness to render her manner piquant.

As for Mr. Ransome, he was a good-looking young man whom I had set down roughly as about thirty years old. The seaside sun had burnt his face, and the brown became him. It was my belief then, as it is now, that he had Indian blood in him, for his eyes were of the dusky hue that spreads like a stain upon the whites, and the whole cast of his face was Eastern, the nose aquiline, the forehead high at the temples, the jawbones long, the complexion sallow, the under-lip full, and so moulded as to convey in repose the suggestion of a slight sneer. He wore a mustache which left a space of clear flesh under the nose; his ears were small, and lay flat against his head; his hair was close-cropped at the back, and brushed up, without a parting, over his forehead. He was a trifle above the average height, but looked smaller than he was owing to the slimness of his shape. His hands and feet were small almost to deformity; he held himself erect as a ramrod, and had a trick of quick, furtive glancing, and appeared to busy himself with details which most persons would overlook.

The mention of his last characteristic hints roughly at a

peculiarity of manner which, because of the subtlety of its
action, is scarcely to be described. It was an effect produced by quick, nervous movements of the body, sharp impulsive glances, abrupt exhibitions of energy taking an
almost passionate character from contrast with the trivial
occasions which exercised them, a restlessness of his hands
and legs, and a habit of beginning a sentence in a clear, decided voice, which would falter and die away, so to speak,
in a singular sing-song cadence, as though his meaning
evaporated before he could fairly pin it down with a full
stop; but no description of this manner and the impression
it produced on me could submit its real character and influence to your mind.

His remarks often bordered on the eccentric, and were
yet qualified again by much good sense and a clear thread
of shrewdness that bound them together and kept them logi-
cal by making them consistent. Phœbe was much amused
by his conversation. He had started with some show of
reserve, but broke through it after a while, and chatted
freely. But, despite his oddities, I was satisfied that he
was a gentleman. His breeding showed itself in numberless little touches, and in a marked degree in his courteous
deference to Phœbe.

I was by no means ill-pleased at the prospect of finding
an agreeable acquaintance in this gentleman during the remainder of my stay at Broadstairs. Having lived much
abroad in my youth, and mixed largely with men, I had
little of the reserve or suspicion that keeps people asunder
among us. Indeed, if the army fails to cosmopolitanize a
man there is no hope for him. I had felt the want of a
companion now and again—some one to smoke a cigar with,
to exchange remarks with on current newspaper topics, to
kill the tedium of the time when Phœbe was upon the water,
or after she had gone to bed.

I went with him on the balcony after dinner. Phœbe
joined us and spoke of her adventure that afternoon.

"I shall never go in a boat again," she said; "I was
much more frightened than I seemed, Mr. Ransome."

"You were nervous, indeed, as the most courageous person in the world would be under such conditions; but your courage could not have been very far off, for you soon recovered it."

"How did you manage?" I asked.

"On reaching Miss Kilmain's boat," he replied, "I got into it and attached my own boat to the stern. I then seized the oars and began to row toward Broadstairs, but I do not suppose that I did more than keep the boat steady against the current. When the other boat arrived Miss Kilmain and I scrambled into her and made up four oars, and in this trim reached home."

I caught Phœbe watching him with a pair of very bright smiling eyes as he spoke; but, happening to meet mine, her gaze fell, and there was an air about her for a brief moment of a sudden confusion. I paid no attention to this, nor, indeed, to various other trifling signs with which she illustrated the pleasure she received from Mr. Ransome's company. We had seen almost nothing of society since my wife died, and it was very natural that Phœbe, in the presence of a good-looking young gentleman who had done her a very great service and treated her with thoroughbred courtesy, should be a little more ingenuous in her behavior than she would have been had she been disciplined by the custom of meeting young men in ball-rooms many nights in the year, as would probably have been her fortune had her mother been spared to me.

It might have been, perhaps, a sensitiveness that made him feel the insufficiency of his introduction to us which set him talking about his mother and relating some particulars of his past. He said that he was afraid he had astonished me by the queer account he had given of his migratory habits.

"Not at all," I answered; "you converted your habits into philosophic actions by the explanation of your reasons for seeking novelty. The first ambition of every young man should be to travel. He can hardly ever hope to think rightly until he has seen the world."

"I am afraid," he exclaimed, laughing, "that I can hardly dignify my excursions by calling them travels. I live at

Guildford—at least my mother has a house there. Do you know Guildford, Miss Kilmain?"

"No."

"There is some charming scenery in the neighborhood. My mother has lived there nearly all her life. She inherited a little—a very little estate just outside the town, from her father, who, by the way," he said, turning to me, "served many years in India—General Shadwell."

"I know the name well," I replied. "Was not he a brother of Lord Carnmore?"

"Yes, the younger brother of a well-entailed family, who had literally to carve his fortune with his sword. My mother is sometimes a little fretful with me for my mysterious disappearances," he continued addressing Phœbe: "but I *cannot* settle. I have been a week at Broadstairs, I talk of stopping here another month, and probably after having persuaded myself into a conviction that I shall serve out my allotted time, will one morning start away for Wales or Scotland. But then I mustn't allow myself to think of this as a possible intention, or I shall defeat all the pleasure of impulse."

He shook his head with a gravity which I thought affected, conceiving that he spoke really in fun.

The sun was now setting, there was a crimson haze in the air, which made the sea a violet color, and the clouds, as they whirled across the sky from the hazy south, had an edging of brilliant gold at their side. I caught myself watching Mr. Ransome, and thinking him, by this flattering purple light, much handsomer than he had at first struck me. There was something that particularly pleased me in the manliness of his face and upright figure; his eyes, though they wanted fire, were filled with a suggestion of active sensibility. But still there was a prevailing oddness in his manner, vehicled by his voice and gestures, and seldom to be gathered from his bare words, which defeated the theories of him I now and again formed as we continued chatting.

The wind fell at sundown, and a calm delicious night came on, with a bright moon, which steeped a broad space of silver in the sea, and made the land and water holy. We kept our places on the balcony until ten o'clock, when Mr. Ransome rose and wished us good-night. I shook hands very warmly with him on parting at the door of the hotel, and assured him that I should be at all times glad to see him both at Broadstairs and at Gardenhurst, where my house was. He thanked me for my hospitality, and implying a neat compliment both to myself and Phœbe in a well-turned reference to his and her adventure, raised his hat and walked away.

I returned to Phœbe, whom I found yawning on the sofa.

"Well, my dear, what do you think of our new acquaintance?" I asked.

"I am almost too sleepy to think," she replied; "but well, he is a very nice—young fellow, is not he?"

"He is gentlemanly."

"Very."

"I can't quite make out that manner of his. I should put it down to nervousness were it not that he is *not* nervous."

"What manner, papa?"

"Why, his odd, quick gestures, and his way of looking at one, and then again his die-away voice when he begins a sentence with energy and falls into a dream before he reaches the end of it."

"I didn't notice this."

"Not his restlessness?"

"He has a habit of twitching his hands a little when he speaks," she answered; "but there is nothing in that."

"That only shows what different impressions the same man will produce on different people," said I, laughing. "He appears to me to be a bundle of nerves, partially controlled by earnestness, which now and again suffers from remissions, and then off go his hands and feet. Has not he Indian blood in him, Phœbe?"

"He is too handsome for an Indian, isn't he?" she replied, with a soft laugh, leaning the sofa and standing at the window with her eyes on the bright moonlight on the water. "Fancy," she continued, pointing to the sea, where

it lay black against the reflection of the silver light, "fancy
my having been alone in a boat out there! Had he not come
to me, where should I be now? Miles and miles away, perhaps, if the boat had not sunk when the wind rose. Imagine
my loneliness when the night fell, and when I should see
vessels passing me at a distance, like phantom ships in the
moonlight, too far off to hear my cries! I must think of
something else," she exclaimed, with a shudder, leaving the
window, "or I shall not be able to sleep."

Her words seemed to rebuke the criticism I had passed
on the man who had helped to rescue her from the dangerous position her fancy was recalling.

"There is no doubt," said I, feelingly, "that we are both
under a very great obligation to Mr. Ransome. He acted
with spirit and humanity, and I shall certainly lose no opportunity of testifying my gratitude by every civility it is
in my power to show him."

"I shall go to bed now," said Phœbe.

I kissed her and she left the room.

II

It was unavoidable that I should see a good deal of Mr.
Ransome. We met on the sands, on the parade, sometimes
walking in the flat green country round about the town. In
spite of our friendly dinner he seemed rather shy at our
first few meetings; but at last gave up all notion of being
regarded as an intruder, and joined us as often as he saw us.

Meanwhile the fright Phœbe had received had effectually
put a stop to her boating. She now went to the other extreme, and refused to enter a boat on any condition. Her
resolution pleased me on the whole, for, though there was
no doubt that the exercise had done her good, the risk she
ran, even with a boatman to take care of her, more than
counterbalanced the benefit she derived from the pastime.

To console her for the loss of this pleasure I hired a phaeton for the remainder of my stay, in which we enjoyed many
drives. Mr. Ransome frequently accompanied us on these
excursions, and on one occasion took the reins; he handled

them capitally; but the horse proving restive, he began to flog him, then urged him into a headlong gallop, which forced me into an indecorous attitude by obliging me to hold on tightly to my seat, though Phœbe appeared to enjoy the swift and menacing motion. I was heartily glad when the jaded beast faltered at last into a trot; and determined to give Mr. Ransome no further chance of breaking our necks, I took the reins from him under the plea that it was my turn to do duty.

I should not have mentioned this but for one circumstance, which left its impression at the time, though I did not then bestow much attention upon it; I mean, that while he was flogging the horse a fierce expression entered his face; he used the whip as a savage woman, mercilessly, and when, the horse pelting along at full gallop, he turned to look at me, I noticed that his face was pale, the smile he gave me almost malevolent, with its strange suggestion of passion, and that his eyes glowed with a light which strongly recalled the expression I had seen in the eyes of natives of India when inflamed with rage.

Now, though Phœbe may not have seen his face at that moment, she could have scarcely failed to notice the extravagant heat with which he had whipped the horse; but when I spoke of this after our drive, she declared that she had not remarked anything excessive in the flogging; on the contrary, she thought Mr. Ransome perfectly understood horses, that he had curbed the restiveness of the animal as only a man thoroughly acquainted with horses could have done, and that as for the headlong speed at which he had driven us, she had always heard that the only way to deal with a horse afflicted with runaway tendencies was to give it its full fling, taking care to keep the animal up to the mark with the whip, and so cure it by exhausting it.

Her defence of Mr. Ransome proved one thing to me—that she admired him, and was therefore likely to find provocation of admiration even in doubtful conduct; but, believe me as you will, I never for a moment suspected that there might be a deeper emotion than admiration at work in her. That discovery was reserved for a later time.

A few days before we left Broadstairs, I found by the merest accident in the world confirmation of the truth of the incidental account he had given of his antecedents. I had received a letter from Dr. Redcliff, inquiring after Phœbe; and in order to fill a page, I mentioned in reply that we had made the acquaintance of gentleman named Saville Ransome, of Guildford, who had helped to amuse us during our stay at Broadstairs; and I then related the manner of our introduction to him. After some time Phœbe heard from Dr. Redcliff, who, in referring to my letter, wrote that a cousin of his, a doctor, was in practice at Guildford, that they sometimes corresponded, and that he remembered his cousin speaking in one of his letters of a patient of his named Mrs. Ransome—a well-connected, odd, old-fashioned lady, whose son was named Saville. She had made rather a joke of herself by her fretful manner of speaking of her son's eccentric habit of leaving her without notice.

I was with Phœbe when we met Mr. Ransome a few hours after this letter had been received. Phœbe, in her outspoken way, told him in substance what Dr. Redcliff had written.

"Oh, then," he said, "Redcliff is Dr. Tobin's cousin, for Tobin attends my mother."

I was afraid, from the uncalculating way in which Phœbe had fallen upon the subject, that he would imagine we had been making inquiries about him; and so, in the best way I could, I explained why it was that Dr. Redcliff had mentioned his name. He appeared perfectly to appreciate my thoughts, and deprecated the implied apology with great good-nature; and then, recurring to what Phœbe had said, exclaimed with a laugh:

"I told you, Miss Kilmain, that my habits sometimes put my mother in a fever."

"But you should correct them if they distress her," answered Phœbe.

There was a freedom in the words, though none in the manner, of her reply, that made me look at her with slightly raised eyebrows. But if she had paid Mr. Ransome a compliment he could not have appeared more gratified.

"You make me very happy," he said, in a subdued voice, "by taking interest enough in my habits to honor them with your reproof. You set my conduct in a new light. I will endeavor to get the better of my caprices."

"Phœbe is rather fond of holding up moral looking-glasses," I said. "I suppose it is my own fault that I am sometimes dissatisfied with the peeps she obliges me to take. Monsieur de Miroir is occasionally an insulting personality, though he is always our nearest and dearest friend."

"How finely the clouds color the sea!" exclaimed Phœbe, changing the subject with a slight air of confusion. "Those long violet streaks look beautiful against the light green out there."

"The wind is in the east; we should be able to see the coast of France," said I; and so we talked of other things.

We left Broadstairs in the first week in August. Mr. Ransome dined with us the day before our departure; and warming to the memory of the agreeable hours we had passed together, I pressed a cordial invitation upon him to see us at Gardenhurst, should he ever find himself in our neighborhood.

Phœbe that evening was not in the good spirits that usually possessed her. I said to Mr. Ransome:

"My daughter is sorry to leave the sea, although she owes it a grudge. Phœbe, would you rather live here than at Gardenhurst?"

"At Gardenhurst certainly, papa," she answered, with a glance at Mr. Ransome.

"But you are sorry to go home?"

"No, though I like Broadstairs."

"We will stop here another week or fortnight if you wish. Shall I write home to that effect?"

She hesitated, swung her foot—Mr. Ransome was looking at her—and replied:

"We have made up our minds to go to-morrow, papa, and so we will go."

"Very well, my dear. So far as I am concerned I have had enough of the sea. I want to get back to my books and pursuits, and the quietude of the country. We have

2

had a pleasant holiday, and next year, please God, we will come here again; where, Mr. Ransome, we must hope to find you."

He smiled and, after a short silence, thanked me for the politeness and hospitality I had shown him, in a curiously impulsive way, beginning the sentence energetically, and ending in the sing-song subdued cadence that made such an extraordinary feature of his conversation.

Phœbe rose and walked on to the balcony. Mr. Ransome exclaimed, "Is the night fine, Miss Kilmain?" and stepped on to the balcony himself. I joined them after a few moments, and saw them standing together; he was pointing to the sea, and raised his voice as I passed through the window to let me hear that he was talking about the lights near the Goodwin Sands.

"They call that the North Sand Head Light," said I, for he spoke of it as the Gull. Perhaps, had I known their conversation before my interruption, I might have considered his inaccuracy very reasonable. "Come, Phœbe," I continued, "it is rather too chilly for you to stand here without any covering on your head."

She passed into the sitting-room without a word, and a few moments after Mr. Ransome wished me good-night, and went away.

III

Gardenhurst was situated within a mile of Copsford, a handsome little town rich in antiquities. All about us were hills shagged with wood, and creating vistas to the horizon, through which, at the setting of the sun, it was a glory to look; for then the land seemed heaped up with mountains of gold with dark-green shadows upon their sides, while their outlines lay shaped in black lines upon the valleys. Very sweet was the summer wind that came floating down these hills, making shifting colors in the sward as it pressed the grass, and bringing to us dwellers above the valleys the fragrance of the hay and the ripe odors of the gardens and orchards of the lower grounds.

Gardenhurst stood midway on the slope of one of the hills called the Cairngorm Mount, because of the strange pale yellow tint it took at sunset, when viewed at a distance, and when all the other hills were ruddy with the expiring light. The slope was very gradual, and contrasted grandly with the sharp declivity of the adjacent hill, which overhung the valley gloomily, and showed a precipitous front with its gray jagged rocks and swarthy verdure. The main road bordered the walls of the estate, turned sharply at its foot, and ran forward in a gentle descent to Copsford.

My house stood in the midst of some thirty acres of ground, and, though of middling size only, was considered one of the prettiest specimens of old-fashioned architecture in that part of the country. The walls fronting the decline were of red brick, of which time had softened the vividness of the color. On either side the door were tall windows with a stone balcony not above two feet high above the lawn, with a little flight of steps to the grass. Above these were bay windows, bold and striking additions, which produced the picturesque effect of overhanging stories, such as you find in gable-roofed houses, without trenching upon the strength of the foundations as overhanging stories do. On the left side was a terrace supported by handsome Doric columns, the roof of which in summer was converted by the gardeners into a parterre. The windows of the drawing-room opened upon this terrace, and the contrast of the blue or crimson drapery with the white pillars and checkered marble pavement was charming. At the back were the greenhouses; on the right was the principal house door, with a carriage-drive from it through an avenue.

This house, not above a hundred years old, stood in grounds which had known the cultivation of three centuries. The result was, the growth of vegetation was extraordinarily luxuriant; for the soil was fat and black with vegetable decay, and so prolific as to keep the gardeners incessantly employed in freeing the beds and walks from the nameless fungi, weeds, and plants which would grow and flourish wildly in a week.

I had followed my father's taste in keeping the flower gardens well-ordered, but in giving Nature her own will under the trees down at the foot of the estate. There the grounds were densely wooded, and the grass was knee-deep, while the ivy and other parasites cloaked the trunks with their tenacious leaves, and swung their curling tendrils from the long boughs. It made a pleasant contrast to pass from the flower gardens, gaudy with brilliant colors, and fatiguing with monotonous uniformity of carefully dug and fastidiously kept beds, to the green, cool, remote tranquillity of the trees, through which the sunshine shimmered soft streams of light at unequal distances upon the high grass, and where from time to time the rich and glorious tones of the blackbird or the thrush would rise and seem to silence and constrain the other birds to listen. Voices and influences gathered about one there to subdue one's heart to deep moods of repose. For many weeks after my wife died, I would haunt the soft shadows and linger among them for hours, finding such soothing inspirations as I could draw from no other sources in the tranquil twinkling of the leaves overhead, in the vague and sleepy murmurs creeping here and there, and originating, I knew not whence, in the broad luminous stare of a rabbit, which a moment after would vanish like an apparition in the long grass.

A fortnight had passed since we left Broadstairs. I had settled down once more to the very placid life I had been leading before Phœbe's illness had interrupted it, and had well-nigh forgotten all about Mr. Ransome.

I need scarcely detain you with an account of my habits, or of the manner in which Phœbe and I managed to pass our days. Interests are created in the country which the denizens of cities might hardly conceive, and which they would laugh at for their triviality were they to be told of them. One may stake a large share of personal anxiety on the building of an outhouse, and the rearing of fancy poultry may absorb one's sympathies quite out of the highway of current political and social events. Do not suppose that we were hermits. The death of my wife, to which I have referred, had given me a distaste for society. I had still many friends and acquaintances in the neighborhood; but my consistent parrying of their invitations had given them at last to understand that I no longer relished the entertainments which had amused me in my wife's lifetime. Phœbe shared in my indifference to society, and so I could not charge myself with selfishness in leading the retired life I then did. But we would now and again spend an evening at a friend's house, or invite a neighbor to a quiet dinner, and sometimes make up a little party for a round game. But balls and large assemblies of all kinds we eschewed with a very sufficient reason; and so, while we managed to keep our friends about us, we contrived to escape the arduous obligations which attend the lovers of society.

One evening near the end of August, I left the grounds, where I had spent half an hour chatting with one of the gardeners, and repaired to a room which I had converted into a study, built over the porch of the door.

Phœbe had left the house shortly after dinner for a walk to Copsford. I was deep in a book that had taken my fancy, and when I gained my study, resumed it with all the sense of comfort that is begotten by a snug armchair and a luxurious silence. But interesting as my author was, he could not detain me from the prospect. Forever my eye was wandering from the pleasant page to the near and distant hills, and the deepening sky, and the magical coloring imparted by the evening to the high trees, the green valleys, the yellow spaces of the harvest fields. There was a wonderful repose in the air. The summits of the higher hills were still purple with the beams of the sun, whose descent they overlooked when their sides midway were dark with the shadow of night. Some of the hills seemed wreathed with foliage. Far down on the left I could trace the mere white line of the London Road veining the shadowy valleys, vanishing here and there under soft dark clouds of trees, and hugging the base of the hill close, round which it twisted its way to Copsford. That town was hidden from me, but many villages speckled the broad hilly landscape, and a few miles distant the smoke of a large manufacturing town clouded the sky of the horizon and gave a curious delicacy of outline to the wooded ridges behind which its houses were packed.

It presently grew too dark for me to read. I put my book down and left my chair, meaning to see if Phœbe had returned; as I approached the door she came in.

"Oh, papa! guess whom I met at Copsford!" she exclaimed.

"Whom, my dear?"

"Mr. Ransome!"

"Indeed!"

"Yes, I was in Queen Street, looking into a shop. A voice said, 'How do you do, Miss Kilmain?' It was Mr. Ransome. I was quite surprised."

"Really?" said I, with a half-smile, and perhaps more dryly than I meant.

She blushed, and laughed, and looked grave all at once, saying:

"Of course I was surprised, papa. I did not know he was in Copsford."

"No, naturally not. And what had he to say for himself?"

"Oh, he was very polite and agreeable. He said that he left Broadstairs two days ago, and ran down here, meaning to spend a day or two in Copsford in order to see you before he returned home. He recalled our strange adventure on the water, and then said, as I was alone, that he would do himself the pleasure to see me home. He walked with me to the gate, and would have left me there, but I could not do less than ask him in. He is down-stairs."

"Where?"

"In the drawing-room."

He was at the window with his back to the door, but he turned with a swift gesture peculiar to himself, when I entered, and came to me quickly.

"How do you do, Colonel? I am very glad to meet you again. I hope you will require no apology for my intrusion upon you at this hour. I could not suffer Miss Kilmain to walk alone, and she was good enough to ask me in."

"You are very welcome," I answered. "Pray be seated.

I should have taken it ill had you come as far as my house and returned without seeing me."

I rang the bell for the lamp.

" You have quitted Broadstairs earlier than you intended, have you not?" I continued.

" To tell you the truth," he replied, laughing softly, and lying back in his chair, but with an air of easy good-breeding, " I found Broadstairs slow. There was nothing to do but bathe, and you know a man can't be bathing all day long. How well Miss Kilmain is looking!"

" Yes, her trip did her a great deal of good. Where are you stopping?"

" At the Blue Boar in George Street."

" You should have come to my house. Remain with us now—I can give you a bedroom, and my man shall go for your luggage."

He reflected a moment, and then declined.

" What I have seen of Copsford," he said, " makes me think I shall like to spend some time here, and——"

I went to his relief, seeing him falter, and exclaimed:

" You can stop here as long as you like without the least fear of being thought an intruder."

" You are extremely good. I am throwing away a happiness——" and he stammered out another refusal.

I had no more to say. He knew his own business best. Perhaps he was right to prefer the independence of an hotel life to the unavoidable restraints our mode of living would impose upon him as a guest. At this juncture a servant brought in the lamp, followed by Phœbe.

She had changed her dress for a white muslin, with a black sash and other half-mourning appendages, which I am not properly qualified to write about. The blush I had brought to her face in the study seemed to have settled there, and her eyes took a fine lustre and a bright vivacity from the contrast. I had good reason to be proud of her. It was not alone her beauty that gratified me; her manner was charming: a mixture of maidenly modesty with womanly dignity. There was just enough of natural languor about her to soften the sharpness of outline which a radically impulsive nature would communicate to behavior, and she could scarcely assume an attitude in which you could not have found a grace.

Mr. Ransome spent an hour with us, and then his manner became spiritless, and he got up quite suddenly and wished us good-night. I did not ask him to stop, having come to the conclusion that he was best pleased when left to act as he chose. I walked with him as far as the gate, and as I shook hands with him, asked him to name a day convenient to himself on which he would dine with me. His time, he answered, was mine; any day would suit him. So I fixed Thursday—that was, three days hence.

Of course I never for a moment guessed that he was likely to protract his stay at Copsford. I merely looked upon him as one of those fugitive acquaintances one makes in one's progress through life, who had taken me at my word to call on me if he passed through Copsford, whom I could not do less than ask to dinner; and who, when he quitted our neighborhood—which I supposed he would do within a week at the very outside—I should never hear of again.

When I returned to Phœbe, I could not help saying:

"There appears to be something very odd about Mr. Ransome."

"What, papa?"

"His manner is so strange. Did you notice how all the life seemed to go out of him just before he jumped up to say 'good-by'?"

"I think he is nervous," she replied, "with a very proper dislike of being thought an intruder."

"Well, there may be something in that," said I.

"I like people with a dash of oddness about them," she continued: "were it not for the peculiarities you notice in Mr. Ransome, his behavior would be as insipid as other men's."

"Oh! and so you don't find his insipid?"

"No."

I was silent a moment or two, and then said:

"I have asked him to dinner on Thursday. You can invite Dr. Redcliff to meet him."

"Very well, papa."

"Did he tell you how long he meant to stop at Copsford?"

"I didn't ask him.   Our conversation as we walked home was all about Broadstairs."

"It seems odd that we should find him in our neighborhood so soon, doesn't it, Phœbe?"

"I suppose he must be somewhere; and Copsford lies in his way home."

"How do you mean?   Copsford is miles out of his way from Broadstairs to Guildford."

She made no answer, and I was going to ask her if she thought Mr. Ransome admired her, nay—I was going to put the question in less doubtful language than this, but thought better of it, and made a remark which changed the subject altogether.

IV

Phœbe and I had our different occupations and interests, which would keep us away from each other a whole morning or afternoon at a stretch.   I might spend two or three hours in the grounds or in my study, while she was out walking with a friend, or reading or sewing in another room.   Then, again, I was fond of riding, and, starting away for a canter after lunch, I would not meet Phœbe again until dinner-time.

She was never dull; it was easy to tell that by her spirits. Indeed, I think that the apparent monotony of her life suited her, and that she would have been discontented had she been taken away from the tame and tranquil interests which she created for herself day by day.   Her character in this respect was a very promising one; and I would sometimes think that the man who obtained her lov⌣ would find her a good wife.   But this was a thought that very seldom occurred to me.   The monotony of our life rendered her marriage a subject that rarely troubled us.   Had we mixed much in society the case would have been different.   I should probably have seen her surrounded with admirers— I may justify my assumption by instancing her beauty

and the fortune she would inherit from me—and then con
sideration of her marriage would have been a permanent one.
But she had no admirers now.   We had withdrawn from
the world, and the world had forgotten us.   I clung to her
as my only child, my only companion, and resolutely blinked
the thought which would now and again enter my mind that
in all probability a lover would one day appear and take her
away from me.

That Mr. Ransome would be that man I had no more conception at the date to which this portion of my story refers,
than I have now of living another fifty years.   Though he
admired her, and of this I had no doubt, I could not imagine that he was in the smallest degree likely to win her
affection.   Of course I fell into the common error of parents.   I saw him with my eyes, and assumed her judgment
to be based on my perceptions.   To me he was nothing more
than a gentlemanly young fellow, odd in his manners, with
a capacity of quick and even fierce passions, amusing, com-
panionable, but essentially a fugitive acquaintance—one
whom we had known by an accident, who would presently
pass away and leave us scarcely a memory.of him.   And so
I dealt with the superficial facts, such as they presented
themselves to my view, instead of adopting Phœbe's sight
and looking deeper, and finding in his dark and masculine
face a beauty that would wonderfully commend itself to
women; in his very capacity of passion an antithetical quality of profound tenderness, not the less agreeable to the
feminine nature because of the capriciousness that dictated
its movements; in his oddness a characteristical flavor which
a girl would relish as a redeeming excellence in a behavior
which she might otherwise find flatly conventional.

Thursday afternoon came, and with it my two guests,
who arrived almost together.

Dr. Redcliff was a man for whom I had a great esteem.
He had attended my family for many years and had faithfully and patiently watched my wife through a long and
painful and fatal illness.   He was a short, stout man,
with a very intelligent face, shrewd blue eyes, and invariably wore a tail coat and a white cravat   He greeted Phœbe

with a cheerful familiar inquiry after her health, and I then introduced him to Mr. Ransome, who had arrived a few minutes before. There was something stiff and almost haughty in the bow Mr. Ransome gave him, but I put this down to nervousness. My friend apparently attributed his manner to the same cause, for he began to speak in his quick, cheerful voice of his cousin Tobin of Guildford, asking what practice he had, and if he had started a carriage yet, and so forth. Mr. Ransome answered him civilly, but preserved his distant manner, and then took an opportunity, when the doctor turned to me, to go over to Phœbe.

In a few moments dinner was announced; I told Redcliff to take my daughter, and we entered the dining-room.

Mr. Ransome was curiously taciturn for some time, responding to my well-meant endeavors to draw him into conversation in monosyllables. I often caught his dark and nimble eyes travelling over us—resting longest, perhaps, on Phœbe, but taking a keener intelligence when they settled on the doctor. I considered his silence owing to the constraint which his nervousness would impose on him in the presence of a stranger amid those who were familiar to him. But all the same I was rather disposed to quarrel with his want of grace; for his behavior was inconsistent, and certainly not in accord with his usual conduct when with us.

The conversation during the first part of the dinner was almost entirely between the doctor and myself; it did not flag, for Radcliff was a most talkative man, with a mind stored with odd experiences, which he related dryly and well.

I happened presently to refer to my daughter's adventure at Broadstairs, and the part Mr. Ransome had taken in it.

"And the tide carried you nearly out of sight of land, Miss Kilmain?"

"Oh no, Dr. Redcliff, but a very great distance; almost two miles, I should think."

"At all events, I had to look through a glass before I could see her, Redcliff," I said.

"I suppose, Mr. Ransome, you found her very pale and frightened?" exclaimed the doctor.

"Rather pale, Miss Kilmain, were you not? but not

frightened," he replied, smiling at her and answering her
as though *she* had put the question.

She raised her fine flashing eyes.

"You found my courage as you rowed from Broadstairs
and brought it to me," she said. "It fell overboard, I
think, when I was about a quarter of a mile from the land,
and found the tide carrying me away."

"I know a man who went mad from an accident of this
kind," said the doctor. "Shall I tell you the story, Miss
Kilmain?"

"Yes, please, doctor."

"He lived in Jersey, and had a little boat of his own in
which he went fishing every day, weather permitting. He
loved the sport, and was his own society, for he rarely took
anybody with him. One day he hoisted his sail and steered
for his regular fishing-ground, reached it, threw his anchor,
and began to fish. One of the sudden dense fogs which
haunt that coast rose and hid the land from him. It grew
thicker and thicker, frightened him at last, and he pulled
up his anchor and began to row—there was no wind—for
the shore, as he thought. He rowed until he was exhausted,
but never approached the land. The night came, the fog
lifted, and he found himself far out at sea, long miles of
water on all sides of him, the glittering stars overhead. You
must follow him in imagination, conceive the agony of his
mind, his sufferings, his terror, as best you may: he never
told the tale himself. Two days, nay, nearly three days
afterward he was discovered by a French fishing-smack.
They described their sighting a little boat, their approaching it, and their observing a man crouched near the mast
counting his fingers. They hailed him, and he looked up
and grinned at them with dry, cracked lips, and went on
counting his fingers. They got him on board, and found
him an idiot, too idiotic to explain that he was dying from
hunger and thirst."

"What became of him?" asked Phœbe.

"His idiocy developed into madness. A few years ago
he was one of the most dangerous lunatics in the asylum
at L——."

"Think, Phœbe, what *you* escaped!" I exclaimed, much impressed by this narrative.

"No—I will not think of it—it is too dreadful, papa."

"That was a terrible misfortune to befall a man," said Mr. Ransome.

"I should have thought his senses would have returned to him when he found himself safe," exclaimed Phœbe.

"Once mad, always mad, more or less, my dear."

"Why do you say that?" demanded Mr. Ransome.

Redcliff looked at him with momentary surprise, and answered: "It is a dogma of mine, but you need not believe it."

"But you should know, as a medical man, whether your dogmas are right or wrong. Are you right in this?"

I saw a queer light kindle in his eyes as he spoke, but there was no temper in his manner.

"My experience of mad people is very small," said Redcliff. "But I don't remember ever having met a man whose unsound intellect had been perfectly recovered."

"What *is* madness?" asked Mr. Ransome, in a low tone, resting his chin on his hand, and revolving a wineglass.

"Now you would pin me down to a definition," responded the doctor, laughing, and looking at me. "Colonel, can you answer Mr. Ransome?"

"No, indeed!" said I.

"Don't mad persons think sane people mad?" asked Phœbe.

"Very often, and perhaps always, if every madman would express his views," answered Redcliff. "For my part, I am inclined to think that there are two sorts of madness—sanity and insanity. The only question is, which is the worst kind?"

He looked at Mr. Ransome to see how the young man would like this evasion of his question; but he took no notice of him; he was looking at Phœbe intently—so intently, indeed, that I wondered she could sustain the fixed regard without a blush. But there was no rudeness in his gaze; nothing but an expression of profound and absorbed contemplation such as might possess a painter's eye in maturing a picture. The silence aroused him; he started hastily, looked around him with a half-scared frown, and then smiled, and addressing me, said that he was thinking of the wretch who had gone mad with fear in the open boat.

I purposely emphasize his behavior by exhibiting these small details of it, that the story I have yet to tell may lose nothing by want of consistency. I recall his behavior now with a particular reference to subsequent events, and necessarily, therefore, witness in it the significance which it certainly did not possess in the days of which I am writing. He was merely odd, in my opinion—nothing more; and there were times when the grace and even sweetness of his manner, and its perfect keeping with all established theories of good breeding, would entirely qualify and even obliterate the ideas he had before suggested to me.

We sat awhile over our wine when Phœbe had withdrawn, and knowing Redcliff to be a miserable man without a pipe or cigar after his dinner, I invited my guests to stroll in the garden where we could smoke and enjoy the night.

There was a bright moon over the trees, and the near hills were white in its radiance, and down in the dark valleys the lights of cottages burned, and all about the horizon the heavens were brilliant with stars which twinkled largely through the warm air, but the moonlight made the centre of the sky pale.

We measured the lawn three or four times and then drew near the terrace on the left of the house, where the drawing-room windows were open and the lamplight shone softly on the black-and-white marble of the pavement.

Phœbe, who possibly imagined we were still lingering at the dinner-table, stood in one of the open windows and made a singular picture with her head drooping on her fingers, her left hand supporting her elbow, her eyes bent downward, and the warm yellow lamplight on her back and her left side whitened with the moonshine. She heard my voice and made a movement to join us, but Redcliff exclaimed—

"The dew is heavy, my dear; don't attempt to come upon the grass."

Mr. Ransome threw away his cigar and went to her. I was following, but Redcliff said—

" A moment, Colonel: I must finish this cigar;" passed his arm through mine and walked me across the lawn.

" What do you think of Mr. Ransome, Redcliff?" I asked.

" I'll be shot if I can tell you.   One requires time to make up one's mind about some people.   But I can give you an idea which I'll wager a hat you don't possess."

" What?"

" Your daughter's in love with him."

" Are you in earnest?" I exclaimed hastily.

" Indeed I am.   Do you tell me you cannot see this for yourself?"

" No; and I think you are mistaken.   *He* may be in love with her, for I won't pretend to understand so odd a character; but *her* heart is still her own."

Redcliff laughed.

" This always happens," he exclaimed.   " The head of the family never sees what is going on under his nose. Take my word for it, the young people are in love with each other, and before long you'll be hearing of it from one of them."

" But am I to suppose," I said, " that my daughter has fallen in love with a man whom she met for the first time in her life not a month ago, and of whom she knows *nothing* beyond that his name is Ransome, and that he has a mother who lives at Guildford?"

" My dear Colonel," replied Redcliff, throwing his cigar away, " never take a view of love from the standpoint of reason.   Besides, because a thing is strange or sudden, is that a reason why it couldn't have happened?   You seem to have forgotten, first, that Phœbe is young; secondly, that Ransome is good-looking; thirdly, that he has rendered her a service of some magnitude and of a character which must very eloquently appeal to feminine sentiment; fourthly, that you saw a great deal of him at Broadstairs, had him sometimes to dinner, and treated him with a great deal of attention; and lastly, that during the fortnight of your intimacy with him, his opportunities of seeing your daughter were plentiful enough to account for every apparent erotic impossibility you can name."

"I am perfectly bewildered!" I cried. "Phœbe in love with this young man? Impossible! I never yet introduced a man to her who pleased her. There was young Cornwallis—you remember him—as fine a young fellow as ever wore uniform—she laughed at him; her poor mother could scarcely induce her to treat him with common civility. And now comes Mr. Ransome, with his half-cracked manners and mysterious habits and dubious antecedents—for what on earth more does Phœbe know of him than I know? and all that I know is, he comes from Guildford and that his mother is well-connected—I say, here comes this stranger, with his odd laughter and singular eyes, and gets my daughter to love him in a few weeks—I might say a few days! Impossible!"

I had quickened my pace as I spoke and approached the terrace. I was looking anywhere but straight before me, when I felt Redcliff's hand upon my shoulder.

"See them!" he whispered.

The windows were open. A cool breath of air was bellying one of the curtains inward and exposing a portion of the room; and where the curtain, but for the wind, would have screened them, I saw Ransome stand close by Phœbe, in the act of kissing her hand.

"There, Colonel, you have confirmation strong as proof of holy writ," said Redcliff.

I walked quickly forward and entered the room. I longed to say something, and yet, for the life of me, could find nothing to say. I wanted an excuse to consider that Ransome had been acting an underhand part, that Phœbe had been deceiving me, but no excuse presented itself, for the very good reason that there was none.

No! indignation, pain, temper would not do. What had happened was my own fault. I had made much of Mr. Ransome at Broadstairs; I had invited him to Gardenhurst. I had never considered the probability of his falling in love with Phœbe, of her falling in love with him, and it was proper that I should pay the penalty of my shortsightedness.

Phœbe looked at me as I entered, and I was struck by the expression in her eyes, at once wistful and mutinous. Redcliff came in chafing his hands, and admonished me with a brief intelligible glance to keep my counsel and my temper.

"I am going soon, my dear," said he, "but before I leave you must sing me a song."

"Yes, gladly. What shall I sing?" she answered.

There was an undoubted reference to me in her manner. Perhaps my face conveyed a little story to her. I was certain she *felt* that I had guessed her secret.

"Sing me a Scotch ballad, no matter what so it be Scotch."

She smiled, gave me another glance, and went to the piano.

"I don't know music, and so cannot offer my services to turn the pages," said Ransome in his most affable manner to Redcliff, presenting an odd contrast with the demeanor he had assumed when I first introduced him. "Perhaps you will officiate."

"Miss Kilmain won't require either of us. She sings from memory."

And Redcliff seated himself while Mr. Ransome leaned against the mantelpiece and there stood without movement, his eyes on the floor, all the time Phœbe sang. It was impossible to watch her fine figure, her graceful attitude, to hear her rich and thrilling voice lending the subtlest significance to every note she delivered, and not find an apology in it all for his love, if love he really felt for her. I could never hear her sing without a strange feeling of tenderness coming upon me. Her voice was very full of memories to my ear. My mood softened as she continued singing. I leaned my face on my hand and scanned Mr. Ransome as he stood opposite me, recalling special points in his behavior to make the present issue consistent, and discovering a quite new interest in him as one who had the most forcible claims upon my attention that any man could come to me armed with.

Redcliff clapped his hands as Phœbe ceased, and then, looking at the clock, jumped up and said he must be off.

3

"Don't let my departure hasten yours," he exclaimed, seeing Mr. Ransome come to us.

"Thank you—it is past nine," answered Mr. Ransome, who then thanked me for my hospitality and shook hands with Phœbe. I did not press him to stop. We walked to the hall. I should have liked to exact a parting consolation from Redcliff, but even an "aside" was impossible, for Ransome kept close to us.

I shut the hall door upon them and returned to Phœbe.

She seemed prepared; she stood at the table with her hand upon it; the lamplight was full on her face, and her shining eyes met mine with a straight, steady outlook as I entered. I am not sure that I should have spoken at once of the matter of which my mind was full, but her attitude was a challenge not to be waived, so I said:

"Phœbe, as I crossed the lawn I saw Mr. Ransome kiss your hand at the window there. What does that mean?"

Instantly a violent blush suffused her face; it was clear she did not know that I had witnessed Ransome's action. She pursed up her mouth to disguise or control the tremor of her lips, and after a pause of some moments answered in a low tone:

"Papa, we love each other."

"Is it really so?" I cried, somehow startled by the answer for which, nevertheless, I was prepared. "Redcliff told me the truth then. His eyes are keener than mine. Phœbe, is it possible that you can be in love with a man whom you met but the other day—a perfect stranger to you?"

"She made no answer.

"How long has this been going on, tell me?"

"We loved each other before we left Broadstairs."

"But why did you not tell me? Why keep such a secret from me? You could have helped me to guard you from this danger. What friend have you in this wide world but myself? Who loves you, who has your happiness always at heart, but your father? You should have taken me into your confidence, Phœbe."

"Oh, papa, do not be angry with me!" she exclaimed

"If I have kept this secret from you it was because I knew you would reproach me for loving him. Why do you call it a danger? Is he not a gentleman? Is he not my equal and my better? You know him only by his manner: but I know his mind—I know how tender, how affectionate, how high-minded he is, how unobtrusive and shy and sensitive. It was as much to guard *his* feelings as to spare my love from your reproofs that I have kept the truth hidden from you."

I was amazed by the passionate energy with which she spoke, and above all by her profession of knowledge of him, which was as emphatically expressed as though they had known each other for years.

For some moments I could not speak, during which she watched me with the dark blush suffusing her cheeks, and her eyes absolutely liquid with emotion.

"But you don't know anything about him, Phœbe. You talk of him as though you were *sure* of the qualities you name."

"I am sure, papa."

"You have literally no proof in the world beyond the bare hints Redcliff gave you in his letter that his antecedents are even respectable. What do you know of his mother, of his family, of his past? But these things are nothing. The real miracle is that of a girl of your spirit, who has never before allowed a thought of love to trouble her, whom I have sometimes thought I should never be able to find a husband good enough for—that *you* should fall in love with a perfect stranger, a fortnight, nay, a week after you had met him. It is incredible. Where is your pride, Phœbe? Where is your affection for me?"

She shook her head quickly to drive the tears from her eyes, but remained silent.

Then my own mood changed. I felt that I was speaking with unnecessary severity, and certainly exhibiting but small knowledge of human nature in expressing astonishment at the suddenness of her love. The fact of my not being able to witness in Ransome the attraction and fascination which had conquered Phœbe could supply me with no argument

If I was to reason her into what I chose to consider common sense, I must not only not lose my temper but I must take care to fasten upon and strictly confine myself to the really weak point of the affair, and that was our total ignorance of Mr. Ransome as man and boy.

"We will discuss the subject no further to-night, Phœbe," I said; "I am positive you will require only a very little reflection to bring you over to my view of this matter. You have allowed your generous impulses to hurry you into an error. You have considered yourself under a serious obligation to Mr. Ransome for putting off to your assistance at Broadstairs, and your resolution to feel grateful has misled you into a sentiment which *cannot* be deep, considering that it has had no time to take root. You are right to feel grateful to Mr. Ransome for the service he did you; but really, were the obligation fifty-fold heavier, you could discharge it abundantly by a much more trifling tribute than the gift of your heart."

I turned away, but she sprang forward and seized my arm.

"Papa, you may think I mistake my feelings; but as I hope to go to heaven, I swear I love Mr. Ransome. I have promised to marry him, and not even my love for you shall prevent me from keeping my promise."

An angry answer rose to my lips, but I forbore to speak it, and left the room, but more agitated, vexed, and astonished than I can well find words to express.

V

I did not see Phœbe again that evening. She went to bed shortly after I had left the drawing-room, and I passed the rest of the hours up to hard upon one o'clock in the morning alone.

I did my best to mentally fasten a quarrel upon Mr. Ransome. I endeavored to convince myself that he had acted meanly and dishonorably in taking advantage of the confidence I reposed in him as a gentleman, to make love to my daughter. But my arguments brought no satisfaction with them. It was idle to call him dishonorable for falling in love. The fault of it all was entirely mine. So far from his showing any boldness in putting himself forward, I had had much trouble to get him to come forward; he had hung back with a modesty or bashfulness that was almost phenomenal in a man of his age; my invitations to dinner, my cordial receptions and greeting only had set him at ease at last, and then I suppose he fell in love with Phœbe, and, having regard to my polite and considerate treatment, concluded that his advances for her hand would meet with my approval.

The suddenness of it!—but then I had made up my mind not to consider *this* extraordinary, remembering how very quickly and easily *I* fell in love, and how very abruptly numberless persons of both sexes are smitten.

So I turned my attention entirely to him, his character, and to what I could recall of the little domestic disclosures he had sometimes made me in moments of mellow intimacy at Broadstairs.

My reflections ended pretty well as they had begun, in mingled bewilderment and anxiety. Not just yet could I feel the pain which would attend the conviction that my daughter had absolutely surrendered herself to Ransome, and that I must lose the only companion whom God in His mercy had left me to soothe my solitude.

Next morning at breakfast Phœbe was very silent. She was pale, and the hollows under her eyes were dark, while the eyes themselves were dull, and proved either that she had shed many tears, or had passed a sleepless night. I was pained by this contrast with the bright sweet vivacity that usually kindled in her face and never shone more fairly than when she had just risen, and said, gently:

"Phœbe, you are looking ill. Have you been fretting over what I said to you last night?"

"You spoke harshly, papa."

"My dear, I did not mean to speak harshly. I have only your happiness at heart—I told you so last night. I considered that you had acted hurriedly and without judgment in allowing yourself to fall in love with Mr. Ransome with-

out taking me into your confidence and not giving yourself
time to learn his character."

" I do know it, papa."

" You *think* you do, Phœbe; but it is impossible that you
should really know it, considering how brief has been the
time of your acquaintance with him. I who have lived
much in the world, and should therefore possess shrewder
penetration than you, am puzzled by him. He seems to me
to have many good qualities, and, so far as outward bearing
goes, he is undoubtedly a gentleman. But there are many
strange characteristics mixed up with these good points, and
they render his nature purely problematical. I have doubts
of his temper. He has the eye of a man who is easily mastered by fiery and dangerous passions. I may be wrong,
but how can you expect me to sanction your love until I
have satisfied myself that he is worthy of it?"

" But you *can* satisfy yourself."

" How? He is only stopping here for a few days."

" He would not be in a hurry to leave if he thought you'd
sanction his love. He would visit us often, and then you
would see I was not mistaken."

"Has he actually asked you to be his wife?"

She answered " Yes," in a low voice.

" When?"

" The day before yesterday."

" He did not call here?"

" No, I met him."

" By appointment?"

" Yes."

I felt myself grow pale. Here had been a real deception.
She had never before deceived me in her life, and this first
deceit shocked me as a bitter discovery.

" Have you appointed to meet him again?" I asked
quickly, and with a frown.

" Yes, papa."

" To-day?"

" This afternoon."

" Phœbe, you are right to tell me the truth. I thank you
at least for that. But I cannot permit you to meet him alone."

She gave me a sharp rebellious look and then bent her eyes downward.

"Since it has come to this," I continued, leaving my chair and pacing the room, "my resolution must be taken at once. God knows I would preserve you if I could from your own inexperience of life. But if you are determined not to heed my advice, then you shall not receive my countenance, for under no circumstances can I allow you to contract an engagement of this kind but as a lady. Understand me, Phœbe; my sanction is not voluntary; it is extorted from me because I feel I can no longer trust you, and that only by sanctioning your love can I save you from lowering your dignity by stealthy meetings and deceitful practices. *These* things must not be. You have chosen your own course, against my wishes; but your desertion of me shall not give me an excuse for ceasing to protect you whilst you still remain under my care. There shall be no shame in your love at all events; since you *will* meet Mr. Ransome, you shall meet him in my house, in the presence of my friends, and with my professed consent, not in secret, not in such a way as to supply the gossips with tittle-tattle."

I spoke vehemently but decisively. She watched me earnestly, with compressed lips, and when I ceased, lowered her eyes again, but offered no remark.

"At what hour is your appointment?"

"At three o'clock."

"Where?"

She felt the shame of this examination and hesitated, but was mastered by my emphatic manner.

"Near Rose Common," she replied; and then the same dark burning blush that had suffused her face the evening before mounted to her cheeks.

"I will keep this meeting for you," I said. "If my explanation does not satisfy Mr. Ransome the fault will not be mine."

I turned to the window, whereupon she left the table and walked out of the room. She sobbed once as she passed through the door. She had left her breakfast untasted, and for my part I had scarcely broken bread.

I was too much disturbed in my mind to care about riding that morning, and I passed the time as best I could in
my study, where I gave myself up to much bitter reflection
on the unfair and undutiful way in which Phœbe had treated
me in withholding her confidence. She did not come near
me, as I hoped she would, that I might sound her thoughts
and prepare myself for my interview with Mr. Ransome. I
presume she kept her room all the morning, for the servant
found her there at lunch-time when I sent him to call her
to the meal, and returned with the message that her head
ached, and that she did not feel well enough to join me.
This excuse, of course, merely meant that she was ashamed
to meet me.

I seated myself at the table with a sorrowful heart. This
was the first quarrel my daughter and I had ever had. It
was an ominous quarrel, because it initiated a scheme which,
so far as I could possibly foresee, must end in parting us.
There appeared to me, besides, something of ingratitude
mixed up in her behavior. She had been ungrateful not to
trust me, in shunning me when I was about to repay her
deceit by setting her love for Mr. Ransome on an honorable
and candid footing. A feeling of loneliness came over me;
I felt myself wronged by her to whom my life had been devoted; I realized the truth, that the thanklessness of a child
is sharper and crueller than a serpent's teeth, and my emotion was so great that it forced me into shedding a few un-
manly tears.

I presently conquered my weakness and sat a while, until
it was half-past two, when I took my hat and walked in the
direction of Rose Common.

This common was situated at the foot of the hill that
bounded Copsford on the west, and was a good twenty minutes' walk from my house. The afternoon was lovely; the
sun's heat was tempered by the moderate breeze that swept
the slender stems of the ripe cornfields, and a brief fall of
rain in the morning had laid the dust in the road and freshened into vividness the green of the hedges and the emerald
coating of the hills. The country, golden with harvest,
was now to be enjoyed; early as the season was, the chink

of the sharpened scythe stole through the breast-high fields: on the far-off hills the hand of autumn had pressed a pale red tint, and the trees in the valleys had a richness and fulness of foliage rarely to be seen in the less mature periods of the summer.

But I was in no temper to relish the ripe and swelling scene. I walked forward moodily, engrossed in thoughts of the language I was to hold to Mr. Ransome. A few minutes before the hour I reached the common, a broad tract of grass on which some goats were browsing, with a cottage or two peeping out from the dense shrubbery on the left, and the hill rearing its vivid bulk on the right and completely hiding the town that lay on the other side of it.

A narrow walk skirting the base of this hill took you to Copsford; along this walk, ere I had waited two minutes, came Mr. Ransome, slowly. He saw me at once, and stopped, for an instant only, then approached me swiftly.

"Colonel," he exclaimed, "I have come to meet your daughter—you know this?"

"Yes," I replied, "and am here instead of her."

"Hear me!" he cried, subduing his voice, but looking at me with glowing eyes; "Miss Kilmain loves me, and our love for each other is assured. I have staked my happiness upon making her my wife. Have you come to separate us?"

"I have come merely to tell you this, Mr. Ransome; that from a conversation I had with my daughter this morning I discovered that she loves you, and that she is in the habit of meeting you secretly; that I think her love ill-advised, hasty, and insecure; and that had her pride restrained her passion from indecorum, I should have resolutely withheld my sanction to her love; but that, since she has already committed herself by meeting you, since I judge by her language that I am unlikely to possess further control over her in this matter, I have determined, at least, that no impediment she can find in *me* shall supply her with an excuse for forgetting the position she holds as a lady and as my daughter. I have come, then, to tell you that you need be no longer under the embarrassment of meeting each other

by stealth. My house is open to you, and *there* your inter-
views need not alarm me with apprehensions of gossip,
which, long as my family have resided in this neighborhood, no member of it has ever, until now, in the smallest
degree excited."

"Until now. Who has been talking, Colonel Kilmain?"
he exclaimed.

"I have yet to learn," I answered.

"Your daughter's reputation is as dear to me as to you.
I would not commit her to an action that could provoke a
whisper from malice itself," he said hurriedly and tremu-
lously. "What manner of delicacy is to be outraged by the
meeting of lovers in secret? Can such meetings, which are
thought harmless in others, be guilt in us? We dreaded
your knowledge of our secret, because we guessed the arguments you would use against it. Our love was too young
to be risked on an act of honesty of which you might have
misconstrued the motive. I begged Miss Kilmain to meet
me in secret, that, by strengthening her love by companionship, I might defy your objections, ay, Colonel, and your
influence when you should find our secret out."

He spoke rapidly, fluently, without a pause, ending in
the sing-song tone that was now familiar to me. Had he
been dealing with any other topic he would have amused
me, for his odd rhetoric was irresistibly suggestive of the
declamation put into the mouths of stage lovers on precisely
such occasions as we were then acting in.

"Mr. Ransome," I answered, "no arguments can be of
use now. The matter has gone too far. I tell you candidly
that I do not approve of this hasty love-making, these pre-
cipitate engagements. We are scarcely more than strangers
to each other. I do not question your honesty, nor will I
charge you with deception in keeping the truth from me,
because I look for protection from such painful situations
to my daughter—to no one else."

"I had no wish to deceive you. I have had no time, even
had it been my wish to do so. Your daughter consented to
be my wife only three days ago."

"I have said all discussion must prove useless. Will you

walk? I am returning to my house, and I invite you to accompany me."

"Colonel, if I enter your house I must be welcome," he said, drawing himself up.

"Welcome!" I exclaimed, forcing a smile; "what man is welcome to a father who would take from him his only child?"

He softened with extraordinary impulse.

"I do not take her love from you. As my wife she is still your child."

"No, you alter love when you change its conditions."

I turned and walked a few paces away, thinking he would follow me, but he stood still.

"Tell me I shall be welcome," he said, "and I will join you. I must assert my claims as a gentleman. If I am not that, I am not fit to marry your daughter, and in this respect you shall not get me to disqualify myself."

I hesitated. I scarcely knew what to say or do. I thought him right to insist upon my recognition of his self-respect; but then how could I pretend, after what I had said, that he *would* be welcome?

"You have hitherto, I believe, always found a welcome in my house as a guest," I said.

He made no answer, and almost losing my temper on finding how absurdly our positions were reversed, I exclaimed:

"I wish you to understand, Mr. Ransome, that my daughter shall not meet you again secretly. I give you, for the reasons I have already stated, the option of seeing her at my house. You may accept it or not, as you please."

So saying, I turned, and resolutely walked away. In a few minutes I heard his quick step behind me. He came to my side, and said:

"You are right, Colonel. I am sensitive and obstinate. You have met me as a gentleman, and I am therefore bound to accept your offer."

Vexed and agitated as I was, I had to bite my lip to restrain a smile. Indeed, there was something ridiculous enough in the notion of his making a favor of courting my daughter in my own home. But my light mirth was very short-lived. I was harassed, tired, and offended, and would willingly have walked the whole way to my house without opening my lips again. But he soon forced me into conver‑sation.

"Colonel," he said, "why did you call your daughter's love for me ill-advised?"

"If you will but consider, you may easily answer that question yourself," I replied.

"Is it because I am poor? if that is your belief, Colonel, you are mistaken. I am not rich, but I am independent, and could support your daughter without the help of one penny from you."

"You misunderstand me. I am not one of those fathers who take a mercenary view of their children's prospects. I would first seek in my daughter's engagement a more fruit‑ful, and a more permanent source of happiness than money can supply. I would know if the man she has chosen for her husband is truly fond of her, not merely taken by her beauty, but resting his affection on other and more durable qualities; if their tempers agree; if he is a moral man with common sense enough to appreciate the weight of the obli‑gation he incurs by assuming the charge and taking upon himself the happiness of a human life."

"One must hope for the best," he answered with a queer little shrug of the shoulders. "There are some things quite impossible to find out before marriage, and character is one of them."

"I don't agree with you. Some infirmities may indeed be concealed, but as much will be apparent as we need know to base our judgment upon, if the man or woman be not a mere actor. But then you must have time to make such dis‑coveries, and that explains my meaning when I speak of Miss Kilmain's love as ill-advised. She does not know you."

"She does, Colonel; she does, indeed," he replied, ear‑nestly.

"We need not argue the point," I said. "She is quite old enough to know her own wishes, and to judge how wise or foolish they are. I leave her to her own judgment, only stipulating that, while she remains under my roof, she will never forget her dignity as a lady."

"Good God, Colonel!" he cried, excitedly, "would you imply that she loses dignity by loving me?"

"I have implied nothing of the kind," I answered, chafing under his stupid misapprehension of my meaning.

He did not offer to speak for some minutes.

The more I considered the false position my daughter's folly had placed me in, the more vexed and anxious I grew. I could never have anticipated for myself a more disagreeable lookout than the prospect of having to argue and quarrel with the man who should ask her to be his wife. Such a possibility could never have occurred to me, because I considered that she was never likely to accept the offer of any man whom I should disapprove of, or contract an engagement without giving me plenty of leisure to consider its propriety before being called upon for my decision. So far, indeed, unless I except the absurdity of his making a favour of attending me to my house, I could find nothing to object to in Mr. Ransome's reception of my remarks. I had said a good deal which a quarrelsome man would fasten upon and fly into a rage over; but he had shown no temper. He was warm only when he spoke of his love, and prejudiced as I was, I could not deny to myself that his love seemed perfectly sincere, for I found the chief exhibitions of it more in his manner than in his language. In truth, had I been asked the real cause of my annoyance, I should have put it down to the suddenness with which the discovery of Phœbe's love had broken upon me, and to the artfulness its concealment illustrated.

He interrupted my reflections after a long silence by saying:

"Colonel, it is my duty to be perfectly frank with you. If I have not sympathized with your misgivings on this subject, it is because it has not occurred to me before now that while Miss Kilmain knows as much of my history as I know myself, you are in entire ignorance of it. You will allow me to assure you that so far as my birth is concerned, I am a gentleman."

"Oh, Mr. Ransome, I never doubted that."

"My father," he continued eagerly, "was a barrister, and came of a good Lincolnshire family. My mother—but a man doesn't take his position from his mother—I can only promise that you will find her a lady."

"Indeed, Mr. Ransome, these confidences are quite needless."

"I do not think they are; you must remember that you have said you consider Miss Kilmain's love ill-advised, because you know nothing of me. You *cannot* believe that I have been influenced by the least mercenary motive in making love to your daughter. She has made me very happy by consenting to be my wife; but she would make me happier still by taking me as I am—I mean by sharing in what I possess and allowing me to be under no other obligation to you than what I should acknowledge in your consent to our marriage. I am totally ignorant of your means; and were you to tell me that you are worth a million I should find as little to interest me in the statement as I find in this stone."

He kicked a flint out of his path with a highly melodramatic gesture, and fastened his dark eyes on me. He seemed honest enough, and certainly his words were strongly flavored with manly disinterestedness; but that peculiar manner of his, which no words can express, and which was as elusive to the faculty of definition as the thread of a spider's web floating in air is to the fingers, curiously qualified to my *instincts* the impression his words should have produced, and made me more secretly restless than his "confidences" had found me.

But by this time we had entered the gates of the grounds, and were approaching my house along the avenue. I scarcely realized the full embarrassment of the position in which I was placed until we were in the drawing-room. Mr. Ransome had seated himself and was looking at me with speculative, watchful eyes. Meanwhile I had rung the bell and desired a servant to inform my daughter that I had returned with Mr. Ransome. What was now to be done? Nothing better, it seemed to me, than to assume an easy manner,

treat Mr. Ransome as an afternoon visitor, and after that
to leave matters to shape themselves as they might. So by
way of breaking the ice, and letting him guess my resolution, I called his attention to the richness of the trees at the
bottom of the grounds, and the charming contrast of the green
with the pale yellow of the further landscape. He came to
the window and at once adopted my tone, commenting upon
the beauty of the flower gardens and praising the taste they
exhibited. My sense of the ridiculous smarted to the absurdity of all this; and yet what other course could I have
taken consistent with the part I had made up my mind to
play? To be hard upon him, to say bitter things, to reproach him now that he was under my roof, was not to be
dreamt of. He was here at my own invitation. On the
highway I might say what I pleased; but in my house,
whither he had accompanied me with reluctance, he was in a
measure sacred as my guest.

So for some minutes we stood conversing as though there
was nothing in the world between us to cause either of us
the smallest uneasiness, and then the door opened, and
Phœbe came in slowly, with hesitation in every movement,
her large full eyes luminous with hope and doubt and surprise. But that subtle expression of determination which I
had noticed in her face the night before was not absent now.

I watched him approach her and take her hand. If ever
I had doubted the sincerity of her love, my doubt must have
vanished before the swift, beautiful glance she gave him,
the momentary leaning forward, the bashfulness thinly
icing her deportment for a moment and then melting away
under the smile which parted her lips and enriched her
cheeks with a bright spot of red. Then she looked at me,
and an expression of misgiving and even fear, almost pitiful
to behold, crept over her face.

"Miss Kilmain," said Mr. Ransome, slowly and in a clear
voice, "your father disapproves of our meeting in secret.
We must both think he is right. He has given me permission to see you here, and our thanks are due to him for removing the only unpleasant obligation that has attended our
intercourse."

"With that explanation," I exclaimed, "I must beg, **Mr.** Ransome, that you will allow the subject to drop. I have put my daughter in full possession of my motives, I think I have been sufficiently explicit with you, and since you can reconcile my attitude with your happiness there can be no possible need for further recurrence to the subject."

Mr. Ransome bowed, handed a chair to Phœbe, and resumed his seat; but let him mask his emotions as he would with urbanity he could not prevent his eyes from expressing his thoughts; and the brief glance I received from them ere he bent his gaze downward enabled me quite to understand what is meant by the expression "looking resentment with a smile."

The small scene that followed would have amused a disinterested spectator, but there was something painfully disagreeable in it all to me. We conversed upon matters as trivial as the weather and the crops, and Phœbe joined in the conversation, forcing upon herself the easy manner that sat lightly on Mr. Ransome, but which needed a great effort of my will to preserve in me.

VI

It did not take me long to discover it was my daughter's destiny that she should marry Mr. Ransome. The privilege he now possessed of calling to see her when he pleased would strengthen their love and render it more durable by supplying it with a conscience. My wishes had been defied, my control set at naught, I could not take interest in a matter I did not approve. My daughter had developed a quite unsuspected quality of headstrong, rebellious resolution; I felt the powerlessness of my parental authority to cope with or divert her from her passion; and dreaded any exercise of severity lest it should hurry her into an elopement and so bring disgrace upon me and sorrow and remorse upon her. I therefore left her to herself, believing that her pride would draw its best sustenance from freedom, and that her self-control which the liberty I permitted would make obligatory, would save her from the commission of any worse disobedient act than what she had already committed in engaging herself to Mr. Ransome without my knowledge.

But, as I have said, the one result of the liberty was to deepen her love by placing her constantly in the society of her lover. I rode, I went about my pursuits, I loitered in my study as usual; I dared not, nor indeed did I choose to act the part of dragon. A man *must* trust his child. Truly enough Goldsmith has said, that the virtue that requires a sentinel is not worth the guarding.

I had taken Redcliff into my confidence at an early stage in the story of this love affair, and to my surprise got no sympathy from him.

He allowed that Phœbe had acted unfairly in consenting to marry Ransome before speaking to me; but, if I would bate that, all the rest was human nature.

" When men get old," said he, " they forget that they were once young. How often was I in love from the age of fifteen to thirty? Don't talk to me of fathers and mothers and guardians! I would have laughed at them all. Why, your stealthy meetings, your furtive kissings under the moon, are the real poetry of love. What song is so sweet as the words of the heart set to a nightingale's tune? When do eyes look dearer than when they reflect the starlight? Would you have people make love under chandeliers, in the highways, in the society of relations? Be charitable, and this you can be by subtracting twenty from fifty and thinking out of the balance."

" This may be very well; but suppose I tell you that I don't like Ransome?"

" *Why* don't you like Ransome?"

" One reason is, I think him half-cracked."

" Because he wants to get married?"

I laughed, though God knows my humor was grave enough.

" Suppose he *is* half-cracked—Phœbe should know; if he is, he keeps his madness well under—suppose, I say, he is half-cracked, what better evidence would you require of his aristocratical descent? Isn't he a gentleman?"

" Yes. He is a gentleman."

" Isn't he good-looking?"

4

" Well?"

" Hasn't he means of his own, enough to lift him above
the possibility of his turning out a mere hungry adventurer?"

" He says he has."

" Isn't there a lord in his mother's family? Isn't he unmistakably fond of Phœbe? Isn't she dying for him?
What more would you have in this nation of mésalliances?
When Addison's Dutch philosopher fell from the masthead
of a ship and broke his leg, he thanked God it wasn't his
neck. Phœbe might have married a man entirely after
your heart—and she might have married a man very much
the other way. She has married neither. She is not the
fiancée of a duke, nor is she planning an elopement with
your gardener. She has found a well-looking, middle-class,
educated young gentleman to fall in love with. He is satisfied; she is satisfied; and all that you have got to do is to
rest satisfied yourself."

All this was quite in reason. There are really few objections a man may have to his child's marriage which his
friends will sympathize with, although there is no other
matter in which they are more disposed to interfere. That
Redcliff, perceiving my uneasiness, could honestly think
the match a good one for Phœbe, I will not believe. He
had sense enough to see that Phœbe meant to marry Ransome whether I liked it or not; and in a true spirit of friendship set the affair before me in the brightest colors he
could invent to console me, in some sort, for the anxiety
and depression I would not conceal from him.

Meanwhile the days were passing rapidly, and still Mr.
Ransome remained in Copsford. He had shifted his lodgings from the Blue Boar to a farmhouse on this side of the
town, and here it was plain he meant to stop until his marriage with Phœbe should consign him to a house of his own.

By this time the engagement was generally known and
talked about. I was frequently stopped out of doors and
congratulated, and several persons who had not visited me
since my wife's death called, no doubt under the impression
that my daughter's engagement was to initiate our return
to society. Of course my pride would never permit me to

suggest that I was not satisfied with Phœbe's choice. I was asked questions about Ransome with a great show of interest by my acquaintances, and I told them how Lord Carnmore was his uncle, and how he was sprung on his father's side from an ancient Lincolnshire family, which was true enough. His appearance and manners they could judge of for themselves. Indeed, Phœbe received many compliments on the good looks of her lover, and on his bearing and behavior. Whether he was rich or poor our friends could not discover, nor on this point did I think proper to enlighten them. He was quite rich enough to please me could I have satisfied myself with him in other respects. It had always been my intention to give up Gardenhurst to Phœbe on her marriage, and settle half my fortune on her. My old home would cease to be tolerable to me under changed conditions. Memory would make it painful without the companionship of one or the other of the two whose presence had thronged it with its sweetest associations, and I could not tolerate the idea of sharing it with the master whom Phœbe's marriage would put in possession of it.

So that, with this plan in my mind, the idea of Mr. Ransome having but a small income could not have prejudiced me against him, since the fortune I was able to give her would make her rich enough to support her position with dignity and elegance. My real objection to Mr. Ransome lay in a secret and fixed dislike, not to be explained by any effort of my judgment. Often, I will admit, my prejudice seemed unjust to me because of my inability to refer it to a motive. Redcliff once attacked this antipathy, and pretended to prove that it could not exist, because nothing I could say against Mr. Ransome was sufficiently conclusive to account for it. He made out a catalogue of virtues belonging to the man—his modesty, his good breeding, his deference to me, his obviously sincere devotion to Phœbe—to every item of which I had to assent. How then could I justify my dislike of a man so deserving of esteem? But the enumeration of his good points did not soften my prejudice. Were he less deserving I might find him more deserving.

" You are angry with him," Redcliff said, " for being the
cause of your daughter's disobedience, and for diverting her
love for you into a new channel."

"Perhaps so," I replied.

I could not explain an instinct. Why I did not like him
I knew not; I could only say and mean that I did not like
him.

Matters had been going on in this way for over a month,
when one afternoon Phœbe came to me in the grounds to
tell me that Mrs. Ransome was in the drawing-room, and
wished to see me.

I had often wondered to myself how long it would be
before this lady came upon the scene,—whether, indeed, it
might not end in my having to go to her. But her visit
now surprised me, for I had no idea that she was at Copsford, and neither Phœbe nor Ransome had hinted that she
was likely to visit us.

I was walking toward the house, when Phœbe said:

" Papa, I did not know that Mrs. Ransome was in Copsford."

" I could not assume you were ignorant by your not telling me," I replied.

" I have no secrets from you now," she exclaimed, quickly. " You wrong me if you think I have.

" Is Mr. Ransome with his mother?"

" Yes."

" Did _he_ know she was coming to Copsford?"

" No. She arrived at half-past twelve to-day, and took
Saville by surprise."

I asked no more questions, but went straight to the drawing-room. I heard Mrs. Ransome's voice before I opened
the door—a shrill, eager, excited voice, so characteristic
that I think I could have formed a tolerably accurate idea
of the woman it belonged to before seeing her.

I entered the room, followed by Phœbe, and found mother
and son standing together by the table—the son looking a
giant beside the dwarf who had given him birth. She was
the smallest woman I ever saw outside a travelling circus.
But no part of her was out of proportion: her head, arms,

and body were in perfect keeping one with another. So far as I could judge, she was about sixty years old; she had a long, aquiline nose, her eyes were a light moist blue; her cheeks were pale, and the skin of the face tight upon it, so as to take a polish from its contraction over the cheekbones and chin. Her forehead presented the most delicate network imaginable of wrinkles, which crossed and re-crossed each other, each wrinkle as fine as the line of a spider's web. She wore sausage curls confined to their place by stout tortoise-shell combs. Her bonnet was large, and made larger yet by a big gray feather; her dress consisted of a rich silk mantle and a black satin gown. There was exquisite neatness in her attire; her gloves were new, and fitted her faultlessly; her collar was of fine lace, her parasol lined with crimson.

No description would better express her than to say that she resembled a large, well-formed woman viewed through the wrong end of an opera-glass.

She was rattling away shrilly and volubly when I entered, but instantly held her tongue and approached me with a short flighty walk, consisting partly of a hop and partly of a stride. Mr. Ransome introduced us; but she was not satisfied with bowing; she ran up to me holding out her hand.

"Extremely glad to meet you, Colonel Kilmain. Have heard so much of you from Saville, that I seem to know you as well as if we had been acquainted for years. Pray tell me, now, aren't you surprised to see me? Saville was quite astonished when he found me in his sitting-room at the farmhouse, weren't you, my dear? You see, I didn't know whether to come or not. Of course I was anxious to meet my dear daughter-in-law who is to be—ah! Colonel Kilmain, you are indeed fortunate in having such a beautiful girl for a child. Well, as I was saying, for the last week I had been making up my mind to come to Copsford. I wouldn't say a word about it to Saville for this reason: if I couldn't come on the day he expected me, he would be disappointed. But here I am now, and oh, those horrid coaches! I was never so jumbled and shaken in all my life. My dear, can you oblige me with a fan?"

Phœbe took one from the table, and Mrs. Ransome sank into an armchair, having delivered the above speech in a breath.

While Phœbe rang the bell for wine, the old lady atten-tively observed me, and then asked her son to name the per-son I reminded her of. She gave him no time to answer, but instantly said, "Sir Percival Sheldon, her husband's dearest friend. I was the living image of him. Ah! he was a fine gentleman, one of the old school—people must go a long way to meet men of his stamp now."

Garrulous as she was, still she was a lady. She articu-lated her words with a refined and cultured accent, she fanned herself with just the sort of air with which one would imagine a fan to have been used by a lady of fashion and distinction fifty years before, and there was an antique grace in the very attitude she adopted when she sank into her chair. Her littleness seemed to purify her. Her minute manners, her trim affectations were like miniature paint-ing on ivory; the same subject transferred to larger canvas would have borrowed a quality of coarseness from the mere effect of size.

She sipped her wine, chatting away freely. I watched Phœbe to observe the effect the little old lady produced on her; but she seemed merely amused, laughed often, while her heightened color showed her by no means insensible to the direct bits of praise she from time to time received from Mrs. Ransome.

Mr. Ransome was silent, as indeed he could hardly help being, seeing that it was almost impossible to edge in a word amid his mother's swiftly uttered sentences; but he had an unconcerned face, and appeared in no wise embarrassed by her volubility.

Presently she turned to them, and said—"Go into the garden, my dears. I wish to have a private chat with Colo-nel Kilmain."

Phœbe laughed outright, but rose nevertheless and went to the window, which she opened. I was rather astonished by the old lady's cool dismissal of these two, but offered no remark. Ransome looked at me, and, after a slight hesitation, exclaimed: "I hope, Colonel, that our withdrawal will not be disagreeable to you?" He chided his mother with a quick glance.

I answered, "Certainly not. But there is no necessity for you to leave the room. Mrs. Ransome and I can converse in the library."

"Ah, you are too amiable," she cried. "I expect the young to oblige the old—that is, their elders. Why should we leave when *they* can leave?"

"I want to speak to the gardener; and thank you for giving me an opportunity to go to him at once," said Phœbe, laughing; and out she went, followed by her lover.

It struck me that she would not have been pleased with so peremptory a dismissal from anybody else—certainly not from me.

Mrs. Ransome ran to look at them walking together, and came back exclaiming—

"Are they not a handsome couple? Are they not beautifully matched?" and then cackled on, "I thought I would lose no time in calling upon you and talking this marriage over. I give my heartfelt sanction, because Saville is quite too clever to be mistaken in his choice. Your daughter is a delightful lady, and I am persuaded they will be happy."

"I suppose," said I, "you know that we met your son accidentally at Broadstairs, and that he and my daughter profess to have been in love with each other before we left the seaside, which would scarcely give them a fortnight to become acquainted in?"

"Yes, Saville wrote that it was love on both sides at first sight. And you see they are not mistaken. They have shown great constancy, have they not?"

A little triumphant light shone in her eyes as she cast them around the room. Where *his* great constancy was I could not see; but Phœbe had certainly shown obstinate constancy in persevering in a cause which had cooled my heart toward her.

"As the parents of these young people," I exclaimed, stirred somewhat by the thought I have just written, "there

should be no lack of sincerity between us, and you must
therefore allow me to say that I think this engagement in-
judicious, for the reason that it was entered on without
either of our consents having been asked, and, I may add,
persisted in in opposition to my implied wishes."

She opened her little eyes wide, and turning up her small
face, marked with a striking expression of gravity, exclaimed, shortly :

"What makes you averse to your daughter's marriage
with Saville?"

"My daughter knew nothing of the character of your son
at the time of bestowing her love on him.   There was an
impulsive haste in this secret surrender of her affections
which annoyed and filled me with anxiety when I eventually discovered it."

"Well," she replied, coolly, "I thought the same thing
when Saville wrote to tell me that he was engaged to be
married, and how long he had known your daughter.   What
did *he* know of her character?   How was *he* to judge that
she would make him a good wife?   But *there* is Saville's
weakness.   His confidence is too generous; he distrusts
nobody but himself; he is all intellect and sensibility."

I controlled the irritation which this highly maternal view
of Mr. Ransome excited, and said :

"What has happened is, I am afraid, past the time of
cure, if not of regret.   My daughter is old enough to be her
own mistress; she has taken her course and must walk in it,
since she will not acknowledge my direction."

I waited to receive her reply, but finding her silent, exclaimed, leaving my chair—

"I don't think we need keep the young people from the
room any longer?"

"No reason at all why they shouldn't join us.   I am glad
to have had this conversation with you.   It is proper for
parents, situated as we are, to understand one another.   I
do hope that Saville and dear Phœbe" (there was some
acrimony in the pronunciation of that word "dear") "will
be happy.   They deserve to be, I am sure.   Their affection
is quite beautiful.   I noticed their greeting when I called

with my son; and an old woman like me doesn't require to see much to judge by."

She gave me an odd look, and turned her eyes upon the window.

I was anxious to cut short her chattering, and called to Phœbe, who was pacing the lawn hand in hand with Ransome. What particular object the old lady had had in inviting me to a "quiet conversation," as she called it, I could not guess. There had been nothing of the slightest importance in what she had said, nor in what I had said. It might be (subsequent events will show that the harshest suspicion cannot wrong her) she meant to inquire into the commercial aspect of her son's engagement, and was deterred by my manner, which was certainly stiff and grave enough to suggest that she would blunder if she showed herself the least bit too curious.

But this is a mere surmise. If she did not strike me as being as eccentric then as I afterward found her, she exhibited quite enough oddness to make me see where Ransome had got his character from; and it was quite possible that nothing but craziness was at the bottom of her wish to talk with me in private.

"Your conversation has not lasted very long," said Phœbe, entering the room with a smile.

"I hope, mother, you have not wearied Colonel Kilmain?" exclaimed Ransome, sending a sharp glance first at the old lady and then at me.

"My dear son, how can you ask such a question?" answered Mrs. Ransome, slapping her dress and then fanning herself. "You young lovers will never allow that your poor old parents may take as much interest in your marriages as in any of your other affairs. Yet they come to us in their troubles, don't they, Colonel Kilmain? They find out their best friends when they want them."

I looked at Phœbe, but she avoided my eye. It was nearly five o'clock, and I had a letter to write before the quarter past, ready for the postman, who called at that hour in the afternoon. So, having mentioned this to excuse myself for leaving the room, I asked Mrs. Ransome to stop to dinner, inviting her out of pure form, and most inhospitably hoping that she would decline. It seemed to me certain that she would have accepted but for her son, who regarded her fixedly. She smiled—caught her son's eye—and declined. Then *he* stepped in, thanked me for my politeness, but regretted that his mother's health was wayward, that she was used to regular and primitive habits, etc., etc., to all which she said, "Yes, it is so."

I bowed to her and left the room, and when I passed the drawing-room twenty minutes afterward they were gone.

VII

Phœbe asked me, when we met, what I thought of Mrs. Ransome. My answer was—

"What do *you* think? My opinion is nothing. She will be your relative, not mine."

"I like her," she replied. "She is quaint and old-fashioned, and is the oddest little body to look at that ever I heard of. But I am quite sure she is good-natured, and would be thought a model little lady by the people of her generation."

"Very well, my dear; if you like her, that is enough."

"But don't you like her?"

"I should not fancy her as a mother-in-law," I replied shortly.

"But I am not going to live with her. And she is certainly not a connection to be ashamed of should she visit me after my marriage."

The confident way in which she spoke of her marriage, as though my consent were perfectly genuine, and I could find no single ground for dissatisfaction, always irritated me. But I never permitted myself to lose my temper with her. For what good? as the French say. I had been forced by her covert actions at the beginning of her engagement into acquiescence in her wishes; the attitude I had then taken I had never departed from. If the days which were passing over her head were not modifying the conclusions she had formed of Ransome's character, temper, and

virtues, her want of perception was not my fault. Had she
permitted me, I would have done my duty by her faithfully;
but she had rejected my advice, she had thrust me aside
from her counsels, and there was simply nothing for me to
do but let matters take their course.

Any attempt at forcing her away from her wishes must
have ended in my defeat. I lacked the moral power to
make my love wise with severity. Besides, I knew enough
of her character to fear the effect of determined behavior,
had I not been too weakly soft-hearted to exercise it.

Having once met Mrs. Ransome, I expected to see her
every day at my house; but I was agreeably disappointed.
She seemed to be inspired with the same bashfulness that
had restrained her son when we had first known him; and
during the three weeks she stopped at Copsford, she dined
with us once and called four times only.

On these occasions she had talked with her accustomed
volubility, and I had noticed that she always seemed best
pleased when her son was out of the room; for he decidedly
influenced her choice of topics, though when she was free
to speak as she chose, nothing ever escaped her which her
son could have found fault with.

So garrulous a lady would soon make acquaintance in the
neighborhood; and before she was at Copsford a fortnight,
people were talking of her as the mother of the gentleman
Miss Kilmain was going to marry. I learned, from the way
she discussed the affair, that she was very proud of her son's
engagement, and I was also told that she spoke in high terms
of me, affirming that I was a man after her own heart, with
other compliments which I need not repeat.

The day before she returned to Guildford, Mrs. Ransome
called to say good-by. She caught me as I was about to
mount my horse. I accompanied her to the drawing-room,
but fortunately the horse at the door was too broad a hint
for her to miss, and she did not stay above ten minutes.

" I don't know," she said, in the course of our brief conversation, " if Phœbe has named the day. Saville is close;
I can't get to hear from him when he is to be married."

" My daughter has hitherto acted quite independently of

me," I replied; "so there is no reason to suppose that she
has not fixed a day for her marriage because I am ignorant
of it."

"Do I understand, Colonel Kilmain, that at this eleventh
hour you still withhold your consent from your daughter's
marriage?" cried the little lady, staring at me with vague,
dilated eyes.

"I thought I had explained," I answered stiffly. "My
consent *has* been given—after a manner. Phœbe exactly
knows its character, and how far she may congratulate herself upon its cordiality."

She left her chair, shaking her head and exclaiming, "The
course of true love never did run smooth!" And then, looking at me very steadily, and with quite a sinister expression
in her eyes, she added, "If *I* were Saville, I would not lower
myself by deigning to accept a gift so grudgingly bestowed
as Phœbe's hand. I only hope that his wife will appreciate
the sweetness and temper he has shown throughout this
strange engagement."

I received her satirical courtesy in silence, shrinking from
the skirmish her words threatened to involve me in. I accompanied her to the hall; she dropped me another curtsey,
and went away.

A week or two after Mrs. Ransome had left Copsford, her
son called upon me. From the dining-room window I saw
him come along the avenue. He asked the servant if I was
at home, and this inquiry for me at once decided in my
mind the object that had brought him to the house.

He was nervous and pale. I requested him to be seated,
and remained silent, determined not to help him one jot
toward an issue I had never more sincerely deprecated than
at that moment.

"I'll not beat about the bush, Colonel," he began, locking his hands to steady the nervous twitchings of his arms,
and regarding me with strange and almost pathetic wistful-
ness. "Phœbe has consented to marry me on the second
of next month, and we only wait to receive your approval."

"Very well," I answered. "She knows better than I
whether that will give her time for her preparations. If

you have fixed on the second of next month, let the cere-
mony take place on that day. What will satisfy her will
satisfy me."

"I wish we had your sympathy. I do not speak for myself, but for her. So far as *I* am concerned, I do not hope
to remove your prejudices to this marriage; though I protest before heaven, I am ignorant of the reasons you have
for your special dissatisfaction with Phœbe's choice."

"This is hardly fair to either of us, Ransome," I exclaimed, forcing a smile. "Of one thing be assured—you
wrong me if you think you have not my sympathy. I wish
you both all joy, and shall prove my sincerity by doing my
utmost to contribute to your happiness."

He bowed, but my tone was too constrained to permit him
to accept my words with the significance they would have
taken from a cordial manner.

Observing him silent, I continued:

"It is proper I should explain my plans to you with respect to my daughter's settlement, from which it was never
my intention to depart under any circumstances. I shall
resign this house to her, and settle upon her a fortune that
will enable her to support her position with dignity and comfort. In the event of her dying without issue, the property
reverts to me, or, in case of my death, to my next-of-kin.
I intend no disrespect by these arrangements. Had Phœbe
married the first lord in the country, I should have insisted
upon the same conditions."

"You are quite right. I would much rather she should
keep what she brings. There is no sacrifice, short of re-
linquishing her, which I would not make to prove that I
marry Phœbe for herself only."

"Oh, I could not question your sincerity in the face of
her convictions. She must know you better than I, and
her constancy should prove yours."

Here all that need be repeated of our conversation terminated. I think he was surprised to find how easily I had ac-
quiesced in his arrangements. But he was greatly mistaken
if he supposed I should review my objections in the teeth
of an opposition which I knew must eventually defeat me.

But I had still one final word to say to Phœbe. I joined her in the drawing-room after Ransome had left the house, and said:

"Mr. Ransome tells me you have fixed upon the second of next month for your marriage."

She colored up, but answered steadily:

"Yes, papa. Is it too soon?"

"You should know better than I. Have you thoroughly considered the step you are about to take?"

"Thoroughly; and I am happy."

"You are not disturbed by the thought that the sanction of my heart does not accompany you?"

"Papa, if I understood your prejudice, I should respect it, though it would not influence me, because there is nothing in Saville to justify any prejudice. But I do not understand it. You were annoyed in the first instance by my loving Saville without your knowledge. But I could not help loving him, and I was afraid to take you into my confidence for the very reason you afterward proved to me I was right to fear—the dread of your ridiculing my love by declaring it could not exist in so short a time. And then my secret meetings vexed you, and though I knew I was to blame, yet I felt I was sufficiently punished by your severity afterward. These things prejudiced you without reason against Saville, who surely did not act wrongfully in falling in love with me. Your sanction would make me happier than I am if I had it; but your disapproval *does not* pain me, because I feel sure that the time will come when you will find out that Saville's nature is honorable and good, and that I was right in giving him my love."

I listened to her without interruption, and then said:

"I pray God that that time may come, my child. But whether it comes or not, never, until you are a parent, will you understand the anxiety and grief you have caused me since you first confessed your love for Mr. Ransome. No!" I continued, holding up my hand to silence her, "I must say this; but do not let it provoke a discussion. We are all the sport of circumstance, and though my heart has misgivings which you are right in saying I cannot so convey as to make them intelligible, yet I have a humble trust in God's providence, and resign your future into His hands with a prayer that He will watch over you. May He bless you and guide you, and make you happy! Our separation may be lasting—for on the day of your marriage I leave this house never to return to it but as a visitor, whose coming must be altogether dependent upon the welcome he receives— but rest assured that my love will follow you while my life lasts. Let your future be what it will, on one friend you may always count who will never betray nor forsake you."

She ran to me and I folded her in my arms. We both of us shed tears, but I will own that my words had relieved my heart of a weight and that I felt happier for having spoken kindly to my daughter.

But a very few lines need be devoted to the marriage. A few of my best friends were present, but Mrs. Ransome wrote a letter at the last moment to say that the state of her health would not permit her to join us. Phœbe seemed perfectly happy. She cried a little when we parted; but I caught a glimpse of her face in the carriage just before it drove off, and she was smiling with an expression of triumph and devotion at her husband.

I now lay down my pen for the present, leaving the interval between my introduction and the story I have yet to relate to be filled up with the narrative of Miss Avory, my daughter's housekeeper, who was an eye-witness of events and actions of which only the rumors reached me.

Part Two

THE HOUSEKEEPER'S STORY

I

THE share I had in the story to which I have been asked
to contribute begins in the summer of the year 18—.

In the first months of that year I was housekeeper to a
gentleman and his wife named Mortimer. My wages were
liberal, my duties small, and I was congratulating myself
on the ease and security of my situation, when Mr. Mortimer
suddenly died. His wife, through grief, fell seriously ill;
her relatives—she had no children—took charge of her; her
home was broken up, and I was dismissed with a gift, to
procure, if I could, another situation.

My having to obtain a livelihood by employment of this
kind was owing to the villainy of a lawyer who robbed me
of the small fortune — two thousand pounds—which my
father had left me. My father was a Dissenting minister,
who, by great care and self-denial, had succeeded in laying
by a sum of money sufficiently large, as he thought, to supply me, his only child, with a competence for life. He had
entrusted his will to the custody of one Mr. Williams, a
solicitor practising in the town in which my father dwelt,
a man in whom he had the utmost confidence, and whom he
would hold up as a pattern of honesty and sincerity. I
was twenty-one when my father died, and three days after
his death Mr. Williams left the country, having, as I afterward ascertained, sold the whole of the securities which my
father had placed with him for me, and leaving me not one
sixpence even to pay the expenses of the funeral. Fortunately the house in which my father had lived and the fur-

niture were his own; these were sold by auction to pay off certain debts, and the remainder of the money was given to me, with which I went into lodgings, and shortly after obtained a situation as governess. My duties were so arduous, and the treatment I received so bad, that I threw up the post in disgust, and on the recommendation of a friend of my father, applied for the place of housekeeper to a family, with whom I lived for six years. My work was comparatively menial, and at first my pride revolted; but I soon found out that what apparent indignity may lie in humble avocations depends altogether upon fashion and not at all upon fact—that a governess, taking a higher stand in the social scale than a housekeeper, substantially does work which no housekeeper is ever expected or desired to do. Good sense should free us from such silly prejudices as these.

The Mortimers' house had been in London. When the old gentleman died and I was thrown once more on the world, my health was not good. I thought a change in the country would benefit me, and wrote to a respectable farmer's wife, Mrs. Campion, who lived at a a place called Copsford, about forty miles from town, asking if she could spare me a bedroom for a week or two. She replied that there was a room at my service whenever it pleased me to visit her. So next day I packed my trunk, took the coach, and with thirty pounds in my pocket, all the money I had, went down to Copsford.

I recall this journey by coach for the sake of the impression one of the passengers made on me. When we had gone about fifteen miles, the coach was stopped, and a gentleman scrambled down from the roof and got inside. He was a dark-complexioned young man, with very black eyes and a short mustache, and I thought he was a foreigner, until he exclaimed in good English against the dust and the wind, the first of which he said was enough to choke him, and the other to cut his ears off. He might have been right about the dust, for it rose in clouds under the wheels, and the gentleman's hat and coat were white with it; but if he meant that the wind was keen, he talked nonsense, for the

5

day was oppressively hot, and the atmosphere of the interior of the coach suffocating.

An old gentleman, with a very red face, who sat in the corner of the coach, with a blue cotton pocket-handkerchief over his head, asked him if he really meant that the wind was cold by saying that it was enough to cut his ears off.

"I didn't say cold, nor am I aware that I addressed myself to you or anybody else," replied the young man.

"I really beg your pardon," said the other, bobbing his head in a kind of contorted bow, "I mistook you. I thought you a gentleman, or I should not have spoken."

"What do you mean, sir?" cried the young man.

The old gentleman pulled out a book and began very gravely to read. The other muttered something inaudible through his teeth, but finding that his staring produced no impression whatever upon the old gentleman, he jerked his hat off, fanned his face with it, and grumbled that the place was hot enough to cook a goose in. A moment after he roared out to the guard—"Let me out! I shall die here." The guard said that he couldn't stop the coach again; the gentleman must wait until they arrived at L——.

"We'll see about that," said the young man, who jumped up, seized the door, and began to rattle it with all his strength, crying at the top of his voice: "Stop! coachman. I'm being murdered!"

I could hardly forbear laughing at the consternation his outcries would excite among the passengers outside, but they produced the effect he desired; the coach was stopped, and the young man, firing off a volley of curses at the guard, sprang out, and presently I heard his feet clattering on the roof.

There were several of us "insides," and you may believe, now we knew that the young man could not hear us, that we made very free with him in our remarks. The ladies unanimously agreed that he was no gentleman: a young fellow in spectacles declared that a minute more, and he would have knocked him down; and the old gentleman in the corner suggested that he was a madman, and bade me, **who sat near the door**, to keep a sharp lookout for the keepers, who were probably in full pursuit of the coach in a chaise.

However, I heard no more of the dark-faced gentleman until I alighted at Copsford. A phaeton waited for him, into which he jumped, and was driven off; while I hired a fly, and was carried with my luggage to the farmhouse.

On my arrival Mrs. Campion came out to meet me, and I walked through a pleasant garden to a large, white-fronted, thatched-roofed building, with a porch rich with woodbine and honeysuckle, and many handsome trees at the back where the outbuildings were, and where the hens were cackling and fluttering as they strove for their perches, while the air all about me was deliciously aromatic with the smell of hay and flowers. The house, indeed, with the sheds at the back, of which I had caught a glimpse as I passed along the road, was just a farm of the real kind, exquisitely neat and picturesquely rustic, without one ornate touch of any description to make a "model" of it.

Mrs. Campion welcomed me cordially, and led me into her kitchen parlor, which the house door directly opened into, where I found her husband—a big, honest-faced man, who nodded pleasantly to his wife's introduction of him. This parlor made a picture it perfectly soothes the memory to recall, and I only wish my story lay in this house, that I might have a good excuse for describing it fully. I could desire no better Paradise in this life than such a place to live in, with the sweet-smelling porch close against the sitting-room, the room itself cosily decorated with burnished brass dish-covers and candlesticks, and a capacious fire-place, in which one might sit and look up, when the fire was out, and see the stars as from the bottom of a well, and a broad, solid table, scrubbed to the purity of snow, and an evenly tiled floor and comfortable armchairs, and cheerful prints upon the brown walls.

Mr. Campion went to fetch my trunk, and his wife took me to my bedroom and sat with me while I removed my bonnet and shawl.

"Now, Miss Avory," said she, folding her arms upon her plump figure, while the kindliest smile lighted up her

comely face; "what I want you to know at once is, you are
my guest and not a lodger, which I should be ashamed to
allow your dear father's child to be.   Please don't thank
me; for if I oblige you in this, you oblige me just as much
by coming, and so we're equal."

Her kindness of course involved us in a little amiable
dispute, which ended in my giving in, and then we went
down-stairs, where a servant-girl was preparing the table
for tea.   And what a tea it was!   Rich brown bread and
delicous butter, and new-laid eggs, and fragrant bacon, and
sweet cream, and tea the like of which I have never since
tasted.   Even had my appetite not been good, Mr. Campion's must have proved contagious.   Such a tea as he
made I never should have thought lay within the power of
mortal man.   His honest, cheerful laughter rang merrily
across the table; through the open door came the delicate
perfumes of the garden; the setting sunshine glittered in
ruby stars in the dish-covers and candlesticks, and the air
was vocal with the songs of birds singing among the trees
at the back of the house.

I need not tell you how I, who had been cooped-up in
London for many months past, enjoyed this radiant scene,
this peaceful, exquisite change.

When tea was over we drew our chairs to the porch,
while farmer Campion lighted his pipe, and his wife drew
forth a bundle of knitting.   We talked of many things,
and I related some of my experiences as housekeeper, and
explained that I could not possibly remain long idle, since
my stock of money was slender, and I had nothing to depend on but my calling.   Farmer Campion looked concerned, and asked me why I did not get married; to which
I replied that nobody had as yet done me the honor of offering for my hand.   He pulled his pipe from his mouth in
order to laugh freely, and, striking his knee, cried out that
if it wasn't for Sally, meaning his wife, I might depend
upon not being obliged to remain single long; which, as it
was the only compliment of the kind I ever received in my
life, I consider it due to myself to repeat.   As Mrs. Campion's face looked doubtful, I changed the subject by

speaking of the extraordinary behavior of the gentleman I
had travelled with from London.

"If that wasn't Squire Ransome, it was Old Nick!" exclaimed the farmer, who had listened to me attentively, and
now addressed his wife.

"Was he dark-faced, with a bit of hair over his upper
lip, and a queer black eye?" asked Mrs. Campion.

"Yes," said I, "and he had a strange sort of voice that
died away at the end of his words."

"That's him! that's him!" cried the farmer. "And he
called out murder, did he? I reckon it was a mercy that
he didn't make some one else call it out."

"Who is this Squire Ransome?" I asked.

"Why, a bit of a mad chap that came among us two
years ago, and married poor old Colonel Kilmain's girl—
Phœbe she was called, as likely a lass as you'll see in these
parts," answered the farmer.

"Not so mad as you think," replied Mrs. Campion,
quietly. "More of a fool than a madman; though it was
always my belief as his mother was wrong in the inside.
He lodged with us two years ago, the time he was courting
Miss Phœbe, and often and often I've had 'em standing in
this very porch holding each other's hands, and whispering
under their breaths as though they were really dying of
love; which they might have been in those days. But time
brings wonderful changes."

"Mrs. Ransome was with us three weeks," said the farmer; "as queer a little body as ever I saw—no higher than
that," he added, holding his hand above the floor, "with
just the sized face yours would show were you to look into
one of them dish-covers."

"It was a queer affair, the courting between that couple,"
Mrs. Campion went on. "I used to say that the Colonel
hated the thoughts of Miss Phœbe marrying her sweetheart,
though there was a deal of pride in him—there was no getting at his feelings by his face."

"But the truth came out once, didn't it, wife?" said the
farmer. "I heard Johnson, the chemist over at Copsford,
say as how Dr. Redcliff, who was very often at Gardenhurst

in the Colonel's time, told the young people, when he was
in a rage with them for quarrelling, that they were badly
matched, and didn't deserve to prosper, because the Colonel
never wished to see them mated, and that he blamed himself for not helping his old friend to put a stop to it, instead of pretending it was all nature and the likes of that.
That came to Johnson by Mary, the housemaid, as overheerd
the parties talking."

"You never told me that before," exclaimed Mrs. Campion.

"Oh. it went out of my mind; other people's business
don't trouble *me* long," answered the farmer, shaking the
ashes out of his pipe. "Redcliff was a good man, and,
I believe, stuck to the lady while he lived. But, lor' bless
me! taking sides never does in marriage. No good ever
comes of pitting man and wife against each other. If they
can't agree, let 'em separate—nothing else 'll do, as any
lawyer will tell you."

I was about to ask some question, when farmer Campion,
suddenly wheeling his big body round until he faced his
wife, and giving the arm of his chair a mighty slap, cried
out: "It's just come into my head, Sally, that they're
wanting a housekeeper at Gardenhurst."

"Are you sure?   Who told you?"

He scratched the back of his head, and said that he was
blessed if he could tell, though he *did* think it was Mr.
Simmons, the baker. But, however that might be, he'd
find out and let me know.

"It would be curious if they *do* want a housekeeper," said
Mrs. Campion to me. "You'd be pretty sure to suit Mrs.
Ransome; but I don't know," she added, shaking her head,
"whether it's a family that would suit *you*. That was the
master, recollect, who came down with you in the coach."

"But I should have nothing to do with him."

"No, that's quite right!" exclaimed the farmer. "He's
very little at home, they say: always tramping or riding
about the country. No one sees much of him excepting his
wife, who, I dare say, wouldn't break her heart if she had
to dispense altogether with his company."

Saying this, he left us to look after his men. My curios·
ity had been excited by what I had heard of the Ransomes,
and by their want of a housekeeper, and I asked Mrs. Campion some questions about them; but she knew very little
to tell me. All that she could say was, that they had the
reputation of being a very unhappy couple; that Mr. Ransome had a very bad temper, and that his temper had quite
spoiled his wife's.

We went early to bed at that pleasant farmhouse, and
my mind does not hold a prettier memory than that of the
sweet, fresh, pink-and-white bedroom in which I slept that
night. There was a great moon over the hills, and I sat
long in its gentle light at the open window, drinking in the
rich night air that crept over the whitened flowers to me,
and thinking that I could hardly wish for more happiness
than to find a comfortable berth in this delightful neighborhood, that I might sometimes climb those noble hills and
live in the presence of the gracious scene into which chance
had led me.

I was awakened by the noise of the farmyard, and opened
my eyes upon a room brilliant with sunshine. It was long
since I had enjoyed so healthful and refreshing a sleep.
There was a bouquet on the toilet-table, for which, I afterward learned, I had to thank Mrs. Campion, who had brought
it into my room before I was awake. A hearty greeting
welcomed me when I got down-stairs, and soon we were
seated at breakfast, with a blackbird singing loudly in a
cage in the porch, and the breezy morning air perfectly
melodious with the humming of the wasps and gold-ribbed
flies among the flowers.

"I mean to inquire about that housekeeping matter for
you this morning," said farmer Campion; "and I hope
you'll get it, for then you'll be near us, and we shall see
something of you."

I told Mrs. Campion that, while she went about her work
after breakfast, I would go for a walk, and inquired the
way to Gardenhurst. But before I started she must first
show me over the farm; and I was taken to a great open

space at the back, with a little forest of stately trees all
about it, where countless hens scratched and grumbled and
cackled, and kept the scene moving with their restless bodies.
Here were the cowsheds, but they were empty, for the cows
had been milked, and were away munching the buttercups
and daisies in a distant paddock; here was a dirty pond,
with ducks sailing upon its dirty bosom; and in a long
range of styes a great concourse of pigs were fretting the
woodwork with their punctured snouts, climbing on each
other's backs, squealing with voracity, and contributing a
curious bass to the sharp trebles that rang from other portions of the enclosure. But I would no longer detain Mrs.
Campion from her duties, and so, promising to be back in
time for dinner at half-past twelve, I passed down the garden and entered the road.

II

I walked straight forward, and arrived at a broad stretch
of grass, sheltered by a hill, and faced by some dense shrubbery, which I afterward heard was called Rose Common,
and then, proceeding along a level road for a short distance, gained the bottom of the lane which led up the side
of the Cairngorm Mount.

The prospect, as I advanced, unfolded itself, and I repeatedly stopped to dwell upon its beauties. The hills lay
heaped all around me, but scarcely any two of them presented the same color. The sides of some were densely
shagged with wood, and I pictured the delicious coolness
and solitude under the shadows of the leaves, the squirrels
frisking among the boughs, the sweet wind rushing from
the hill-tops through the trees. The little villages peeping
out of the valleys were sharply defined in the brilliant atmosphere. Yonder, on the spire of a church, a gilt vane
shone like a gold-colored flame against the rich background
of the dark green hill. The month was June, and the crops
were still green, though high and wavy, and the larks soared
over them, inviting the eye to seek them in the air, where
the vain search was rewarded by the spectacle of the soft

olue heavens, with here and there a cloud, as wan as the moon and no bigger, melting in the azure depths.

After I had walked and loitered awhile, I got into a main road, and came presently to a wall, which ran a long distance up this road and terminated at a gateway. The gates were open, and did not look as if they were ever closed. From the description of the estate which Mrs. Campion had given me, I knew this to be the residence of the Ransomes; but I could see nothing of the house, owing to the trees of the avenue, which wound away to the right and afforded no glimpse even of the grounds behind them.

The idea now occurred to me that I might as well call and inquire if the family were in want of a housekeeper since I was on the spot. Even supposing Mr. Campion had been misinformed, I could hardly be thought intrusive if I explained that the farmer had told me the situation was vacant. It was certain I could not long afford to be idle; nor could I trespass beyond a week at the outside on the Campions' hospitality. To be sure I had not been greatly prejudiced in Mr. Ransome's favor by his behavior in the coach, supposing that queer individual to have been Mr. Ransome. But my experience as housekeeper had shown me that I should have little to do with the master. One place might prove as good as another. All about Copsford was delightful country; it would be pleasant to have such friends as the Campions in the neighborhood; and so, everything considered, if I could obtain the post of housekeeper at Gardenhurst, I might consider myself lucky.

But it was too early to call yet; indeed, it was not yet ten. In an hour's time I might venture; so I walked slowly forward, and, coming to a grassy plot, sat down near the hedge, finding that the road branched off, and began to look dusty and hot as the sun mounted. A cart came by presently, the driver asleep, with his back to the horse and his head on his knees; but the horse went up the hill more steadily than had his master held the reins. Then several tramps came down the hill, walking in a line, and kicking up the dust with their dogged lazy feet. They did not see me, or I should have probably had them swarming about me to beg for money. There was a woman among them with her bonnet on her back, and her hair glued in black streaks upon her forehead with perspiration, who took strides as long as any man among them, and spoke in a thick voice, and had a wonderfully coarse laugh, and was, I think, the most unwomanly woman I ever saw in my life. I speculated upon their intentions as they swung down the hill *en route* for Copsford, until they had tramped themselves out of sight; and then an old pedler, with his pack on his back, came by, leaning on his stick and stopping ever and again to peer among the stones at the side of the road, turn the thing that arrested him about with his stick, kick it viciously, and march forward again, working his under lip.

When presently I looked at my watch I found that a whole hour had slipped by since I first seated myself; so I got up and walked down the hill to the gates, not without a misgiving that I was acting boldly in assuming the family's want of a housekeeper on the mere strength of an unaffiliated report.

There was no lodge and no bell; so I passed through the open gates along the delicious avenue, where the hard ground I trod on and the velvet sward under the trees were twinkling with the shadows of the leaves. On coming to a bend, I saw the house in the sunshine, with the conservatories gleaming at the back, and a broad lawn stretching in front of it like a carpet. A footman came to the door.

"Does Mrs. Ransome live here?" I asked.

"Yes, mem."

"I have been told that she is in want of a housekeeper. Is that so?"

"Quite correct. Do you apply for the situation?"

"Is Mrs. Ransome to be seen at this hour?"

"Yes."

"Then ask me no questions, but go and tell her I am here."

The footman stared, then sauntered off, and disappeared through a door. He returned in five minutes, and asked me to accompany him, and conducted me through a small

anteroom into what seemed to me, and which really was
another hall, with doors on either side. He knocked on
one of these doors, threw it open, and in I walked.

I found myself in a large room, pleasantly though plainly furnished, with pretty pictures on the walls and flowers
on the sideboard. A young lady with a small, handsome
face, dark eyes, and narrow, well-defined eyebrows, sat
near the open window with a book in her lap. She inclined
her head when I entered, and told me to take a chair.

"You have applied for the situation of housekeeper?"

"Yes, madam; I have been told that you are in want of
a housekeeper, and took an early opportunity of calling to
offer my services."

She said that her housekeeper had left her in May, and
that she had been making inquiries since that time for some
one to replace her. What was my name, and my age? and
where had I lived? and what salary did I expect? and did
I thoroughly understand my duties?

While I answered her questions she observed me narrow-
ly, and while *she* spoke I examined her. Her conclusions,
as the issue afterward proved, were satisfactory; mine, I
will confess, were somewhat doubtful.

First of all I was struck by her haughty manner, expressed not so much by her speech as by her lofty uphold-
ing of her head and the deliberate gaze she fastened upon
me, as though her scrutiny was in no sense to be regulated
by the embarrassment its intentness might cause. Her eyes
were very fine and flashed as she moved them; her mouth
was small and the lips compressed; her complexion quite
colorless; her dress simple in fashion, but rich in material,
and it fitted her fine figure exquisitely. Her face was thinner than the peculiar character of her beauty admitted; in
health (I thought), or were she happy, those dark lines under her eyes would not be there, nor would her lips look
pallid with habitual compression.

I was with her not longer than a quarter of an hour, during which (having exhausted her questions) she had observed
that her household was a small one and that her reason for
engaging a housekeeper was not to save herself trouble, but

to obtain help in her efforts to economize. I told her that
I thought myself qualified to assist her in that, as my
knowledge of servants was great, and in my last situation
I had the entire control of the housekeeping duties, and had
done so well as to save Mr. and Mrs. Mortimer a fair sum
of money a week out of the amount they had allowed me for
keeping house. She would write to Mrs. Mortimer and
communicate her decision. Where was I stopping at Copsford?

"At Rose Farm," I replied.

"Oh, then you know the Campions?"

"Quite well. I am their guest at present."

"They are worthy people," she said, and her eyes wandered to the window and she fell into deep thought. I remembered then that Rose Farm had been the scene of her's
and Mr. Ransome's love-making. She looked up in a few
moments and exclaimed, " I will write to you when I have
heard from Mrs. Mortimer. Should her answer justify me
in engaging you, you can enter upon your duties at the beginning of next week."

Upon this I bowed and left the room.

I got back to the farm by twelve o'clock. Farmer Campion was in the porch when I approached the house, and
called out:

"It's quite right, Miss Avory. They're in want of a
housekeeper up at Gardenhurst. I saw Larkins the butcher
who serves 'em, likewise Miss Reddish, who keeps a sta-
tioner's shop in King Street, and knows all about everything, and they both said t'other housekeeper left in May,
and a new one was wanted."

"Very well," I answered; "I'll see what's to be done in
a day or two."

"My interview with Mrs. Ransome had taken place on a
Tuesday. On the Friday following the Ransomes' footman
called at Rose Farm with a note addressed to me, which, on
opening, I found to contain this formal communication:

"Mrs. Ransome, having received a satisfactory reply from
Mrs. Mortimer respecting Miss Avory's character and ex-

perience, begs to say that Miss Avory may consider herself
engaged from Monday next."

"No answer," said I to the footman; and gave the note
to Mrs. Campion to read.

"I don't doubt you'll suit them," she exclaimed, handing
me back the letter; "and I only trust they may suit you.
But I'm pretty sure before you have been at Gardenhurst
a month, you'll have seen some queer goings-on. I'm much
mistaken if the young wife don't want a good friend at her
back with such a husband as the Squire to deal with. If
she hasn't wonderfully changed since she used to come here
and chat as pleasantly as yourself with me, you'll like her.
But mark my words, you'll have seen some rare goings-on
before you're a month older."

So I did, and within the time my friend had prophesied.
What these "goings-on" were I will endeavor to relate as
faithfully as I can, bating no jot of the truth, and I trust
that my frankness will never be mistaken for freedom by
the gentleman who has requested me to write down all that
I know about his daughter and son-in-law.

III

Monday morning having come, I was driven over to Gardenhurst by Mr. Campion, who carried my box to the house.
The footman treated me with proper respect now that he
knew I was housekeeper, took my box, and asked me whether
I would see the mistress at once or go to my bedroom.

"What is your name?" I asked him.

"Maddox—John Maddox," he answered.

"How do they call you here?"

"Maddox."

"Then, Maddox," said I, "put that box down and send
one of the housemaids to me."

"Yes, mem," he replied, and went away.

I was determined to let him see by my behavior that this
was not my first place. Never in my life did I attempt to
conciliate the servants I have had to rule by bland manners.

A good-looking housemaid arrived and conducted me to

my bedroom, which, though at the top of the house, was no
great distance to climb, as the building consisted only of
two stories. On the first landing I passed a large room on
the left, the door of which was open, and enabled me to
catch a glimpse of a handsome bedstead richly draped, satin-
covered chairs, and other luxurious furniture.

"Whose bedroom is that?" I asked the girl.

"Mistress's," she answered. "Yonder is the master's;"
she pointed to a door on the right.

"Stop a moment," I said to her as she was leaving my
bedroom. "I shall want you to show me down-stairs to the
housekeeper's room."

I took off my bonnet and smoothed my hair with my
hands, and then threw a brief glance round to judge the accommodation I had been provided with. I could not grum-
ble. The bedroom was neatly furnished and in front of the
house; that is to say, it overlooked the grounds, which
sloped for nearly a mile, it seemed to me, down the hill;
at the bottom were the dense trees entirely blotting out the
prospect in that quarter; between them and the house were
the flower-gardens, and all on the right was the kitchen-
garden, where the gardeners were at work. The left was
clear and submitted a magnificent prospect of hills stretching to the horizon.

"How many indoor servants are there?" I inquired.

"Four," answered the girl.

"Do Mr. and Mrs. Ransome see much company?"

"Hardly no one. They did when they were first married, but they don't seem to have no friends now."

"How long have you been in your situation?"

"A year and ten months, this week, miss."

This looked promising. I followed the girl downstairs
and reached the basement, where the housekeeper's room
was, adjoining the kitchen. The cook, a middle-aged
woman, came in to see me under the excuse to get a piece
of newspaper, and while I was questioning her about her
work that I might obtain some insight into mine, a bell rang
and presently Maddox came to say that I was wanted in the
dining-room.

I went upstairs, and after a little hesitation, owing to the two halls, which puzzled me, found the door to which I had been conducted by the footman on my first visit, knocked and entered.

Mrs. Ransome was alone, walking up and down before the open window with her hands behind her. There was a slight flush on her marble-colored cheeks, and an angry light in her eyes. The smell of a newly lighted cigar lingered in the room, but the smoker was not visible.

She turned her head with a strangely haughty gesture, and, forcing a composure upon herself, said in a rich, tremulous voice:

"When did you arrive, Miss Avory?"

"Just now, madam."

"I wish to say at once, that you will recognize no other superior in this house but me, that you will obey no other orders but those you receive from me. You understand?"

"Certainly," I replied, somewhat surprised.

"The reason I discharged my last housekeeper was because she thought fit to disobey my orders by obeying those of another person, who visited us in April. If I die for it," she exclaimed passionately, "I will claim my own rights to the last."

I was silent.

"The lady I wrote to, Mrs. Mortimer, told me that you are the daughter of a Dissenting minister. Have you seen much trouble?"

"I had much trouble when I began life; but since then my troubles have been commonplace enough."

She bent her eyes on me with a frown of earnest scrutiny. I was struck by the intentness of her gaze, which, so far as I could read expression, seemed indicative of habitual distrust. Her beauty at that moment was very striking. She swept her hair behind her ear, and, pulling an envelope from her pocket, exclaimed:

"I received this letter an hour ago from my husband's mother. She was here in April—she is coming to stop here again next week. She is a meddlesome woman, Miss Avory. I put you on your guard against her. If you value my pleasure suffer her on no account to dictate to you."

This frankness must surprise the reader more than it sur-prised me. I own that I was not so astonished by it—stranger as I was to her, and occupying as I did a humble position in her household—when I looked at her and saw that her mind was struggling with a painful grievance, and that her candor was the result both of helplessness and irritation.

"Madam," I replied, Mrs. Campion's words coming into my mind; "depend upon it I shall recognize no mistress but you while I remain in your house. I have had some experience of meddlers, but was never influenced by them in my life."

"Thank you," she answered simply; and the hard expression went out of her face, and she looked at me with something almost of gentleness in her eyes.

She then spoke of my duties, of which she explained the nature fully; and which, greatly to my satisfaction, I found would give me more liberty than I had ever before enjoyed. There were no more outbreaks of temper; but several times, when she was silent a moment or two, I heard her sigh bitterly; and once, when one of the gardeners passed the window, she turned quickly, evidently mistaking his footstep, with a glance of scorn and dislike that made her face tragical.

I left her and went down-stairs, where I found the house-maid whom I had before talked with sewing in my room. Being anxious to learn as much as I could of the characters of the people I had come to live with, I resolved to put a few judicious questions, concluding that the two years she had lived in the house would qualify her to satisfy me on most of the points I considered it my policy to learn.

"Is this your regular time for sewing?" I inquired, by way of opening the conversation.

"Yes, miss, from twelve to one, after I have helped Susan to finish upstairs."

"Do you like your place?"

"Why, yes, it suits me pretty well. Mistress is kind, though she is often put out by master."

"Has Mrs. Ransome any relatives living in the neighbor-hood?" I asked.

"None that I know of. She has a father who is an officer, and lives somewhere in France. He came here six months ago to visit his daughter, but the quarrels was so constant that they made the poor old gentleman dreadfully uneasy. I *did* think it hard that he couldn't find hisself comfort-able here considering it were his house before he gave it to his daughter. He said to Mrs. Simpson, as were then housekeeper—'For God's sake,' he says, 'be a friend to my child and protect her as much as you can from her own temper,' he says, 'and the aggravating man she's married.' I don't know what he expected Mrs. Simpson to do, but Mrs. Simpson told me this herself."

"Perhaps the quarrels were caused by his interference," said I, rather doubting that little bit about "the aggravat-ing man" which she had put into the Colonel's mouth.

"No, indeed, they were not. I can answer for that my-self. The Colonel's a perfect gentleman, and was always trying to pacify them."

"But what is the reason of these quarrels?" I exclaimed, disposed to consider them largely due to Mrs. Ransome, who had struck me as possessing a very dangerous temper.

"Nothing but wickedness," answered the girl, sewing quickly, "and I don't care who hears me say so."

"Who is to blame?"

"Why, the master," she cried, looking up. "I heard it said at Copsford—that's where I belong to—before I came here, that there was a good deal of love between them, but most on her side; and for a time things did go on very pleasantly, but they got arguing at last, and then took to quarrelling; and sometimes, I'm truly grateful no one can hear 'em but those in the kitchen, for he talks so madly and she screams, you'd hardly think you were in a gentle-man's house. I've heard a thing or two since I've been here, though not through listening, but because the secrets was forced upon my ear by the loud voice they were spoken in."

"These secrets are nobody's concern."

6

"No, certainly not, and I never talk of them, only when I'm questioned like."

"Do you know Mr. Ransome's mother?"

"Her that was here in April? Yes—she's no bigger than my sister's child who was eleven in December," she exclaimed, bursting into a laugh. "Such a bit of a woman, miss, you might hide her in a fish-kettle."

"Does she attempt to order you about when she comes here?"

"That she does, but *I* never mind her. I forgot to make her bed once, and she came running into the kitchen after lunch calling for me, and was in such a passion, I thought she'd go off in a fit. 'Oh, you wicked girl!' she says, 'Oh, you bad-hearted thing! how dare you neglect me?' she says. After she had stormed at me, she climbs up-stairs again, and I heard her complaining to mistress, and just to make sure that she told no lies, I listened in the hall; and mistress says, "My servants are engaged to wait upon me; if you want proper attendance, you may get it in a lodging." This pleased me, for it served the old lady right for abusing me for forgetfulness. Well, out flounced old Mrs. Ransome, and I had to hide behind the hat-stand to prevent her seeing of me; and she ran up-stairs calling, 'Saville! Saville!' meaning her son; and soon she comes down again, followed by the master, and then they both go to where the mistress was, and such a dreadful quarrel followed that I was quite scared, and went into the kitchen where the servants stood listening with white faces expecting I don't know what."

I was really too interested to silence her before she stopped of her own accord; but when she had done, my judgment stepped in and warned me against encouraging this gossip. I thereupon changed the subject, and shortly afterward left the room for the kitchen, where I got into a very homely conversation with the cook upon prices, tradesmen, and such matters.

When I left the kitchen I went up-stairs to my bedroom to unpack my box. There was nobody about, and I peeped into Mrs. Ransome's bedroom when I passed it, where I saw, hanging on the left-hand wall, a half-length portrait, the size of life, of a gentleman in military uniform, the face fair-complexioned, the eyes brown, and the hair short. I had no difficulty in telling by the eyes alone that this was a near relative of Mrs. Ransome, if, indeed, it were not her father. Other pictures were around the room, chiefly of a devotional character. I was again struck by the luxuriousness of the furniture—the satin-covered sofa at the foot of the bed, the rich, pink-lined window drapery, the carpet that felt like piles of velvet beneath the foot, the elaborate bedstead, and the beautiful knick-knacks—smelling-bottles, ivory hand-glasses, etc.—upon the toilet-table. These things impressed me only so far as they contrasted with the plain furniture of the other rooms. They pointed, I thought, to a quality of selfishness which made the personal comfort of the occupant of the bedroom an affair of essential importance.

I reached my bedroom, and set to work to fill the chest of drawers, and give a look of habitation to the apartment. While my hands were busy, I constantly found my thoughts running on the gossip the housemaid had bestowed on me; but I must own that I found little to interest me in the mere narrative of quarrels, in the account of old Mrs. Ransome, and of her son's evil temper; what troubled me was, how long could I hope to hold my situation in a house where so much bad passion was rife, and where collisions of a most irritating nature might be of hourly occurrence? I was quite sure the place would suit me if Mr. and Mrs. Ransome would allow me to do my work without interfering with me; but I made up my mind not to submit a moment to any ill-usage.

Having finished with my box, I started upon an exploring expedition through the house. The servants' rooms were next to mine; I examined the women's and found them tidy enough, but Maddox's presented a most dissipated appearance. There was a pair of trousers under the bed, and a waistcoat in the fender, and by the bedside, on a chair, was a flat candlestick richly festooned with grease, and beside it a volume bound in sheepskin, which I examined, and discovered to be "The Life and Adventures of Mr. Jeremiah Abershaw," with a horribly coarse woodcut for a frontispiece representing a gallows surrounded by a crowd eagerly observing a procession apparently emerging from a wall, the procession consisting of the Ordinary (labelled), Jack Ketch (labelled), some figures in the rear, and the Felon with his face turned to the mob, and a balloon coming out of his mouth inscribed "I die game!"

"Mr. Maddox keeps good company," I thought, and proceeded on my *tour d'inspection,* meaning presently to have a talk with my footman.

I reached the second landing where Mrs. Ransome's bedroom was, and knocked on the door facing hers. No answer; so I was about to turn the handle when the door flew open, and a gentleman dressed in a light suit presented himself. The moment I saw him I recognized him as the hot-headed individual who had travelled with me from London.

His dark eyes fastened themselves upon me with a look of surprise, and he exclaimed, "What do you want?"

"I beg your pardon," I replied, "I did not know you were in this room."

"Who are you?"

"Miss Avory, the housekeeper."

"Oh, my wife's choice, aren't you?"

"Mrs. Ransome engaged me on Saturday."

"Why did you knock? does anybody want me?"

"No, sir; I was looking into the rooms merely to see how the servants did their work."

"Oh, I understand. And you are the new housekeeper, eh? my wife's choice, are you?"

He stared at me with his strange eyes, running them over my figure, and after a short silence said:

"Where have I seen you?"

That he should have had the smallest recollection of my face, considering that I had been one of a number and in no manner attracted his notice in the coach, showed that he possessed a good memory. But I was not going to help

"THE DOOR FLEW OPEN AND A GENTLEMAN DRESSED IN A LIGHT SUIT
PRESENTED HIMSELF."--Page 84.

him, for the reason that he might take a prejudice to me for having witnessed him make such a thorough donkey of himself.

" Where have I seen you?" he repeated.

" I think I meet you now, sir, in this house for the first time," I replied.

" I've seen you somewhere," and he looked annoyed and frowned as he fixed his eyes on the ground.

I gave him a bow and turned away, but he stared after me until I was on the stairs, and then I heard him shut his door by slamming it to.

I had not seen enough of him yet to enable me to describe him fairly, but his blunt, unfortunate manner did not prevent me from thinking him a very good-looking man. His eyes were the most peculiar part of him, restless, glowing and black, the whites a darkish pearl-color. His forehead was high, but the shape of his head was not good; the brows were narrow and the back of the head flat. I particularly noticed that he twitched his hands incessantly while he stood asking me questions, and he had the same nervous affection in his lower lip, which he would draw sideways and disclose the teeth under his small black mustache. Another peculiarity: he invariably raised his voice in the beginning and sank it into a drawl at the end of a sentence. This might have seemed nothing but habitual indolence, as though a sentence tired his voice before he had done with it, had not the numberless suggestions of excitable activity which appeared in his gestures and manner flatly contradicted the idea. I chafed a little when I reflected on the imperious and offensive way in which he had asked me what I wanted, but tranquillized myself presently by allowing that I had annoyed him by breaking in upon his privacy and in a measure deserved his impatience.

I was resolved to carry out my programme, and the next room I came to was the drawing-room, the door of which was ajar. I peeped in, and seeing nobody advanced and gazed about me. This was undeniably the most charming room in the house, although here again the furniture was

not nearly so costly as that in Mrs. Ransome's bedroom.
There was a tall window facing the door, which led on to the
lawn, and more windows on the right, through which I
could see a row of pillars. A stream of sunshine lay upon
the carpet, and I approached the window through which it
shone to draw down the blind.

Just then Mrs. Ransome came in.

"That's right, Miss Avory," said she. "I am glad to
see you so careful. Have you been over the house yet?"

"I am now going over it," I replied.

"Have you any fault to find with the servants?"

"No," I answered, not choosing to do Maddox an ill-turn
before speaking to him.

"I can see that you will not require to be instructed in
your work, and 1 am very glad of it, for reasons you can
guess from what I have already said. Your experience
will always enable you to remember who the mistress of
this house is. My last housekeeper's ignorance on this point
was, as I have told you, the cause of my dismissing her."

Why this extraordinary jealousy of her position? It
seemed to me that she would better consult her dignity by
insisting less upon her mistresship.

"When my father lived here," she continued, "we used
always to occupy this room; but we chiefly use the dining-
room now; and I would not use that if I could help it. I
would lock up the house and save it for its real owner, my
father—do you hear, Miss Avory? He gave it to me, but
I don't wish to keep it, and should like to be a beggar!"

She made this singular speech with her eyes flashing as
they rested upon mine. Her frankness surprised me; there
was a want of dignity in it which I could not reconcile with
her haughty bearing. Could she not reserve her complaints
for an equal?

She may have read my thoughts, for she drew close to
me and exclaimed, throwing her handsome obstinate face
back:

"I don't know how long you may stop with me, Miss
Avory—perhaps a year—perhaps a week; but though you
should remain no longer than a day, you are certain to find

out the secret of this house, and you shall learn the truth
from me at once, before your mind is poisoned by falsehoods. Answer me a question: Did the Campions speak
of me?"

"Yes, madam."

"What did they say?"

I would not tell her what they said for many reasons, so
I answered:

"They spoke of you as wanting a housekeeper, and suggested if I applied that I might obtain the situation."

"I don't mean that," she exclaimed impatiently. "Did
they speak of my husband, and me?"

"I scarcely remember," I stammered, really confounded
by this examination.

"I ask you because, when Mrs. Ransome was here, she
did not scruple to go about telling the most wilful falsehoods of me. Thanks to her and her son I have lost my
friends, my house is shunned, and though I can prove
nothing, I know that my character has been atrociously
misrepresented."

She stamped her foot and frowned, but not more from
temper than from an effort to repress her tears.

"Although I cannot pretend to remember accurately
what the Campions said," I replied, "I can assure you that
not a syllable was breathed by either of them that did not
flatter your character, and make me eager to serve under
you."

She watched me distrustfully, then sighed bitterly, and
murmured:

"It *must* be so! How can I have such grief and not
speak it? I am friendless—those who would serve me are
afraid to hear me—my own poor father dare not come to
me. Oh, my God! if I knew how to end it!"

She put her hands to her face and burst into tears. Her
grief seemed to bring her to my level, and to justify me in
offering her my sympathy. But what could I say? I
knew nothing of her sorrow, nor would my own self-imposed
rigid training suffer me to endure the thought of permitting
the removal, for a moment, of our distinctions, by attempt-

ing to soothe her. I stood irresolute and silent, listening to her sobs, and wondering how much of the grief that racked her was of her own making.

Suddenly Mr Ransome came into the room. He entered quickly, walked right up to us, and stood for some seconds fronting his wife and staring at her before she was conscious of his presence.

" What now?" he exclaimed.

At the sound of his voice her hands dropped from her face, she drew herself slowly erect, looking at him from foot to head with an indescribable expression of scorn in her eyes, then wheeled sharply about from him. Contempt was never more fiercely expressed than in this quick action.

" What is your name?" he said to me; " I forget it."

" Miss Avory."

" What has my wife been saying to you, Miss Avory?"

" That is my business!" she exclaimed, turning upon him. " Miss Avory, leave the room if you please."

I hurried away, only too glad to make my escape; but before I reached the door Mr. Ransome called out:

" Stop!"

" Go!" cried his wife. " Miss Avory, remember who is mistress here."

" I insist upon your answering my question," he exclaimed, coming to the table.

I looked from one to the other of them; they were both watching me with passionate eyes; one or the other was to be obeyed; I ranged myself with the weaker side, reckless of consequences.

" I was engaged by Mrs. Ransome, and am bound to consider her my mistress. I therefore obey her orders." And out I went.

She came after me and caught my arm when I was in the hall.

" Miss Avory, I shall not forget your courage," she said in a feverish whisper. " Thank you!"

IV

I gained my private room in the basement, and was thankful to find it empty. I threw myself into a chair with a mind as weary and upset as if I had been engaged for hours in violently quarrelling. These people, from what I had heard, had been married two years. Two years ago they were making love in Rose Farm, standing hand-in-hand in the porch, while Mrs. Campion watched them as they whispered, and thought, to use her own expression, "that they must be dying of love." And now they were living the life of cat and dog, and behaving as though not even a memory of their love survived in them to give some sort of dignity to their mutual hate. I had not been in the house three hours, and yet more had been revealed to me than I should have expected to hear and see in a twelvemonth. Since they were so miserable together, why did not her father take her away and keep her with him? What was at the bottom of these quarrels—Temper? Jealousy on one side or the other? Had the precious idol that love had reared been found the veriest plaster of Paris?

I sat in this room, which, to distinguish it, I will for the future call my room, moralizing and speculating until I had recovered my composure, and then, wondering if they were still quarrelling upstairs, I went to the door and listened, but all was quiet.

Maddox was in the pantry cleaning the plate. I called to him, and he came to my room, holding a spoon in one hand and a piece of washleather in the other. He was a wiry man, about as tall as Mr. Ransome, and, bating the mustache, not unlike his master in his complexion, the shape of his nose, and the length of his jawbones. His hair was dark brown, his eyes the same color, sly, shrewd, and vigilant. They twinkled when he stood before me. He had an idea, I suspect, that I was going to pump him about his master.

"I went into your bedroom just now," I said, "and found it in a disgraceful state. When you have finished cleaning the plate, go and fold up your clothes—I should be ashamed to ask the housemaid to do it for you—and pray give me no further chance of detecting your slovenliness. Do you read in bed?"

He was staggered by my address; his eyes ceased to twinkle, and his mouth slowly opened.

"Read in bed?" he echoed.

"Yes. There is a greasy candlestick on a chair close to your pillow, and a book near it which, were Mr. Ransome to see it, he would order you to burn."

"Burn!" he exclaimed, trying to become indignant. "I should like to see any one burn it. It's my book, and that's my bedroom, and it's law for a man to do wot he likes with his own. And if I choose to keep awake all night, and beguile the time with reading, wot's that to you, mem?"

"We'll see," I answered calmly, for Maddox was by no means the first footman I had had to deal with; "if you like to hide that book in your box, you may; but if I find it by your bedside again I shall take it to Mr. Ransome, and ask him if it is his wish that works of that kind should be introduced into his house. You had better do what I tell you; I never argue with servants I am hired to control. Do your work properly, keep your bedroom in order, and we shall get on; but be quite sure that no impertinence will check my interference when I find things going wrong; and I consider that things are going very wrong when I learn that the footman sleeps with a lighted candle and a book about thieves against his pillow, and leaves his master's clothes heaped about the fender."

"I don't know what you refers to, mem," said he, doing his best to speak with lordly contempt; "but master's clothes are in his dressing-room, and not in the fender, if, mem, you'll be pleased to look for yourself."

"The waistcoat in the fender belongs to your livery. Do you find yourself in clothes, or is your livery paid for by your master?"

"Oh, I see your meaning!" he exclaimed, tossing his head, but looking at me very angrily; "and it does you very great credit, mem, to be so hobservant of your betters' interest. And I hope, mem," he continued, edging toward the door, "for your betters' sake, as you'll go on as you've begun, and not deceive of their expectations," he said, gaining the passage, "by turning out worse nor them as you've pleased to abuse. And hI'm blowed——" His voice died away in a growl, and presently I heard him hissing over the plate in the pantry with great ferocity, and intermingling his sibillation with angry exclamations, to which I paid no more attention than I did to the flies that buzzed about the ceiling.

But that first day of my arrival was not yet ended. At half-past two Maddox came to my room to lay the cloth for my dinner. He snuffed through his nose as he glided round the table and slapped the knives and forks down angrily, and now and again I caught him glancing at me morosely out of the corners of his eyes.

"What will you be pleased to drink?" he inquired with an air of frigid obsequiousness.

I told him ale.

"Oh, I thought you might hev been a water-drinker," he observed, evidently intending to be cuttingly sarcastic.

How was it that I could not think of him but with reference to his volume on Jerry Abershaw? The gallows, the procession, the crowd of that coarse frontispiece always came into my head when I looked at him, and I wished, to save the prejudice that had grown in me and that had really nothing to do with his behavior, that I had not found that book in his bedroom.

There was nothing for me to do about the house that afternoon; so I told the housemaid named Mary to give me the work she had been upon in the morning, and spent an hour in sewing.

My room was not a cheerful one. The window facing the avenue was sunk below the ground, and the grass upon the cutting was long and obscured the light. A great linen closet occupied the whole of one side; there was also an old-fashioned safe for the plate, a clock with a hoarse tick on the mantelpiece, some prints, a couple of wooden armchairs, and a big glass case containing a number of shelves loaded with handsome crockery.

It was nearly four o'clock when I heard a quick step descending the kitchen staircase, and a moment after my door was pushed open and Mr. Ransome stepped in.

I put down my work and rose. There was a wandering expression in his eyes as he surveyed me some seconds before addressing me; his face was pale and he held his hands behind him.

"Will you be good enough to tell me your name?" he said; "it's always going out of my head."

"Miss Avory, sir."

"Avory—Avory—Ivory—Avory—very well! now I'll remember. Sit down—you needn't stand."

I seated myself.

"Who told you to obey my wife before me, Miss Avory?" he continued, twitching his mouth oddly, and shifting the weight of his body first on one leg and then on the other.

"No one, sir."

"Then when I told you in the drawing-room to stop, why didn't you stop?"

"I obeyed the first command that I received," I answered, controlling as best I could the nervousness his curious eyes inspired.

"Did she tell you not to obey my orders?"

"If you mean Mrs. Ransome—certainly not, sir."

He looked at me angrily and exclaimed:

"How the deuce do I know that you are speaking the truth?"

I colored up at this ugly speech and bit my lip. He saved me from speaking the sharp answer that was on my tongue by saying:

"Are you a trustworthy person? Have you ever been housekeeper before?"

"Mrs. Ransome has received my character. I have been housekeeper fourteen years to various families."

"Are you a lady by birth?"

"Sir," I answered warmly, "my origin has nothing to

do with my duties.   If I serve you properly my birth cannot matter."

"Come, madam, I desire no airs.   My reason for making these inquiries is to learn whether you are a proper person to confide in.   Let me hear whether you can keep a secret or not."

"I would rather not know any secrets, sir."

"Look here," he exclaimed, holding up his hand, "do you give me to understand that you would rather believe my wife than me?"

"I am afraid, sir, I do not understand you."

He looked cautiously toward the door and closed it.   He then returned to me, approaching me so close that I shrunk back in my chair, while my heart began to beat quickly and I felt myself grow pale.   He bent his face forward and whispered:

"My wife is mad!"

When he had said this he drew himself erect, frowned, and stood watching me with his arms folded.   I stared at him with astonishment.

"That's the secret," he went on, drawing a chair to the table and seating himself; "and now you can understand why I asked you if you were trustworthy."

Whether he spoke the truth, or whether he himself was mad and thought his wife so, I couldn't yet tell; but to judge from what I had seen of their conduct, I think, had my opinion been asked, I should have pronounced them both mad.

"Follow me, if you please," he resumed, holding up his hand with one finger extended.   "All mad people are cunning.   Madness begins first in hallucinations accompanied by violent outbreaks of temper.   This is my wife's case.   She imagines herself both master and mistress in this house, speaks of me, her lawful husband, as an intruder, and is forever threatening to lock up the home and go forth into the world as a pauper.   What is this but madness?   Is it sanity?   You look a clear-headed woman—answer me."

"I cannot venture to give an opinion until I have seen

more of **Mrs.** Ransome," I answered, utterly confounded
by the man.

"But you have seen something of her."

"Yes, sir."

"What was she talking to you about when I interrupted
her conversation in the drawing-room?"

I could find no reply to make. One of his feet beat softly.

"Was she not insisting upon her being sole mistress
here, and cautioning you against obeying anybody else's
command?"

I dared not, with his glaring eyes upon me, remain silent.
I answered, "Yes."

"Ha!" he exclaimed triumphantly, springing up and
resting his hand upon the back of the chair. "Continue—
recite me all that conversation."

"Sir, I beg you not to press me; there was nothing in
that conversation which would interest you to hear."

"Did she talk of locking up this house?"

"She meant——"

"Answer me," he cried harshly.

"Yes," I said, my reply wrung from me by the fear his
manner had renewed.

He lowered his head and said in a gentle voice—

"Miss Avory, I entreat you not to attend to what she
says. She is mad, poor girl, on this subject of mastership—
nay, on other subjects; but this is the central hallucination round which other delusions cluster. She thinks my
temper passionate; but she herself is all passion, and con-
founds my remarks with her own wild speeches. Her
madness takes the form of extraordinary aversions. There
is my mother—a harmless, tender-hearted old lady—my
poor wife hates her. The sight of her, nay, the name of
her, flings her into a fury. Has she spared you? Wait
a while. I only ask you that, when by some innocent action
or speech you have kindled her passion, bear with her.
Remember *how* she is afflicted; but never heed her calum-
nies, her temper, her wild, ungovernable wishes."

He raised his forefinger mysteriously, smiled **softly,**
bowed with singular grace, and quitted the **room.**

The manner of his leaving me gave to his words a significance that utterly deceived me. There had been sense and tenderness in his final words, and these, taken with the precision with which he had counted off his wife's "delusions," thoroughly disposed me to believe that Mrs. Ransome *was* mad. His statement was not to be weakened by recollection of his behavior in the coach, by his rude and even insolent manner to me, by my sincere doubts even of his own sanity. I had to consider that what he had said of his wife was true; that she *had* insisted upon my recognizing her sole authority; that she *had* declared her wish to lock up the house; that she *had* implied her husband was something very much worse than an intruder, and that she abhorred her mother-in-law. Were these things signs of madness? Why, yes, if I put myself in his place, and argued with a presumption of her madness; if I considered that the temper that was shown was always on her side, and that her grievances were entirely imaginary. As yet I could not suppose otherwise. But what could I know of the truth in the short time I had been in the house? *His* behavior might mean no more than an offensive mannerism; but hers, so much at least as I had seen of it, was better to be explained by madness than any other reason I could assign to it.

Determining not to allow my mind to dwell upon these matters until I was able to form a definite opinion of them, I went into the kitchen where the cook was getting ready the dinner. Maddox had been rung for by his master, and was upstairs. I asked one of the housemaids where Mrs. Ransome was. "In her bedroom," was the answer.

"Has she been out this afternoon?"

"Oh, she never goes further than into the grounds now."

"It were otherwise when the Colonel lived here," said the cook. "Him and her used often to be out riding or walking together. I've met 'em, when I've been coming over from Ulverston in my brother Tom's cart, as fur as Thorney Mount, a good eight mile from here, walking for their entertainment an' looking as cheerful as young lovers."

Just then Maddox came in.

" Master don't dine at home to-day, cook," said he.

" What! an' his favorite jint down too! Well, it's poor cooking for people who's up and away when you're striving your best to please."

" I've put my room to rights, mem," said Maddox, sardonically. " It's open to your inspection now."

" Very well," I replied.

" Where's master going to to-day, I wonder," remarked the housemaid Mary. " Last fortnight he told Maddox he'd be back for dinner, and didn't come home for a whole week. He's a rare gentleman for travelling. If I had his money I'd travel too."

" It isn't often he comes into this part of the house," said the cook, looking at me with an eye full of curiosity.

" One would think," observed Maddox, sitting down and letting his head fall backward under a Dutch clock that wagged its pendulum over his nose, " that he'd quite forgotten there was other rooms in the place beside those he's used to."

" He came to-day, though," said the cook.

" Yes, I heerd him," returned Maddox.

" Did you listen?" I exclaimed, turning sharply upon him with a profound conviction in my mind that he was capable of greater meannesses.

" Listen!" he answered suddenly; " of course I didn't; but as the pantry's not a mile off, and your door ain't fitted for a dungeon, it wasn't my fault if his words struck upon my ear and obliged me to take them in."

" What did he say?" asked the cook, who was bursting with curiosity.

" Why," said the footman quickly, so as to prevent my silencing him, and giving me an extravagantly cunning leer as he spoke, " he told Miss Avory as mistress was mad."

He laughed, hummed a tune through his teeth, and while I was striving to find fit words for the indignation that possessed me, walked slowly out of the kitchen.

" Mistress mad!" cried the cook. " That I don't believe."

" Nor I!" exclaimed both housemaids together.

" No more mad," continued the cook warmly, " than I

am. But I'll tell you what she is, miss; she's a ill-used woman, and I don't care a farden if master hears me say so!" she cried, polishing a soup-plate with great excitement.

"That footman," I exclaimed energetically, "must have a very mean nature. I wonder what Mr. Ransome would say if I told him that his man listened to his private conversation with me."

"He'd kick him," said one of the housemaids.

"It wouldn't be the first time," said the other.

"Such languidge," continued the housemaid who had first spoken, "as goes on between them two sometimes of a morning, I never heard the likes of. It's enough to make one downright wicked to listen to it."

"Only think of the sinfulness of calling mistress mad! Poor dear lady who was as happy as the days were long when she lived with her father, a perfect gentleman, and his wife a sweet lady who had a kind word for every one," cried the cook, who was clearly her mistress' partisan.

"We have no right to talk of these things," I said. "You have only the footman's word to go by, and the word of a man who can listen to a private conversation is not to be taken on oath." And I ended the subject by starting Mary on an errand, and recommending the cook to look to her joint.

The rest of the day passed without my seeing either Mr. or Mrs. Ransome again. The young mistress dined alone, which I learned was much more the rule than the exception. Mary gave me this piece of information when she brought me my tea, but I offered her no encouragement to talk.

After tea I went up-stairs to the bedrooms, where I lingered a while, and returned to my room, not having met Mrs. Ransome. I thought she must feel very lonely upstairs, and wondered how she managed to get through the time, if she amused herself no better than she had amused herself that day.

I inquired of the cook, who came to ask me a question, if Mrs. Ransome played the piano.

"Why, yes, miss," she answered. "Mary, who's been here longest of any, says she plays and sings beautifully;

7

but I've not heard the piano since I've been in the house, an' that'll be getting on for four months."

"I suppose she passes her time in reading."

"I am sure that's more than I can tell you. She's a poor lonely lady for certain, and I can't get what that Maddox said out of my mind. *I* know who's the mad one of them two."

This reference silenced me, and the cook withdrew. At ten o'clock the footman passed my room bearing a tray containing water and glasses. He went up-stairs, and shortly after I heard the sound of excited voices which came out through the dining-room door that Maddox had opened. I could not distinguish the words that were spoken, but the voices belonged to Mr. and Mrs. Ransome, and of the two, hers was decidedly the loudest and most impetuous. They were hushed on Maddox closing the door. When he came downstairs, I said:

"Has Mr. Ransome returned?"

"Yes, he hev, mem."

"What time do the servants go to bed?"

"Half-past ten," he answered shortly, and scarcely able to address me civilly.

"Does Mr. Ransome lock the house up?"

"No, mem, he don't; specially when he doesn't come in all night."

I told him he could go; and presently a bell rang violently, and after a while Mary came to tell me that mistress was going to bed, and wished me to see that the doors were fastened, and the lights out before I went to my room.

I asked the cook to accompany me, lest I should overlook a door; and when the other servants were out of the kitchen, we went up-stairs and locked the hall-doors, and closed the drawing-room windows, and then entered the dining-room, where the windows were wide open. The smell of tobacco-smoke was still strong in the room, and I looked into the little balcony that stood a foot or two above the lawn to make sure that Mr. Ransome was not smoking there. There were some bottles on the table with the corks out, and a man's hat on the sofa. While I placed the bot-

tles in the sideboard I looked about me for signs to suggest
how Mrs. Ransome had spent the evening. But there were
no books, and no work-table or basket, and in the absence
of these I could only conclude that she had sat with her
hands before her.

"Strange," said the cook in a whisper, "what pleasure
master can have in going out an' leaving his wife alone.
It isn't as if there was theaytres, and the likes of that to
entice him. He does nothing but walk. The milkman
told me the other morning that he was coming to Copsford
by the Dawling road at half-past nine at night, and who
should pass him, walking all by himself, but Mr. Ransome."

"He certainly chooses odd hours for his excursions," I
replied; "will you close that window, cook? Thank you."

I extinguished the lamp, and there being no other room
to look to, bade the cook good-night and went to bed. The
night was sultry. The moon was in the south, and the hills
under it were black, but its silver light lay pale in some of
the valleys. I went to the open window to breathe the air.
So deep was the silence that I could hear the wheels of a
vehicle upon the London road away down on my left, in
the further valley, which was a mile off. Some big clouds,
resembling motionless volumes of steam, hung overhead,
and presently one of them approached the moon, and then
the fine white light that floated in a silvery haze over the
land went out, and the outlines of the hills were swallowed
up in the darkness.

I was about to leave the window when I heard a woman's
voice exclaim:

"If you knew how hateful the sight of your face is to
me, you would never come near me!"

A man's voice answered, but the tones were smothered,
and I could not catch the words.

My first impression was that the speakers were below on
the lawn; and I stretched my head out of the window to
see them. A faint atmosphere of light was reflected from
the window exactly under me, and, recalling the situation
of the apartment I was in, I at once perceived that the
room under mine was Mrs. Ransome's bedroom. Her win-

dcw was open; she must have stood near it to enable me to hear her so distinctly.

"My father?" I heard her exclaim; "how dare you mention his name? He hated you from the first! He knew you were a madman; and I should have known it too, but you deceived me with your madman's cunning—lonely, miserable creature that I am! But he *shall* know—he *shall* know, though it break his heart, for I cannot go on enduring this terrible life!"

His answer was still inaudible, but he had evidently drawn nearer to the window, for I clearly remarked the emphasis of savage contempt in the tone of his voice.

"Keep away from me!" I heard her cry. "You want to drive me mad, and you shall be answerable for what I do in my madness. Why do you come to my room?—no, not one word! not one word!—but to-morrow she shall know more—take your hand off!" she cried with a half-suppressed shriek. "Oh, coward! coward!" There was a trampling of feet for a moment, a low fierce laugh, and a door was banged. Then followed a profound stillness, presently disturbed by sounds of piteous sobbing.

I had listened without a moment's reflection that I was acting dishonorably in doing so. This thought could not occur amid the intense agitation which these intelligible words, the startling shriek, the pitiful after-sobbing had excited in me. I shrunk away from the window with my heart beating wildly, my hands cold as death, my forehead damp with perspiration. For many minutes I stood near the toilet-table listening for further sounds with strained and painful attention, but soon the sobs died out and I heard the window closed.

What horrible quarrels were these? Was I in a madhouse? Such sounds, and above all, that strange fierce laugh, by whomsoever uttered, would seem only possible in a lunatic asylum. Long after I had heard her close the window, I found myself still standing and listening. My hands trembled violently when I began to undress myself, and the looking-glass reflected a face as white as a sheet. It was one o'clock before I fell asleep, and throughout my slumbers that horrible laugh, that half-suppressed shriek, mixed their wild part in my dreams, and made my repose more unrefreshing than had I lain sleepless in my bed.

V

The sunshine awoke me; it was seven o'clock. The morning was glorious, the birds sang loudly from the trees, and numberless butterflies hovered about the rich flower-beds, and gave life to the bright verdure of the lawn.

The moment I recalled the quarrel of the night I became as agitated and nervous as if the conversation I had heard had passed but five minutes before. The servants were busy in the rooms downstairs when I descended, and I found Maddox in his shirt-sleeves cleaning the dining-room windows. He bestowed a sour glance upon me as I stood for a moment watching him, but made no response to my "Good-morning."

I did my best to abstract my mind from the unpleasant memory that haunted it by going busily about my work; and at eight o'clock went to breakfast. Mary had prepared my table, and when I sat down she lingered at the door and said:

"Did you hear anything last night, miss?"

"Why do you ask?"

"I only thought, as you sleep over mistress' bedroom, that you might have been frightened, being new to the ways, if you *was* disturbed."

"Did *you* hear anything?"

"Oh!" she exclaimed with a shrug, "we're always hearing something."

I was anxious to know if the quarrel I had overheard was unusual. If the thing was frequent I might take courage and compose my nerves.

"What do you hear?" I inquired.

"Why, the most dreadful quarrels between master and mistress. It's enough to turn one's blood cold to hear 'em sometimes. What with him with his laughs, and her with her screams, it's truly awful."

"Then these quarrels often take place?"

"Ay, pretty near as often as they are together. I ought to know, for I act as lady's-maid to mistress; and sometimes of a mornin', when I'm doing her hair, if master comes in, the words between 'em so scares me that I often don't know whether I'm standing on my head or my heels."

"How long have these quarrels been going on?"

"Oh, for a good while now. They're *his* fault, mind you, miss. He *do* say the most outrageous things; and once——"

"And once what?"

"Once he caught her by the hair and clenched his fist, and made as though he would hit her on the face."

"Is it possible?" I exclaimed. "Why doesn't her father interfere? Why doesn't she leave him?"

"Oh, she's been going to leave him ever so many times to my certain knowledge. But there's a wonderful deal of pride in her. You see, miss, if she was to go in for a divorce all the truth would come out, and everybody would be talking of her. An' as to leaving him—well, I don't know anything about that. Her father hasn't any idea of what she has to go through. I heard her tell master she'd rather die than that the Colonel should learn what a dreadful mistake she had made in marrying of such a man. But he must have seen a good deal when he was here; quite enough to make him understand that his daughter was the reverse of happy."

As I had heard all I felt disposed to learn from her, I told her she might now leave me and go about her work. Although servants are not very veracious sources of information, I did not doubt that what Mary had told me was substantially correct; and I might now console myself with reflecting that in spite of the cry and the laugh that still rang in my ears, there had been nothing more tragically significant in the quarrel I had overheard than in any other of the quarrels which were perpetually occurring. But surely, I thought to myself, these are scenes that must soon come to an end. Mrs. Ransome's piteous reference to her loneliness and misery, her wild cry, "I cannot go on lead-

ing this terrible life," shou'd lead me to conclude that any
near day would find her home broken up, herself seeking
her father's protection. I could not doubt that there had
been too much real anguish in her voice last night to mislead me on this point. What had forced that shriek from
her?—that bitter exclamation, "Oh, coward! coward!"
Had he struck her? The thought sent the blood tingling
through my veins.

I was afraid, should he remember that I slept over his
wife's bedroom, he might suppose I had overheard the
quarrel and would seek me with some fierce explanation. I
therefore kept to the lower part of the house to avoid re-
minding him of my existence by meeting him, until I heard
one of the servants say that he had gone out.

I asked if Mrs. Ransome had breakfasted, but was told
that she had not yet left her room. It was then nearly ten
o'clock. I was going upstairs when I met Mary coming
through the hall.

"Oh, if you please, mistress wants you. She's in her
bedroom."

"Alone?"

"Yes, miss."

The girl's manner was strange, though I scarcely noticed
it at the time. She hurried off when she had made her
answer as though she wished to avoid further questioning.

I found Mrs. Ransome reclining on the sofa at the foot
of her bed. A tray was on a little table at her side with
some tea and dry toast. She had on a handsome dressing-
gown which was unbuttoned at the neck and displayed the
exceeding whiteness and purity of her skin. But her face
was so miserably pale as to neutralize the effect of her
beauty. She turned her eyes about with slow, weary
movements, and kept her left arm motionless by her side
as though it pained her.

"Sit down, Miss Avory," she said languidly.

I took a chair near the door, but she exclaimed:

"Come nearer, sit there," and pointed to a chair opposite
the sofa. She was silent for some moments, during which
she kept her eyes fastened upon her right hand, which lay

on her lap. Then turning to me: " You saw enough yesterday, Miss Avory, to know the kind of life I am leading.
I was maddened when I sent for you in the morning by a
dispute I had had with Mr. Ransome over the letter I received from his mother; and in the fulness of my bitterness I spoke my thoughts aloud. I do not regret having
done so. I do not recall a single word. Was I not right
in saying that you could not be an hour in this house without learning its secrets? I could not endure the thought of
your imperfectly knowing the truth, of your getting one
version from a servant, another version from your own observation. If I had any pride left—God knows I have none
now—I should not be the less plain with you. I *must* have
sympathy. It is horrible, amid the bitter loneliness of my
present life, to feel myself misjudged."

She sighed heavily.

" I am sure you will not consider my sympathy the less
sincere," I replied, " if I use it to entreat you respectfully
to consider that you may be showing a want of judgment in
taking strangers into your confidence. You have received
no assurance that I am one jot better than the majority of
the persons in my station of life, who have little feeling
outside their own interests, and are incapable of appreciat-
ing the suffering that puts them in possession of the heart
secrets of their employers."

" Oh, you are different—you are very superior to such
persons—but understand me, Miss Avory : what you heard
from me yesterday was forced from me by the anger which
Mrs. Ransome's threatened visit excited in me. To-day I
should have confined myself to your duties—well, but I
have told you I do not regret my frankness. But whether
I am deceived in you or not," she continued, a sudden light
coming into her eyes, " you shall know the truth. You
have already heard a terrible falsehood—I have called you
here expressly to tell you how infamous is the lie my husband told you about me yesterday morning."

" This is Mary's doing!" I thought to myself. **Now
what mischief was that girl's wretched love of gossip about
to occasion?**

"I paid no attention to what he said," I replied.

"Oh yes, you did!—reflect—when he told you I was mad, you thought he spoke the truth."

"Why should you think this?" I exclaimed, not the less conscience-stricken because there was something in her manner now that convinced me of the profound wrong I had done her in harboring a moment's doubt of her sanity.

"Pray answer me!" she cried, shaking off her languor, and eying me with jealous eagerness. "Did you not believe him?"

"No, I will not go so far. I considered his assertion barely probable only."

"Because of my temper yesterday?—because of my blurting out my grief almost at our first meeting?"

"Yes, madam."

"But do you think me mad *now*, because I wish to remove from your mind the horrible suspicion my husband's words created?"

"Certainly not. I would only ask, taking my humble position into consideration, why my opinions should in any way be of the least importance to you?"

She started from the sofa and stepped across the room, holding her dressing-gown tightly about her, by folding her arms on her bosom.

"I cannot explain," she said, stopping and looking at me from the end of the room. "I do not sometimes understand myself. When my mind is full, my thoughts will find utterance, and I cannot help myself. But do I humiliate myself by wishing you to know the truth?"

"I should have found it out soon, madam."

"No; you mistake!" she cried passionately. "He would have won you over, and it is agony to me to feel that his cunning can make people think that all the wrong-doing is on my side."

She came close to me, pulled the sleeve of her dressing-gown above her elbow, and exposed her bare arm.

"Look at those marks!" she said, through her compressed lips. "They were made by his fingers last night.

Did you hear me cry out? You sleep overhead—you **might** nave heard me."

There were five small livid marks upon her arms just above her elbow, and where they were the arm was swollen.

"I heard you cry out," I answered.

"Who would believe," she moaned, adjusting her sleeve, "that he is the savage he is? I was awake all last night with the pain in this elbow. My father would shoot him if he knew how he treats me."

"Why do you not go to your father?" I exclaimed.

"Mr. Ransome is too dangerous a man for any woman to live with."

She made no answer at once, but resumed her seat on the sofa, and leaned her cheek on her hand.

"If I leave him," she said, speaking in the tone of one who thinks aloud, "I must abandon my old home, the home my dear father loves, and I must own that I was guilty of a miserable sin in loving him." She stopped and looked at me. "Miss Avory, the story of my marriage is a long one. The telling of it would show you that my father abhorred the thought of my becoming Mr. Ransome's wife, and that I was madly obstinate and deaf and blind to signs in the man which my instincts perceived and warned me against. How I advocated him! how I strove against my father to save the sensitiveness I thought he possessed! How I proved, knowing all the time that my father's misgivings were merely sterner forms of my own secret doubts, that he was sweet-tempered, manly, upright, generous, and a gentleman! Can I unsay all this to my father? Above all," she cried, "shall I allow my husband to drive me from my own home and make me a subject of the gossip which my father detests?"

These words explained everything to me.

Had she spent hours over the narrative she could not have made me see the story of her marriage more clearly. The indignation the sight of her arm had raised in me had forced me into offering her one piece of advice; but now that my temper had cooled I would not take it upon myself to express any further opinion unless challenged to do so.

Her frankness astonished me; but it did not render our relative positions the less defined nor offer justification for any expression or behavior on my part that should not be in perfect keeping with the situation I filled in her household.

"Can you understand me?" she continued, softening her voice, and speaking with one of the saddest smiles I ever saw on the human countenance. "It is easy to advise husband and wife to separate, but who but a wife can appreciate the humiliation, the misery, the lonesomeness that horrible alternative involves? Do not mistake me! I hate my husband—ah, God help me! I am a wretched sinner to say this; but he has made me hate him. If *he* only should prove the sufferer, I would separate from him this day. But I think of my poor father—the shame of it! . . . my hand shall not do it! The child he loved and honored must not break his heart!"

She sobbed and pressed a handkerchief to her eyes angrily. "He knows that I am unhappy, but he does not know *how* unhappy. I could not help his finding out much of the truth when he came to see me. I did not want him to come. I dreaded the discovery he was bound to make; but I dared not urge him to stop away, for that would have told him too much. In no letter of mine has he ever read a single line that would make him think I was the miserable woman I am. There is a secret he suspects, but is not sure of. Must I tell it you? . . . My husband is mad! . . . Miss Avory, tell me—you know this?"

"I should conclude he was, if on no other evidence than those marks on your arm."

"But when he told you *I* was mad, did you not guess the truth about him?"

"Indeed, madam, I was bewildered—I have had no time for reflection—I am so great a stranger to you—I so little anticipated these disclosures——"

She raised her head haughtily.

"There it is, Miss Avory. You are like the rest of the world—discreet. The life I am compelled to lead, which every morning brings to me regularly, you are afraid to hear. You feel that safety lies in ignorance."

"You wrong me," I exclaimed, flushing up. "I am pained but not frightened. Your experiences are very new to me. If I knew how to help you—with the deepest respect I say so—there is little you could command which you would find me unwilling to perform. But I trust I have sense enough to perceive that yours is one of those cases in which the sufferer must help himself. No good wishes, no advice, no interference can be of use. Your reason for not leaving your home, that you may not give pain to Colonel Kilmain, does honor to your heart as a child; what purpose could be served by my urging you to weigh your present unhappiness against the unhappiness your leaving your husband would cause your father? You would still be guided by your own judgment, and my arguments, by being impracticable, would become officious."

"You speak reasonably," she answered thoughtfully; "but I beg, Miss Avory, that you will not let me feel that I have acted foolishly in talking of my troubles to you. I have been forced into these disclosures. Yesterday morning, before I sent for you, my husband had cruelly insulted me. My bitterness lay close to my lips. I could not help giving vent to it. It tormented me all day, and when I saw you again in the drawing-room, I was impelled, I could not silence myself, to speak to you as I did. But when I heard that my husband had represented me as a madwoman to you, I felt that I should go mad indeed if I did not instantly send for you and speak as I have done. No, I regret nothing! Judge me not! As I live, I am the most miserable woman in the world!"

She flung up her hands and burst into a passion of tears. There was something very piteous in the spectacle of her wild grief. I knelt by her side and took her hand, and endeavored to soothe her; but many minutes passed before her tears ceased, and then she leaned back on her couch with her handkerchief pressed to her face sobbing convulsively.

Her words, her grief, the injury done to her arm, had completely won me over to her side, had obliterated all memory of the disagreeable impression she had left on me the day before, and had opened my eyes to the character of the man she had married.   And now that my sympathy was with her, I found all those actions which I had been prepared to assume as illustrations of a disordered mind, perfectly consistent, womanly and spirited.   This man and his mother should not drive her from the home her father had given her; and hence her jealous, passionate determination to be obeyed as the mistress.   I could feel surprised no longer by her opening her heart to me ere I had been an hour in her house, now that she had shown me what mad and bitter impulses her husband's treatment might set working in her breast.

She let fall her handkerchief presently, and sat up; whereupon I rose from her side and stood near the door.

"Thank you for your patience and attention," she said, in her rich, low, tremulous voice.   "I will promise to shock you no more with my troubles.   I only beg you to remember how events, which were out of the power of either of us to control, have forced you into the ungrateful position of confidante."

"Not ungrateful, Mrs. Ransome."

"Oh yes; you are no young, talkative girl, thirsting to find out home-secrets that you may be wiser than your neighbors.   I suppose the servants constantly speak of these quarrels?"

"You must expect that," I replied.

"My husband is wholly to blame; were I on my death-bed I should say that.   He takes a vile pleasure in insulting me for the sole purpose of exciting my temper, and then he finds an excuse for his own mad passion, and you may hear him laughing in his rage, as though the quarrels he creates between us were his sole enjoyment.   Why, Miss Avory, all this is nothing but a madman's paltry scheme of revenge.   My father was cold to him, and never scrupled to let him know how averse he was from our engagement.   The mother never forgot that.   She has taught him to recall it as a bitter insult—and the coward avenges himself on me!"

"You should not allow the mother to enter the house."

"I cannot prevent her. They are two to one."

"But you have friends who would take the responsibility of advising your husband upon themselves."

"Not one!" she answered, with a little stamp of her foot. "The one dear friend I had, Dr. Redcliff, died; I have no others. One by one the people who were visitors here when my father and I lived together have stopped calling. I may have some secret sympathizers, but there is not one I would deign to tell my troubles to, for there is not one who would not shrink from interfering—and interference can do no good. Miserable and helpless as I am! she exclaimed, her eyes kindling, "I will still fight my own battles. These horrible days *must* end!—only what pride I have remaining will not endure that he should misrepresent me. *You* know the truth now. Oh, I have been keeping you standing. Pray forgive me. I need not detain you longer. Thank you again for your patience."

She forced a smile and lay back on the sofa. I opened the door and quitted the room, with spirits as much depressed as if I had endured some painful personal trouble.

VI

So far, I have closely related the particulars of my first day's residence at Gardenhurst. Much of my story lies packed in that first day and in the morning which followed it, and there was scarcely an incident that did not bear directly upon the singular issue toward which we were blindly pressing.

But I can now for a while afford to be less minute; and the brief review of a few days will fitly serve as an introduction to the most extraordinary portion of this story.

After I had left Mrs. Ransome I devoted much thought to what she had told me; and, with no doubt in my mind as to her perfect sanity, furnished forth the history of her married life in this form: That the grounds on which Colonel Kilmain had based his dislike to the marriage were his suspicion of the soundness of Mr. Ransome's reason; that his daughter, blinded by love, had adhered obstinately to her resolution to marry him; that for some months his insanity lay hidden or quiet, and then took a positive character; and that now, after a year and a half or longer, of daily, subtle growth, his madness had ended in exciting her bitterest hate. I speculated upon the nature of the madness whose actions were too sane to qualify the abhorrence they excited by pity for the affliction that produced them. There should, I thought, be deep malice and great cunning mixed up in the insanity that could induce no other emotion in the sane mind than scorn and rage. For instance, any wildness, any want of logic in Mr. Ransome's insults, would blunt their barbs by representing them as expressions of an irresponsible mind. Misery, not hate, would follow these outbursts. Mad he undoubtedly was; but, I assumed, with such a leaning to reason that the consistency of his language would render it as detestable to her as if his brain were as healthy as her own.

I saw very little of him. He was out nearly all day, and then the house was quiet. Three days after my arrival I was in the grounds when I met him, at the very bottom where the trees were, and where I had been sauntering for ten minutes past. He came out from among the trees, with his eyes bent down, humming a tune. Could I have hidden, I should have done so. I will plainly own that I was afraid of him. He stared doubtfully at me, and then his eyes sank, and then he stared again. It struck me that my gaze embarrassed him, but I attached no significance to the fancy; nor did I look at him sufficiently long at a time to satisfy myself on this point.

"Well," he exclaimed, standing still, "has my wife insulted you yet?"

"No, sir," I answered.

"Ha!" he said, holding up his finger, and looking cunningly, but not at me, "you remember what I told you and are humoring her, eh?"

I could not say yes, and I was too frightened to say no, so I forced a smile, which I hoped he would interpret according to his wishes.

"Pass on!" he exclaimed, frowning and motioning me

toward the trees. " You are one of those ladies whom the dumb devils are fond of."

He stepped out of my way and stood with his hands hanging down. I pressed forward with a beating heart, not knowing how mad he really might be, and considering that the least show of obstinacy would be the most foolhardy exhibition I could at that moment indulge in. When I was well among the trees I peeped over my shoulder, and saw him standing where I had left him. When he caught me looking, he turned quickly on his heel and hurried away. This action, of which I afterward understood the import, merely seemed to me a part of his general extraordinary behavior.

Again, on the following day I met him in the hall, as he was leaving the house. His manner was very different. He smiled, asked me if I did not admire the surrounding country, and after one or two civilly expressed remarks, bowed with the utmost affability and walked away. Such conduct, based on good sense, would have modified, if not obliterated, all my theories about his insanity (until perhaps the next outbreak) if I had not heard and seen enough of his treatment of his wife to persuade me that the man was not in his right mind. Only the night before another quarrel had taken place in the bedroom under mine, not, indeed, so fierce as the one I have recorded, but bad enough to have shocked me had it been the first in my experience. For a long two hours afterward I had lain awake, striving to conjecture the reasons of these insensate scenes. I conceived that his mother's approaching visit might be at the bottom of the quarrels that had taken place since I had been in the house; but, so far as it was possible for me to judge, there was positively no reason to be assigned to the constant wrangles that had raged between them ever since a few months after their marriage but wickedness, a mere mad perversity on his part—a vicious mind unhallowed by one softening memory, finding insane pleasure in goading his wife into a moral condition little superior to his own.

Whether in accordance with her promise to shock me no more with accounts of her misery, or whether because of the hint I had given her that she made a great mistake in communicating her troubles to strangers, and above all to persons beneath her in position, Mrs. Ransome became very much more reserved after that interview I had had with her in her bedroom. She did not ask me if I had overheard her second quarrel with her husband. She did not mention his name. Once only she referred to his mother's approaching visit, when she told me that old Mrs. Ransome would occupy the spare bedroom between her husband's and her own. She looked, indeed, when she spoke, as though she had more in her mind to add, but she seemed to recollect, and quickly changed the subject, drumming sharply with her fingers on the table, as though the effort of repression cost her something.

I thought the change a good one, and flattered myself with having contributed to it; but there was a bitter hardness in her reserve that made me doubt the wisdom of the motives which had prompted it. I do not mean to say that one reason of her silence was not her conclusion that, having set me right as regarded her relations with her husband, any further explanations or bewailments might weaken the mpression she had produced. But all the same, this sudden change in her was curious—this abrupt departure from a profound self-abandonment to grief to a reserve that was frigid. I was sorry for her own sake that she had been so candid with me. I considered that I now beheld her in her natural character, and that her pride, which she professed was dead, was secretly bleeding over my knowledge of her secrets, and particularly over the manner in which I had become acquainted with them.

Mr. Ransome's mother was expected to arrive on the Monday.

On the Sunday evening Mrs. Ransome had gone to church alone. During her absence Mr. Ransome, who was smoking on the lawn, seeing me pass the open dining-room windows, called to me and said:

"My mother arrives to-morrow. Did you know?"

"Yes, sir."

"What room is she to have?"

8

I told him.

" You will see that it is made comfortable for her. "

" Certainly, sir."

" And be careful to let nothing that my wife says inter-fere with your duty to make my mother feel herself per-fectly at home in this house."

He said this sternly, in one of those odd gusts of passion which it seemed a law of his moral being should disturb him when he was speaking on matters that could furnish no excuse for temper. I answered yes, and left him, think-ing that in that very tone I had found the key to the quar-rels between him and his wife. *I* might endure such a manner now and again; but how would the quick, haughty spirit of his wife brook it? Her answer was bound to be pitched in the same note, and then would come the disso-nance, the uproar, the fury.

He had left the lawn before Mrs. Ransome returned from church, but whether he was in the house or striding across the country I could not tell. His actions had no reference to the ordinary standard of behavior.

I opened the door to Mrs. Ransome, being on the stair-case when she rang. She was pale with the heat and tired, but looked a beautiful, commanding woman, her bonnet in exquisite taste, her dress a blue silk. I thought her mind would take notice of some pathetic irony involved in this visit to church and this return to a home of bad passions and aching trouble.

She entered the dining-room and called my name lan-guidly as I was going. I went to her.

" To-morrow, Miss Avory, my husband's mother arrives. It is not my intention to live with her while she remains in my house. But do not suppose that I am to be driven from my home by her. I want to consult you. Please sit down. Now, tell me how I am to manage."

She sank into an arm-chair, slowly fanning herself. There was a hard, obstinate look on her face despite her languor, and she kept her eyes fixed on me.

" I do not exactly see how you can avoid living with Mrs. Ransome if she occupies this house with you," I answered.

"Very easily. Mrs. Ransome can use the library, as we used to call the next room, and take her meals there with her son. We never need meet. She comes to see my husband—not me; and she *shan't* see me."

" But do you consider the embarrassment——?"

" I consider myself, no one else," she exclaimed, plying the fan quickly. " I have made up my mind *not* to meet that woman, and there's an end to it. I shall retain this room for my own use. Meanwhile you will see that the servants just attend to her—no more. For yourself, Miss Avory, you will take no notice of her, and if she attempts to order you—tell me. I want an excuse to turn her out of the house."

Had I traced the least lurking softness in the expression of her face, I should not have scrupled to represent to her the deplorable unwisdom of the course she meant to adopt; but I was as effectually silenced by her obstinate, haughty, resolute eyes, by her hard, tightly compressed lips, by her slight but suggestive frown, as if her most passionate command had been addressed to me.

"I hope you thoroughly understand my wishes?"

" Yes, madam."

" You know enough to require no further explanation. Indeed, I should pay no compliment to your common sense by supposing that you desired me to explain. I am mistress here, and mean to assert my position. That is all. If Mr. Ransome is displeased, he can tell his mother to go; if his displeasure is very great, he can go with her. Happen what will, my resolution is taken. I will not sit at the same table with that woman, nor countenance her gross intrusion upon *my* home by the smallest act of civility."

" You know best, madam."

" Yes, I do know best. She shall not have the chance she had last April of exciting more bitterness even than we naturally feel between Mr. Ransome and me; of championing him against me though he was never so cruelly in the wrong, of maddening me by her atrocious innuendoes, her direct charges, her criminal falsehoods, and then walking to Copsford and telling everybody she knew—even my

tradespeople—that I was an evil-hearted woman, that I was
not a lady, that my wicked conduct was breaking my husband's heart, and such infamous talk as that. Would you
meet such a woman were you in my place?"

"I certainly should not. But I should require certain
proofs of her guilt before I condescended to resent her
falsehoods."

"I have had proofs. She abused me to my last housekeeper. She talked to the servants about the suffering her
poor Saville endured through my heartless treatment. She
will talk to you if you will let her."

"She will not talk long."

"You will take care to strictly carry out my instructions?"

"Certainly."

These were her orders; and now it was evidently to be
war to the knife between this unhappy couple. I do not
think that she had any clear anticipation of the consequences of her action. It seemed to me that she wanted to
push matters to a crisis, taking no thought of what form
that crisis might assume, resolute only to bring about a
change of which her husband would be burdened with the
whole responsibility.

Mr. Ransome remained away from the house all that
evening and returned at ten o'clock. Ten minutes after he
had arrived Mrs. Ransome's bedroom bell rang. She was
evidently acting wisely for once. When I looked down
from my window half an hour later her light was out.
Perhaps she was reserving her forces for the morrow. Be
this as it may, I thought that she had it in her power to
pass as tranquil a time every evening, and for the matter
of that, every day too, if she would but hold her tongue
and leave him to do all the talking.

Next morning I obeyed her orders about getting the library ready, with more alarm than, perhaps, I should at
that time have been willing to confess. Every moment I
expected Mr. Ransome to drop upon me and ask me what I
was about. There was no joke even in the idea of a ren-
counter with such a man. Of course I should obey Mrs.
Ransome, let him countermand her orders as he pleased;

but suppose he told me to leave the house? I should have to go. He was master, view him as I would, and with his disregarded dismissal hanging over my head, my situation would be too intolerable to make it worth my while to keep. These thoughts greatly flurried me as I superintended the cleaning of the library. The room was a small one, and faced the avenue; the trees threw their shadows upon its one window and obscured the light. Dark, and commanding no better prospect than the compactly grouped trunks of the trees, the apartment was sufficiently dreary, and I could not wonder that it was never used. There were some old oil-paintings against the walls which, in the imperfect light, were scarcely decipherable, appearing, indeed, no better than streaks of yellow and red upon a black ground. There were no books, and why the room was called "the library" I could not conjecture, unless it had been used long ago as a library and kept the name.

Mrs. Ransome's folly in forcing her mother-in-law into this room took deeper meaning from contemplation of the darksome chamber. I was very glad when the job of getting it ready was finished. I breathed freely when I closed the door, and had scarcely reached my own room when I heard Mr. Ransome's footsteps in the hall.

I had no idea at what hour the old lady was expected to arrive, but was not kept very long in suspense; for while Mr. Ransome was still at breakfast, Mrs. Ransome summoned me to her bedroom. I crept, in a manner that would have convicted me of a most sneaking gait, past the dining-room where Mr. Ransome was breakfasting, being, in view of the storm which his mother would bring along with her, honestly afraid to meet him.

Mrs. Ransome was seated before the toilet-glass, and Mary was brushing her hair—rich, beautiful hair it was, and it fell over the girl's arm like fine black silk with a lustrous blue sheen upon it. I had never seen her look more beautiful. Her noble white neck showed like marble through her muslin dressing-jacket, and her small, superbly shaped head was fully disclosed by her hair being down. The curtains had pink linings, and the light, therefore, exactly suited her complexion, the pallor of which, in the clear sunshine, would have appeared almost ghastly from contrast with her brilliant black eyes and hair.

She saw me in the glass, and addressed me without turning her head.

"Oh, Miss Avory, I forgot to tell you last night that Mrs. Ransome is supposed to arrive here between half-past twelve and one. Be on the lookout for her, please. I mean, be ready to receive her when the door-bell rings; then call Susan and tell her to take Mrs. Ransome to her bedroom—you understand?"

She was fond of putting that question. It seemed as if her passionate resolution and anxiety to carry that resolution out made it difficult for her to suppose that her wishes were exactly intelligible to those she addressed.

"Quite," I replied; "and should she ask for you?"

"Tell her that I am very well—not dead yet, nor even dying," she responded, with a loud satirical laugh, at which Mary tittered and glanced at me.

"You would not wish me to make that reply, madam," I said, taking her seriously.

"Oh, dear, no! preserve your p's and q's, Miss Avory, and tell her with all the ironical courtesy you can summon, that the young mistress is not visible."

"I shall obey your instructions literally," I said, meaning to imply the hope that she would not render my duties more ridiculous than her temper made positively necessary.

"I expect you to do so," she replied sharply, turning her face toward me and wrenching her hair out of the girl's hand by the movement. Then softening her voice instantly and smiling, she added, "Remember!"

I knew she referred to my promise to recognize no other authority but hers, and answered:

"I do remember, madam, and you may trust me. I am anxious about my instructions simply because I mean to carry them out to the letter."

"Well, those instructions are as you have heard. When she leaves her bedroom she will be shown into the library. If she asks to be taken to the dining-room, tell her that I am there, and that the library is for her use while she chooses to honor us with her presence. As to the drawing-room, the door is locked. There is the key."

She drew it from her skirt pocket and held it up, watching my face to see how I would receive her manœuvre. I merely inclined my head. She knew her business better than I did, and no possible result but irritation could have been produced by any attempt to reason with her while that obstinate, defiant expression lighted up her eyes, and that faint, bitter smile made her mouth hard with obdurate meaning. But foolish as her plans were, she made them, in my opinion, more foolish yet by speaking of them before the housemaid. Had she seen how the girl took her words in, the grin of expectation that widened her mouth, her anxious glances at me lest I should interfere with the thunderous programme her mistress had prepared, and so spoil much delightful sport, Mrs. Ransome might have been satisfied with directing me in the briefest terms, and allowing me, for the rest, to use my judgment.

"Is the library ready?"

"Yes."

"You quite understand that Mrs. Ransome and her son take their meals together in that room? Let Maddox wait upon them. He is more Mr. Ransome's servant than mine. Mary will attend upon me."

"Then two separate trays are to be prepared for every meal while Mrs. Ransome remains here?"

"Of course. Mr. Ransome has choice of either room. It will matter little to me whether he chooses to live with his mother or his wife. But no earthly power shall induce me to occupy the same room with that woman, to sit at the same table with her. This house is mine; I therefore select the rooms which please me. And should Mrs. Ransome *dare* to complain, tell her that I am willing to pay the rent of a lodging for her at Copsford, where she may have her own way and be as much mistress as she chooses. That will do, Miss Avory."

Mr. Ransome lingered in the grounds until eleven o'clock, and then left them, no doubt for Copsford to meet

his mother. As the time approached when I should have
to receive the old lady, I grew absurdly nervous. Indeed,
I considered it unfair to myself that I should submit to
execute orders so entirely repugnant to my own feelings,
and was only restrained by selfish considerations from going
to Mrs. Ransome and declaring that I was unequal to the
duties she had imposed on me.

Mary had evidently been chattering to the other servants,
for they were on the alert every time I passed the kitchen;
though whenever they saw me they pretended to have an
immense deal of work to do, which utterly engrossed them
from all paltry consideration of the business that was none
of theirs.

When it was half-past twelve, I went into the library
and stationed myself at the window, whence I commanded
a sight of the avenue and could observe the carriage approach. The matter is of no importance, but I ought to
have mentioned in my description of the house that it had
no stables. The Ransomes did not keep a carriage, but Mr.
Ransome, I believe, jobbed a phaeton at Copsford, which
would be brought to Gardenhurst from time to time.

It was a quarter to one when I heard the sound of wheels
coming along the avenue. Soon afterward the bell rang.
Maddox went to the door, and I followed him and stood on
one side as he threw it open.

An old rumbling "cottage upon wheels," as Sydney
Smith used to call the flies of that period, had drawn up,
and Mr. Ransome was helping a very little woman to get
out of it. So small and fantastic an object I never before
saw, and I wondered that Mr. Ransome did not catch her
under the arms and swing her into the hall as he would a
child. She alighted with great deliberation, and catching
sight of Maddox, called to him in a shrill voice to take her
trunk. Mr. Ransome paid the coachman his fare and came
up the steps, followed by his mother, at whom I could
scarcely look without laughing. That such a fragment of
humanity should give Mrs. Ransome trouble seemed incon-
ceivable. As reasonably might Gulliver have been vexed
by being flouted by a Liliputian maid of honor. Her bon-

net was large and the feather in it larger; but there was no extravagance in the rest of her costume. One thought of her as a doll, and hardly troubled to speculate on the material and style of her costume; but one might see that she was exquisitely neat. The little bow, the little collar, the little shawl, the little gloves, the little cuffs, and the very little sandals—she wore her dress short, after a then fast-expiring fashion—were all faultless in their adjustment, fit, and aspect. Her eyes were blue and dim, but she did not use glasses; they had a wide, staring expression in them, and, like her son's, they travelled nimbly and fell upon you abruptly, and appeared to take in minute details by resting on them. Her nose was long and rather handsome, I thought; but the bones of the face were hard against the skin, and a sad want of fleshiness, coupled with a disagreeable whiteness of complexion, made her appearance cadaverous.

"Where's my wife, Miss Avory?" were the first words Mr. Ransome asked me.

I could not remember that Mrs. Ransome had given me any instructions as to the answer I was to make to that question, so I answered, "I don't know, sir," and turning to the little old lady, said, "Will you let me take you to your bedroom, madam?"

"If you please," she replied, with hopeful alacrity, and added, "You are the housekeeper, aren't you?"

"Yes," I said.

"Lead the way. I'll follow."

Mr. Ransome called Maddox to him and addressed him in a low voice, while I pushed through the anteroom that divided the two halls and ascended the stairs, with the old lady laboring like a short-legged child behind me. I forgot until I had reached her bedroom that it was part of my programme I should call Susan to attend her up-stairs. But I was too flurried to remember such minor matters. However, it gave me an excuse to leave her at once after throwing open her bedroom door, and I was half-way down the stairs before she had time to ask me a question.

Mr. Ransome was in the hall, holding the handle of the drawing-room door.

"Miss Avory, come here, please!" he called out.

"Will you let me send Susan up-stairs first, sir? There is nobody with Mrs. Ransome."

"Do you mean my mother?" he exclaimed, twisting the handle of the door angrily and shaking it.

"Yes, sir."

"Why is there nobody with her, then?" he shouted, stamping his foot. "Go and send one of the girls instantly, and come back to me."

I called to Susan, gave her the requisite directions, and returned to Mr. Ransome. Now that I confronted him, I found my fears gone.

"Where is Mrs. Ransome—my wife?" he asked, frowning savagely and speaking in a fierce voice, suppressed almost to a whisper, but avoiding my eye.

I gave the same answer I had before made:

"I don't know, sir."

"You do know."

"If I did, I should tell you," I replied, folding my hands and looking down out of pure disdain.

"Why is this door locked?"

"I did not lock it."

"Who did then?" And without waiting for my answer, he added, "Go and get me the key."

"Mrs. Ransome has the key."

"Ask her for it."

I was about to go up-stairs, meaning not to reappear until I had considered whether I had not better pack up my box and leave the house; but he cried out:

"There! there! in the dining-room. See if she's there."

I crossed the hall and turned the handle of the door, but found it locked. Much surprised, I pushed with my knee, thinking that the door had stuck with the paint.

Mrs. Ransome's voice within exclaimed, "Who is there?"

"I, madam—Miss Avory."

"I wish to be alone, Miss Avory."

Mr. Ransome came to the door and struck it with his fist.

"I want the key of the drawing-room!" he called out.

She made him no answer.

He struck the door again and his face grew livid. He had no need to strike it a third time, for it flew open and Mrs. Ransome stood on the threshold. Her eyes were in a blaze; her face was white with passion; and there for some moments they remained, confronting each other.

"What do you want?" she said to him.

"You have locked the drawing-room door."

"I have."

"What for? to prevent my mother from entering it?"

"Yes."

"Give me the key."

"I will not."

"Give me the key, you devil!" he repeated through his teeth.

The words were nothing beside the manner in which he spoke them. Had she shot him dead as he stood there, I could have forgiven her. They had a very different effect upon her from what I should have expected. Either her passion was shocked out of her or she mastered it, for she said, coldly and deliberately:

"The library is prepared for Mrs. Ransome's reception. That and her bedroom she may use while she is in my house. The other rooms I keep for myself and my servants. Miss Avory has received my instructions and will see that they are carried out."

Saying which, she shut the door in his face, and locked it.

What would he do now?

Having no doubt that he was insane—and I never saw his madness more clearly than in the expression that had entered his face as he struck the door with his fist—I should have believe anybody who had whispered that there was no action too violent for him to have committed that moment. But my fear was to be disappointed. He stood gloomily staring at me for many moments, though little by little his frown relaxed, the passion went out of his face, and a smile so absolutely indescribable that I feel myself involved in a direct contradiction by calling it a smile, crept about his mouth and set it like a piece of carving.

He held up his finger, and bending his head forward, exclaimed in a mysterious whisper:

"Do you question her madness now?"

As he said this, he looked over my head and went for· ward. I turned and saw his little mother coming quite noiselessly down the staircase. He met her, took her hand, placed it under his arm, and led her without a word into the library, the door of which he closed silently.

VII

The servants had heard the dispute in the hall, and were clustered at the foot of the staircase eagerly waiting for more quarrels. They dispersed when they saw me, and, what was better, had sense enough to judge by my manner that they had better ask me no questions nor annoy me by their gossip.

Two luncheon-trays were to be got ready, as I had told the cook: one for the library and one for the dining-room. It was impossible to tell what new explosion would follow the discovery of this arrangement. Would Mr. Ransome submit to having his mother kept to two rooms in a house full of rooms? It was idle for his wife to talk of herself as sole mistress, etc., of Gardenhurst. Mr. Ransome was her husband and head, and could act as he chose, and she must have known this; and therefore I thought her audacity foolhardy in adopting an attitude which not only repelled sympathy, but which, if Mr. Ransome only chose to act with common resolution, was bound to involve her in a humiliating defeat. Did he really think her mad? Strange, at all events, that that should be the first remark he made to me when I was expecting a very different outburst, and that he should have said it with a smooth face as if pity were at the bottom of the remark.

Maddox and Mary took each of them a tray, and some jokes passed between them as they went up-stairs. I knew I should be summoned in a moment or two by the occupants of one room or the other, and stood at my door waiting for the return of the servants. Maddox came first. Of course that dangerous chatterbox Mary was with her mistress, inventing lies rather than not have something to gossip about.

"Master wants yer," said the footman shortly, without looking at me, and walking straight into the kitchen.

I crept up the staircase very timorously, knocked, and entered the library. The sky had grown overcast within the hour, and what with the absence of sunshine and the gloom of the heavy trees upon the window, the atmosphere of the room was no better than a kind of twilight, in which one had to remain some moments before one's eyes could clearly define objects by it.

Little Mrs. Ransome, perched before the tray, was already at work upon the roast chicken. Her son stood behind her, his hands buried in his pockets and his chin lowered upon his breast.

"If it were not for my mother," he exclaimed, almost before I was fairly in the room, "I would have the dining-room door broken open and force your mistress to explain the meaning of this," pointing to the tray. "You must explain, as you are acting under her orders. No hesitation, Miss Avory. By G——, you'll find me dangerous if you trifle with me!"

"I will tell you what I know, sir," I replied, in nowise daunted by the mixture of bad taste and idle bravado in his speech. "But first of all you must tell me what you want to hear before I can answer you."

Little Mrs. Ransome ate hungrily, without once looking at me.

"What orders have you received from my wife?"

I told him exactly.

His face grew blacker and blacker as I proceeded, and his hands twitched violently in his trousers pockets. He wrenched them out, and exclaimed to his mother:

"What will you do? You hear how she means to treat you."

The old lady put her knife and fork down, and pushing her chair from the table, said:

"It is for you to choose. If I leave, I complete her tr

umph. Saville, she wants disciplining. If she were a man,
I should say she wants flogging."

The blood rushed into my cheeks as I heard her.

"Madam," I exclaimed, "pray consider of whom you are
speaking."

"How dare you interrupt me?" she cried shrilly. "Saville, who is this impertinent woman?"

"Whoever I am," I replied, "I do not acknowledge you
for a mistress. And I tell you, madam, that I cannot
stand by and listen without indignation to the language
you apply to your son's wife."

She looked dumfounded, and, turning to Mr. Ransome,
cried:

"Order her out of the room! You will not allow your
servants to insult me?"

I had caught Mr. Ransome watching me furtively, and
with a veritably frightened expression. I looked him full
in the face, expecting his command, and meditating a reply;
for all my fear had left me, and I felt nothing but utter
scorn and dislike for them both. But his gaze wandered;
he was silent.

"Mr. Ransome," I exclaimed, "I am in no dread of your
mother's temper, nor of your dismissal of me. I am prepared to leave your house at any instant. But while I am
in it, I will not suffer any unmerited and senseless insults to
be heaped upon your wife's head. She is a deeply wronged
woman—your mother knows it. She has been driven by
your conduct into a desperate action; but it is Mrs. Ransome's duty to palliate, not to aggravate it—to reconcile
you, not to deepen the bitterness that already exists."

"Saville! will you listen to her? will you submit to
this?" shrieked the old lady in a horrible fury.

"Hold your tongue, mother!" he exclaimed savagely.
He looked at me, but still I kept my gaze angrily upon
him; and he grew restless, uneasy, shrinking in his manner and attitudes.

I noticed this now decidedly. The full importance of it
rushed upon me. I became, even as the thought seized me,
sensible of my power over him; but whether obtained by

the pure force of will which I had unconsciously in my temper thrown into my language, and which gave steadiness and decision to my gaze, or whether by the mere possession of a pair of eyes which had never struck anybody before as in the smallest degree uncommon, either for their beauty or their ugliness, I could not tell. I only knew that he could not look at me, while the longer I looked at *him* the more scared grew the expression in his face.

His mother found out the secret in an instant. She glanced from one to the other of us, left her chair, and, running to the door, flung it open, and ordered me to leave the room.

I did not even look at her.

"Saville!" she half-screamed, "are you master here or not?"

"Who denies it—do you?" he answers fiercely, addressing me.

"No, sir; but I deny the right of that lady to order me out of the room; I deny her right to expect the smallest obedience from me; and I further declare that she is acting a cruel and unwomanly part in seeking to exasperate you against your wife, and in siding with a man like yourself against a weak, defenceless, ill-used lady. Be assured, sir," I continued, determined to "have at him" now that I had the chance, and taking care not to remove my eyes from his, "that society, sooner or later, avenges such injuries as have been done Mrs. Ransome, your wife. A wife, for her own and her husband's sake, may hide the secret of her misery"—I spoke these words with all the force I could put into them—"but others have eyes and ears to see and hear, and tongues to report; and when I leave this house, I shall consider it a duty I owe to my mistress and myself to relate to the *proper persons* the exact nature of the terrible life you have led Mrs. Ransome, of which I have seen one shocking illustration in the marks of your fingers upon her arm."

"Ah, but how did that happen? She had maddened me, and I grasped her arm while answering her—it was an accident," he exclaimed, while his face grew as pale as his mother's, and the coward's false, forced, vanishing smile twisted his lips, and made his mirthless eyes look wild and haggard.

"She would break his heart if she could!" the mother cried. "Talk of *her* sufferings! Has she not threatened you, Saville? Has she not wished that you would drop dead at her feet? But everybody in Copsford knows her! I took good care that her character should not be misunderstood. The wilful, venomous hussy!"

I glanced at the eager, passionate, crazy-looking little face, and hated the woman there and then, hated her for her falsehoods, her vulgar abuse of her daughter-in-law, her low, miserable malice. This was a touch of nature that made my young mistress and I akin. Her determination not to meet this spiteful little creature had all my sympathy now.

Mr. Ransome was staring at me fiercely; but the moment I looked at him his eyes fell, and he muttered to himself.

"Sir," I exclaimed, "you have heard the cruel words your mother has made use of toward your wife. Can you suffer a stranger like myself to go forth from this room and say to those I meet that Mrs. Ransome's character was grossly insulted in the presence of her husband, and that he did not utter one word in her defence?"

"Don't look at me!" he cried, passionately. "Look at my mother. You are speaking of her—address her!"

"I am addressing you, sir."

He went to his mother and whispered. The action was made extraordinary by the terrified glance he threw at me over his shoulder. She bent her blue eyes, full of malignity, upon me, and said, suppressing as well as she could the shrillness in her voice:

"My son and I wish to be left alone. You are now an intruder, and every moment you stop makes your intrusion the more unpardonable."

This decided me. In the face of this view of my presence I could no longer stop in the room. I went out, closing the door after me, and paused a moment or two outside, considering whether I should go to Mrs. Ransome or to my room. The voices within rose high. I heard him say, "She is a devil! how she looks at me!" And the mother answered, "She cannot harm you. She is your wife's friend, and is in league with her to turn me out of the house and humble you." I would not suffer myself to hear more, but walked to the dining-room.

Mrs. Ransome opened the door herself to my knock, and exclaimed!

"Oh, is it you, Miss Avory? Come in."

Her luncheon was upon the table, but she had not touched it. There was some wine-and-water on a chair near the sofa, and some toilet vinegar. The room was oppressively hot.

"Let me open one of the windows," I said, and suited the action to the word.

She merely said, "I was afraid they would come in by the lawn. My head aches cruelly. Have you seen his mother?"

"I have just this moment left them both in the next room. Did not you hear us talking?"

"No."

"I had hoped to do you a service, but Mrs. Ransome was too cunning, and left me no excuse to remain with them."

"What service?"

"Let me first tell you that I have made a discovery. I do not positively declare that I am right in my conclusions— but I believe I am. Mr. Ransome is afraid of me."

She sank back on the sofa with a faint incredulous smile, which I deserved for putting my theory into such conceited language.

"Pray forgive my manner of expressing myself," I went on; "I do not want you to misunderstand me. I never observed the same behavior in him before to-day. I haven't the faintest notion where my power lies; but I am as certain as that I am standing here that I have been suddenly gifted with some kind of controlling force which, were I resolute in my exercise of it, would make him tractable to my wishes."

She looked at me inquisitively, and said:

9

"I understand what you mean. The nurses or matrons in asylums are supposed to enjoy your power, is that it? I believe you; but I should not have suspected your influence by looking at you. You once suspected my sanity," she exclaimed, with a smile; "see if I can outstare you."

"I don't like the idea of possessing this power. It suggests a disagreeable species of affinity."

"I would to God I could take it from you!" she said. "But do you not see that his insanity must be gaining strength by bringing him within the reach of such power as you can exert?"

"Yes, I see that, madam. But is it not for the best? Your life is unendurable. The resolution you need to end it will be forced upon you by the madness which will compel you to separate from him."

"Oh! I never think of him. It is my father I dread— his horror of scandal—his misery when he reflects upon the ending of the marriage I was so obstinate upon!—But what was the service you hoped to do me?"

"That I could induce Mr. Ransome to persuade his mother to leave the house."

She shook her head, and exclaimed:

"You don't know what a perverse, vile woman she is. They influence each other, and she will persuade him to keep her here until she is tired of stopping. But I *swear* I will not meet her—she shall only use the two rooms I have given her."

"Frankly, madam, I have seen enough of her to make me hate her as cordially as you do. But will you tell me why she is so bitter against you? why she takes pleasure in exciting ill-feeling between you and Mr. Ransome?"

"I cannot explain—I do not understand it. It has been partly the work of time, with her own mad, wicked nature to furnish her with motives. It began by her taking her son's part against me, then we had words, and so it crept on. Her hatred of me is so intense that I really believe, were it not for the consequences, she would incite her son to kill me!"

"God forbid!" I exclaimed, with a shudder; "though if

I thought that, and were in your place, I would have her turned out of the house neck and crop, and obtain such help as would effectually prevent Mr. Ransome from introducing her again."

She made no answer, but walked to the window and stood there, breathing the air, and pressing her hands to her temples. I never felt sorrier for her than I did at that moment. There was something painfully sad in the thought of her great beauty wasting and decaying in loneliness and misery, in her young, ardent nature desolated by evil passions, not one of which, I dared say, but her husband was responsible for.

I was about to entreat her to take some food, feeling persuaded that she had eaten nothing that day, when she turned sharply round, and cried in a bitter voice:

"I wish my husband were dead!" She instantly added, "The grief, the pain, the utter hopelessness he has forced into the two brief years of our marriage no heart but mine can conceive. What I have had to endure—the insult, the neglect, the fierce temper, yes, and the blows—only God has witnessed. Oh, there have been words of his, actions of his, I never can forgive him for! There is not under heaven a woman more wronged than I have been. He had my first love—for a long while I strove with my own temper and bore with his gathering, reckless, crazy taunts, until my patience gave way. What is the use of saying he is a madman? He was not mad when I married him; he has never been so mad as not to know how most cruelly to wound me. And have not the mad their sane moments— when moods of tenderness visit them? Why did he marry me? He has told me over and over again that he never loved me. He saw that my father disliked him, and he determined to make me his wife for that reason only. He declares that my humiliation is the only pleasure he knows. He praised his mother, he thanked her, before me, for going to Copsford and telling the people there every falsehood her wicked heart could imagine. Your distinguished father should be told of this,' he said. 'He once informed me that no member of the Kilmain family for generations

had ever excited one word of gossip in this district. He's
a liar. Phœbe has excited gossip. All Copsford is talking
of her, and saying what a wretch she is to lead her husband
the life of a dog.' Those were his words. When he mentioned my father's name I could have stabbed him. Villain! Coward! Why does not God take his wicked life?"
Her passion was terrible. But the hot blood mounting
to her head racked her unendurably. She groaned and
sobbed, with dry, feverish eyes, and cast herself upon the
sofa, clutching her temples as though she would rend
them.

I knelt by her side and endeavored to soothe the pain by
pressing my handkerchief, damp with the vinegar, to her
forehead, heartily regretting my intrusion on her, since it
had brought about no better issue than this explosion of passion. I did not attempt to speak to her; but when, after
bathing her head for some minutes, I believed the pain in
some measure relieved, I left the room, receiving a faint
"thank you" from her as I opened the door.

VIII

Determining not to be made ill by this excitement, and
my head (in emulation of Mrs. Ransome's) beginning to
ache, I tied a handkerchief, under my chin and sallied forth
into the grounds to breathe some fresh air and recover my
composure, which had been greatly shaken by Mrs. Ransome's outburst.

There was a pleasant breeze blowing from the distant
hills over the great open space where the grounds were un-
protected. I walked toward the kitchen-gardens, where I
should be screened from the house, and paced a long walk
where a forest of peas hid me as effectually as the trees
down at the bottom could have done.

The under-gardener was at work here weeding some beds.
I stopped and had a talk with him. I mention this trifling
circumstance because Colonel Kilmain has communicated the
sequel of this story to me, and for reasons the reader will
ascertain in due course, I am wishful to recall the first occa-

sion I had of speaking to this man. He comes back to me
as a square-built individual, with a brown homely face,
which struck me as honest enough. I took no particular
notice of his appearance. He was very respectful in his
manner, answered my questions with alacrity, complained,
but with moderation, of the hardness of the times, of the
dearness of food, and said that he was keeping company
with the upper-gardener's daughter, but hadn't the heart to
marry her yet, as it was as much as he could do to support
himself on what he earned.

"That shows good sense," said I. "If all working-folks
thought as you do, there would be a deal less poverty and
trouble among them."

The air had freshened me up, and I returned to the house,
but with a real feeling of reluctance and a sincere regret that
the inner life of the old building was not more in keeping
with the repose and serenity of its exterior, and with the
lovely and delightful scenery that lay around it. The
breeze sported with the trees of the avenue, and all on that
side of the house the sunshine flickered and the moving
shadows seemed to fan the building.

I was no sooner in the hall than the story of the place
was renewed for me by the sounds of voices in the dining-
room. Mr. and Mrs. Ransome were quarrelling furiously;
but they were alone, for as I entered the house I had just
caught a glimpse of the little old lady's head vanishing with
great velocity round the turn in the hall where the library
door was. I had no doubt she had been listening.

I made up my mind to seem deaf and interrupt the quarrel by walking into the room as though I had no idea that
anybody but Mrs. Ransome was there.

I turned the handle of the door, making sure they would
suppose I had knocked and that they had not heard me, and
walked in. The moment I showed myself there was silence.
Mrs. Ransome sat on the sofa, one hand to her head, her face
scarlet, and her eyes shining with passion. Mr. Ransome
stood by the table, leaning upon it with both hands, his
body inclined toward her. His face was very pale, but
there was a weird merriment in it, an expression of mali-

cious enjoyment of what he was about, which my hand is
powerless to describe.

I stood at the door, feigning embarrassment, but not
offering to retire. They both looked at me, and Mr. Ransome stood erect and drew away from the table. I watched
him steadily and saw that his eyes fell, that the indescribable expression I have mentioned went out of his face, that
his lips moved as though he whispered to himself.

Mrs. Ransome started up and exclaimed, pointing to her
husband:

"His mother *shall* not come into this room! Tell him
that! Tell him to leave me! My head is driving me crazy.
Tell him he is killing me!"

"You hear Mrs. Ransome, sir?" I said, turning upon him.

"She lies! I am not killing her. I insist upon her receiving my mother in this room—I am master here, and my
wife shall obey me!" he answered, scowling at me with a
look of mingled hatred and fear in his strange faltering
eyes.

"You are not master here!" she shrieked. "The house
is mine."

My ramble is the grounds had given me nerve. If ever
a lingering doubt of his insanity had disturbed my conjectures, that doubt had now ceased. I could no longer look
at him and be ignorant that I was confronting a madman;
though *how* mad he was my total inexperience of this horrible affliction could not decide. Dealing with aberration
of this kind, I felt I need preserve in myself no consistency
of behavior. Could I influence him? If I was to try, I
must drop the housekeeper and assume the manner and tone
of an equal.

As these thoughts flashed through my mind, I fixed my
eyes full upon him and said:

"Mrs. Ransome speaks the truth. You *are* killing her.
You must not stop here."

"How dare you——" he began, and ceased. I had approached him by a step, never remitting my strong, determined stare. I had forced all my will into my eyes. I
was *resolved* to subdue him.

He raised his hand to wave me off; his glance travelled swiftly from the ground to my eyes—there and back again, there and back again, over and over. I saw him struggling to prevent his rage from evaporating into terror, the signs of which appeared in his face and made him a piteous creature. *Now*, by Mrs. Ransome's silence I knew she was watching us. But I could not look at her. I was fighting the man with my eyes, and every instinct warned me not to intermit my resolute gaze for a moment. My own feelings, as I marked my power over him, I can scarcely describe; but I clearly recall a thrill of triumph and an access of new determination with each phase of his gradual subsidence into shrinking, struggling silence and dismay.

Watching him always, I stepped sideways to the door, threw it open and said:

"Mr. Ransome, will you come with me? I wish to speak to you."

He made no answer, but neither did he move. A sudden fright that I had utterly misjudged myself seized me. The fear turned me pale, but this was, happily, the only symptom. I kept my eyes fixed on him and stood waiting for him to act.

"Phœbe," he exclaimed, in a passionate whisper, actually slinking round the room to where his wife was, "tell her to go. She makes me ill with her eyes!" He wiped his forehead with his handkerchief, and his glance fled swiftly from my face to the floor, again and again.

Mrs. Ransome walked to the other side of the room. I stepped up to him and said:

"The presence of your mother in this house makes Mrs. Ransome miserable. I take it upon myself to urge you to advise her to leave."

"Do you know whom you are addressing?" he burst out, looking on the ground.

"Well," I answered. "Better than your mother knows you. Meet my eyes. If you want to learn your secret, you will find it there."

He tried to look at me. I remarked the effort; but a weight of lead seemed to keep his gaze bent downward.

"You know my secret, do you?" he muttered. "Now that you have it, what do you mean to do?"

"Much, for your wife's sake," I replied. "Shall I speak to you before her?"

"No!" he said hurriedly, looking around him with a perfectly white face. "Where shall I go? . . . We must be alone! I understand you now."

"Will you give me the key of the drawing-room?" I said to Mrs. Ransome.

She drew it from her pocket and handed it to me. She then went to a part of the room behind her husband and made a gesture, signifying that I should not trust myself with him. I smiled to let her know that I was as free from fear at that moment as ever I was in my life, hastened across the hall, leaving the dining-room door wide open, and turning the lock of the drawing-room door, motioned to Mr. Ransome to come. He followed quickly, gliding along the floor with stealthy, noiseless tread.

The moment he had entered, I shut the door and slipped the latch, determined that his mother should not interrupt me. Had I given myself time to reflect, I believe I should have been frightened by my own temerity. But I was excited, eager, resolute on having my way. I never thought of danger, and my very fearlessness immeasurably strengthened the power I found that I had over him.

The window blinds were down. I drew them up and flooded the room with the brilliant afternoon light. He stood near the table; I approached him quite close and said:

"Mr. Ransome, you know I have your secret. But you may repose the fullest confidence in my silence providing you will allow me to dictate actions which will prove as much to your advantage as to your wife's."

"She has called me a madman," he said in a whisper, mysteriously raising his finger; "but she does not believe it, or she would not be so free with the word. Why do you keep your eyes on me? Great God! do you not know they put fire into my blood?"

"For your wife's sake, Mr. Ransome, you must request

your mother to leave this house. But I also advise you to do so for your own sake. Listen to this! Your mother makes your position a dangerous one. Her presence sets the servants talking. Terrible quarrels may happen, the rumors of which will get abroad and invite inquiry by making people eager to learn the cause. If your secret is found out, you know as well as I do what will happen."

"Oh!" he shrieked; "don't speak it! it is my horror!"

"Think of your wife's forbearance," I continued; "one word from her——"

"Hush!" he whispered. "Why did you draw the blinds up? Light is treacherous. When I think of my secret I like to be in darkness."

"It is your secret," I said, taking no notice of the irritable glances he flung at the windows, "that drives you away from your home; that forces you to take lonely walks; that compels your tongue to say harsh and cruel things to your wife. Is it so?"

"Hush! my wife does not know. She flings her words out wildly and hits the truth by accident, never guessing that she has hit it."

He chuckled, and said something to himself under his breath.

"I have power," I continued, "over your secret, and can save you from the penalty it will bring if you will suffer me to advise you. Your mother loves you—but her love is dangerous. One incautious word from her will lay you open to the servants."

"You are right!" he exclaimed, speaking rapidly. "I was afraid of her when I was engaged to Mrs. Ransome. The Colonel had keen ears, and I felt that he suspected my secret, and I kept mother cautious by watching and interrupting her."

"You must fear her as you feared her then. You are in greater danger now than ever you were. You have turned your wife's love into hatred, and one provoking word from your mother may cause her to write to her father and beg him to save her from you. You can guess what he would do."

He shrank away from me, twisting his hands. The mad
house, poor miserable wretch, was his terror. That one
threat, in the present phase at least of his madness, was a
weapon by which it might appear he was to be controlled
to any purpose. But only I could use it. He was conscious that I knew his secret, but he believed it was nobody
else's, for just the very reason the cunning of insanity would
suggest—he had been called mad to his face.

"You may trust me," I said, "if you will let me trust
you. I urge you to remove your mother from this house."

"At once?"

"Yes."

"How? There is no coach to Guildford."

"Let her sleep to-night at Copsford. She can take the
coach in the morning."

He walked about the room with feverish restlessness.
He once looked at me sideways with a scowl that should
have thrown my nerves into disorder, but my triumph had
been so easy that I was not to be frightened now.

"Every suggestion I make," I continued, preserving the
same inflexible voice and look I had assumed throughout,
"will be for your good, and I will offer no suggestion that
is impracticable."

"Tell me again what I am to do," he answered, stopping
and holding his head in a listening attitude.

I replied that he must at once request his mother to leave
the house. "If she refuses——"

He interrupted me with a furious exclamation, and I was
glad of the interruption, for though I perceived the necessity, I also felt the inhumanity, of putting the threat that
terrified him into words.

I said no more, but went to the door and threw it open,
giving him one last look as I went out, and entered the dining-room.

Though there were no spectators of this interview, yet
from what Mrs. Ransome had seen of my influence over this
unhappy man, she will bear witness to the truth of the above
scene, while the sequel will also serve to vindicate my accuracy. I would emphasize my veracity in this particular

record, because of the extreme air of improbability it carries
with it.   I cannot pretend to explain the power I had over
him further than the narrative defines it.   Nor, in review-
ing the scene, can I account for the security I felt in that
power, and the strong persuasion I had that, by taking my
cue from his tone, and drawing upon my imagination so as
to accommodate my reasoning to his moods, I must eventually subdue him to my wishes.   Throughout I was actuated
only by the strong desire to serve Mrs. Ransome; and I
dare say not a little of the self-control I exercised on that
occasion was owing to the great sympathy I felt for her
misery.

She was lying with her forehead pressed against the sofa
bolster.   I shut the door and exclaimed:

"Mrs. Ransome will leave us this afternoon."

She started up and said, "How? has she consented to
go?"

I answered her by relating the conversation I have just
detailed.   She looked at me with amazement, and cried:
"Why should he think you only have guessed his secret?
For eighteen months I have known that I am the wife of a
madman.   Over and over again in my passion I have called
him mad."

"He does not believe you mean what you say.   But who
shall follow the logic of the insane?   I cannot conceive what
there is in me to frighten him.   I should have thought such
eyes as yours would have controlled him as minen ever could
do.   But putting these considerations aside for the present,
I should like to address you seriously on the subject of
your husband.   He is not responsible for his actions.   Your
personal safety is really dependent on your taking precau-
tions at once to guard against his violence.   His insanity has
most unquestionably gained ground since I have been in the
house.   Consider his behavior just now."

"But what would you have me do, Miss Avory?"

"You should write to your father, and take his opinion."

"Oh, I *hate* the idea of writing to my father about him,"
she exclaimed, bitterly.   "I have had excuses for doing so
long and long ago, but have always turned from the thought

with dislike and dread.   There is not more danger now than
there was eighteen months ago."

"But *can* you continue leading this life?"

"Do not ask me—do not force me to think!   I have been
supported by a dreamy hope of some chance occurring—of
some event happening, to put an end to it all without my
father's interference, without even his full knowledge of the
unendurable mistake I made in opposing his wishes."

"What change can you expect?   Nothing but his death
can free you, unless you place him where his actions will
be restrained, which I think you ought to do both for his
sake and your own."

She did not answer, and I was struck by her silence; because, though in a moment of passion she had, not long
before, cried out that she wished him dead, the expression
of that wish implied by her silence, now that her temper
was cool, made it sinister.

"It is hard to wish him dead," I ventured to say.   "His
madness must fill him with suffering, we may be sure of
that.   I told him that his secret, as we phrased it, drove
him into his lonely walks, and forced his tongue to offer
insult to you.   What frightful fancies must sometimes visit
him!   His horror of a madhouse is shocking.   Think,
madam, the thought, the dread of it subjects him to a weak
woman like me!"

She interrupted me by exclaiming:

"He is a coward and a devil!   I *hate* him—and what I
have said before I say again—I wish he were dead!   Don't
seek to justify him to me!   Mad as he is, he can calculate
upon the effect his language has on me!   All his time is
occupied in thinking how he can most grossly insult me.
He may be a poor afflicted madman to you, but he is a
coward and a devil to me!"

"That makes it all the more necessary," I replied, "that
you should separate from him."

"Oh, it is easy to say it!" she answered, with great excitement in her manner.   "But the first step is the effort,
and you don't know what reasons there are to keep me
chained to this life."

"One I know to be Colonel Kilmain's abhorrence of scandal."

"That is one; but you commence the list in the middle. Begin it with my pride."

I had always known that to be *the* reason; but I would not tell her. Had she not said that she had no pride?

"I can appreciate the full force of that objection," I said.

"Exclude every shadow of sentiment from the catalogue and make it a compilation of hard, selfish motives—with one exception: I wish to spare my father. Yes! and that too springs from selfishness, for there again my pride is at work. I detest the thought of his learning how great was my miserable folly in marrying Mr. Ransome."

"But ask yourself, madam, if your motive for leaving matters as they are is weighty enough to overbalance the many reasons you have for separating from him."

"Let him separate from me," she said bitterly. And seeing me about to continue, she exclaimed, "Listen at the door for a moment, Miss Avory. I want to know what they are doing."

I opened the door quietly, but heard no sound. I walked some paces down the hall and peeped around the corner; the library was empty.

"They are not in the library," I said, returning to Mrs. Ransome. "I will go and find out what they are doing."

So I advanced to the top of the kitchen staircase and called to Mary.

"Where is Mr. Ransome?" I asked softly.

"I don't know, miss. Maddox, do you know where Mr. Ransome is?"

"No, I don't," answered the man's surly voice. "Ain't he upstairs with his mamma?"

I was determined to know what he and the old lady meant to do, and went up-stairs; but was scarcely on the first landing when I heard their voices in the bedroom. I fancied they were quarrelling, but I could not be sure of this merely on the evidence of the lady's shrill voice. I went into the younger Mrs. Ransome's bedroom to wait, and had hardly pushed the door to, so as to leave it just ajar, when they both came out.

"If you can't walk the distance," I heard him say, "I'll send Maddox for a fly."

"I'll walk it," she answered, fretfully. "I'll not forget what a coward they've made of you."

"Hush! hold your tongue!" he cried, in a fierce whisper. "It's your own fault. You brought the woman upon me by abusing Phœbe. Here, take my arm."

They were going down-stairs and their voices died out. I waited five minutes and then descended to the hall, where I met Mary.

"Only think, miss," she exclaimed, grinning broadly; "old Mrs. Ransome has gone away!"

"How do you know?"

"Why, I heard master call to Maddox and tell him to send one of the gardeners with Mrs. Ransome's luggage to the Copsford Arms; and then they went out by the avenue door."

I popped my head into the dining-room and exclaimed:

"Your little visitor has not made a long stay this time, madam. She has just gone away."

"Thank God!" answered Mrs. Ransome. "I have proved myself mistress this time—they both wanted this lesson! I don't think she'll ever trouble Gardenhurst again."

She came into the hall, and, lookin ground her with brilliant eyes, exclaimed, "Oh, what a hot skirmish it has been!" I could hardly forbear smiling. The victory was hers, indeed; but how had she won it?

IX

When in the silence of my room I reflected on the part I had played, I was amazed at it, and wondered what sort of reception the story would get were I to make a boast of it.

I felt afraid to meet Mr. Ransome again. The dread was owing to my belief that my influence over him had been but a temporary power of which the particular mood

of his mind at that time had rendered him susceptible; that
a greater or lesser degree of madness would break the spell,
awaken him to a perception of the humiliation he had suffered at my hands, and impel him to deal with me with
probably a good deal more fury than he had ever exhibited
toward his wife.

These conclusions, which were perfectly reasonable, were
also, as you may perceive, rather terrifying. My courage
had been taxed to the utmost, and I was quite sure that
nothing short of something highly tragical would enable me
to pass successfully through such an ordeal again. I had
never met a madman before in my life; I do not think my
mind had ever dwelt upon the subject of madness as a
fancy. Some power, quite foreign to my nature, had
buoyed me up during my interview with Mr. Ransome; and
my own tact had enabled me to exert the influence that his
bearing had shown me I possessed over him successfully.
But that power had deserted me now. I felt certain that,
without it, my influence would be worthless; and the mere
thought of having to deal with him again was thoroughly
alarming.

Of course the servants were ignorant of the true reason
of old Mrs. Ransome's sudden vacation of the house. I
heard them attributing it to the mistress' determined opposition, and the cook applauded her courage.

Meanwhile I listened anxiously and nervously for the
sound of Mr. Ransome's footsteps in the hall. Suppose
he came home as sane, let us say, as he was that day when
he paid me his mysterious visit in order to announce his
wife's madness to me? I had no influence over him then,
or signs of it would have appeared, and I should have
remembered them. Or suppose he returned home as insane
as he was that night when he left the marks of his cruel
fingers on his wife's arm?

Six o'clock came and dinner was served, but only one
was there to eat it. When another hour had passed, my
room grew too dark to enable me to continue sewing. I
went up-stairs very cautiously and carefully, listening lest
Mr. Ransome should have returned unheard by me, and

hurried through the hall, meaning to kill half an hour before the twilight should give me an excuse for lighting my
lamp, in taking some exercise in the grounds.

The hall door stood open. I gained the lawn and walked
quickly toward the kitchen-gardens, the least frequented
portion of the estate. How glorious was the summer evening! The heat of the sun was gone, though the sun shone
brightly away on my right, where, upon the level horizon—
for the hills filled the landscape to the left many great
clouds were grouped, and promised a noble sunset. The
sky was a soft blue, and the rich green of the trees stood
out exquisitely against it, and produced a harmony of tints
that was almost saddening with excess of beauty. I chose
the shelter of the pea-beds, and breathed with a bounding
pulse the pure sweetness of the breeze which shook the
homely vegetation around me, and kept the numerous in-
sects constantly on the wing. The house in the distance
looked the picture of an English gentleman's home. There
were brilliant stars kindled by the setting sun in its windows; the bright glare made the walls white, and enriched
with magical effects of shadow the pretty pillared terrace,
surmounted with flowers, the gleaming drawing-room windows and the soft colors of their drapery. Mrs. Ransome
was right in not allowing her husband to drive her from
such a home. The question was, would separation from
him involve her leaving the house? Could she compel her
husband to quit Gardenhurst? I could not say. It seemed
to me that if she separated from her husband, then, in order
to save herself from being persecuted by him if he had a
mind to haunt her, she would have to quit the home she
loved, and either exile herself in some foreign country or
become a kind of fugitive in her own. She had certainly
one remedy—she could have him placed in an asylum.
Such control might be imperative hereafter, if it were not
necessary and merciful now.

Mr. Ransome had not returned when I reached the house.
There was nothing unusual in his prolonged absence, but I
wished he would come home, for I wanted to see what he
would do.

A little before eight o'clock I was astonished by hearing the sound of the piano in the drawing-room—the first time the instrument had been played since I had been in the house. The performer's touch was firm; she played in octaves, and filled the whole house with the music. The air, whether a waltz or not, was played in waltz time, and so cheerful, so gay, so melodious was it, that my feet began to move in the most mysterious manner, and I think through the magic of that tune I could have waltzed accurately without ever having learned the dance.

The servants came out of the kitchen to listen and seemed highly delighted. Mary, the better to hear, went up-stairs, and I was thinking of calling her down, when a new direction was given to my thoughts by the alarming crash of a door being shut, and by the sound of the music ceasing all at once.

"I'll wager her husband's come back and stopped her!" the cook said.

"Could she have seen him coming?" replied Susan. "It isn't two minutes ago since she began."

The girl's remark put an idea into my head. Was Mrs. Ransome swelling her triumph over her mother-in-law with music, and timing the performance so that her husband might just catch her at it? If so, then she deserved what might follow. She knew that his passions were not under his control, and she had no right to anger him. Whatever her motives might be, I considered that she showed bad taste in playing the piano at that particular time, when she might expect her husband's return at any moment; and when the sounds, so very unusual in that house, might be interpreted by him as a kind of crowing over the victory I had won for her.

I was so vexed with her that I shut my door to prevent any sound from reaching me that might excite me into running to them and interrupting the quarrel. However, I was too nervous, and too apprehensive of the man's total want of self-control, to keep myself long in suspense. I opened the door and listened, but could hear nothing; and questioning whether Mr. Ransome *had* come home, and

10

whether the door had not been banged by a draught, I went back to my chair, drew the lamp closer to me, and resumed my needle.

But scarcely had I made a dozen stitches when footsteps sounded on the stairs, and Mary thrust her head into my room, her face quite white, and her eyes reflecting honest terror.

"Oh, miss!" she exclaimed, in a loud whisper, "they're quarrelling awfully up-stairs. I hear mistress tell master she would kill him, and he gave a loud laugh and said that he always knew she was capable of murder, and he wished she would kill him, for it would do his soul good, wherever it were, to know that she was hanged."

"You have no right to listen," I exclaimed angrily, but very frightened too. "You'll get yourself into trouble some of these days with that mean trick."

"I went to listen to the music," she answered; "how could I tell that she'd stop playing? I didn't know master was there. He must have walked in through one of the windows, and, oh! there will be murder done! I'm sure of it! Mistress' passion is something awful."

I pushed past her, heedless of risks in my resolution to stop this dangerous quarrel. I walked hastily to the drawing-room door, afraid that my courage would abandon me if I gave myself time for thought; but I heard no sound as I opened the door, and when I entered I found Mrs. Ransome alone.

She was standing in the middle of the room, her hair in disorder, her bosom rising and falling with her fierce breathing; and scarcely had she seen me when she shrieked out:

"Tell him to keep away from me or I shall kill him!"

"For Heaven's sake control yourself, madam!" I exclaimed. "Where is Mr. Ransome?"

"There—in the grounds! he left me in time I should have killed him!" she panted, pointing furiously toward the open window, at which I glanced without seeing Mr. Ransome.

"*Pray* do not use such expressions," I said. "Why

do you put yourself in his way? Why do you excite
him?"

"What do you mean by excite him?" she cried, turning
her brilliant eyes upon me. " I was playing the piano and
he came in noiselessly and kicked the door to, and ordered
me to stop playing. Of course I refused. I told him to
go away and went on playing. And the wretch," she
said, through her teeth, "seized me by the shoulder and
dragged me away—look at the music-stool! it fell down
when he dragged me—and I felt the coward's nails in my
shoulder! Brute! madman!" she shrieked; "I'll kill him
for his treatment of me! I'll kill him!"

She quivered from head to foot with rage.

Just then Mr. Ransome showed himself at one of the
windows under the veranda. He stared in with his
strange eyes and a white smile twisting his face into positive ugliness. I made a step toward him, meaning to advise
him to keep away; but when he saw me advancing, he
wheeled around and walked off quickly.

She had not seen him, and after standing in silence
awhile, struggling as though to recover her breath, she
went to the piano and closed it with a bang, and stood beside it with her eyes fixed downward.

"Think," she exclaimed, in a low, bitter whisper, "of
his laying his hand upon me! Think that there is no horrible degradation to which I may not at any moment be
subjected by this barbarous man!"

I saw her clench and open her hands, and then she came
toward the door and made as though she would walk away
without further speech, but stopped suddenly.

Pained and harassed as I was, I could not help admiring
the wonderful dignity her vehement resentment, her lacer-
ated pride, communicated to her movements. The light in
the room had not permitted me clearly to see her face before; but now she was close to me I observed how peculiarly the character of her beauty was adapted to the tragical emotions which then possessed her. Her face was
marble-colored with wrath; her eyes glowed; her black,
narrow eyebrows were knitted into a violent frown, which

had the effect of contracting the skin upon her forehead and
bringing her hair appreciably lower, and thus giving shadow
and force to the gloomy expression that darkened her coun·
tenance.   I watched her with much the sort of fear that I
had believed Mr. Ransome would excite in me, and could
scarcely credit that the influence I had exercised over her
husband should be denied to her.

"Are you not sick of these scenes?" she exclaimed.
"Do they not disgust you?   Oh! what words have I to express the sense of utter degradation they fill me with?"

I would hazard no protests.   She was not in the mood to
endure the least reproach—to tolerate the smallest word of
advice.   I held my tongue, keeping my eyes averted.

"Can you imagine," she continued, "what my feelings
are when I look back and think of the respect and affection
which were mine when I was Miss Kilmain?   When I com-
pare what I was with what I am—in those days admired
and petted and followed, and now shunned and ill-treated,
and infamously, O God! *how* infamously humiliated!   It
is my own fault.   I refused the love of a man who would
have honored me as a lady, and gave my hand to a heartless
coward who, mad as he is, pretends to a greater madness
that he may the better insult me and humble me!   How
shall I end this!   I have brought the curse upon myself;
am I not privileged to rid myself of it?   But how? *how?*
Is there no refuge for such miserable women as I but the
publicity that adds shame to the sorrow it does not cure?
Must I take the whole world into my confidence to free myself from this monster?   Oh, there is no pity among men
for women!   The laws men make protect themselves, not
us.   Think now, how helpless I am.   You talk to me of a
madhouse.   Imagine yourself a stranger to me.   You hear
of my husband being in a madhouse; what are your conclusions?   Are they not cruelly prejudicial to me?   I should
have kept him at home, obtained tender guardians for him,
nursed him, watched over him!   Oh, you know how the
world cants! how it gives nothing—how it exacts everything.   Let me tell the world I hate this man; I am judged
and condemned a monstrous sinner for my candor.   Shall

"TELL HIM TO KEEP AWAY FROM ME, OR I SHALL KILL HIM!"—Page 148.

I go into the highway and pull my sleeve above my arm
and exhibit the marks of his fierce hand upon my flesh?
Shall I bare my shoulder and point to the laceration of his
nails there, and invite the crowd to observe these things
and bear witness for me when I call him ruffian and
coward? The world loves such secrets. It would not lose
a syllable of them. Shall I entertain it with a full sight of
my heart, all the misery that lies there, all the bitter memories, the dark hopelessness? Others may do this. I would
rather die a hundred times over!"

She continued looking at me for a moment or two after
she had ceased speaking, with a frown that made her gaze
passionately earnest and scrutinizing; then, gathering up
her skirt, walked quickly across the hall into the dining-
room and closed the door upon herself.

X

That foolish girl, Mary, had been telling the others how
she had heard mistress threaten master's life, and how
master had threatened to kill mistress, and how she had
heard a terrible crash which she made sure was mistress
who had been knocked down (which must have been the
music-stool that had been upset in the unseemly scuffle at
the piano). They were jabbering away in mysterious
voices on these texts when I passed the kitchen, and I heard
the cook make use of the following bloodthirsty observation
with great emphasis: "That if ever mistress did kill the
master, she (the cook), for one, would stand up and say it
served him right, and call upon other wicious husbands to
take warning by his fate."

Rather horrified by this very sanguinary view of the
situation, and hoping to check the conversation, I put my
head in and asked where Mr. Ransome was.

"In the library, ain't he?" answered Maddox, who sat
with his back to the door, and spoke without turning his
head.

"Mary," I exclaimed, holding up my finger, "remember
the caution I gave you just now. Be careful!"

With which solemn admonition I withdrew, leaving it to produce the best effect it might.

At half-past ten the servants had gone to bed, and the house was quiet. Candle in hand, I took my regular rounds, and in the library found signs, in a great quantity of cigar-ash, of Mr. Ransome having spent the evening there. I bolted the hall doors, extinguished the hall lamp, and went to my bedroom.

The moon, which rose late now, was just creeping over the hills, and the red, hot-looking planet seemed to increase by the mere force of appropriate effect the sultriness of the night. Breathless and still, the land lay black under the dark heavens; but all along the west the summer lightning played, and threw out, for breathless moments at a time, the fine, delicate outlines of clouds.

My bedroom was very hot, for the sunshine had been upon it all the afternoon; the candlelight awoke the flies, which buzzed drowsily past my ear, and a great black moth flew in through the window and disagreeably affected my nerves by the harsh slapping noise it made as its wings struck the ceiling or the wall. Once or twice a moan of wind sounded in the chimney—a brief passage of air that filled the black trees with a strange and solemn note, and took a fanciful meaning from the ear by its abrupt cessation and the breathless stillness that followed it.

I left the window wide open, but drew the curtains close, extinguished the candle, and got into bed. The heat kept me wakeful; I tossed restlessly upon my pillow, practising all the artless little fictions I had been taught as a child by which to invite sleep: such as counting, reciting a scrap of poetry over and over again, keeping my eyes fixed on a portion of the room until all manner of lights swam out of the darkness. I heard the bell of St. George's at Copsford strike the quarter before twelve. How exquisite, how fairylike was the dainty thrilling of that clear far chime upon the silence! I strained my ear to follow the tremulous echo until it died—and then quite a different sound jarred an instant upon the silence.

It was subdued and muffled. I should scarcely have

heard it but for the strained attention of my hearing at that moment. It sounded like the turning of the handle of a door.

I listened, not nervously—such a sound was easily accounted for—but heard nothing more. Now, indeed, I must get to sleep. I should feel the effects of this wakefulness in the morning. I planted my head energetically on my pillow—five, six minutes or more passed—I was still wide awake, and distinctly heard the echo of a footstep in the garden. The noise was such as would be made by the heel of a boot crunching the gravel.

I sat up in my bed and listened, to make sure. The sound was not repeated. Could I have been mistaken? Was it the moth scraping the paper of the wall with its wings? I felt nervous, but I knew not why when I asked myself the question. In so calm a night the lightest sound would be audible, and the footstep of a wayfarer on the high-road beyond the walls might strike the ear as though the tread were under the window.

Once again I settled my head on the pillow, and consoled myself with reflecting that, happen what would, there would be daylight at three, and the dawn must bring security. I had fallen at last into the state of semi-unconsciousness which is the delicious preliminary to sound sleep, when I was startled into complete wakefulness by a noise which seemed to have come from the landing just outside my door. My heart beat quickly; I turned my head and listened. The staircase creaked, and then the sense of hearing was occupied by the vexatious throbbing of my heart. Who was outside? Who was moving at this hour? I got out of bed, and hot as I had found the night, my feet were now as cold as stones. I opened the door and looked out. The landing was pitch-dark.

"Is there anybody there?" I called out.

No answer—no sound of any kind. My own voice frightened me. I listened for some moments, then closed the door and returned to bed.

I was not again disturbed. I fell asleep, and when I awoke it was time to get up. The morning was dark. A

strong wind swept through the open window and rounded
the curtains like sails. I drew them apart, closed the window, and saw the sky lead-colored, with heavy rain slanting
across the country, the grounds streaming with wet and the
trees swaying wildly to the strong wind. I dressed myself
and went down-stairs. The servants were about, but not
seeing Maddox, I asked if he had left his room? Evidently
not. I told Susan to go upstairs and call him, and went
into the dining-room, where the cook was dusting the furniture. The scene from the window was a desolate one—
the sweeping rain, the streaming shrubs, the flowers tossed
by the gale and scattering their petals, the gloomy sky with
under-clouds resembling smoke sweeping along it.

Susan entered and said, " I've been knocking at Maddox's
door miss, and can't make him answer."

" What causes him to sleep so heavily? He has always
been punctual before," I answered; and I went up-stairs,
making sure he would get up and answer directly he heard
my voice.

The bedroom door was closed. I knocked heartily, but
got no reply. I knocked again, and then, greatly wondering, turned the handle and peeped in. The room was
empty, and the bed had not been slept in. I looked about
me, surprised out of common sense by his absence, for I
remember stooping and peering under the bed, and then I
opened a closet full of shelves and stared into that.

Since he was not in his room, where was he? Since he
had not gone to bed, where had he slept? I hastened below and exclaimed to the cook.

" Maddox did not use his room last night. His bed is
untouched."

" Not use his room?" she answered quickly. " Why, I
see him go into it myself; I said good-night to him as he
opened the door."

" His room is empty. Is he down-stairs?"

" He's not in the kitchen. I haven't been into your
room. But what should he do downstairs all night?"

" What, indeed? But I'll go and see nevertheless."

Mary was in the drawing-room; the other housemaid was

sweeping the staircase; I would question them presently.
I found the door of my room ajar. If none of the servants
had entered it, the circumstance was odd, because I was
always the last to leave that part of the house at night, and
made a point of closing all the doors before going to bed.
Maddox was not in the room, everything was precisely as I
had left it over-night: the lamp on the table, my work-
basket beside it, the book I had been reading, the chair
drawn close. I looked into the pantry; I went further, I
lighted a candle, and boldly walked into the cellar. Not a
trace of the man was visible. I restored the candlestick to
its place, and went slowly upstairs, pondering over the
noises I had heard in the night. I called the two housemaids, and first I asked them if they had been into my
room since they left their beds? No. Were they sure?
Certain sure. Did Maddox go up-stairs with them when
they went to bed last night? Yes. Susan lighted his
candle for him at her own on the landing, and she heard
cook wish him good-night.

"Did any of you hear footsteps outside your bedrooms
last night?"

"Lor no, miss!" cried the cook, in great agitation.
(She had a room to herself.)

"I didn't," said Susan. "Did you, miss?"

"I want to make sure that *I* did by inquiring if any of
you did," I replied.

"I won't declare that I didn't, though," said Mary
"Mind, I don't say it was a footstep I heard, but it was a
queer noise."

"It was yourself snoring," exclaimed Susan. "I am sure
you couldn't have heard anything if I didn't, for you was
asleep before me."

"Let us hear about this noise," I said.

"Well, it might have been my fancy," answered Mary,
who doubtless found her imagination defied and rendered
useless by the simple evidence of her bedroom companion.
"If Susan didn't hear it, I suppose it *was* my fancy."

"It is very fortunate that Susan *didn't* hear it," I exclaimed, "or you would probably have made a ghost of it.

However, Maddox may take care of himself. If this is a
practical joke of his, the want of his breakfast will bring
him among us soon enough. And if he has left the house,
why, then a very indifferent servant has discharged himself, and Mr. Ransome will have to look out for another
man."

But these easy conclusions by no means represented my
own doubts, and the real surprise that the footman's disappearance had given me. I could not forget the noises I had
heard; and as they were unquestionably real, they only
served to make Maddox's disappearance the more unaccountable, by establishing the theory that he had wandered
about and eventually left the house; and then suggesting
the question—what was the object of his midnight quest
and ultimate flight?

However, at that early stage I had no right to assume
that he *had* left the house; and, for the present, I con-
tented myself by supposing that, mysterious as his absence
appeared, a word would clear up the mystery, and submit
it as an intensely commonplace affair. I will explain what
I mean by an instance. A housemaid in a family, the
housekeeper to whom was known to me, was found missing
from her bedroom one morning, just as Maddox was. At
midday came a letter from her father, filled with humble
apologies for his daughter's behavior, saying that she had
left the house after the family were in bed, to keep an
appointment with her lover; that on her return, she found
the house door had been blown to by the wind; and that,
not knowing what to do, she had walked a distance of seven
miles to where he (her father) lived, and knocked them up
at four o'clock in the morning, to the horror and dismay of
the mother. Some such solution as this, I thought, might
attend the conundrum Maddox had bequeathed us.

I noticed, in going up-stairs, that Mr. Ransome's bedroom door was ajar, and I paused a moment, thinking to
hear him stirring, that I might tell him of his footman's
disappearance. But all was still, and I crept quietly
away.

I couldn't help laughing at the mysterious airs the women

gave themselves. My reference to the sounds I had heard, coupled with the unaccountable behavior of the footman, had frightened them; and it was absurd to see them grouped together in the broad daylight, muttering under their breaths, their superstitious souls grasping at the opportunity to entertain one another with dismal narratives, drawn, no doubt, from books which you only meet in the drawers of kitchen-tables and dressers, but related by these simpletons as though they were personal experiences.

Mary had the most to say, and though both the others well knew that there was not the smallest reliance to be placed upon her most solemn asseveration, yet they listened to her with preposterous eagerness, and swallowed her miserable small-talk with as many "lawks!" "did you evers!" and "fancy nows!" as would fill a whole chapter of this story.

The table was laid for breakfast in the dining-room, and it was now nine o'clock, but Mr. Ransome had not yet made his appearance. This was unusual. He was seldom later than eight, and to the best of my knowledge away out of the house by the half-hour. Thus his wife, by leaving her room at nine, generally had the satisfaction of breakfasting alone.

Her bell rang, and Mary answered it, and I suppose did not get her nose fairly past the door before she was telling Mrs. Ransome all about Maddox's disappearance; for in a few moments she came hurrying to me to say that I was wanted by mistress.

"What is the meaning of the footman's not sleeping in his bedroom, Miss Avory?" Mrs. Ransome asked me.

"I haven't the slightest idea," I replied.

"Are you *sure* he isn't in his bedroom?"

"Quite sure."

"Nor anywhere in the house?"

"No signs of him at all."

"This is very curious," she said, seating herself. "Have you spoken to Mr. Ransome about it?"

"He hasn't left his room yet," I answered.

She glanced at the clock and said:

"Mary, go and tell the cook to get my breakfast ready on a tray and bring it to my room."

Mary went out reluctantly. She longed to hear our conversation.

"You had better knock at Mr. Ransome's door and tell him what has happened," said Mrs. Ransome. "The footman may have robbed the house."

"I thought that myself; but I have looked about me well, and nothing seems to have been touched."

"Didn't you hear somebody walking on the landing outside your room last night?"

"I asked Mary and the others if they had heard the sound of a footstep, but they tell me they did not. I thought myself that I heard the staircase creak, and the handle of a door turned, and then again the crunch of a foot upon the gravel in the grounds."

"You couldn't have been deceived in such sounds."

"Why no, madam. I am pretty sure they were real."

"It must have been Maddox whom you heard," she exclaimed.

"No doubt. I am afraid that something is wrong, unless, indeed, the man walks in his sleep. When I went down-stairs this morning I found the door of my room open. None of the servants had entered before me; and I perfectly remember shutting that door last night, as I do every night, before going to bed."

"Have you looked at the plate-safe?"

"No. At least I have not looked *into* it."

"You should," she exclaimed. "You had better go at once and knock at Mr. Ransome's door."

She was agitated and restless, and made an impetuous gesture as though she would have me be quick.

The door of Mr. Ransome's bedroom was partially open, as I had already noticed. I knocked, but got no answer. I knocked louder, but got no reply to that either. Mr. Ransome must be in a very sound sleep; and I stood irresolute, doubtful whether I should knock a third time or peep in. I did both: I rapped lustily, then pushed the door gently and entered.

Both the blinds and the window-curtains were drawn; and quitting the bright light of the landing, I could scarcely see for some moments in the gloom that filled the chamber. But one thing was immediately apparent: Mr. Ransome was not in his bed. More—his bed had not been slept in.

I ran to the windows, and pulled up the blinds. The clouds had broken, the rain had ceased, and the sunshine was streaming brilliantly upon the soaked grounds. I stood astounded to find the bedroom empty; astounded, because I had not questioned that Mr. Ransome was in the room, and because the exactly similar disappearance of Maddox immeasurably heightened the surprise of *this* disappearance. I hurried to Mrs. Ransome.

"Well, has your knocking aroused him at last?" she inquired.

"He is not in his room," I answered.

She stared, and burst into a loud, strange laugh.

"Has *he* gone too?"

"It seems so. Come and see for yourself, madam. You will find his bed untouched."

She advanced a few steps, stopped, and said, "Are you sure he is not in his bedroom? I do not wish to meet him."

"Quite sure."

She crossed the landing, and I followed her.

"This is one of his mad freaks!" she exclaimed, looking around her. "He was here last night; for he came up-stairs shortly after me, and I heard him shut his door."

"Has he ever left the house before at night?"

"Never. But the past actions of such a man furnish no criterion to judge his present actions by," she answered, in a hard tone. There was no surprise in her face. She gazed about her coolly and walked to the window and looked out. "The height is too great for him to have ventured without breaking his leg or his neck," she said, with a laugh. "If he has left the house, he has gone to work like a sane man by opening the doors. I suppose he'll come back when it suits him."

She walked out of the room, and when on the landing, said:

"Never mind about Mr. Ransome, Miss Avory. I am more concerned about Maddox. Go and thoroughly examine your room and look elsewhere. I have always thought him capable of robbing the house, and I should like to know if he has done so."

I was about to follow her, when my eye caught sight of something glittering upon the floor, close against a chest of drawers. I picked it up and found it a sovereign; upon which I called to Mrs. Ransome, "See what I have found, madam."

She came back quickly, asking, "What?" I gave her the money, and, in doing so, caught sight of a splinter of wood sticking out of one of the locks of the top drawer of the chest. I pulled the handle and the drawer came out, and I saw that the lock had been forced and broken. The drawer contained a few cravats and some stud and pin cases, which were empty.

"This looks like a robbery," I said. "Do you see how the lock has been wrenched?"

"Is this Maddox's doing or Mr. Ransome's?" she answered. "I would as soon believe it my husband's as the other's. There may be some cunning in this to throw us off our guard."

I was rather bewildered by this view of the case, and said:

"What object could Mr. Ransome have in leading us to suppose that he has been robbed?"

"What object has any madman in practising the most stealthy stratagems for the most imbecile ends?" she replied sharply. "He might wish to frighten me by leaving us to suppose that Maddox has robbed and murdered him, for anything I can tell; or the pair of them may be in some wretched conspiracy to get my name about and give scandal-mongers an excuse for inventing falsehoods about me."

"Did Mr. Ransome keep money in this drawer?"

"I don't know. I am perfectly ignorant of his habits."

"His dressing-case used to stand on the toilet-table; I

don't see it there now," I said, looking around me in search of it.

She went to the drawers and pulled them open one after the other. Their contents were tossed, and in such a manner that they might easily have furnished a proof of a thievish hand having routed among them. In looking into the lower drawer, Mrs. Ransome became absorbed in thought; her hands fell to her side, her eyes remained fixed, and she stood motionless. Then she suddenly broke away, stared quickly around, and said:

"Thinking will not explain anything. This leaving the house is an unaccountable act, and I'll not condescend to bestow a thought upon it."

Saying which, with a suggestion of extraordinary perversity in her tone, she passed into her bedroom.

I lingered a few minutes, looking about me for any hints to help to a conclusion. One fact was obvious: Mr. Ransome was gone. But had he been robbed? The sovereign I had found on the floor might have slipped out of his pocket; his own hand might have broken the lock of the drawer in a passion. How could I tell that anything was missing? I did not know what he had in his drawers and wardrobe. The dressing-case was gone, indeed; but he might have taken it with him. As to the rumpled state of the wearing apparel in the lower drawers, this might have been owing to his own impatience. Had he been robbed; and if so, by whom? Mrs. Ransome had heard him shut his bedroom door: a sufficiently conclusive proof that he had *entered* his bedroom. At what hour, then, had he quitted it? If Maddox had robbed him, he could not have robbed him while he was in his bedroom. Neither would he have robbed him before he entered his bedroom, for the obvious reason that Mr. Ransome would discover the robbery on entering the room. It was even more unlikely that Maddox would have committed the robbery after Mr. Ransome had quitted the house; because the sight of the untouched bed would suggest that his master was still downstairs or had not yet retired to rest, and that he might come to his room at any moment and find Maddox there.

Taking these theories for what they were worth, I felt strongly disposed to concur in Mrs. Ransome's view— namely, that the disappearance of both master and man was a conspiracy between them, designed for a purpose I could not imagine, but designed, no doubt, to bring anxiety, grief, and humiliation upon the wife.

The broken lock, the sovereign on the floor, the rumpled drawers, the missing dressing-case, might all be so many cunning details devised for the purpose of complicating the mystery. There might be a special subtlety in the very unobtrusiveness of the signs which had been created to establish a theory of robbery. A great air of confusion and disorder in the room might, by the very officiousness of the details, set conjecture on the right track.

I went to the door and turned the handle to try if the movement would produce the same sound I had heard overnight. But this was a failure, for the handle made no noise at all. I then descended the stairs and entered my room, and had a good stare at the old-fashioned safe in which the plate was locked. There were no external signs whatever to denote that it had been touched.

I had brought the keys of the various closets, etc., with me from my bedroom, whither I always carried them at night; they made a big bunch, and the stoutest and most intricately-cut of them all belonged to the safe, which was of iron, and I should think upward of fifty years old. Hence the lock, as you may conceive, was no very ingenious patent; but it was secure as any old lock can well be, with a stout plate of steel over the bolt which the mouth of the key fitted; while the key was so contrived as to sink below each side of the plate and to withstand any amount of pressure if it was not exactly adjusted to the plate.

I inserted the key and opened the heavy iron door. The safe was empty.

I was struck motionless, doubting the evidence of my own senses. To appreciate the full significance of this discovery you must know that among my other duties was the business of locking the plate away every night. Every night before going to bed Maddox brought me all the silver that had been in use throughout the day in the plate-basket, and remained in my room while I counted it, after which I put it in the safe and locked it up. He had done this every night since I had been in the house; he had done this the night before. The only portion of the silver that had been left out were some spoons, which went up on the tray with the water and glasses. But these spoons I had found in the dining-room and library, and they were now in the kitchen. The plate in use represented but a very small portion of the silver contained in the safe. To find this safe empty, then, was a discovery that perfectly overwhelmed me.

I ran upstairs.

"All the plate is stolen!" I exclaimed; "the safe is empty!"

Mrs. Ransome uttered an exclamation, while the brush with which Mary was operating on her mistress' hair fell from her hand and her mouth flew open.

"All the plate gone?" cried Mrs. Ransome.

"Yes," I replied; "every bit of it!"

"Then this accounts for Maddox's disappearance! He must have stolen your keys."

"No; he couldn't have done that. The keys were in my trunk, and I am positive nobody entered my room last night."

She was silent, and then said, "What's to be done?"

"The police ought to be told," said Mary.

"Certainly," I replied. "Are there any police at Copsford?"

"Oh yes," cried Mary. "I know the inspector well. He's a friend of father's. Shall I run for him, ma'am?"

"Yes." But she must first finish doing Mrs. Ransome's hair. She achieved her task with extraordinary celerity, and then hastened away.

The conversation between Mrs. Ransome and me was very discursive and scarcely worth chronicling, being on my side, at all events, chiefly ejaculatory. But one notion Mrs. Ransome had got into her brain—which my latest discovery seemed rather to confirm than shake—and that was,

11

that the whole business from beginning to end was a conspiracy against her, planned by her husband, and helped by
Maddox.

"I don't know what it means—what his object is," she
exclaimed, as we went down-stairs; "but the mere fact of
their having left the house together is conclusive that this
double disappearance is a planned affair.   Oh, Miss Avory!
my husband is wicked and mad enough to do anything."

"I believe that myself," I answered.   "But allowing the
largest license to the actions of madness, I cannot see how
Maddox's stealing the plate can help any plot against your
peace of mind that Mr. Ransome may meditate."

"Nor I; but Mr. Ransome can explain, I dare say, and
with his mysterious forefinger and brutal smile show us
how utterly mad he is by this his last scheme."

"What shall we say to the inspector when he comes?
Suppose he hits upon your idea, but without guessing the
motive of the act, that Mr. Ransome and his man have gone
off and taken the plate with them; what will be the effect
upon the neighbors when they hear the mutilated story?
Will they not declare that Mr. Ransome has actually
robbed his own house?"

She laughed, and looked grave in a moment.

"We should have thought of this before sending for the
inspector.   I am sure I don't want such people here.
They seldom do any good, and his visit is certain to set
people talking.   It is Mary's doing.   The girl is a perfect
fool and runs mad on the merest hint of excitement.   We
ought to have deliberated a little before sending to Copsford."   She grew uneasy and left her chair, and moved
restlessly about the room.   We were in the dining-room,
and I was talking to her while she waited for her breakfast.

"Perhaps," she suddenly exclaimed, "this is a part of
Mr. Ransome's plot.   He judged that, on our discovering
the robbery, the police would be summoned."

"There is nothing humiliating in summoning the police
in order to point out a robbery," I answered, seeing her
pause.

"But there is in the gossip that will follow. People are
so detestably knowing. They put two and two together
and make five. 'If the footman had quitted the house
alone, we could understand,' they will say; 'but why
should Mr. Ransome run away on the same night, and no
doubt at the same hour?' and not being able to find an answer, they will invent one; and who can tell what monstrous fictions may get about?"

The entrance of Susan at this juncture interrupted the
conversation, and I left the room. While Mrs. Ransome
breakfasted I occupied the time by further explorations,
and by asking the servants questions. But neither my
researches nor my interrogations were of any use. The
two servants could throw no light on Mr. Ransome's disappearance. I asked them if they had ever noticed Mr. Ransome and Maddox conversing together with any air of
familiarity. Never. Had it struck them that Mr. Ransome
had treated his man with more forbearance latterly? No—
quite the contrary. A day or two ago Susan had heard Mr.
Ransome storming at Maddox in his bedroom. How had
Susan heard this? In passing the bedroom. Was she sure
that Mr. Ransome did not know that she was passing?
Not unless he could see through a wall.

I was in the kitchen when Mary, after nearly two hours'
absence, returned with the inspector. The girl, who was
breathless but in high spirits, came running down-stairs to
tell me I was wanted. I heard her cackling like a hen to
the cook as I made my way upstairs, and gathered, even in
that brief time, enough to lead me to suppose that the inspector had been put by her in possession of a very great
deal more information than it was possible for any living
being, in the present state of knowledge, to communicate.

The inspector was a bald, big man, with strong whiskers,
a frogged coat, pantaloons tightly strapped down over his
boots, and small black eyes lodged in deep caverns and
protected with a regular furze of eyebrow. He sat on the
extreme edge of a chair, opposite Mrs. Ransome, who looked
nervous and pale and worried.

The moment I entered the room the inspector told me to

sit down, as if that were an indispensable part of the proceedings, without which there was no getting on at all.
He then opened a broadside of questions upon me, deeply
puzzling himself occasionally by the magnitude of his knowingness. I was to describe Maddox. I was then to relate
my habits—-when I locked the safe, where I put the keys—
with a great number of other questions all having regard to
Maddox only; whereby I was led to believe that no reference had been made to Mr. Ransome's disappearance, until
he suddenly turned to Mrs. Ransome and said:

"You're husband has gone too, ma'am, hasn't he?"

"He did not occupy his bedroom last night."

"How might that be now?"

"I really do not know."

"It's not to be supposed that he was acquainted with this
here footman's intention to rob the house?"

"It would not be a robbery if the plate were removed
with Mr. Ransome's sanction."

"Just so," answered the inspector, looking enlightened;
"that's just what I am driving at. Anything suspected?"

"What?"

"I ask, ma'am——-"

"I desire the benefit of your suspicions," said Mrs. Ransome restlessly.

"Then, if you please, I'll search the house."

"Will you take the inspector upstairs, Miss Avory?"

The man followed me to Mr. Ransome's bedroom. I
showed him the broken lock, and told him how I had found
a sovereign on the floor, and how I missed Mr. Ransome's
dressing-case. Did I know what was in the dressing-case?
Valuables, for instance? Bank-notes, say? No; I was
quite ignorant of the contents of the box. He opened the
drawers; he peered under the bed; he shook the window-
curtains; he looked out of the window; he folded his arms
and gazed sternly around him. He was a very knowing
inspector indeed. He went to my bedroom, and I showed
him my trunk where I put the keys, and I explained to him
that it was impossible for Maddox or anybody else to have
entered my room when I was in bed, and pulled the trunk

from under the bed, and opened it, and taken out the keys, which were certain to jingle, all without my hearing him. And he agreed with me. After this he examined Maddox's room, where in a drawer we found a piece of candle, a pipe, a box of lucifer-matches, a portrait of a lady in bronze paper, and the book concerning the adventures of Jerry Abershaw. The inspector eyed the book gravely, but made no observation, and desired me to take him to the plate-safe. So we journeyed down-stairs, where the safe stood open; and he looked inside it and outside it, and examined the key and applied it to the lock, and then scrutinized the lock—all with an air of profound wisdom, as though he should say, "Everything is clear to my mind, young woman; but that is *my* secret."

However, his face wronged his judgment, for, so far from everything being clear to his mind, he exclaimed, smiting his knee, that he couldn't make head or tail of the business —that it looked like a robbery, but that it mightn't be a robbery; that if Maddox worked alone, he was the thief; but that if Mr. Ransome set him to work, he wasn't the thief; that he was puzzled when he thought of them both going off the same night; and that he would like to speak to the mistress, please.

I took him to the dining-room, and there left him. He went away after he had been alone with Mrs. Ransome for about a quarter of an hour, and she came down-stairs to my room.

Her discomposed manner was easily attributable to the uncomfortable vocation of her recent visitor.

"Close the door, Miss Avory," she said; "I don't want the servants to overhear us."

I did as she bade me, and said:

"What does the inspector think?"

"Oh!" she exclaimed, pettishly, "he is a very stupid man. He asked me a great number of useless and unnecessary questions, and then had to request me to give him directions after all. We ought never to have sent for him. He will now return to Copsford and tell everybody that Mr. Ransome has run away from his wife, and that the footman

has run away with the plate, and I shall be as much talked
about as if I had run away myself."

" But did not he express an opinion?"

"No; he said he was puzzled. That was substantially
all he said, though he wrapped up his meaning in such a
variety of arguments and questions that one would suppose
he saw the whole thing as clearly as I can see through that
window."

" Does he mean to start his people in pursuit of Maddox?"
I asked, struck by the air of indifference with which she
discussed the subject.

"I'll tell you, as well as I can, what passed between us.
He asked me at what hour I supposed the robbery had been
committed. I told him it must have happened last night
after half-past ten, because you did not go to bed before
that time. He then put some irrelevant questions about
you, which I cut short, because they were silly. Then he
wanted to know if Mr. Ransome had ever before left his
house at night without communicating his intentions to do
so to me. I answered yes, and that he was in the habit of
leaving his home sometimes for a day, sometimes for a
week, without a word: and as he could do it in the day, so
he could do it in the night. What sort of character did
Maddox bear? I said I knew very little of the man. He
was his master's servant, and had been engaged by him,
and that he had been in our service six months. After a
number of questions of this kind, he said, 'Do you charge
this man with having robbed you?' 'The plate has been
taken,' I answered, 'and I suppose Maddox took it. But
I will tell you plainly that it is quite as likely as not that
he was an instrument in Mr. Ransome's hand.' There I
stopped, not choosing to enter into further explanations.
'My duty is very simple,' he said. 'If you charge this
footman with having robbed you, I will have him apprehended if he can be caught. If you tell me that he has
acted in concert with your husband, then you give me to
understand that Mr. Ransome is as guilty as he, and that
there are two parties to be followed. But that can't be;
for if the footman acted on Mr. Ransome's instructions, he

is no thief, because he is his master's servant, and is bound
to obey him; and the plate is as much your husband's as
yours, and every man has a right to his own.   That's law.'
By this time I was thoroughly tired of the man, though I
quite appreciated his bewilderment in not being able to get
a direct charge from me.   It was out of the question that I
should go into family matters with him, and explain that
Mr. Ransome was mad, and that all this might be a scheme
of his to revenge himself for my treatment of his mother;
and I firmly believe this to be the case.   So, in order to
get rid of him, I told him that I would consult my friends,
and let him know my determination.   But I don't mean to
consult my friends, Miss Avory.   I shall leave matters as
they are and wait."

"But suppose," I suggested, "that Maddox has really
robbed you; suppose that Mr. Ransome knows nothing
about the robbery."

"I can't suppose anything of the kind.   There are seven
nights in a week.   Is it not too much of a coincidence that
they should both take it into their heads to leave on the
same night, perhaps at the same hour?   I tell you I can't
conceive Mr. Ransome's object.   As a madman, his actions
must be unaccountable; but that this double disappearance
is some insane conspiracy against me I am as certain as
that I am now looking at you."

"What do you propose to do, madam?"

"Nothing.   What *can* I do?   Suppose my theory is
right.   I start the police in quest of Maddox, and he is
captured; he then confesses the conspiracy between himself
and Mr. Ransome.   Could I ever hold up my head again?
God knows, I have been sufficiently degraded as it is.   I
rarely leave the grounds for a walk—I have a horror of
meeting people who used to know me; the scandal would
be *too* crushing should it be said that my husband could
engage a menial like Maddox to join him in a scheme
against me."

"But when it is known that your husband is mad, would
not people be sorry for you, and visit what shame the
thing involves upon him?"

"It would not save my name from being mouthed," she cried bitterly. "Let Mr. Ransome go; if my freedom had been purchased by the loss of my whole fortune, I should not be one jot less glad than I am now to feel that he is gone. I have but one dread—that he will return. Pray God he will not! Pray God he will not!" she exclaimed, with startling vehemence.

I was silent for some moments, and then said:

"If you really believe that Mr. Ransome's and the footman's disappearance is a conspiracy against you, you are wise in maintaining a dignified reserve. His action is an extraordinary one—much too extraordinary to be reconciled to any theory it is possible to form of his ultimate intentions."

"But never forget that he is mad," she interrupted.

"No, and that fact *only* can make your conjecture probable. But still, assuming him to be as mad as we will, what possible reason can he have for getting Maddox to steal the plate, or for carrying the plate off with him? What can he do with it?"

"Bury it, perhaps."

"Maddox must expect a large reward for running the risk of being taken up for the robbery. To tell you the truth, madam, I have always doubted that man's honesty from a discovery I once made, but which I never chose to repeat, as I had no wish to be thought a talebearer." I then spoke of the book I had found by his bedside.

"Oh, people in his sphere read anything," she said. "They delight in stories of murders and robberies. I should lay no stress upon that."

"Well," I exclaimed, somewhat disconcerted. "But now comes another question: How did he open the safe?"

"That's one reason I have for believing Mr. Ransome to be in the secret," she answered. "Before you came, he used to keep the key of the safe—that was when we had no housekeeper. There was nothing to prevent him then from having another one made."

"But this notion implies that he has had the scheme in his head for some time."

"I dare say he has."

"But he would be using the key constantly. How could he leave it at a shop while it was being copied?"

"He would take the impression of it in wax. House-breakers manage so, I have read, don't they?"

She suppressed a yawn and got up suddenly.

"We have talked more about this matter than it deserves, Miss Avory. I shall do nothing—merely wait. I have plenty of patience—when he is not with me; more than he. At the end of some weeks, if I find he still keeps away, I will write to papa. He is the only friend I should dream of consulting—the only friend whose opinion I would take. But I'll not write yet. I am afraid my troubles are not over. They *will* be over when I find he does not mean to come back."

She walked out of the room abruptly, and I heard her call to Mary to bring her hat from her bedroom, as she was going to walk in the grounds.

XI

There would have been no mystery in Mr. Ransome's disappearance had he left the house alone. His habits were capricious and unaccountable, well known to us all; and his empty bedroom would merely have suggested the question, "Where is he gone *now?* and how long does he mean to stop away?"

The mystery was created by the simultaneous disappearance of Maddox. The coincidence of their joint departure furnished such strong presumptive evidence of collusion that the detail of the robbery merely served to complicate the enigma of the madman's motive without shaking the belief that the two men had acted in concert.

There was indeed another view to be taken of the matter: it might be supposed that Maddox had robbed the house without knowing that it was his master's intention to quit it on the same night. But this seemed difficult to realize; because (speaking for myself) I could not imagine that two men occupying the same house—the house itself by no

means a large one—could be stirring on their legs in the
dead of night, and in the profound stillness of such a night
as that on which these events had happened, without the
one hearing the other; and as the necessity of secrecy (supposing them to have acted independently of each other)
was strong on them both, the mere idea to either of the men
of the other being about would be enough to frighten them
both back to their beds and force them to defer their several schemes until another opportunity.

The sounds that *I* had heard convinced me as much as
anything else that Mr. Ransome and Maddox had acted together; because the noise resembling the turning of the
handle of a door had come from the landing where Mr. Ransome's bedroom was; and this had been followed by the
creaking of the staircase outside my room—in other words,
the stairs belonging to the landing where Maddox's bedroom was. They had followed each other with but a short
interval; hence, then, I suppose that Mr. Ransome had first
left his bedroom, and had been shortly afterward joined by
Maddox.

But the fact of Maddox having run away was no reason
why Mr. Ransome shouldn't return. He might walk in at
any moment, and enjoy the disappointment of the hope he
had kindled in his wife. Meanwhile I wondered what
would be thought over at Copsford when the inspector
whispered about that Mrs. Ransome meant to take no action
in the matter of robbery?

The day passed, the evening came; but not Mr. Ransome.
We were somewhat embarrassed for spoons and forks, and
Mrs. Ransome had to make what shift she could for her
luncheon and dinner with those which were used in the
kitchen. Mary said that she had never heard her laugh so
merrily as when she took up one of the two-pronged iron
forks which had been placed on the table.

"It's my belief," the girl said, "that she looks on the
loss of her beautiful plate as quite a joke."

I thought the joke that amused her lay in the loss of her
husband.

I had a short conversation with her before she went to

bed. Her mood rather puzzled me, for her vivacity was
made at times inconsistent by abrupt lapses into anxious
gravity. She excused herself once for bursting into a laugh
when I was talking gravely about Maddox and putting it
to her, as I had before done, whether it was not very probable that the man had committed the robbery on his own
account, by saying that, somehow, she had a feeling that
she would never see her husband again. She had no reason
to give for this notion; it might perhaps, she said, be owing
to the secret and curious way in which he had left her;
but, however it might be, the feeling was strong in her. I
am afraid I did not echo her laughter; not because I thought
her fancy improbable, but because I considered that her
husband being mad, common humanity demanded that we
should take a sober view of his situation, which might be
that of a fugitive irresponsible for his actions and likely
to come to serious harm if suffered to wander at large without control. I did not express my thoughts, hoping, indeed
believing, that she shared them, but that her pride and hate
of him would not permit her to take any part that might in
the smallest degree be suggestive of hypocrisy.

Before I went to bed that night I carefully examined
the fastenings of the doors. If Mr. Ransome should return
while we were in bed, I was determined that he should
play no tricks with my nervous system, but enter the house
through the proper channels. A pleasant thing to find
him in bed next morning with one of the lower windows
burglariously forced!

But the night passed quietly. I remember going down-
stairs in the morning with much curiosity, scarcely knowing what startling discovery I might make. But all was
safe. I was up before the other servants, and frightened
the cook nearly into hysterics; for she, not knowing I had
left my room, came into the kitchen where I was, and catching sight of me, ran away with a shriek; nor, until I had
called her several times, could I persuade her that I was
not a burglar whom she had just caught in the act of walking off with the kitchen-table and the whole of the crockery.

At midday the postman brought a letter to the house

addressed to Saville Ransome, Esquire. The handwriting was a woman's, big and scrawling. I took it to Mrs. Ransome, who said, "It is from his mother."

"I wonder if he has returned to Guildford?" I observed.

"At all events, she doesn't know he has left the house, or she wouldn't address him here."

And as she said this, she tore open the envelope and read the contents. Her face grew dark, and she threw the letter violently on the table when she had read it.

"The hateful old creature!" she exclaimed.

She took up the letter and began to read it aloud:

"'I reached home safely at two o'clock, and lose no time to tell you of my arrival. I met Mrs. Emmerson on my way from the coach, and she was quite surprised to see me; and no wonder, for I had told her I should be away for a fortnight. I explained why I had left—that your wife was an insulting, common woman, who locked up the rooms in *your* house and put the keys in her pocket, and would not give me even decent accommodation. "Poor Saville!" she said. "What a terrible life he must have of it with such a creature!" "You may well say that," I answered. "She is a most infamous person, with a temper that would disgrace a fishwoman, and proud like all parvenus."'"

"Pray read no more, madam," said I, regretting the angry passion that flamed in her eyes and this perusal of a coarse, uninteresting letter not addressed to her. "She is a stupid woman, and quite beneath your notice when she is from under your roof."

She crumpled the letter in her hand and flung it into the grate.

"That's how I would serve her," she exclaimed. "A parvenu! Oh, think of it!"

She walked about the room and suddenly crossed to the drawing-room, where, a moment after, she began to play the piano, bursting into a loud, noisy air, which she presently changed into a melody wonderfully sweet and soft. If that tune showed the variation in her mood, I thought, I might safely speak to her on the subject I should have commenced in the dining-room but for that letter.

"Are you going to tell me that I should not play, Miss Avory?" she exclaimed, as I approached her.

"Oh, dear no, madam."

"The right thing to do, I suppose, under these afflicting circumstances, would be to sit with my hands crossed, and, by way of a coiffure, the nearest approach to widow's weeds my milliner could invent. But then I must first consider what I have to mourn. The loss of my plate? *That* is a serious matter. My dear husband's amiable flight? That should make me wear bright colors and sing and play all day long."

She had raised her hand to strike the piano again, when I said:

"I was thinking, madam, I should like to call upon the Campions. I have not seen them since my arrival here. They were very kind to me when I first came to Copsford. Shall I inconvenience you by leaving the house for an hour or two?"

"Not in the least. Never trouble to speak to me when you wish to take exercise. I shall sometimes join you, I hope, if *he* stops away. I used often to walk long distances with papa; but since I have been companionless I have kept to the grounds. What shall you tell the Campions about Mr. Ransome and his man?"

"As little as I can. To speak the truth, my motive in calling on them is to find out what people are saying. I may perhaps be able to check a few fictions. The Campions know a great number of persons."

"That is a good idea. I should like to know what people *are* saying. But do not trouble to contradict anything. Bitterly as I hate the idea of my name supplying the neighborhood with a subject for tittle-tattle, I would rather that the most absurd falsehoods be circulated than the truth."

She nodded and recommenced her playing. I left the room, and in a few moments was walking toward Rose Farm.

I found Mrs. Campion at home. She was knitting in the garden under the shade of an apple-tree, and gave, by her snug, round, healthful presence, a finishing detail to the whole picturesue scene.

She ran for a chair, and told me that her husband had gone over to some village in his cart; and then she asked me how I was getting on, which brought our chat to the subject of the Ransomes.

"Is it really true," said she, "that Mr. Ransome has run away from his home, and taken all the plate with him?"

"Are people saying that?"

"Oh," she answered, trying to suppress a laugh, because she would think the topic a grave one to me, "all sorts of things are said. I heard this morning that the footman had murdered his master and hid his body, expressly that people should think he had helped him to steal the plate and was gone off with him! Such nonsense, to be sure! But living in the country is not like living in London, Miss Avory. In places like Copsford we are bound to know everything our neighbor says and does. But it's a strange thing to happen, all the same, supposing, of course, it's true."

"If what is true?"

"Why, that Mr. Ransome and his man-servant have gone off and taken the plate with them. *Is* it true?"

"I give you my word, dear Mrs. Campion, that I am as ignorant of the truth as you are. All that I can tell you is that Mr. Ransome and Maddox the footman left the house— I don't say together, but pretty nearly at the same hour— and that all the plate has been stolen out of the house-keeper's room. Nothing more is known at Gardenhurst than this. If you can tell me more, I shall be grateful."

"Bless you! what should I know?" she exclaimed. "It's everybody's talk just now, and that's how I came to speak of it. And how does the young mistress bear it all?"

"Why, it is not a very pleasant thing to happen in a house. Have you heard whether anybody like Mr. Ran-some or Maddox has been met?"

"No, I have heard nothing. I doubt if they've been seen. I should have heard else."

"**Do you know if people have thought it worth while to**

mention, among other things, that Mr. Ransome is a madman?"

"Oh, it's well known he was crazy-like. It's only a
madman would rob his own house, sure! And what's Mrs.
Ransome going to do? I suppose she has set the constables
after them?"

"What! after her own husband?"

"Why not? If *my* husband was mad and was to run
away with the footman and things belonging to the house,
wouldn't I send after him? I'd have him caught for his
own sake; and I'd have the footman put into prison for
helping his master to make such a fool of himself."

"Rather hard upon a wife to have to give her husband
into custody!" said I, laughing.

"Oh, that's right enough. But if he's mad, my dear?
He ought to have a keeper—as I was only saying to John
last night, when he was telling me of the fierce quarrels
that were always going on between Mr. and Mrs. Ransome;
dreadful enough, he said, to make him wonder how you can
stand living in such a house. That's just the truth, my
dear, and you'll pardon me for saying so."

"How do you know they quarrel?"

"Oh, it was always known. They lost their friends by
it long before you came, as I was told by one of the servants
up at the Rayners', where the family were often talking of
Mr. Ransome, and saying as how they and people like them
couldn't visit a house where they were never safe from being
shocked by angry words between the master and mistress.
But *you've* seen enough, Miss Avory, I dare say, to prevent
you from wondering why they have no friends."

"I have seen enough to convince me that Mr. Ransome is
mad; and if I were in Mrs. Ransome's place, I should have
a very poor opinion of the sincerity of the friends who
could visit my lunatic husband's sins and temper on my
head."

"Oh, but you'll confess," she exclaimed, smiling and
stooping to pick up the ball of worsted that had rolled off
her lap, "that Mrs. Ransome can be very aggravating
when she pleases."

"I thought you liked her."

"So I do—at least, so I did when she was Miss Kilmain
But I've seen very little of her since she was married,
She was a pleasant lady then, and I tell everybody who
speaks of her the same. But right is right; and though
I firmly believe that her husband is altogether to blame for
spoiling her temper, yet that don't alter the truth that she
picks quarrels with him when he'd be quiet, and treats him
and his mother in a way that isn't right, considering that
she knows he isn't sane. And besides, a mother's a
mother, and there's no reason why a lunatic shouldn't have
the feelings of a son."

There was a prejudice implied in these remarks which,
remembering how kindly Mrs. Campion had before spoken
of Mrs. Ransome, somewhat disconcerted me.

"How do you know all this?" I asked her.

"I'll tell you. I drank tea last night at Mrs. Evans',
her whose sister is along with you at Gardenhurst."

"You mean Mary?"

"Yes, Mary. When the girl was sent for the inspector
she met Mrs. Evans in the road, and told her what her
errand was, and all about Mr. Ransome's disappearance and
the robbery and everything. And then she spoke of Mrs.
Ransome locking up the rooms that her mother-in-law
mightn't go into them, and of the dreadful quarrels that
took place and were always taking place, and how Mrs.
Ransome had once, in her presence, declared she would kill
him, and such awful words. She said that she often felt
sorry for her mistress, but that there was no denying that
she constantly aggravated her husband; and as Mrs. Evans
afterward said, putting it to me, wasn't her locking up the
rooms and forcing her husband and mother to take their
meals almost in darkness enough to anger a saint? I'm sure
I should be sorry to say an ill word against Mrs. Ransome;
but right is right, and when I heard Mrs. Evans talking I
had really nothing to say; for wicked as Mr. Ransome may
be, he deserves pity for wanting his senses, and oughtn't
to be made madder than he is by having his mother treated
as if she were no better than a common servant."

I suppressed the indignation which the thought of Mary's dangerous gossip had excited in me, and answered:

"You may take my honest word for it that, though all that Mary has repeated is substantially correct, Mrs. Ransome has been most inhumanly treated both by her husband and her mother-in-law, and that there is not a single action she has committed since I have been in her service which I am not prepared to justify. Though you should learn ten times more from Mary than what you have already heard, you would still know but a very small portion of the truth. I have less reason than Mary to sympathize with Mrs. Ransome, having known her but a few weeks against the two years Mary has been with her. You may therefore believe me when I say that the gossip that represents her as having aggravated or in any way offended or injured her husband is a direct falsehood; and that her treatment of her mother-in-law is angelic in comparison with what that offensive, false-tongued little woman deserves."

"Well, well, Miss Avory," exclaimed Mrs. Campion, taking my hand and pressing it, "we'll not speak of them any more. You know the truth better than I do, and I am sorry to have said anything to have vexed you. I wonder if there are any strawberries left. Come and see. I can give you a rare treat of cream with any we can find. I wish John would come home. You'll stay to tea?"

This I said I should not be able to do. However, I walked with her to her strawberry beds, and there we found as much fruit as would have lasted me a week. I was grateful to her for having checked a conversation which might only have resulted in leaving upon us both an uncomfortable impression. I stopped with her until four, talking of my duties at Gardenhurst, and hearing her tell about her farm, and the wages her husband paid, and the earnings he averaged, pacing the while her garden, where the beds were edged with high box, and filled with old-fashioned flowers, stocks, pansies, sweet williams, with glorious shining roses intermixed in abundance, and lilies baring their breasts of snow to the sky. I brought the conversation again to the Ransomes, by begging her not to

12

heed the gossip she might hear, and to remember my honest assurance that Mrs. Ransome had lived a miserable life with her husband, and deserved the deepest compassion.

"Didn't I tell you," said she, evading the point, "that you would hear of queer goings on in that house before you had been there a month? You haven't been there that time yet, and I don't suppose anything more singular could have happened in any family in England than the running away of the master and the footman with the plate and such-like valuables."

"That is the theory," I said, "but it is not proved yet, and until some kind of evidence turns up, I, for one, shall refuse to have any opinion one way or the other upon the subject. I suppose we are sure to hear something soon. Somebody who knows one or the other of them is sure to meet them and report. The world is very small, and we are always falling in with acquaintances, go where we may."

Saying this, I shook hands with her, received a warm invitation to come again soon, and walked toward Gardenhurst.

I had not reached the house ten minutes before Mrs. Ransome sent for me. She was in the drawing-room; a portfolio of music lay on the sofa beside her, and she was turning the sheets over as I entered.

"Did you find the Campions at home?" she asked.

"Yes, madam."

"What a pretty place Rose Farm is! I used to like Mrs. Campion very much, and wonder that she doesn't come to see me. Did she speak of me?"

Her manner was full of undisguised eagerness to hear what I had to tell.

"Yes, and had she lived in this house, I don't think she could be more perfectly acquainted with the *facts* of everything that has happened both before I came and since I have been here."

"How is that?" she asked, flushing up.

"The plain truth is this, madam: your servant Mary is a gossip. She has a sister at Copsford to whom she has related the whole story of Mr. Ransome's disappearance and

the robbery. The story, taking, no doubt, many exaggera-
tions from its transit through the sister, has become formidable enough to prejudice so amiable a person as Mrs.
Campion."

"Ring the bell, Miss Avory," she exclaimed, starting up
with a face full of anger.

"One moment, madam. Do you mean to dismiss Mary
or reprimand her?"

"Dismiss her, and at once. How dare she talk out of
my house? Ring the bell, if you please."

"Pray forgive me for offering an opinion. I would not
dismiss her. Have you ever cautioned her before against
this dangerous habit of hers?"

"Certainly not; I would not trouble to caution her. I
have a horror of these gossiping creatures, and the servant
whom I find guilty of talking of my affairs out of my house
must leave me."

"I have not one word to say in her defence. But I
would strongly recommend you, madam, not to dismiss her
on these grounds. She might grow malicious and invent
falsehoods out of revenge."

"What falsehoods? What have I to fear?" she cried,
staring at me.

"You have to consider that Mr. Ransome's disappearance may have a vicious purpose; and I should take care
not to strengthen his hands by creating enemies of people
like Mary, who know enough of what has passed in this
house to be able to erect formidable fictions on the basis of
certain truth."

"I don't understand you," she exclaimed, "Mary knows
that my husband and I quarrel—that I hate him—that he
is a madman—that his treatment of me has been monstrous
ever since she has lived with me. Let her go and tell people that. I am not afraid of the truth. But I will not
suffer an eavesdropper to remain in my service. How
dare she go and gossip about my affairs, knowing how I
detest to have my name discussed!"

"She has the excuse of having spoken only to her
sister."

" I don't care. She has no right to speak to her sister."

" Will you not try what a reprimand will do? If that fails, then let me give her notice under the excuse that you do not require three servants. I am convinced," I exclaimed with energy, "that it is not your policy to let her know you have dismissed her for talking. People will wonder what secrets you have which you are ashamed of hearing repeated."

This was a bold and unlucky remark.

" People are more likely to wonder," she cried scornfully, "that I could submit to have my home affairs talked of by a senseless servant. Will you ring the bell, Miss Avory?"

Her impetuous order was no longer to be disobeyed. I had not yet received a more convincing proof of her sensitiveness to the opinions of others than her present anger.

Susan answered the bell.

" Send Mary to me," exclaimed Mrs. Ransome; and when the girl had gone, she added: " Surely, Miss Avory, you do not want me to be afraid of my own servants?"

" If the motive of Mr. Ransome's disappearance were clear, I should not dream of opposing your dismissal of Mary," I answered. " But since his absence puzzles us, how must it puzzle others who would readily swallow any inventions they might hear? For that reason I would deal with Mary cautiously."

" But what can the girl invent?" she demanded impatiently.

" She can set people talking."

" Of what?"

" Of you."

" Yes, of me! She can tell the truth or she can tell lies; and what then?"

" But you do not wish to be talked about, madam."

" No; and that is why——"

Mary knocked and entered. I was about to leave, but Mrs. Ransome signed to me to stop.

•" When is your month up?" she inquired, frowning at the girl.

"On Wednesday week, ma'am," answered the girl, look-ing at her.

"Miss Avory will pay you your wages up to that time, and you can leave to-day."

"What have I done?" asked the girl, turning pale.

"You have talked of me among your friends—told the secrets of this house, and gossiped to everybody who will listen to you."

"I've not talked more than other people," answered the girl sulkily, and with a glance at me that said, "I have to thank you for this."

"Other people may say what they like," cried Mrs. Ran-some angrily. "But you, who live in this house, who see and hear things which other people know nothing about, act with unwarrantable impertinence, and prove yourself totally unfit for any place of trust in carrying your mean and dangerous gossip into the streets. That will do!" she exclaimed, waving her hand. "You will leave my house at once."

The girl walked to the door and, I thought, was going straight out; but she stopped and said—

"Wherever I go I shall tell the truth."

"Mind you do!" responded Mrs. Ransome. "And now leave the room."

She was about to say something more; but Mrs. Ran-some sprang up, and she hurried out, slamming the door after her.

"Now let her go and tell the others," said Mrs. Ran-some, with her eyes gleaming. "She will save me the trouble of cautioning them to mind their own business. Miss Avory, please pay the girl what is owing to her, and see that she is out of the house by six o'clock."

I found Mary crying when I went down-stairs, but she wiped her eyes when she saw me, and turned away.

"I am sorry——" I began.

"Don't speak to me!" she cried. "You tale-bearer! you've done this for me."

I bit my lip and answered, "You have done it for your-self. I cautioned you some time ago against opening your

mouth so wide about your master and mistress. You are
properly treated, and your manner now satisfies me that I
have done my duty in telling Mrs. Ransome the truth about
you."

I then handed her her wages and went to my room. In
less than half an hour she had left the house.

XII

Mary was not replaced. Two servants were quite enough
to do the housework. Indeed, I began to think that I was
of very little use to Mrs. Ransome, and said so when I
asked her if she wished for another girl to attend upon her.
She answered that I was mistaken; she could not do without me; and was good enough to say that she regarded me
more as a companion than a housekeeper. Susan took
Mary's post, and pleased Mrs. Ransome more than the
other had done. This girl was an excellent servant, quiet,
respectful, and diligent.

On the fourth day following the disappearance of Mr.
Ransome, an old gentleman named Skerlock, a magistrate,
called at the house, and had an interview with Mrs. Ransome. She afterward told me the object of his visit.

He had heard of the robbery, of Mr. Ransome's and the
footman's flight; could he be of any service to Mrs. Ransome? He had the honor of a slight acquaintance with the
Colonel, and should feel proud to receive her commands.
The inspector had acquainted him with the result of his
visit to Gardenhurst, and now Mr. Skerlock would like to
learn whether Mrs. Ransome wished for some definite action
to be taken in the matter? There was so much mystery involved in the whole affair that he (Mr. Skerlock) respectfully submitted that it should not be suffered to rest without
inquiry. It gave him extreme pain to allude to the very
delicate point that, it seemed to him, formed a prominent
feature of this singular occurrence; but he must be permitted to refer to the report that from time to time had
reached him of the unsoundness of Mr. Ransome's intellect.
Of course Mrs. Ransome might have special reasons for not

choosing to pursue the man Maddox with a charge of robbery; but basing his judgment on the reports that had obtained circulation, and which accredited the robbery to an inexplicable caprice on the part of Mr. Ransome, he (Mr. Skerlock) would deferentially submit to Mrs. Ransome the need of having her husband followed, since common humanity demanded that a man not master of his reason should not be suffered to wander at large.

Mrs. Ransome thanked the old gentleman for his visit, and assured him that her husband's absence gave her no uneasiness. It had often been his humor to leave her without notice; and it was probable that these eccentricities had given rise to the report of his madness. She was much obliged to Mr. Skerlock for his sympathy and advice; but some time must elapse before she could consider herself justified in viewing her husband's disappearance in a grave light. With regard to the apparent robbery of the plate and Maddox's flight, she would reserve her opinion until her husband returned.

She described Mr. Skerlock leaving her in an amusingly mystified state of mind.

"Ought I to have told him," she exclaimed, "that my husband is a madman, with the passions of a devil? that I *hate* him? that my prayer morning and evening is that he may never return—that we may never meet again? That would have shocked the amiable old man; but it is true—it is Heaven's truth! I will not lift a finger to have him followed. But I am bound to feel grateful to Mr. Skerlock for taking the trouble to call," she added satirically.

As the days wore on other people called; persons, I was told, who had not set foot in Gardenhurst for a year. They came to sympathize, to offer their services. One or two of these visitors had been on intimate terms of friendship with Mrs. Ransome before her marriage. Of course I could not tell how she received these visitors or what their conversation was; but I know she believed them more curious than friendly, a view of them which would make her very hard and obstinate and reticent on the subject that had attracted them. Had I been in her place, I would have denied my-

self to these callers. They had forfeited (as old acquaintance) all friendly claims upon her, whether rightly or
wrongly matters not; and this would have given her a good
obvious motive for keeping herself out of sight.

I am not sure that the state of suspense in which she
was then living was not more secretly trying to her than
the misery and trouble which were presently to come. The
worst was known then; but now the vexations and harassing doubts as to her husband's object and whereabouts and
return to her must have galled and fretted her impatient
spirit inexpressibly. So, at least, I would think when
talking with her sometimes. She forced a cheerful manner
upon herself; was often at the piano; would laugh loudly
over trifles; but there was an artificiality about her good
spirits I could not mistake. Her resolution to enjoy her
freedom drove her behavior beyond the limits of becoming
mirth, and thus I felt the unsoundness of her light-hearted
manner. She was as a reveller who, conscious that the
morrow must bring trouble, seeks to drown thought in
clamorous merriment. I have seen her enter the drawing-
room, laughing loudly over some trifling rejoinder she has
made me; I have heard her strike the piano and dash into
a merry, boisterous tune; but in a few minutes the jovial
air would be silenced, her fingers would wander absently
over the keys, the sounds would cease, and peeping in, I
have seen her leaning her cheek on her elbow, lost in
thought, motionless as an image.

A week passed—ten days—a fortnight. I began to wonder how this would end. A woman possessed of Mrs. Ransome's youth and beauty and fortune must soon tire of
migrating, like the Primrose family, from the Red Room to
the Brown. She would want change; she would want society; and for two years she had had neither.

But certainly she could do nothing until she had heard
of her husband and knew his intentions. By and by she
would get news of him, of course; but of one thing I was
confident, she would never consent to live with him again.
His desertion had provoked as much gossip as ever a divorce
could have done; and her professed objection to scandal she

could no longer advance as a reason for not putting an end
to her misery by separating from him.

About this time she received a letter from her father,
who was living at Boulogne, telling her that he had met
Mr. Hastings, one of the curates at Copsford, and had
learned from him the story of the robbery and her husband's
disappearance. How was it she had not written to him of
this? Was it true? If so, then he could only suppose
that Mr. Ransome's conduct was one more illustration of
his eccentricity, and that she did not attach the significance
to it which, to judge by Mr. Hastings's account, it deserved.
Let her answer him promptly, and set his mind at rest.

She read me this letter in her bedroom, and said that in
reply she should tell him not to be uneasy; that he was
right in supposing this to be another instance of her husband's capricious character; that he must not pay any heed
to gossip, and so forth; Saville had left her a fortnight ago,
she expected him home every hour, and then she hoped the
queer little mystery of the stolen plate would be explained.

"This is enough to tell for the present, Miss Avory," she
added. "My husband *may* come home—this very day, for
aught I know. If I were to suggest to my father that the
man had probably left me for good, I should have him here
at once; and what would happen if my father should be in
the house when my husband returned? . . . No, papa
must be kept in ignorance for the present. God knows, it
will be bitter enough for me to have to tell him the truth
when the time comes!"

I could not appreciate this reasoning. Surely she was
carrying her obstinate pride a little too far in determining
to fight her mad partner to the bitter end; in resolving to
take no counsel of those who would have befriended her in
the only effectual way that was possible—namely, by removing her out of the reach of her husband, or by confining
him in a madhouse. But I did not possess the secret of
Mrs. Ransome's character. She had many points with
which I had no sympathy, and many which I could not
comprehend. Certainly I never could reconcile her undissembled hatred of her husband with her nervous and pas-

sionate dislike to having the truth of her married life known
to her friends.

The circumstance I am now about to relate, and which
was in an extraordinary degree to complicate the mystery
which was already sufficiently puzzling, happened one
Tuesday morning, not quite a month after Mr. Ransome
had left the house.

I was helping Susan in the bedrooms, when I was startled
by the violent ringing of the hall bell. My first thought
was—Mr. Ransome has returned!

Susan ran down-stairs to answer the summons. Five
minutes had scarcely elapsed when the girl returned in
great haste to tell me I was wanted by mistress, and who
did I think was down-stairs?—old Mrs. Ransome!

There was nothing surprising in her visit but the impertinence of it. It was natural that she should wish to hear
of her son; only, instead of calling, she should have written.

Where was the mistress? In the drawing-room. To
that room I hastened.

Long before I reached it I heard the old lady's excited
cackle. I pushed open the door, and the younger Mrs.
Ransome cried out:

"Miss Avory, I have refused to allow that woman to ad·
dress me without a witness. Be good enough to draw near,
and take particular notice of what she says."

She was very pale, but quite collected. They both of
them stood, one on either side the table. The old lady was
pale too; but never did I see such a venomous little face as
she turned upon me when I entered. She was pointing
with her parasol to her daughter-in-law. In some odd way
her black satin gown stood out as though it covered a bar-
rel, and gave her aspect a ludicrous character of small,
swelling rage.

"Where is my son?" she screamed, flashing upon Mrs.
Ransome, and keeping her parasol pointing. "You know!
tell me now! tell me now!"

"I do not know," answered Mrs. Ransome.

"Do you mean to say," the little old woman screamed
out, "that he's been away a month and never once written

to tell you where he is? Do you mean to tell me that you
can't put your finger on the exact spot where he is at this
moment? Wretch that you are! you have murdered him!
Look me in the face and deny it!"

Mrs. Ransome turned as white as a sheet, and involuntarily I made a movement toward her, thinking that she
was about to faint. Then my passion boiled up; before
Mrs. Ransome could answer, I had turned upon the old
woman.

"How *dare* you make such a charge? Are you so mad
with temper that you do not know the horrible words you
are uttering?"

"No observations that you can make will in the smallest
degree signify to me," she answered, looking at the wall
over my head. And then, lowering the key of her voice a
full octave, she exclaimed deliberately, "I have come here
to see my son. He is not here, and I will find out where
he is. His wife knows, and I expect her to answer me."

I crossed over to Mrs. Ransome, out of whom the life
seemed to have been shocked, and said in a whisper:

"You had better retire and leave me to manage this lady.
She is as mad as her son, and her only purpose is to insult
you."

"Ah! You are right in advising her to answer my question!" cried the old lady, shaking her parasol at us.
"Have you murdered him? You are capable of it. I can
prove you capable of it!"

Mrs. Ransome's simplest and perhaps only course would
have been to walk out of the room. Anybody else would
have done so. But she never *would* cut short a quarrel by
this easiest of processes. She must answer; she must have
the contemptible triumph of the last word. Nobody should
drive her out of her own room—which was as bad, to be
sure, as being driven out of her own house. Hence the
violence of the quarrels between her and her husband.
Hence the useless and crazy passage of words that now took
place.

She leaned upon the table, her face like a carving in
marble, and her tone, manner, and sneer as hard too—all

but those wonderful eyes of hers, which shone with sparks
of fire in them.

"I have told you," she said, slowly forcing her words
through her pale lips, "that I do not know where your son
is. But I pray that the coward and the madman may never
come back to me. I pray that he is dead, that I may be
sure he will never come back to me."

"You hear her!" exclaimed the old lady, turning to me
with her face brimful of malignant triumph. "She says she
wishes him dead. She speaks as though she knew he was
dead. Bear witness to those words—I shall remember them!"

"Do *you* know where he is?" I said, looking at her
steadfastly. "The malice in your language suggests that
you can answer your own question?"

"As I believe in God," she cried fiercely, "I have not
heard of him nor seen him since that day he accompanied
me to Copsford. *She* can tell," pointing to Mrs. Ransome,
"if you are ignorant. Let her answer me. Did she not
threaten my son's life on the day of his disappearance? In
the drawing-room that evening—in this very room—when
he asked her to stop the strumming that was making his
head ache, did she not turn upon him and cry out that she
would have his life?"

I glanced at Mrs. Ransome, who was watching the passionate little woman intently, and paused a moment to give
her time to reply; but as she did not immediately speak, I
said:

"Your knowledge of that quarrel proves that you must
have seen your son since that day. How otherwise should
you know of it?"

"Let *her* answer! Is she dumb? Is she conscience-
stricken?" She brandished her parasol and repeated, "Did
you not threaten to kill him? Look me in the face and
deny it if you dare!"

"Yes, I would have killed him! The coward buried his
nails in my shoulder! His brutal hand is a pollution—he
made me as mad as himself, and I would have killed him!"
she replied, quite deliberately, but with the tremor of pent-
up passion in her voice.

"'GIVE ME BACK MY SON,' SHE SHRIEKED."—Page 189.

"Ah!" raved the old lady, "you dare not tell a lie now! Wicked as you are, you dare not add to your guilt by a lie! You are known to me—you shall be known to the world soon! Give me back my son," she shrieked.

"Let this end, for God's sake!" I implored Mrs. Ransome. "If you will not order her to leave the house, give me leave to do so."

"Look at her!" continued the old lady. "Do you see how white her face is? Do you see how scared she is? Oh, you may cover your terror with sneers, but I can look through such masks—I can see your guilt in your heart! You have a mother to deal with in me who has lost her son; and I say to you, miserable woman that you are, give him back to me, or shall hold you guilty of his death and prove you his murderess by your own words."

This reiterated charge affected me in a manner I can scarcely describe. The woman looked crazy enough, in all conscience, with her dim blue eyes, her bloodless face, her excited gestures, her strange writhing smiles which came and went; but there was also a tremendous earnestness in her manner—if one can possibly conceive anything tremendous in so small a person—that lent an extraordinary significance to her words, and without inclining me for an instant to view her accusation gravely, qualified the intensely disagreeable impression of madness her demeanor was calculated to produce.

I looked at Mrs. Ransome, and doubted if she quite understood the nature of the astounding charge her mother-in-law was screeching at her.

"What reason have you," I said, addressing the old lady, "for supposing that Mrs. Ransome has anything to do with your son's disappearance?"

"Has she not threatened to take his life over and over again? Has she not threatened this?" she cried. "Now he is gone—and I ask her where he is—and she will not tell me."

"She cannot. Nobody in this house knows where he is," I answered.

"*She* knows!"

"It is false!" said Mrs. Ransome.

"You know his habits as well as we do," I continued. "He has left the house before now, without giving notice."

"Not for a month at a time!" shrieked the old lady. "Sometimes he has left me for a week, but never without writing and telling me where he was. But this time, though he went to his bedroom—though he was heard to go to it and closed the door—when the morning came he was not found in it; he was gone; and he has not returned—and a whole month has passed and he is still missing. *She* knows why this is! *she* can answer me! Give me back my son! give me back my son!"

She beat the air with her parasol, and almost howled out her entreaty.

"You have the particulars of his flight at your finger-ends," I said. "How do you know that he was found missing in the morning?"

She made no answer to this, but ran to the bell and pulled it violently; and then, turning to Mrs. Ransome, cried out:

"You shall be confronted with your servants. I'll force them to own that you are capable of killing *my* poor boy!"

"Miss Avory," said Mrs. Ransome, "show this woman out of the house."

"I shall confront you with your servants!" cried the little old lady.

Mrs. Ransome went up to her.

"Leave my house," she said.

"This is your way," I exclaimed, throwing open the door, and motioning to Susan, who stood outside, to go away.

"Coward!" screamed the old woman through her teeth. "You dare not let me examine your servants! You dare not stand by and hear them answer me! Look at her!" she continued, pointing derisively at Mrs. Ransome; "see how white she is! Miserable creature! You dare not meet your servants before me!"

My first impression, when I saw Mrs. Ransome move, was that she was about to strike her; and I involuntarily threw up my hands to petition her, by that dumb show, not to touch the crazy little thing. But I misjudged her intention; she grasped the old lady's arm, and as you would swing an infant, so did she swing her mother in-law to the door—into the hall—then to the hall door—then on to the steps. The door banged, and she came back to me.

The whole thing was done before I could have counted ten. The feat involved no particular strength, although passion would have supplied enough; for I don't suppose the old lady weighed more than a girl of eight or nine; but never while I live shall I forget the scene. Compared with her mother-in-law, Mrs. Ransome looked a giantess; could I have seen the faintest twinkle in her eyes, I should have caught at it as an excuse to relieve myself of the laughter which internally shook me. She walked into the room with a firm tread and a patch of deep red on either cheek; but she staggered before she reached the table, and the color went out of her face and left it a deadly white. She put out her hand to the table to steady herself, and said in a difficult whisper:

"Is this his reason for leaving the house? Is this—the conspiracy—to charge me——"

Her head fell forward, her hand dropped to her side; I ran and caught her, a dead weight, in my arms. She had fainted. I had to lay her at full length on the floor, not having the strength to carry her to the sofa. There was a bottle of toilet-vinegar in the next room; I fetched it, knelt by her and bathed her face. There was no mirth left in me now. I was about to ring for assistance, but reflected that I should be acting more judiciously in not bringing the servants into the room. Even while I was endeavoring to restore the poor lady, the thought that old Mrs. Ransome had got all her information from Mary struck me as a revelation. For a quarter of an hour she remained unconscious and then regained her senses. I led her to the sofa and ran for some brandy, of which I obliged her to take a good sip. This braced her up; she recollected herself, and asked me if old Mrs. Ransome had re-entered the house? I said no, but, to make sure, went to the hall door and looked out;

but of course she was gone; it was hardly to be supposed
that she could stand on the doorstep all that time; though
her astonishing exit might have given her an excuse for
wanting leisure to adjust her faculties and her apparel.

Mrs. Ransome complaining that her head ached, I
drew a chair to the sofa and cooled her forehead with
vinegar.

"What do you think of that dreadful woman's visit?"
she asked faintly. "Do you suspect that it is a part of the
conspiracy I always believed was my husband's motive for
leaving the house?"

"Do not let us discuss the subject yet," I replied. "Take
time. Rest yourself a while. When you are better, we
will talk of that crazy woman's visit."

"I must talk of it now. I am well enough. Her hideous accusation seems a dream to me. Can she really think
I have *murdered* her son?"

"Not unless she is raving mad. For heaven's sake do
not allow your mind to dwell on such a preposterous idea.
Let us think of her only as regards the mischief she may
design you."

"Ah! it comes back to me," she said slowly. "I see it
now. My senses left me when I was about to speak of it.
She is an instrument in her son's hands. She plays her
part cheerfully, for she hates me—she hates me unforgiv-
ingly—she will never rest until she has revenged herself
upon me for my reception of her in this house. How
awful! Oh, God! to think of her going about with this
charge in her lying mouth. She knows where he is—she
must know. He is somewhere concealed, and she has
waited a month, and now she has begun her horrible work.
Oh, think of it!"

"But what can she do? Who will believe her?" I exclaimed, marking with grief and helpless indignation the
expression of misery and suffering on her face. "Let her
devise some less ridiculous charge, and she might obtain
credit. But such an accusation as *this!* She will be
laughed at—she will be insulted for her monstrous malice.
Have no fear. I would to Heaven I could change places

with you. You must oppose the completest insensibility to such absurd fabrications."

"I cannot cope with her—I must write to my father—I must have his help," she muttered, closing her eyes, evidently having paid no attention to what I had said.

"Yes," I cried eagerly, "you must write to him to-day. You should have done so before."

"I will write at once; no, not yet," she replied, raising her hand to her forehead. "My head is too confused." She put her feet to the ground, but sank down with her back against the sofa, whispering like one talking in a dream. "Murder him! What can she mean? Base and cruel pair—murder him! Did he leave me for this? What a shocking scheme!"

She stared around her with a startled light in her eyes, and once again strove to gain her feet, but staggered and fell back, whispering the incredible thought again and again—"Murder him! Did he leave me for this? Murder him!"

Presently she began to complain of her head; I soaked the handkerchief and laid it on her forehead; then pulled down the blinds, and saying that I must not permit myself to converse with her any longer, I left the room.

XIII

Two hours had passed since old Mrs. Ransome was whirled out of the house, when, sitting in my room, I was startled by hearing one of the bells just outside in the passage ring violently. I ran out and saw that it was the house-bell and called to Susan to answer the door and deny Mrs. Ransome, who, I believed, was asleep. The girl returned after a short absence, and with a look of consternation exclaimed that old Mrs. Ransome had returned with the inspector and a constable; that Mary was with them; and that they were all waiting in the outer room—she meant the room dividing the two halls.

Hardly suspecting the import of this visit, I was, nevertheless, so greatly astonished by it that for some moments I could do no more than stare at Susan.

13

"Did they ask for me?" I exclaimed.

"No—for mistress; but I thought I'd come and tell you they were here first."

"What on earth does that wretched little woman mean to do now?" I wondered to myself as I went up-stairs. The room being small, and the inspector and the constable being very large, I beheld what I took, for the moment, to be a crowd of persons; but they soon resolved themselves into four only.

The inspector was seated, drumming impatiently with his fingers on the arm of his chair; behind him stood the constable, a large countryman, whose profoundly provincial aspect no amount of buttons nor officialism of costume could in the smallest degree modify. Mary, shawled and bonneted, was at the outer door, and was excessively pale. Little Mrs. Ransome was holding forth to the inspector, but held her tongue when she saw me, and honored me with a smile, the exact counterpart of the indescribable expression I had seen on her son's face that day when I had brought my influence to bear upon him in the dining-room.

"Where's the mistress, young lady?" inquired the inspector, leaving his chair.

"She is at home. What have you to say to her? I can take your message."

"You're very kind, mum, but on the whole I think I would rather take it myself," replied the inspector; whereat the constable laughed.

"I will go and tell her you are here."

"You may do that, young lady; but I hope you won't keep me waiting long. My time is rather important."

"I must tell her the object of your visit. What is it?" I asked, looking at Mary (who averted her eyes), and then at Mrs. Ransome, who seemed bursting to speak, but kept herself under, it appeared, by holding on tightly to her skirt.

"You may tell her," answered the inspector, "that I've come to search the house."

"Search the house? What for? What do you expect to find?" I cried.

"Do you see that, Mr. Inspector?" called out the old lady. "Do you see how frightened she is? Mr. Constable, please notice that; and you, Mary."

"Well," rejoined the inspector, with a great air of condescension, "there's no reason why you shouldn't be told; though mind, it's not my business to give *you* information. That lady," pointing with his thumb to Mrs. Ransome, "says that her son, Mr. Ransome——"

"Mr. Saville Ransome," interrupted the old lady, gazing intently at the inspector.

"What's the difference?" exclaimed the inspector contemptuously—"that Mr. Saville Ransome has been missing for a month; and she's asked me to come and look over the house and see what's to be seen."

"Do you see how frightened she is?" said the old lady, trembling with eagerness. "Mr. Inspector, please notice how pale she is; and you, Mr. Constable; and you, Mary."

"Is it necessary that those two women should intrude upon the mistress?" I asked, taking no notice of Mrs. Ransome.

"They came of their own accord. They said they was coming this way. There's no law that I know of to prevent 'em coming any way they please," answered the inspector.

"You pretend that it is your duty to search this house. Mrs. Ransome need not be disturbed. I can take you over the house."

"Never you mind what my dooty is," exclaimed the inspector, wagging a fat forefinger at me. "You attend to your own business, young woman, and do what I tell you, or you'll get yourself into trouble."

Saying which, he bestowed a frown upon me and walked into the hall, followed by old Mrs. Ransome and the constable; but Mary lingered, whereat the old lady called sweetly, "Come along, my dear; don't be afraid, Mr. Inspector will prevent her from flying at you."

I pushed past them, walked quickly into the drawing-room, closed the door after me, and approached Mrs. Ransome, who had not moved from the sofa since I had left

her, and whose eyes showed that she had been sleeping. I
told her hurriedly that the old lady had returned with the
inspector and the girl Mary; that the man's object was to
search the house; that they were outside, and were waiting
to see her. I begged her to be calm, to say as little as she
could, and to let the man have his way, since I was sure
the old woman counted upon opposition to strengthen the
villainous suspicion it was manifestly her object to create.

She started up with an expression of mingled wonderment and horror in her face, and springing off the sofa,
cried out:

"They dare not search my house! They dare not force
themselves upon me! Tell them to go! O my God! how
can she treat me like this?"

But at this moment the door was pushed open, and the
inspector and the old lady walked in, leaving Mary and the
constable at the door.

Mrs. Ransome stared at the constable, who in a peculiar
manner brought home the sense of the insult her mother-
in-law designed, as though questioning the evidence of her
senses; looked at her former servant quickly, then at the
old lady, and raised her hand as if to ward or motion them
off, with a gesture of singular dignity.

"What is it you want?" she exclaimed.

"My son!" cried the old lady. "Give him back to me!
You turned me out of your house just now, but here I am
again; and as often as you turn me away so often will you
find me returning, until you tell me where my son is or
what you have done with him."

"Mr. Inspector," said Mrs. Ransome earnestly, "I do not
know where this woman's son is. I swear that I am ignorant of his reason for leaving this house; whether he is hiding, whether he will return, whether he is dead. This
person has a malicious motive for bringing you here. I
entreat you to consider the injury you will do me by beginning a search which I assure you will result in nothing and
which is instigated only that it may give that woman pleasure by degrading me."

I rejoiced to hear her speak without temper and ration·

ally, and watched the inspector anxiously to observe tne effect of her words upon him.

The old lady interrupted him as he was about to speak.

"You are not to believe her," she shrieked. "She will try to disarm suspicion by soft words; but do they not all do that? Do they not all say, we are not guilty! we are not guilty! until the truth is examined into, and then they are found guilty? She would not let me confront her with the other servants just now. She is afraid of the questions I can ask them. But yonder is one who was in her service two years and who will speak the truth. Mary," she vociferated, "have you not heard this woman threaten to kill her husband?"

"Yes," answered Mary boldly, looking around her, "over and over again."

"Weren't you driven out of the house because she knew you could tell stories about her that would help to bring the truth to light?"

"Yes," replied the girl.

"Liar!" I exclaimed passionately. "You will not dare repeat that statement on oath!"

"I can't have this noise," said the inspector, raising his hand. "This lady," he continued, addressing Mrs. Ransome, and pointing to the little woman, whose nostrils were working like the gills of a fish, "came to my office this afternoon and said she had reason to believe that her son had never left this house in the way that had been given out; that she believed he had been murdered; and called upon me to search this building. My dooty is clear. I must act upon her information. I am very sorry, for it's no pleasure to me to disturb gentlefolks with inconvenient calls; but the house must be searched, and if you'll give instructions to that young woman [meaning me] to follow me and my mate with the keys, and lose no time, I shall feel obliged. The sooner this here unpleasant business is disposed of the better for all parties concerned."

A brief silence followed this speech; the old lady looked eagerly at her daughter-in-law, hoping, with all her malig-nant little heart in her face, that she would offer opposition.

Mrs. Ransome glanced at me piteously—had I dared speak, I should have counselled her to let the man have his way. But I was afraid to open my mouth, lest some intemperate word should damage her interests.

The color had died out of her face long ago; she was now of a marble whiteness.

"Dare you search this house without reason?" she asked the inspector in a low voice.

"Attend to her, Mr. Inspector! she defies you!" cried the old lady.

Mrs. Ransome's passion exploded like gunpowder on which a spark falls.

"Are you men," she burst out, "that you can suffer yourselves to offer me this insult on the accusation of a wretch like *that*? See how she takes a cast-off servant of mine into her confidence to further her barbarous end! Must I endure their presence in my house? Is this my home, and am I compelled to let those women remain in it and listen to their atrocious falsehoods? Leave me!" she shrieked, stamping her foot. "If I were a man, you would not *dare* take this liberty!"

"Is she not capable of murder? Hear her! Watch her!" cried the old woman, sputtering her words through her lips and chuckling in sheer enjoyment of her daughter-in-law's rage; and looking with her little body, her long nose, her cadaverous face, her pointing finger, as much like a witch as any portrait of that species of creatures I ever met with. "Give her a knife," she screamed, "and she will stab any one of us to the heart! Search! search! Mr. Inspector. Don't be afraid of her! Search high and low! In some such a fury as this she has killed my son! Mark me! I am his mother, and can read his death in her face!"

Her transports, her gesticulations, were much more likely to dismay the inspector than any passion Mrs. Ransome could exhibit.

"You mustn't object to this search, ma'am," he said to Mrs. Ransome. "It'll do you no good. I can tell you that."

I drew close to her and whispered, "He is right. For God's sake oppose him no further."

"Has she a right to whisper?" bawled the old lady, pointing to me. "What is she saying? Ask her!"

"I am ready to accompany you," I said, turning to the inspector; "but first I must take leave, on Mrs. Ransome's behalf, to request that these two women quit the house. Your license does not extend to insisting on their presence. Their insults form no portion of your duty."

"I don't want them," answered the inspector. "They needn't stop for me. The old lady *would* come and bring the other one along with her because, she said, the young woman knew the house. But I can look about for myself, without their being by to point out the road."

"You hear what the inspector says?" I exclaimed, going to the door and holding it open. "Leave the house if you please."

"No, no!" cried the old lady, stepping backward into the middle of the room. "I see the trick. You'd like to blind the inspector. I'll search as well as he."

"You can't stop if they don't want yer," said the inspector gruffly. "And as they *don't* want yer, you must go."

"Mary," she shrieked, "tell them what you know—tell them again that you heard that woman threaten my son's life! Tell them that you were turned away because——"

"*Are* you going?" exclaimed the inspector angrily. "If you think I've got time to listen to all this talk, you're very much mistaken. I'll tell you what it is," he continued, growing more angry, "if the mistress here likes to order the constable to turn you out, she can, and he'll obey."

"Now then, mum," said the constable. "This way, please."

He went out and threw open the hall door. Mary vanished; the old lady began to expostulate, crying out that we wanted to trick her; that if she chose to remain, she could, for she knew the law as well as anybody; and made use of so many crazy observations that I hoped the inspector's slow intelligence would see what sort of a person he had to deal with in her. All that he did, however, was to stretch forth his hand, intending, probably, to conduct her to the door; but she skipped out of his reach, and crying to Mrs. Ransome that her secret was known, and that she'd never rest until she had had her punished, hurried out of the house.

Mrs. Ransome had resumed her seat on the sofa and was looking downward with a stony face. I told the inspector that I was ready; but the absurdity of the whole proceeding struck me as so very great that when we had gained the hall, I asked him whether the house could not be as well searched without me as with me.

"It's only your acquaintance with the keys that I want, ma'am," he responded; "we don't wish to break no doors open if we can help; and I haven't time to be trying of a lot of keys and always finding the right one out last."

One might have thought his time of immense consequence, to hear his repeated references to its value; but I had reason to believe that there was little to occupy him at Copsford but his toothpick.

"Where will you begin?" I inquired.

"Atop first and come down regular."

"And what do you suppose you are going to find?"

"What we shall, and never you mind," he retorted, mingling sarcasm and reproof in a breath very impressively.

I took them upstairs, mourning as I went over the grinding of the carpets under their thick boots. There was no use in offering further protest against this invasion. Undoubtedly, the consistency of such an intrusion on the strength of any heavy accusation it might please a malicious or fanciful person to prefer with the celebrated boast that every Englishman's home is his castle, and Britons never will be slaves, was very remarkable.

I corked up my indignation, and looked on while the inspector and the constable peeped and pulled and opened and kicked and shook. They went into every room; they opened every closet and cupboard; they ransacked Mrs. Ransome's wardrobe; they probed into holes, they squinted up chimneys. What on earth were they looking for? I submissively asked the question.

"We're looking," responded the inspector, "for some sign as will help us to learn that the little old lady's suspicion is right. *That's* what we're looking for. And don't you ever try to stop officers in the execution of their dooty, or you'll find the law one too many for you, as a good many others have done."

"But what signs do you expect to find?"

"I'll tell you when I come to 'em."

"Do you really, think, because Mr. Ransome is missing from this house, that he has been murdered in it?"

"I'd advise you not to say too much, ma'am. It's my dooty to caution yer. You never know what goes in evidence."

Such is the effect of buttons upon the unaccustomed mind, coupled with stolid faces, creaking boots, and the spirit of the law as demonstrated by supercilious self-possession and the right to handle, shake, upset, hold up, and throw down things which even a thief might regard as in some measure sacred, that I found myself growing nervous, wondering whether anything suggestive *would* be brought to light, and even attaching weight to the very suspicious manner in which the inspector and the constable went about their work, as though there really must be some reason. some especial reason not to be fathomed by the unofficial understanding, to justify their elaborate inquiries. Sometimes, when they opened a stair-closet, I found myself stretching forward, imagining that I should see the dead body of Mr. Ransome staring at us from the twilight of the recess. The two men particularly scrutinized Mr. Ransome's bed, and the hangings, and the carpet around it, and the furniture near it—for spots of blood, I think.

In a word, they literally acted upon the suspicion that had been put into their heads by Mrs. Ransome. Her son was missing; his wife was capable of murdering him or of procuring his murder; they must search the house; and so they did, I will do them the justice to say that. They searched every nook and cranny in it, omitting only the

drawing room, where Mrs. Ransome was, and passing
lightly over the dining-room, as though the deed could
hardly have been committed there, but redoubling their
vigilance in my room and throughout the basement.

The inspector came back to my room after he had searched
the scullery and pantry, and said he would like to have a
talk with the servants. Would I please send them in, one
at a time. I suppose he had a right to order this; but I
could not help wondering how far he would have to go before he should overstep the limits of his legitimate duties.
The cook protested against being called upon to answer any
questions, on the grounds that she hadn't been engaged for
it; but on my representing to her that the sooner the interview was over the sooner the men would be out of the house,
she consented to be shut in with the inspector, whom
she regarded as a very high legal functionary, a kind of
country Lord Chancellor, who had it in his power to
sentence and hang her out of hand if his temper were so
disposed.

I don't think he got very much information from either
of the servants, for his face looked gloomy and his eyes
extraordinarily knowing when he begged me to step that
way and tell him what *I* knew.

"All that I know," I replied, "you heard when Mrs.
Ransome sent for you about the robbery of the plate."

"I don't mind that," he said, with stupid pomposity.
"A month ago isn't to-day."

"I shall tell you nothing more," I exclaimed, bridling
with difficulty my rising temper. "You know your privi-
leges better than I do; but it seems to me that you have
gone far enough already. You are not a magistrate. You
have no right to examine me. You came here to search the
house; you have made the search, and what now should
prevent you from returning to Copsford?"

"Take care," he cried, holding up his forefinger. "I've
cautioned you before against trying to teach me my duty.
You'd better tell me what you know. Nothing but aggra-
vation can come of obstinacy."

"What do you want to know?"

"They say you heerd a noise that night Mr. Ransome is supposed to have left the house?"

"I did hear a noise."

"What sort of noise?"

I told him.

"Now about the turning of the handle of the door. Which handle was it do you think as was turned?—the husband's or the wife's door?"

"You advised me just now," I answered, "to be careful of my words, lest they should go in evidence. I don't know what you mean by evidence; but I will take your advice to me to be careful. I am certain you have no right to ask me these questions, and in that persuasion I decline to give you any more answers."

He turned to the constable and said:

"You hear that? That's what is called contoomacy. If a warrant *is* granted, I shall remember this young woman when the magistrate asks my opinion. Come along, William."

They tramped heavily up-stairs, heavily through the hall, heavily out of the house. When they were gone, I went to the drawing-room and found Mrs. Ransome walking up and down, with her head in a listening attitude and her face haggard with the effect of tears.

"Oh, Miss Avory!" she burst out, running up to me, "do you see his conspiracy now? Did I not tell you, on the very morning we discovered he had gone, that he had left the house to revenge himself upon me? Could any one but a demon hit upon such an awful plan to ruin me? His mother is playing the game for him! What shocking wickedness! Will God permit it to be successful? Will people really believe that he has been murdered?"

She uttered the word with a gasp. I took her by the hand and led her to a chair.

"The inspector has left," I said, "after ransacking the house. I do not suppose he would dared have done this were he not empowered by his position to do so. But atrocious as his conduct is, I do not regret it. It is sure to create indignation when it is known, and any prejudice

against you which that wicked old woman has excited will
be forgotten in sympathy."

"But what could she have said to justify the man in such
an extreme proceeding?" she cried. "Does she actually
charge *me* with the murder of her son?"

"I fear she does. I can scarcely conceive that the inspector would act in this manner on a small accusation.
But is it not monstrous that such a man as that should be
privileged to use his own judgment on the first malicious
fabrication that is reported to him? He examined the servants, and tried to examine me; but I would not answer
his questions. He *cannot* have authority for acting as he
has done."

"If he can believe her," she moaned, burying her face in
her hands, "will not others? They have long tried to degrade me—they have done it at last! My house has been
searched—it will go forth to the world that my house has
been searched, and that I am accused of murdering my
husband! My God! what a scheme to enter his head!
How can I prove my innocence? He may keep away from
me for years and years, and remain hidden, and then die
and no one of all the world who believes in my guilt hear
of his death! How can I clear myself? What am I to do?
I shall go mad!"

She sprang from her chair, with her hands clenched, her
head thrown back, her eyes with a wild, hunted expression
in them. Her action, her attitude, her look, was madness
itself.

"You must be calm," I implored. "Remember the
character of the persons you have to deal with. They
must be matched with their own cunning or they will triumph. I cannot advise you yet—I must have time to
think. But it is imperative that you should write to your
father and urge him to come to you without a moment's
delay."

"I have done so," she answered. "There is the letter."

She pointed in a bewildered manner to the table.

"I will post it at once," I continued. "They have reckoned on your defencelessness. Long ago I saw that you

could not cope single-handed with Mr. Ransome. There is no limit to his wicked ingenuity, and one had need to be as wicked, and as mad too, as he is to match him."

"Will they not believe me when I tell them that this is a conspiracy between the mother and son?" she exclaimed wildly, eagerly staring at me. "Will they think for a moment that I am capable of taking his life?"

"No," I answered decidedly; "do not dream of such a thing. That woman has done her worst in getting your house searched. But she has overreached herself. They very magnitude of her accusation will defeat its purpose."

"But the inspector believes it, or he imagines me capable of conniving at Mr. Ransome's death, or would he *dare* search my house?" she cried.

"His belief will not be the belief of others. He is a pompous, foolish man, and would act, I dare say, on any information that should be given him. No doubt he is empowered to enter a house and search it if he thinks proper; but in this case he may have exceeded his duty. Your father will find that out, and will know the remedy against such insolence."

"That woman has done all she can," cried the poor lady, weeping bitterly. "She has cast a horrible suspicion upon me, and her son will take care that I shall not clear myself from it."

She hid her face in her hands and sobbed piteously. It was imperative, however, that the letter to her father should be posted at once; for the post-bags were made up twice a day at Copsford, and in those primitive times, or at all events in that primitive town, it was necessary to post a letter some time before the departure of the cart to insure its despatch.

"Does this letter," I asked, "urge your father to come at once?"

"Yes," she sobbed.

Without another word I hurried out of the room.

𝔓art 𝔗hree

THE COLONEL'S STORY
(*Continued.*)

I

I TAKE the liberty of interrupting Miss Avory's story, in order to relate myself this portion of the narrative, the particulars of which I am better acquainted with than she.

After quitting Gardenhurst, I had fixed upon Boulogne as a place of residence. My chief object in leaving England was to place the sea between Phœbe and myself, that I might have a reasonable excuse for seldom visiting her. My own common-sense persuaded me that my opposition to her marriage would hardly endear me to her husband. I felt that I should always be an unwelcome visitor to *him;* and having no opinion of his temper or generosity, I was determined that no intrusions of mine, at least, should give him an excuse for quarrelling with his wife.

I heard from her frequently during the first eighteen months of her married life. There was never a syllable in any of her letters to lead me to suppose that she was unhappy. But I took notice that, after a little, she entirely omitted her husband's name from her correspondence. I regarded her silence on this point as ominous, but it was negative: it might be owing to other causes than quarrels or unhappiness; she might conceive that I took no interest in him and his doings, and certainly there was a forced tone in such references as I made to him which could not mislead her in this respect.

At last I received a letter, in which she begged me to

spend a few weeks at Gardenhurst. I should have been glad to excuse myself, for I had strong misgivings that my presence might create dissension, and as I had no reason to suppose that she was unhappy, I was for letting well alone. My longing to see her, however, triumphed over my hesitation, and within a week from the date of her invitation I was at Gardenhurst.

I will not dwell upon this part of my story further than to say that I was not in the house a day before I discovered that she was unhappy. I questioned her, but her answers were evasive. She confessed that her husband's caprices troubled her, but more than this she would not admit. She was looking well, and, in my opinion, had gained in beauty since her marriage. But her old pride and obstinacy were still with her, and were now sharply cut features of her character. These, I saw easily enough, were the secret of her reticence. She had learned her mistake in opposing my judgment, but would not confess her discovery; nay, rather than endure the mortification of such an admission, she would have me believe she was happy. On the whole, I considered her wise to make the best of what was unalterable. The disclosure of her sorrow would only have grieved me, without putting it into my power to help her.

I have observed that, in Miss Avory's narrative, it was implied or stated to her that Mr. Ransome had made me very unwelcome. This was an exaggeration that must be attributed to the heat or prejudice of the accusing person. I cannot pretend that Mr. Ransome received me cordially; but he met and treated me throughout my stay in the house with as much politeness as I had reason to expect, and with more than I had hoped to receive. Sometimes I thought he was afraid of me. His behavior when with his wife and me in a room would corroborate the suspicion of fear which was suggested by his resolute shunning of me if we met in the grounds. I saw very little of him; but I witnessed nothing in his manner or conversation to cause me to imagine that, if he ever had been insane, which I had once solemnly believed, his insanity had gained ground since I last met him.

Two or three days passed without any quarrels taking place; and then a quarrel that shocked me exceedingly occurred at the luncheon-table. There was more of sarcasm and sneering contempt than of rage in Mr. Ransome's language; but my daughter's behavior was pure passion. She had provoked him in this instance by some unfortunate reference to his mother. Though her words were very intemperate, I could not have divined that the hate they expressed toward him was positively her only sentiment. Anger made her bitter, and she might not have meant what she said. I told her I could not submit to witness such scenes, and threatened, if they were repeated, to leave the house. I blamed her for provoking him; but by this time her passion was expended; she looked at me attentively, but offered no defence for her conduct.

My threat of quitting the house, however, did no good. A day or two afterward they quarrelled in my presence again; and again I considered Phœbe to blame; for, though a good-tempered man, perhaps, would not have noticed the remark that had fired Mr. Ransome, yet there had been something singularly aggressive in her manner, in the look she gave him, in her short, hard laugh, in the quick shrug and insolent turn of the head.

She had kept me so entirely in ignorance of her life with her husband that it argued no want of perception on my part not to conceive that in these quarrels she was retaliating his cruel insults and even barbarous behavior to her when they were alone. To me he maintained his doubtful attitude of frightened courtesy, and in my presence never behaved to his wife offensively nor said one word, up to the time of quarrelling, which would have justified me in offering a protest. Even when their quarrels were at the highest, his manner was smooth, his language unimpassioned compared to hers; but he would turn very pale, the sinister gleam I remembered shone in his eyes, and his retorts and charges would not be the more reassuring because they were spoken deliberately and even with difficulty.

I tried to draw Phœbe into a confession, but she was on her guard. She was not unhappy—no! Saville was capri-

cious and angered her; but she dared say most of their
quarrels were owing to her own temper. She did not like
little Mrs. Ransome—she admitted that; and said that
many of the quarrels between her and her husband were
owing to that woman's interference. How did she interfere? I asked. Oh, when she came to the house she
ordered the servants as though she were their mistress.

"I am mistress here, am I not, papa?" she exclaimed,
with the old obstinate look in her face. "You gave me this
house, and the money I spend here is my own. While I live
no one shall dispute my right to regard myself as mistress."

I endeavored to point out that she could be mistress
without insisting too strongly on her rights; that there was
something ungracious in her emphatic assumption of privi-
leges, seeing that her husband and his mother well knew
that the property was hers; that the best-natured man in
the world might object to play second-fiddle in his home,
and that, indeed, her fortune was as much her husband's as
hers; and that the settlement of it upon her did not make
it the less his, but only prohibited him from touching the
capital.

She did not press the argument, and soon contrived to
change the subject.

I noticed several bad signs during this visit, all concur-
ring to make me uneasy; though I never could get her to
be frank with me. They occupied separate bedrooms; they
had no visitors to the house; Phoebe was constantly out,
and sometimes remained away all day. Had I chosen, I
might have obtained enough information from the servants
to satisfy me that my daughter was leading an unhappy
life; but not even my child's interests could force me to
stoop to so mean and unfair a device. What she refused
to tell me herself I would not hear from a menial's lips.
My visit lasted scarcely a fortnight; and when, offended at
last by quarrels which were conducted on my daughter's
side with a heat which I considered inexcusable, I quitted
the house, I was as ignorant of the truth to which one word
from her would have opened my eyes, as I was at the moment of entering it.

14

Six months or thereabouts had elapsed since I returned
to Boulogne, when I happened to meet Mr. Hastings, who
had been appointed curate at Copsford a short time before
my daughter's marriage. He remembered and crossed the
street, glad to meet with a familiar face in a strange town.
We walked together, and he told me about the robbery at
Gardenhurst, and the strange disappearance of Mr. Ransome. I was amazed by this piece of news; for I had heard
but a few days before from Phœbe, and she had not mentioned the circumstance. Mr. Hastings was equally amazed
by my ignorance. He told me that this was the one topic
now at Copsford; that all sorts of surmises were current;
that some were for having that Mr. Ransome had been
murdered by his footman, and others that the footman had
been murdered by Mr. Ransome. He further added (very
courteously) that regret was felt by Mrs. Ransome's well-
wishers that she had not taken steps to discover the truth,
since her indifference both as to the robbery and her husband's disappearance had been much commented on and
given rise to many idle rumors and prejudices. He said
that, had he been less a stranger to my daughter, he would
have called upon her and advised her to place the matter in
the hands of the police, which, however profitless the step
might be so far as regarded the solution of the mystery,
would silence gossip and rescue her from the charge of
heartlessness.

I hastened home and wrote to Phœbe, mentioning the
news I had received from Mr. Hastings, and asking her to
explain her silence. I had to wait some days for her answer. When at last I received her letter, it was to the
effect that I must not allow myself to be made uneasy by
any reports that reached me; that this disappearance of
Mr. Ransome was only another illustration of his capricious
character, and that it was quite likely he would have returned before I received her letter. The robbery, she said,
was the real mystery; for she could not guess whether the
footman had actually stolen the plate on his own account or
whether he had acted on the instructions of Mr. Ransome.
When her husband came home he would clear up this diffi-

culty, and she would hazard no conjecture until he had returned.

I had to be satisfied with this answer, which was no explanation. It was plain that she must think her husband very mad if she could suppose he would order his man to rob his house. To my common-sense it seemed that she was bound to assume that the footman had stolen the plate; and I could not understand why she hesitated to start the police after him. There was a reserve in the tone of her letter which made me fancy that the so-called mystery was no mystery to her. It seemed very idle to pretend that her husband could connive at this robbery. I knew very well what plate they had, and if it were all gone, then the loss would amount to not less than seven or eight hundred pounds.

However, I forebore troubling my mind with conjectures, living in daily expectation of receiving a letter that should explain the whole affair. Meanwhile, I frequently met Mr. Hastings, and from him gathered, by very slow degrees, the estimation in which my daughter and her husband were held at Copsford. I was greatly concerned to find that their habit of quarrelling was well known; that in consequence of Mr. Ransome's eccentric and often insolent reception of his wife's friends, few, if any, persons visited the house; and that it was generally understood he was insane, though various degrees of insanity were ascribed to him.

All this was extremely mortifying for me to hear. I have before written that, owing to the loss of my wife, I had withdrawn from society, and preserved the acquaintance of but few people; but I believed I had left a name that was thoroughly respected throughout the neighborhood, and I cannot describe the distress and annoyance with which I heard that my daughter and Mr. Ransome were incessantly creating gossip, and that this last vagary of Mr. Ransome had brought upon his wife as much scandal, had excited as many rumors, and generated as much prejudice, as if she had very seriously committed herself.

Three weeks passed before I again heard from Phœbe;

and then one afternoon, on returning to my lodgings, I found the following letter from her:

"DEAREST PAPA:—For God's sake come to me at once. I am the victim of a horrible plot, and am helpless while you are from me. I cannot write more now. An unendur-able insult has been offered me. On receipt of this letter leave Boulogne."

The handwriting was an agitated scrawl, and the wild appearance of the letter was completed by the rough way in which it had been folded and crammed into the envelope. You may conceive I was greatly agitated. The hasty, un-satisfactory words offered scope to all kinds of conjectures. My ruling impression was that she had violently quarrelled with her husband. I imagined that he had returned home, assigned some discreditable motive for his disappearance, and that she had been driven into a passion by this confes-sion, and dashed off this letter to me when her temper was at its height.

I had to wait until the morrow to cross the Channel. The packet started at nine, and after being blown about for nearly six hours, we made Dover. I posted to Canterbury, where I caught the coach to London; slept at Southwark that night; early next morning booked myself for Copsford; and reached that town at four o'clock in the afternoon, three days after the receipt of my daughter's letter.

I engaged a bedroom at one of the chief inns at Copsford, where I left my portmanteau, and, hiring a fly, was driven over to Gardenhurst. The familiar scenery through which I passed, amid which I had spent so many years of my life, recalled many associations mournful and happy. I remem-bered how I had climbed yonder hill; how, as a boy, I had fished in the silver trout-stream in that dark-green valley down there; how often I had traversed this road I was now journeying along, with my wife by my side; how in later days Phœbe had been my one dear companion. I thought of her folly in marrying a man of whom she had known so little, but in whom I had witnessed characteristics which furnished me with but poor promise of my girl's happiness with him. As I approached the house, my agitation increased. My ignorance of the nature of my daughter's need of me rendered my imagination painfully active, and I felt as if I should not have the courage to meet her.

I alighted at the gate and walked along the avenue. My hand trembled as I raised it to the knocker. I was mastered by I know not what indefinable dread, and waited with miserable anxiety for my summons to be answered. The gloom of the evening had gathered under the avenue; but away down on my left the grounds were shining in the light of the sinking sun, and the rooks were noisy in the soft dark clouds of trees at the bottom.

The door was opened by a plainly dressed, but neat, kindly faced woman, who might have been twenty or forty, for she had an odd look of youth and middle-age in her face. Her hair was brown and brushed smoothly over her forehead; her eyes were gray, clear, and singularly honest and penetrating; her complexion pale. She started on seeing me, and before I could speak, exclaimed:

" You are Colonel Kilmain, sir?"

" Yes. Is my daughter at home?"

" Yes, sir; she will be very glad to see you," she said. "She is in the drawing-room. Have you no luggage?"

" I have left my portmanteau at Copsford. Mr. Ransome has not returned?"

" No, sir."

" Does Mrs. Ransome expect me?"

" Yes, sir; but she was afraid you would not arrive before to-morrow."

She closed the hall door and I walked to the drawing-room, first knocking and then throwing open the door. Phœbe was seated at the table in a most listless attitude, mechanically turning the leaves of a book, with her eyes directed at the window. She looked around, saw me, sprang from the chair, and in a moment was sobbing upon my breast.

" My darling," I exclaimed, kissing her and leading her tenderly to the sofa, " you see I have lost no time in coming to you. You have caused me great anxiety, for your letter was very hurried and short, and has terribly exercised my imagination. What is the plot, Phœbe? **What has your** husband been doing?"

" Oh, papa, I cannot tell you yet," she answered, holding my hands with a clinging attitude, and pressing against me in a way strangely suggestive of the need of shelter and protection. " You are tired—you must rest yourself a while. You are not prepared to hear the story yet. I will ring for some tea—that will refresh you."

"No, my child, I want nothing," I said. "Tell me everything at once. I have been in suspense long enough— begin now, Phœbe."

She breathed quickly, and a look of wild fear came into her eyes. Her face was very thin, the hollows under her eyes dark, and there was an expression of passionate dis· tress and weariness, and lines of care that made her older· looking by ten years.

I repeated again eagerly my wish to hear the truth at once. Her hands trembled in mine and I felt them turn cold and clammy. Then she began her recital. She told me how, on a certain morning, above a month ago, her husband and the footman, Maddox, were found missing; how the housekeeper, Miss Avory, had found the plate-safe empty; how the inspector had been summoned, and how, after he was come, she regretted having sent for him when she considered that the disappearance of the two men might be a scheme of her husband's, and that it was impossible for her to explain her suspicions to the inspector without entering into family secrets which her pride abhorred the thought of making public; how she suffered the matter to rest in the full persuasion that Maddox had acted in concert with Mr. Ransome, and that the latter would return any day, when, if Maddox was really guilty of stealing the plate, the police could be started in pursuit of him; how but a few days ago, Mrs. Ransome had entered the house and denounced her as her husband's murderess; how, shortly after she had been turned out, she came back with the inspector, a constable, and a dismissed servant, who declared that she had frequently heard her late mistress threaten to kill Mr. Ransome; how the inspector and the constable had searched the house, implying by the act that they deemed her capable of the crime imputed to her; and how, at that very time of speaking, she was actually lying under the suspicion of having murdered her husband with her own hands or of having connived at his death by the hands of another.

Such was her story to me.

I listened to it without a word, too astounded to utter even an exclamation.

When she had made an end I looked at her. As I live, I believed at that moment that she was mad; that her whole story, consistently related as it had been, was a hideous delusion.

"Do you mean to tell me, Phœbe," I exclaimed, "that the inspector searched this house on the information of Mr. Ransome's mother, for the purpose of finding proof of your guilt?"

"Yes, papa. Miss Avory will bear witness. Let her join us. She has been my only friend!"

"Stay!" I cried, restraining her. "Answer me first some questions, and then we will call her. What kind of life have you led with this man who has deserted you?"

"As I believe in God," she answered, wringing her hands, "the most miserable life that ever woman led in this world."

"And you never told me!"

"He has driven me mad," she continued, rocking herself to and fro, "with wild and dreadful insults. He has struck me with his fist. He has buried his fingers in the flesh of my arm, and left marks there which have lasted for days! He has cursed and spat upon me! Ruffian! coward that he is! he has tried to drive me mad—and he has done it, I think! for this last act of his has forced a weight like burning iron into my head, and I have scarcely closed my eyes in sleep for six days."

"My God!" I cried, grasping her arm, in the passion that mastered me. "Why did you not tell me this before? Why have you allowed his madness to play itself into this last atrocious act?"

She made no answer, and continued rocking herself to
and fro, moaning as though her heart would break.

"Was it your obstinate pride that kept you silent?" I
continued. "Am I so great an enemy to you that you will
never take me into your councils until it is too late?
Would real pride suffer itself to be trampled upon and
crushed while it had a voice to lift up to summon the help
which a single syllable would have obtained? And now
what has come of it all? The deadliest suspicion is upon
us! Your husband's villainy has made this house accurst!
Though all be made clear as the daylight, yet the suspicion
will always haunt us, the foul memory will never depart!
The ruffian has done his work! Why have I been spared
to witness this awful disgrace?"

I paced the room in a frenzy. My pride had received a
terrible wound, and the torment of it drove me wild. I
grasped the whole situation as though I had been an actor
in it from the beginning. *Now* I understood the significance of those whispers to which Mr. Hastings had referred. My daughter was terrified by my passion, and
stared at me with wide-open eyes.

"Why did you not tell me that your husband was a villain? Why did you not tell me? long ago I would have
taken you from him!" I cried; and I repeated these exclamations again and again, feeling the blood in my head,
and clutching at my collar, which seemed to strangle me,
until, breathless and exhausted, I sank into a chair.

I felt her hand upon my shoulder—I motioned her away.

"Not yet," I muttered. "Give me time! this is an
awful blow. I should not have believed I could bear it
and live."

Then I looked at her. There was something heartrend-
ing in the misery and pain expressed in her face.

"Oh, Phœbe!" I cried, extending my arms, "this is
hard—hard upon us both!"

She fell at my feet.

I pressed my lips to her forehead and raised her.

"God knows you have suffered enough. How can I hear
you tell me of your husband's behavior and remain calm?

Was he ill-treating you six months ago? If so, he hid his villainy well, for how often did I tell you that you were the transgressor in the quarrels between you! How little did I guess the provocation he gave you in secret! You have said that Miss Avory has been a friend to you. Ring the bell and let her join us. She will be cooler than you, and tell me clearly all that I must know without delay."

"Papa, you are tired—you have travelled a long distance —rest yourself awhile."

I had assumed a calm for her sake, but my agitation was so great that it needed the utmost effort of my will to enable me to speak quietly. I rang the bell myself, and paced the room while I endeavored to realize our position and make myself master of the details of Mr. Ransome's plot against his wife—for a plot, on the assurance of Phœbe, I considered it. She watched me wistfully, but without the fear that had hitherto made her face almost pitiful to see.

Miss Avory probably guessed that the summons was for her, for she answered it herself. There was something so quiet and steady in her manner and appearance that the mere sight of her seemed to soothe my agitation. Though her features were irregular, yet there was so much intellect and delicacy and firmness expressed in her pale face that one would never dream of noticing that she was not pretty. She was as much a lady as any one I ever met, with her self-possessed manner, her calm gaze, her gentle, but not timid, air. At any other time I might have wondered to find her occupying the lowly position of housekeeper, but I had other things to think of.

I begged her to be seated. She closed the door and took a chair facing one of the windows, perhaps that I might see her face and know that she spoke the truth in her answers.

"I have just heard from my daughter," I said, "the story of the wrong her husband and his mother have done her. Do you think with her that this is a conspiracy on Mr. Ransome's part, and that his mother is helping him to carry it out?"

"I cannot make up my mind to take that view, sir," she

answered. "I have no doubt that Mr. Ransome's insanity is great enough to account for everything; but there is one feature in this affair so purposeless as respects any issue Mr. Ransome may contemplate, that, until I can find a reason for it, I cannot persuade myself to regard Mr. Ransome's disappearance as a conspiracy. I refer to the robbery of the plate. He could have no object in taking the plate himself or in getting the footman to take it."

"But Miss Avory will not consider that Mr. Ransome is mad," exclaimed Phœbe petulantly.

"Miss Avory does, my dear," I answered; "I think her views very sound. The same thought occurred to me when I read your letter. The fact of your husband and the footman leaving the house on the same night proves only a coincidence. Had there been no robbery committed, one might assume that they had gone off together; but the missing plate convicts one of them of theft. Your husband could have no motive in taking it; he would not burden himself with it; he could find no use for it. Hence Maddox must have stolen it; and the robbery, in my opinion, proves the two men to have acted independently of each other."

"I must tell you, sir," said Miss Avory, "that I was talking to some people of the name of Campion a day or two ago, and they assured me, from what they had heard, that Mrs. Ransome is perfectly sincere in her belief that her son has been murdered. Monstrous as her theory is, since it involves an abominable charge against the members of this household, yet it is well to know that she is conscientious in professing it, because it proves that she is not in league with her son."

"But how do you know she speaks the truth?" cried Phœbe. "Did she not make Mary tell an infamous lie by suggesting that she had been discharged because she knew too much? I will never believe," she exclaimed passionately, "that she and her son are not in a conspiracy against me. She brought the inspector to my house that she might degrade me and create a suspicion against me in people's minds; and is the word of a wretch who could act like this to be taken? She wants to revenge herself; and there is no lie she would not tell to disgrace and ruin me."

"What have you done to make her revengeful?" I asked.

"When she visited us, she would act as if she were mistress here, take my authority out of my hands, and set the servants against me, besides aggravating the bitterness that already existed between my husband and me. I determined to show her and everybody else that I was mistress, that this was my house, and that no orders but mine should be obeyed. At her last visit I gave her the use of two rooms, and refused to let her occupy the others. This is her reason for hating me."

"You did not tell me this before," I exclaimed.

"Well, papa, it is true; and on the same day of her arrival she left us, and that night her son disappeared. Do I not prove the conspiracy by showing you why it should exist?"

"Did she leave you voluntarily?"

"No. Miss Avory frightened Mr. Ransome by threatening him with a madhouse. She found that she had power over him, and used her influence to oblige him to take his mother away. This was a defeat she could not forgive. Oh!" she cried impetuously, "it is blinding one's eyes to the truth to pretend that all this isn't a conspiracy. *I* see through it plainly enough."

"Are you sure he was frightened of you, Miss Avory?" I said; "or do you think his fear was feigned and a stratagem of his madness? He might have wished his mother to go, and pretend that he was afraid of you as an excuse to remove her."

"No, sir; he was afraid of me; I am sure of that. He ruled his mother, and would not require any excuse to request her to leave."

"You actually threatened him with a madhouse?"

"Not actually; he confessed his horror of the thought, and I worked upon his fear by implication in order to get him to remove his mother."

I recalled his manner to me six months before; how he had shunned me, how he had avoided my gaze. I had often felt that he was afraid of me. A strange idea seized me.

"Do you think, Miss Avory, he ran away *because* he was frightened of you, and dreaded that your threats of a mad-house might really be carried out?"

She was silent, and bent her eyes down thoughtfully.

"Consider," I went on; "he would understand that you knew of his behavior to my daughter; he might believe that, having guessed he was mad, you would acquaint me with your discovery of his madness and of the ill-usage my daughter was subjected to; and not doubting how I should act, he ran away—a madman's fear acting upon him."

"That might be his reason," she replied, drawing a long breath.

"He knew," I exclaimed, with excitement, "as certainly as that he lived that, had I guessed he was the madman I have found him out to be, I would have saved my daughter from his brutality by using the only remedy I am per-mitted against him. He is fit only for a madhouse, and there I would have had him lodged. Phœbe, can this have been his reason for leaving you?"

"No! his reason is to disgrace me. He has done so, through his mother!"

Her answer recalled me from my speculations to the sense of our present position.

"What is thought of Mrs. Ransome's charge against my daughter, Miss Avory? Is it credited?" I exclaimed.

"I must tell you the truth, sir," she answered. "There is much gossip about it, and until the old lady's accusation is disproved, people will continue wondering and talking."

"Disproved?" I cried. "What shape does the accusa-tion take? Does she actually charge my daughter with murdering Mr. Ransome?"

"She declares it is her full persuasion that her son is dead; that your daughter knows he is dead, and can tell, if she chooses, how he came by his death."

"She called me murderess to my face, papa," Phœbe shrieked, starting up and holding her clasped hands out before her.

"But," I burst out, "how can she found a charge of this kind on the mere disappearance of her son, knowing that it was his habit to leave her without hinting his intention? Are they all crazy at Copsford that they listen to this woman's stuff?"

"She made the inspector search the house expressly that people should suspect me," moaned Phœbe.

"A serious mistake was made in the first instance," said Miss Avory, "by Mrs. Ransome omitting to give instructions to the inspector to follow Maddox. People are dwelling upon that. They think something is hidden behind this indifference to the robbery."

"Yes," I answered; "I see how this indifference might be misconstrued. Why, Phœbe, did you not treat the matter as a robbery? Of course people wonder that you should not take a single step to recover your property."

"How could I explain the truth to the inspector?" said Phœbe, beginning to sob; "I believed then, as I believe now, that the removal of the plate was a part of the conspiracy—perhaps to account for Maddox's disappearance—to throw us off our guard—as the apparent robbery of Mr. Ransome's room was designed to do; and I would not play into the coward's hands by exposing my secrets to strangers. I thought he would come back; every day I expected him. *Then* I should have found out the truth about Maddox."

"Where is Mrs. Ransome living? Do you know, Miss Avory?" I asked.

"She has a lodging in Dane Street, I believe. I heard last night that she was ill. The news came by a friend of the cook, who also added another startling piece of gossip."

"What was that?" I exclaimed, seeing her look earnestly toward Phœbe.

She hesitated some moments, and then answered:

"The day after the inspector searched the house, Mrs. Ransome applied for a warrant against your daughter; but her application was refused."

"A warrant to bring my child before the bench on the charge of murder?" I cried.

"Yes, sir. I beg your pardon, madam," Miss Avory

said, addressing my daughter, "for not having told you this before. I thought it best to wait until Colonel Kilmain had arrived. She applied in person, and on its being refused, fell into a passion and called on all present to take notice that the law refused to help her to bring her son's murderess to justice. A few such scenes, sir, would do good, by convincing people that she was mad."

"But is she not known to be mad?" I exclaimed, almost paralyzed by the hideous and overwhelming pertinacity the old woman had exhibited.

"I am afraid not—at least by the majority," she replied. "Some sympathy is felt for her. She is a poor, heart-broken mother, they say, mourning the loss of her son; the law ought to help her to find him. She is now ill, seriously ill, it is rumored; and whether her illness is feigned or not, the report is sure to increase the sympathy she has excited."

I felt myself for the moment utterly helpless in the face of the astounding situation in which my daughter was placed. It was now half-past seven; the evening was fast drawing in, and the room was so gloomy that I could barely see the faces of my companions. For seven or eight hours no food had passed my lips: I felt faint but had no appetite. I asked Miss Avory to get me some brandy-and-water, and she hurried away, and after a short absence brought, in addition to what I had requested, some sandwiches and biscuits. While she was gone not a word had passed between my daughter and me. She was terrified, I think, by the misery she had brought upon me: and I was too agitated by conflicting passions to utter a syllable. I forced myself to eat and drink, and then, jumping up, announced my intention to go at once to Mrs. Ransome.

"I *must* see her," I exclaimed, "though she be dying; I must extort the truth from her, and force her to own that either this is a conspiracy to ruin you, or that she actually believes her scoundrel son has been murdered in this house."

I heard Phœbe addressing me in beseeching language, but I paid no need to her; with a feeling as of a fever raging in my blood, I hurried into the hall, seized my hat, and in a few moments was walking impetuously toward Copsford.

II

The evening was fine, the sun had set, and in the east the sky was heavy with stars. The cool air fanned my heated face as I walked, but I saw no more of the rich and glorious landscape that lay around me, with its wreathed hills and black valleys, than had I been in a cell. The blow that had been dealt me was a stunning one. The significance of the position my daughter had placed both of us in by her fatal choice of a madman for a husband grew deep and appalling now that I was alone, and could give my whole mind to it. From any charge, however insignificant, so that it gave provocation to gossip, my pride would have recoiled with horror; but *this*!——

In half-an-hour's time I had reached Copsford. I entered the High Street with a dread of being recognized, and poorly lighted as the thoroughfare was shrank as I advanced close against the shops, and passed forward hastily, keeping my face bent downward. The little town was as familiar to me as my hand. I reached Dane Street, and, looking about me a moment entered a chemist's shop, and asked the man behind the counter if he knew where Mrs. Ransome lived.

"Why, Colonel Kilmain," he exclaimed, with a smile, "you ought to know where Gardenhurst is, sir."

"I don't mean my daughter," I answered, foolishly dismayed by finding myself known; "there is another Mrs. Ransome who lodges somewhere in this street."

"Oh, to be sure, sir. I beg pardon. I was thinking of Mrs. Ransome of Gardenhurst. The other Mrs. Ransome— she's your daughter's mother-in-law, I believe, sir—lives at Number Three, a private house, at the bottom of this side. They say she won't live, sir. I've been supplying her with a deal of medicine for the last few days, one way and another. That's a bad job about her son. Oh, I beg your pardon," he exclaimed, coloring to the roots of his hair.

"What about her son?"

"Oh—really—I forgot who I was talking to, sir. Number Three, sir—last house but one on this side."

"It is reported that her son is murdered, isn't it?"

"Why, yes, so they say, sir. I am quite vexed with myself for forgetting."

"Murdered by whom?"

"I'd rather not talk of it, sir," he answered, with a great air of confusion. "It's not a pleasant subject," he added appealingly.

"But you can answer my question."

"If I *must* say it," he exclaimed, forcing his words out with reluctance, "they report that he was murdered up at his own house."

"And are you fool enough to believe this report?"

"I? Lord bless you, sir! I've got other things to think of."

I wheeled round and walked out of the shop. Better for me, perhaps, had I always acted so.

I reached the house to which the chemist had directed me and knocked. It was an old but clean house, with black gleaming windows on a level with the wall, and a door decorated with a brass knocker and handle. I stepped backward, after I had knocked, and looked up. A light shone upon the second-floor windows, and the shadow of a figure walking in the room moved upon the blinds. In a short time the door was opened, and a thin, ghostly looking man in a sleeved waistcoat stood forth, leaving a candle burning on a table in the passage.

"Does Mrs. Ransome live here?" I inquired.

The man looked attentively at me for some moments, and then answered in a voice resembling a raven's:

"No."

"Where does she live? I was informed that she was in lodgings at Number Three."

"So she were," croaked the man, "and this is Number Three. But she don't live nowheres now. She's dead."

He wagged his head slowly from side to side, struck his nose with his finger, and fell back a step, repeating, "'Cos she's dead."

"Dead!" I exclaimed. "When did she die?"

"As the clock was a-striking twelve," he answered. "My wife's attending of the corpse now. You can't see it." The strange suspicion that this might be a trick of the old lady's, though God knows for what end, was put into my head by the man's words. Unfortunately, I could not see his face clearly, for the candle behind him flickered in my eyes, and the street which he confronted was quite dark.

"Can you tell me the name of the doctor who attended her?" I said.

"Mr. Eastwell."

"Thank you."

I knew Mr. Eastwell by sight, and where he lived. I turned away, and the ghostly-looking man shut the door. I crossed the street, and looked at the windows where the light was. The shadow moved restlessly upon the blinds. Was she really dead? If so, her death must have been sudden. How came it that the news had not been brought to Gardenhurst? Those who attended her would be sure to know that Phœbe was her daughter-in-law, and they would naturally look to her for instructions with respect to the disposal of the body.

This reflection increased my suspicion. I walked hurriedly into the High Street, where Mr. Eastwell lived, trying to imagine in what manner the supposed death of the old lady would strengthen the plot of which Phœbe declared herself the victim. On my arrival at the surgeon's house the door was opened by a page, who took me for a patient and led me to a small, close-smelling room, with a table on one side covered with glass bottles and the walls hung with anatomical drawings.

Mr. Eastwell, probably sharing the impression of his page, kept me waiting some time.

He was a fat young man, in spectacles. He brought into the room with him a strong smell of tobacco, and catching sight of me, suffered the stereotyped gravity to melt out of his face, while he exclaimed:

"I have the honor of seeing Colonel Kilmain?"

15

I told him he had; whereupon he seated himself, clasped his hands over his knee and posed himself in a listening attitude.

"I have called to know if it is true that Mrs. Ransome is dead," said I.

"Quite true. She died this morning."

"So I was informed by the man whom I suppose the house belongs to. Surely her death is very sudden?"

"No," he answered. "She lived a night longer than I thought she would. I was with her last evening and gave her up then."

"Am I right in supposing," I said, satisfied by his manner and answers that she *was* dead, "that she did not wish any communication to be made to her daughter-in-law, Mrs. Ransome of Gardenhurst?"

"Oh, the lady is your daughter, of course. It did not occur to me before. To be sure—she was Miss Kilmain! I understand the motive of your inquiries now. Your conjecture is quite right: Mrs. Ransome emphatically prohibited any notice of her illness or death being given to your daughter. She has left very complete instructions about her funeral and so forth. She puts her body into the hands of Mr. and Mrs. Wadgett, her landlord and his wife, with orders to place it in a coffin and despatch it to Guildford. Mr. Wadgett will accompany the corpse and consign it to the custody of some intimate friend of the deceased."

"Who is that intimate friend, I wonder—her son?"

"No, sir," he exclaimed, looking at me sternly through his spectacles; "that intimate friend is not her son. And, sir, you'll pardon the liberty I take in venturing to feel surprised that, knowing the very grave suspicions which afflicted Mrs. Ransome, and which I have no hesitation in saying, aided by her maternal attachment and grief, hastened her death, you should venture to suppose that that intimate friend *should* be her son."

"I arrived at Copsford this afternoon," I exclaimed, "and heard for the first time of the accusation which your patient in her madness thought fit to level at my child. I so strongly suspected that woman's honesty that I would

not be satisfied with her landlord's assurance of her death,
but came to you to have the news confirmed, believing her
capable of any extravagant deceit. *That* is the object of
this visit; not to discuss a subject so utterly preposterous
as Mrs. Ransome's delusion."

"I know nothing more than what she has told me. I
decline to pass an opinion one way or the other."

"I have not asked you for an opinion," I answered
warmly. "Had that woman lived, I would have forced her
to confess herself either mad or utterly wicked. My charity disposes me to think her mad. Human wickedness of
the worst description would stop short, I think, of charging
an innocent lady with the crime of murder! One question
you can answer me: Is it your belief that Mrs. Ransome
was mad?"

"I will not say," he replied deliberately, "that her grief
at the supposed death of her son had not unsettled her
mind; but I would not call her mad. Far from it. Her
reasoning was as sane as anybody's I ever listened to."

"Is it possible," I cried, "that you can reconcile her
sanity with the charge she brings against her daughter-in-
law?"

"I would really—I would really, sir," he answered, waving his hand and smiling, "prefer not to enter upon this
subject. It is no affair of mine. I have given you my
opinion of Mrs. Ransome's sanity. I may be wrong—we
are all apt to mistake. The unfortunate lady *may* have
been a raving madwoman. I can only say that she struck
me as a healthy minded person who talked with incoherence
only when she cried out, in her grief, for her son to be restored to her."

I got up, bowed to him, and left the room. He accompanied me to the door, remarking upon the freshness of the
night, and suggested that, since I was just returned from
abroad, I must feel the difference between the climates. I
barely answered him, and hurried into the street.

His testimony to Mrs. Ransome's sanity indescribably
vexed and agitated me. Was he sincere in declaring that
he believed her sane?

I stood a while in the street, considering what I should do. It was past eight o'clock; the night had fallen but the pavements were brilliant enough with shop-lights, though here and there some of the shops were being closed. I had an extraordinary reluctance to return to Gardenhurst without having taken some decided step; without having prepared some measure that would enable me to go to work resolutely on the morrow. A man turned to look at me after he had passed, and I shrank some paces away out of the light of the shop before which I had unconsciously halted while I debated my next action. My unfortunate sensitiveness made me suffer as much as though I myself had done some great wrong.

I was about to advance, with a half-resolution in my mind to call there and then upon a solicitor and submit my daughter's position to him, when a little elderly man, passing at that moment, stopped, looked at me attentively, and exclaimed:

"Why, Colonel Kilmain! is it possible that you have come to live among us once more?"

"Mr. Skerlock!" I said; "I hope you are well, sir? It is some time since I had the pleasure of meeting you."

"Oddly enough," he replied, "you were in my mind not an hour ago. And yesterday I asked my wife if she had heard whether you had arrived at Gardenhurst."

"I reached here this afternoon, having hurried from Boulogne in consequence of a pressing letter from my daughter. You do not require to be told of the extraordinary business that has brought me here."

"No, indeed," he excaimed; "and I want to have a chat with you on that very subject. Which way are you walking?"

I answered that I was anxious to have some conversation with him, and proposed that we should turn into the White Hart, the inn where I had hired a bedroom, and which was but a few steps up the street. He asked me to go to his house, but I declined, and we repaired to the inn, where we found the coffee-room empty. I called for some wine, and drew my chair close to Mr. Skerlock. He was a spare

man, of a dry and dusty aspect, a great consumer of snuff;
his face was full of amiability and kindness. He put his
hat upon the table, and pulling out his snuff-box, opened
the conversation by trusting that I would not misconstrue
his meaning if he should be frank with me; he felt that he
should be thought guilty of presumption in offering either
his sympathy or his advice to a gentleman with whom he
had not the honor of an intimate acquaintance—and so
forth.

"I can assure you," I replied, "that I was never more in
need of sympathy and advice than I am at this moment.
When you met me, sir, I had been standing for full ten
minutes pondering on how I should act."

"Understand me at once, Colonel," he exclaimed; "I
utterly scout the monstrous supposition which your daughter's mother-in-law has been trying to establish—I suppose
you know the old lady is dead?"

"Yes, I have just heard so."

"I may tell you plainly," he continued, "that her death
does not and will not promote your daughter's cause. It
has already excited sympathy, and we shall find that persons who were before incredulous of her assertions will now
doubtfully shake their heads. As chairman, I have incurred some abuse for refusing Mrs. Ransome's application
for a warrant."

"As chairman?" I exclaimed, not understanding.

"Have you forgotten that I am a magistrate?"

"I remember. I beg your pardon. I have only visited
Copsford once during the last two years, and then my stay
was a short one."

"I have provoked much criticism," he said, taking a
pinch of snuff, "for not acceding to the old lady's wishes.
But we live in a very small world here. There are a good
many poor; and they are clamorous on the inequalities of
justice, saying that, if Mrs. Ransome had been a rich woman and your daughter a pauper, the warrant would have
been granted. Was ever such nonsense talked? As if a
warrant *could* be granted on such evidence as the old lady
offered!"

He rapped his snuff-box excitedly, and then smiled and nodded.

"But do you really believe that Mrs. Ransome was sincere in supposing that her son had been murdered?" I asked.

"I am afraid that cannot be doubted."

"Did she not strike you as being mad?"

He sipped his wine, dropped his head on one side, and answered mysteriously:

"Mad as a March hare. But no one will believe me. There was the excitement of lunacy in her eye, sir, when she was refused her application; and then she began to argue with amazing vehemence—though, mind you, not without logic—and eventually had to be ordered out of the room."

"But you know her son is mad?"

"Oh, yes; that *is* known."

"You also know that her son was in the habit of absenting himself for weeks at a time from his mother, without apprising her of his departure or return?"

"Yes, she admitted that."

"Then in God's name!" I cried, "what can she mean by charging my daughter with having killed her husband?"

"Now we come to the point, Colonel," he answered, holding up his fingers and telling them off as he spoke. "You must first of all know that her evidence was to this effect: that your daughter (as she was prepared to prove) had been repeatedly heard to threaten Mr. Ransome's life; that she used him like a dog and never neglected an opportunity to insult and degrade him before his servants; that, though it was true he was in the habit of leaving the house without communicating his intention of doing so, yet never before had he quitted it in the dead of night, and never before, in her experience, had he been longer away than a fortnight at the very outside without writing to say where he was; that she had herself seen enough of Mrs. Ransome to persuade her that she was capable, in her passion, of committing murder; that her conviction was, either that Mrs. Ransome in a fury had killed her husband, or procured some assassin to do the work for her; that the latter conjecture was rendered highly probable by the mysterious disappearance of the footman on the night of Mr. Ransome's disappearance, by the abstraction of the plate, which would serve to mislead suspicion and fix it upon the obvious commission of a comparatively small crime by which Mr. Ransome, in seeming to be concerned in it, would be shown to be alive; and by Mrs. Ransome, from that hour to this, never having taken any steps for the recovery of the plate, for the apprehension of the thief, or for the pursuit of her husband."

The old gentleman had checked off his fingers, and now plunged them into his snuff-box, his eyes on my face.

"All these arguments can be met and silenced," I answered. "But I am sure that you have disposed of them in your own mind, and I have no right to inflict a long and superfluous explanation upon you. The one point I have to consider is—how am I to clear my daughter's character of the suspicion Mrs. Ransome's accusation has left upon her?"

"The great mistake your daughter made, Colonel," he answered, "was in neglecting to instruct the inspector to follow up the robbery of the plate. It is her total silence, her withholding from all action, that has given foundation to reports and started the curious and vicious theories people are promulgating. I took the liberty of calling on her and representing the necessity of having the matter inquired into; not because I anticipated the sinister result that has attended her inaction, but because I considered it mercifully necessary that her husband, being an irresponsible person, should not be suffered to wander at large."

"She tells me she believed he would return to her any day," I replied. "She also believed that the robbery of the plate was a part of his scheme to bring shame and sorrow upon her; and wild as the theory appears, yet nothing is impossible to madness. She refused to instruct the inspector because her pride abhorred the thought of taking any step which might ultimately lead to her confession of the miserable life she led with Mr. Ransome. Knowing her character as I do, how proud and self-willed she is, I believe in her explanation firmly; and I believe it to be all the more true because of the very inconsistency, perversity, and singularity of motives it forces her to avow."

"And I believe her too, sir," exclaimed the old gentleman earnestly. "Let any man look at her, speak to her, and imagine her guilty if he can, of *any* crime—let alone this!"

I seized his hand and shook it warmly.

"Thank you," I said, "for the courage your words put into me. I would ask you now if I have no remedy against the inspector for his unwarrantable intrusion on my daughter?"

"I am afraid not; he can only be charged with excess of zeal, and the law looks softly upon such transgressions. But will you allow me to recommend the course I consider the only advisable one for you to follow?"

"If you please."

"Your first step should be to call on the inspector, formally charge the footman with the robbery of the plate, and explain that your daughter's ignorance of such matters was her reason for not directing him to pursue the man before."

I at once saw the policy of this.

"That suggestion shall be carried out to-morrow morning," I exclaimed.

Mr. Skerlock looked pleased.

"The next thing," he continued, "is to find your son-in-law, dead or alive."

"Undoubtedly."

"That you must endeavor to accomplish by advertisements, offers of reward, and by putting the matter into the hands of men accustomed to this sort of work. My friend Mr. Clements has had to employ a man of this kind. If you will call on him, he will give you the man's address and you can write to him."

I thanked him for his practical advice.

"Some," he continued, "would recommend you not to act in the matter; to treat it with silent contempt, and so forth. But contempt (and you could not feel it) would be mistaken for indifference, and would therefore be rash.

Your daughter's name is dear to you. It would be very dear to me if I owned her for a daughter. Though your inquiries should prove fruitless, yet when people hear that you *are* inquiring, they will find evidence of innocence in it; and they will have no further cause to complain of your daughter's inhumanity in suffering a crazy husband to wander at the mercy of the world. Mankind are very full of cant," he exclaimed, with a twinkling eye; "we must recognize, we must bow to it, if we want to seem either what we are or what we are not."

This said, I looked at the time and debated within myself whether to return to Gardenhurst or send a messenger there to tell my daughter I should sleep at Copsford. I finally resolved to bear Phœbe company, having much to hear from her and Miss Avory. However, I did not want to lose my friendly companion in a hurry. It was still early; he showed no impatience to be gone, but drank his wine with relish, and seemed to have made himself very happy by cheering me up.

It was a source of great comfort to me to know that he utterly discredited the old woman's accusation, for I could converse with him on the subject on the thorough understanding that the whole thing was either a conspiracy between the mother and son or an extraordinary and incredible misapprehension on her part of the facts. The great interest he took in the matter, and the hearty sympathy he expressed, determined me on being perfectly unreserved with him. I told him the story of the marriage, my objection to it, my grave doubts as to Mr. Ransome's sanity, my daughter's obstinacy, which forced me to yield to her. I pointed out that there might be good reasons for old Mrs. Ransome's antipathy to my daughter and myself in the aversion I had shown to the engagement, which she had no doubt regarded as an insult, since I had never the courage to tell her that my objection was based on my doubt of her son's sanity; so that, from my avoidance of the truth, she might have drawn conclusions highly obnoxious to her pride, which was that of a woman who had a very high opinion of her station in life. I explained to him that, on

Phœbe's testimony, many of the quarrels that had arisen
between her and her husband were owing to the mother,
who had been intrusive, insolent, and meddlesome. In
short, I recounted all the facts I could remember to justify
my suspicion of the old woman's having acted from a
malicious motive. He agreed with me that the evidence
was strongly in favor of such a supposition, and he did not
doubt that a great deal of malice had been at the root of
her persistent accusation; but he would have to assume an
incomprehensible degree of wickedness if he denied her
sincerity in believing that her son had met with his death
by violence. She had never swerved from that view from
the moment she had communicated with the inspector.
Unless she was sincere, could we believe she would have
had the courage to take upon herself the enormous responsibility of such a charge? She never professed to have
received intimations of his death by supernatural means:
such as by his ghost having appeared to her, or by a dream,
or by a mysterious voice, or by any other nonsense by which
an old woman, and a crazy old woman, might endeavor to
fortify her statements. She founded her arguments on the
most prosaic premises, as a counsel would; on the circumstantial evidence of her daughter-in-law's fits of passion,
her repeated threats to kill her husband, her inaction in the
matter of the robbery, and the double disappearance—
all which, there being nobody to confute her, had filled
the public mind with foolish fancies and preposterous
prejudices.

As I listened to Mr. Skerlock, one idea impressed itself
upon me—that the old gentleman's familiarity with Mrs.
Ransome's arguments, and his knowledge of the state of
public feeling, proved that the subject was a notorious one.
This conviction emphasized the need of immediate action.

Our long and friendly conference was terminated by his
repeating his advice to me to start the inspector without
delay after the footman, and to employ every means in my
power to discover Mr. Ransome's whereabouts.

"If," he said, "the footman can be found and the robbery proved against him, the theory which has obtained

that he was an instrument in your daughter's hands will be exploded, and such a discovery is certain to bring about a revulsion of prejudice. Flatter the inspector by placing the matter in his hands; he is a talker, and will unconsciously serve your ends by telling everybody his commission. But do not let the matter rest with him. The man who is to search for your son-in-law may as well search for the footman also. The police are sharp enough; but there is no sharpness equal to that of the man whom you pay highly for his discoveries."

We bade each other good-night.

Part Four

THE HOUSEKEEPER'S STORY
(*Continued.*)

I

It was hard upon ten o'clock before the Colonel returned from Copsford. I did not expect him, for he had told me that he had engaged a bedroom at the inn, and I thought he would sleep there.

He drove up in a fly, his portmanteau was handed out, and calling to me (for I had been attracted to the hall by the ringing of the bell, never hearing the summons now without conceiving that Mr. Ransome had returned), he asked me to be so good as to prepare a bedroom for him, and then join him and his daughter, as he wished to speak to me.

He was very pale, with a tired and yet an agitated expression in his face. I felt very sorry for him, as much so as ever I felt for his daughter.

I got ready the bedroom that old Mrs. Ransome was to have slept in, and having lingered long enough to give him time to relate the result of his visit to Copsford to his daughter, descended and entered the dining-room where they were.

He was addressing her earnestly, but broke off when he saw me, and instantly Mrs. Ransome exclaimed:

"She is dead, Miss Avory! She died this morning."

"Is it possible?" I answered, knowing perfectly well whom she meant.

The Colonel rose, and, with an air of great courtesy, placed a chair for me near to where they were sitting.

"I doubted the news at first," he said, resuming his seat; "but it is unquestionably true, for it was confirmed by the doctor who attended her, and by Mr. Skerlock, a gentleman," he added warmly, "who, by his sympathy and advice, has placed me under an obligation to him I shall never forget while I live."

"I would to heaven," cried Mrs. Ransome, "that that miserable, wicked old woman had died two years ago. I should have been saved all this misery."

Her father rebuked her vehemence with a glance, and addressing me, said:

"I desire to thank you, Miss Avory, for the sympathy and kindness you have shown my daughter since you have been in this house. It consoles me to think that she should have found so sincere a friend in you in the absence of myself, whom she has thought fit to keep in ignorance of the very wretched life she has been leading since her marriage."

I made some suitable reply, and then he related to me the story of his visit to Copsford. I listened to him attentively, and was much struck by the strong common-sense the suggestions Mr. Skerlock had offered him illustrated.

"We cannot improve upon that advice, I think, Miss Avory," he remarked.

"No, sir."

"It will cost me some prevarication," he said, looking at me anxiously. "I shall have to tell the inspector that my daughter objected to the idea of having her name brought forward, and that that and her ignorance were the reason of her omitting to tell him to follow Maddox. But I *must* be guilty of some deceit to deal successfully with this overwhelming suspicion. Could we learn where Mr. Ransome is, then the strict and whole truth would be our only policy; but while he remains in hiding, we can prove nothing; we can only illustrate our innocence by our actions, and we must be very cautious to do nothing that can strengthen the prejudice and doubt which already exist."

"I should consider any precaution justifiable under such circumstances," I exclaimed.

He turned to his daughter.

"Phœbe, it is your violent temper that is the cause of all this.   You have been heard to threaten your husband's life. How could you say such a thing?"

"There were times when I could have killed him," she answered, turning pale.

"But that is an awful threat," he said, "and it has been wrested to an awful purpose.   Even Mr. Skerlock, whose heartiest sympathy is with us, declares that the old lady was sincere in believing that her son met with his death through you; and it was on those reckless words of yours that she most insisted."

"I would have killed him!   I would have killed him!" she muttered.   "I once showed Miss Avory the marks of his fingers on my arm.   Before she had even entered the house, he had struck me across the face with his hand.   Ruffian!   I would have killed him, and his mother knew it."

He looked at her intently, and then, in a voice so strange that I cannot attempt to describe it, he exclaimed:

"Phœbe, do you know what has become of him?"

She started, looked up, the blood rushed into her face; she answered shrilly and wildly:

"No—no!   Why do you ask me?   My God! do you mistrust me?"

He pressed his handkerchief to his face, and his hand trembled violently.

"You should not speak as you do," he said in a hoarse whisper.   "You terrify me.   Thank God, others have not questioned you."

He still looked at her fixedly, and there was silence between them.   Suddenly she shrieked out:

"Were I on my death-bed, I would still say there were times when I could have killed him.   Did I know that he was dead now, I would fall on my knees and thank God. I hate him as never woman hated a man!   But," her voice sank and she dropped her head, "I do not know where he is."

He continued looking at her for some moments, and then waved his hand.

"Miss Avory, to-morrow I commence business. There is much to be done. I suppose I shall have to go to London to see the man whom Mr. Skerlock's friend is to recommend to me. On my return I shall reside here. Phœbe, have you a likeness of your husband?"

"Yes," she answered."

Her face was very white, and there was a shocked expression in it. Indeed, I myself had turned pale in remarking the manner in which the Colonel had asked her if she knew where her husband was. Could I doubt old Mrs. Ransome's sincerity when I saw how *he* had yielded to the quick prompting of suspicion? Could I wonder that the town had taken up the tale to the prejudice of Mrs. Ransome when her own father could doubt her, though but for a moment?

"Let me have it," he said, speaking in a softened voice. She left the room. He followed her with his eyes to the door, watching with the admiration of a stranger, in which was mixed the deep anxiety he felt, her graceful movements and the peculiar sweeping action of her gait, so strangely suggestive of her pride and resolution and the haughtiness under which even I, who knew how much was to be forgiven her, often winced.

The moment the door was closed he turned to me swiftly and said:

"Miss Avory, do you think she knows more of this mystery than she chooses to tell?"

"No more than I do, sir," I answered, staggered by the significance of the question.

"She says *now*—now to my face, that she could have killed him!" he continued, in a loud whisper. "What made the old lady so persistent? . . . Look at her! her temper may have been brutalized by her husband's ruffianly treatment. I saw a dangerous fire in her eyes when she spoke of him. What would not such hate as hers prompt?"

He left his chair and paced the room, and then exclaimed:

"My God! what madness am I talking! No, no! I am extravagant! The horrible anxiety I have undergone since

I first heard the story from her has upset my mind. Poor
girl! she should have told me before; I would have taken
her from him. Poor girl!" he repeated, and smiled at me
wanly.

" You must not allow the faintest doubt of her innocence
to possess you, sir," I exclaimed. "Believe me! I watched
her. I have been by her side throughout this dreadful
affair; as I believe in my own innocence, I believe in hers.
She has no more conception whether her husband is living
or dead than I have. I cannot say more, sir."

He stepped up to me, grasped my hand, and walked to
the window, where he stood with his back to the room. I
was glad to have said I what did and to have said it
at once. Suspicion is as contagious as fever; and had I
given myself time to think, I might have faltered in my
answer.

She came back with a large plain gold locket, which she
gave to her father. He looked at the portrait inside it
attentively, and asked her if she knew what her husband's
age was when the likeness was taken. She thought about
twenty-five. The mother had sent it to her shortly after
her marriage. She had never worn it. She only remembered having it by being asked for a portrait of the man.
It was fortunate that she had not come across it before—
she would have destroyed it.

He paid no attention to this outbreak, but, handing me
the locket, asked me if I thought the portrait was sufficiently like to enable a stranger in search of Mr. Ransome
to identify him. I drew close to the lamp, and, after a
short inspection, answered that it might help out an accurate
and minute description of him; but that he appeared in the
likeness at least ten years younger-looking, and that he
was represented with his hair parted, which very much
altered him.

"Have you not a more recent portrait of him?" he asked
his daughter.

"No," she answered.

"Then this must do. As Miss Avory says, it will help
to illustrate a description. His was an uncommon kind of

face," he said, addressing me   "Eyes such as his are not often seen in Europeans."

"He might disguise himself," I replied.

"Yes, I have thought of that."

"But suppose he has left the country," exclaimed Mrs. Ransome.

"If I can obtain proof that he has done so, I shall want nothing better. If I can only get evidence to show that he was seen alive on the day following his disappearance from this house, I shall be satisfied. Let us look at our position; suspicion has been excited that this man has met with foul play; it has been brought to bear straight upon you by the mother in causing this house to be searched and in applying for a summons against you. We have to choose between two alternatives: we can sell or let Gardenhurst and quit the neighborhood; or we can strive the uttermost in our power to prove the suspicion a monstrous and false one. If we quit the neighborhood, we shall appear to justify the woman's accusation."

"I should not consent to go," exclaimed Mrs. Ransome passionately. "They shall not drive me away."

"Certainly we must not leave until we have done everything that can be done to prove that Mr. Ransome left this house of his own accord. Any day he may return; any day Maddox may be captured. But I have made up my mind," he added vehemently, "the moment this wretched mystery is cleared up, to separate you from your husband and sell Gardenhurst. Let the issue be what it may, our name is dishonored, the darkest shame that ever fell upon a family has fallen upon us. This very evening I entered Copsford as a felon might, dreading the eyes of those I met, slinking past shops, and cowering in the gloom; and by one man— Eastwell—was met with an insulting commiseration such as I might bestow upon a wounded dog. I will have no argument," he cried passionately, seeing that she was about to speak; "you have called me to you and I will protect you. But there must be no opposition to my wishes. My will must be your law—my weakness with you has borne its fruits in his. Nevermore shall I be influenced by considerations of

16

what *you* may call your happiness; you have qualities in
you which render you unfit to act for yourself, and I have
registered a vow to suffer no other judgment than my own
to direct me in the future."

She raised her gleaming eyes to his face, let them drop
suddenly, but made no answer. She was cowed by his im-
petuosity, and sat with her hands tightly clasped upon her
knee, quite still.

I considered that my presence was no longer necessary,
and rose to bid them good-night. The Colonel opened the
door for me, and I was touched by the courteous smile he
gave me, which only served to light up the deep grief and
anxiety that had already made his face as haggard as his
daughter's.

After I had been in my room twenty minutes I heard
them come into the hall and bid each other good-night. I
sent the servants to bed and locked up the basement as usual
and went up-stairs, but was surprised to find the hall door
open, and the Colonel standing on the threshold, smoking.

He looked round leisurely, saw me, and threw his cigar
away.

"I see you are locking up, Miss Avory. Shall I close
and bolt this door for you?" He did so as he asked the
question. "I am going to bed in a moment. I am very
tired. It is strange to me to stand under this familiar roof
again—but what pleasures, what years of my life, would I
not gladly forfeit to change the circumstances under which
I find myself in this house!"

"We must hope that this trouble will soon pass, sir," I
said. "I live in constant expectation of seeing Mr. Ransome return."

"I wish he would! I wish he would!" he exclaimed.
"You noticed the unjust suspicion that seized me in the
dining-room? I did my poor girl a grievous wrong in that
brief moment. But *why* will she not curb her temper?
Why will she, in the face of the horrible doubts that hang
over this house, recklessly persist in declaring that she
could have killed her husband, and in wishing him dead?
But he is a great villain!" he added, clenching his hand.

" My daughter has been treating me to a passage or two out of her married life. Wonderful that she should have held out so long—that she should have kept these miserable secrets so entirely hidden from me!"

He approached the hall table, took a candle, and lighted it at mine.

" There *cannot* be a doubt," he said, " that she is utterly ignorant, not only of his whereabouts, but of his motive for leaving her—unless the misery that has followed his disappearance was his motive, which I will not believe."

He looked at me so inquiringly that I easily saw, despite his assurance to the contrary, that he could not rid his mind of a lurking suspicion of his daughter.

" Unquestionably she is ignorant," I answered earnestly.

" Yes, unquestionably," he repeated. " The robbery of the plate is a genuine piece of thievery on the part of the footman—of that I am persuaded—Mr. Ransome knows nothing about it. The execution of their respective plans fell upon the same night; but that they acted without knowledge of each other's intention I am as convinced as that I am now addressing you. More than this—I utterly disagree with my daughter in viewing her husband's disappearance and the subsequent accusation of his mother as a conspiracy between them. The woman was crazy; she hated my daughter, and believed her capable of murdering her son—a mad woman's hallucination, which is not to be reasoned upon. Enough that it existed; that she argued from her barbarous premise with enough logic to render people credulous; that she has cast upon my daughter a suspicion that, in the absence of the ruffian who is the cause of all this unhappiness, it may tax the subtlest mind in the world to disprove. The motive of his absence I cannot conjecture. I only hope he is not dead. If he has committed suicide, for instance, or gone abroad under an assumed name, my daughter's lookout will be a desperate one. One year from this date I shall dedicate to the unravelling of this mystery. If by the end of that time nothing has happened to explain the puzzle, I shall sell this property and take my daughter abroad."

He seemed to find relief in speaking thus freely; but he suddenly perceived that he was keeping me from my bed, and, with an apology for his thoughtlessness, he again wished me good-night, and went up-stairs.

He came down-stairs very shortly after me next morning, and went into the grounds while his breakfast was preparing. From the dining-room window I saw him conversing with the under-gardener, Poole, and then I observed him eye that portion of the house where Mr. Ransome's bedroom was critically. He then walked with the man to the bottom of the grounds, where I lost sight of him.

The morning was a bright one, autumnal in coloring and perfume. I went out to collect some of the fruit which the wind shook from the heavily laden pear and apple trees in the kitchen gardens, to set the best of them on the breakfast-table; and as I returned with my apron full, I saw the Colonel approaching the house.

He found his breakfast ready, and seated himself to it; and when I entered the room, bearing some of the fruit I had collected, he said:

"It has occurred to me, Miss Avory, that our shrewd inspector only half did his business when he ransacked this house. Why did he not search the grounds? I have told Poole to look among the trees at the bottom yonder. In matters of this kind it sometimes happens that the apparently wildest surmise is the true one. Suppose Mr. Ransome should have taken it into his head to go and hang himself on one of the trees over there, or shoot himself among them."

"That is a dreadful fancy!" I exclaimed, with an involuntary shudder.

"So it is, and a foolish one too, I dare say. However, Poole has promised to search the grounds. He seems to take a great interest in this affair. His theory is that Maddox, in stealing the plate, encountered his master and killed him. By the way, I forgot to ask you—when you came down-stairs that morning and found Mr. Ransome gone, did you find any window or door open?"

"No, sir; and in my surprise at the time, I never thought

of asking the question. But on my making the inquiry a few days afterward, Mary (the girl who was dismissed) told me that she had found one of the drawing-room windows leading on to the terrace open, but had forgotten to mention it."

"I wonder if that girl knows anything that will throw a light on this mystery? Do you think she does?"

"No, sir; nor would I ask her; for rather than not seem to know, she will tell a falsehood and mislead us."

"She was the woman who swore to hearing my daughter threaten her husband's life?"

"Yes, sir."

"Did she tell the truth in that?"

"I fear she did. I myself have heard Mrs. Ransome use the same threat."

"Reckless, foolish girl!" he exclaimed. "How our idlest words come home like curses to us! *That's* the foundation on which the ugly structure of suspicion is erected. When will she learn to moderate her miserable temper?"

He looked at his watch, then hurriedly applied himself to his breakfast, and I left the room.

Half an hour afterward he went out. From a bedroom window I saw him trudging toward the avenue, with his head bowed and his hands clasped behind him. He looked a thorough gentleman. Some might have found fault with him for a certain want of life in his manner; but speaking for myself, I am always best pleased with a grave deportment in a man who has reached to middle age. The Colonel was tall and slender, with gray whiskers and mustache, an aquiline nose, and a full, mild, dark eye. His voice was very pleasing, with even a note of sweetness in it. As I watched him disappear among the trees of the avenue, I heartily wished that good luck would attend his efforts.

Shortly after he was gone, Mrs. Ransome came downstairs and asked me if her father had left the house.

"I wish he had asked me to go with him," she exclaimed, on my answering her. "I should like to face that impudent inspector and demand how he dared enter my house.

With papa at my side, I should have the courage to do any·
thing. Indeed I have a great mind to go out riding for
several days a week for the next month. I would gallop
right through Copsford, and let the people see how much
truth there is in the old wretch's accusation by my utter
indifference."

"If I were you, madam, I would do nothing without first
consulting Colonel Kilmain."

"But am I to make a convent of this house and die here
like a poisoned rat in a hole, because a vile and wicked old
creature chooses to hold the most monstrous and ridiculous
opinions respecting her son's disappearance?"

I made no answer, being quite satisfied that all this talk
was mere bravado. She looked at me steadily, and after
a pause of some moments, said:

"Did you notice the strange way in which my father,
last night, asked me if I knew more about my husband's
disappearance than I chose to tell?"

"I heard him ask you a question of that kind."

She was silent again; and then burst out passionately,
while her face grew pale:

"How can I wonder that strangers suspect me to be guilty
of all that the old woman charged me with, when my father
doubts me?"

"You must not think that he doubts you," I answered
gently. "He was prompted to ask the question by the
words you made use of."

"What words?"

"You said you could have killed your husband."

"It is God's own truth!" she cried. "Over and over
again I could have killed him! and so much do I hate him—
thinking of him now—though he may be dead for any·
thing I know—that, had I killed him, I never should have
felt one jot of remorse or horror in recalling the deed."

I threw a hasty glance around, and exclaimed:

"Pray, madam, be cautious. Think what construction
would be placed upon your words should they be overheard."

I looked at her shrinkingly, and even with a feeling of

dread. The intensity she threw into her utterance made her declaration almost as startling as if she had confessed to having killed her husband.

She tossed back her head with a smile filled with obstinacy and scorn. The light was on her, and I noticed the violet hue under her eyes, the thinness of her throat, the paleness of her lips. Indeed, a great change had come over her since the day on which the inspector had been brought to the house by the old lady; a change subtle and physical, exhibited by the wasting, not only of her face, but of her whole figure, and by a hard, subacid expression which appreciably modified the character of her beauty. With her head thrown back, and that strange, scornful smile about her lips, she stared at me with obstinate intentness; and when, neither understanding nor relishing her protracted gaze, I was about to turn away, she said:

"You too suspect me!"

"You wrong me by thinking so," I answered quickly; "nor is there warrant for your belief in anything I have said or done."

She drew a deep breath, and exclaimed:

"You seemed afraid of me. Why should you be scared by the truth? Is it not true that I hate my husband? When I showed you my arm—you remember?—you thought my hate justified. If I were to tell you how he has made me suffer, not with his hands—though God knows he has not spared them—but with his tongue, before I had half gone through the catalogue of his brutalities you would be telling me that you too could have killed him had you been in my place. But have no fear," she added, changing her voice and resuming her scornful smile, "if he has been murdered, his death is owing to no contrivance of mine."

"My only reason in urging you not to speak of yourself as having been sometimes tempted to kill him is that no further excuse may be furnished to people to preserve the abominable suspicion which I fear is current. The Colonel has a very difficult matter to deal with, and looks to you for help. I, who know you, and know how you have suffered, put a very liberal construction on your references to

the past. Your assurance is nothing but a mere form of
words. You could have killed him!—that is, the provocation he gave you was so unendurable that, when you recur to
it, you feel that he goaded you to passions which might
have tempted you to any act of violence. I can sympathize
with the memory—but other people are not so generous.
They will take your words literally, and establish them as
a premise from which to·deduce the crime that the mad old
woman charged you with."

She shrugged her shoulders and turned away, humming
a tune. The movement was a chilling one. I left the
room, resolute, however, not to judge her harshly, knowing how bitter had been her past sufferings, and how heavy
was the trial she was now undergoing.

II

The Colonel returned at one o'clock. I happened to be
in Mrs. Ransome's bedroom, which was over the dining-
room, and heard him call to the under-gardener, who was
at work on the lawn:

"My man, go round to the kitchen and tell them to give
you my portmanteau, and carry it at once to the White
Hart."

"Yes, sir," answered the man; and he added, "I've
searched as you told me, and haven't found nothing."

"Oh, well, I did not expect you would. Give the portmanteau to the people in the bar, and tell them I have
booked for the coach at half-past two. Also request them
to send a fly to be here at two precisely."

These orders announced his speedy departure, and I ran
down-stairs with the intention of hastening forward the
lunch, but met him as I crossed the hall.

"Where is my daughter?" he asked me.

I looked into the drawing-room, and, seeing one of the
windows open, went to it and caught sight of her walking a
little way beyond the terrace. Her head was uncovered,
and her abundant hair gleamed with a violet sheen in the
sun. She was lost in thought, and neither heard nor saw

me until I was addressing her at her elbow. She instantly
followed me to the drawing-room, where her father waited.

"My dear," he exclaimed, in a voice of mild reproof, "I
thought you would have been on the lookout for me."

"I did not know when I was to expect you, papa."

"I have passed a busy morning," he began; but I interrupted him by asking if he meant to lunch at home, that I
might give orders to the cook.

"Susan knows all about that," he answered. "Do not
leave the room, Miss Avory. I have nothing particular to
tell—and if I had you would have every right to hear it.
I went straight to the inspector's office on leaving here, and
had a long interview with him."

"I hope you spoke your mind to him, papa," exclaimed
Mrs. Ransome, firing up at the mention of the man. "I
should like to have been with you. I want an opportunity
to tell him what I think of his conduct."

"You must put aside all resentment," he answered.
"Your cause will not be helped by passion. I caution you
that our situation is more critical than you suppose it. I
forced myself—God knows how reluctantly, and with what
pain—to speak to several persons this morning, and though
it was impossible for me to extort their real opinions from
them, I found, unmistakably, that the prejudice is strong
against you. I cannot explain my discovery by using their
words, but I felt in their superficial sympathy, in their
evasive answers, in their recurrence to Mrs. Ransome's
death, which, it is now going about, is owing to her heart
being broken by the loss of her son."

She stamped her foot, crying, "What an impudent
fiction!"

"You speak of the inspector's insolence," he continued.
"The man met me with great respect; regretted the necessity that had obliged him to enter the house, and pointed
out that, had he not acted on the strong evidence of Mrs.
Ransome and the girl Mary, his enemies would have reported him as unfit for his duties, as wanting zeal and
energy, as being intimidated by rich people, though never
scrupling to enter a poor man's house (which he had occa-

sion to do, he told me, only a fortnight ago). It was not
my policy to be angry with him. It is not my policy to be
angry with anybody just now. The dead woman has raised
up a number of cacklers against us, especially among the
poorer classes. I have to conciliate these people, not insult
them. Is it not so, Miss Avory?"

"Undoubtedly, sir."

"Why should they be conciliated?" cried Mrs. Ransome.
"They must be wretches who can believe what that vile old
thing said of me; and if I only knew how to punish them
for daring to suspect me, I would."

He held his hand up, as if to silence her.

"You must not interrupt me," he exclaimed. "My time
is very short here, and if we get upon these senseless arguments, I shall not be able to explain my intentions to you."

He looked at his watch, and continued:

"I first of all went to the inspector, and was with him
for an hour at least. I told him all about Mr. Ransome
and his madness, and how, among his other habits, was that
of leaving the house mysteriously; that he had often left
his mother's house in this manner, and that she very well
knew it to be one of his eccentricities. I carried out Mr.
Skerlock's suggestions faithfully, by pointing out that it
was owing partly to your ignorance of such matters, and
partly to your dislike to having your name mixed up in a
police affair, that you had not instructed him to follow
Maddox on a charge of robbery. I said that you had no
idea where your husband was, and that you daily expected
his return. I then declared there could be no doubt that
the footman had stolen the plate, and I begged him to lose
no time to make every possible inquiry for the man, since
continuance of the terrible suspicion that had fallen on you
might altogether depend upon his apprehension."

He watched his daughter attentively as he spoke.

"What did the inspector say, sir?" I ventured to ask.

"That he would do his best," he answered; "but that I
mustn't hope for much, seeing the long time the man had
had to make off in." He paused, and added bitterly,
"Miss Avory, that fellow is the most suspicious of the lot."

"But that will not prevent him from obeying your instructions?"

"I do not say," he exclaimed, shaking his head, "that
what I have done has been for the best. In speaking to
him, I more than once doubted the wisdom of my visit.
Respectful as he was, he yet contrived to suggest that he
regarded my instructions as an effort to blind him; and if
he thinks *that*, then, by heaven! he must conclude that I
believe my daughter guilty, and am trying to save her from
detection."

Mrs. Ransome exclaimed, "That man would *oblige* himself to believe me guilty, merely that he might justify himself for his daring outrage."

"That is highly probable, sir," I said. "I do not think
it necessary to allow one's self to be troubled by *his* conclusions. He is a muddle-headed man, with a slow mind,
that would require a long time to rid itself of an impression."

"But," replied the Colonel, "there are many wiseacres
in the town who are satisfied to form their judgments by
his. It is lucky, perhaps, that I *did* assume him suspicious
in my conversation, otherwise I might have been led into
explanations from which, his conclusions being foregone,
he might have picked many details to strengthen his own
views with. I must be chary of explanations. The mere
truth, in the absence of Mr. Ransome and Maddox, cannot
improve our case, and portions of it are likely to injure us,
if those points upon which suspicion is based are kept
back."

"What points?" asked Mrs. Ransome.

"Your wretched quarrels," he answered, flushing up;
"and above all, your reckless, passionate, evil threats."

She hung her head. He took a turn about the room, and
pulled out his watch for the third time, but was so deep in
thought that he kept his eyes fixed upon it for some moments without seeming to know what he was doing.

He looked up suddenly and said:

"Phœbe, I leave at half-past two. I have the address of
the man I want from Mr. Clements." He drew forth his

pocket-book, but replaced it without opening it. "I may be away for a day or two—I cannot say how long. I shall probably employ others as well as this person. Of course I shall return to Gardenhurst and continue living here. But take one caution: unless you can trust your temper, keep yourself hidden. This is a frightful time for me—a horrible term of suspense remains beyond; you must help me hand and heart. You will ruin us both, utterly prejudice your case, and defeat all my efforts, if you suffer your dangerous temper to obtain a mastery over you in your conversations with strangers. We," he exclaimed, pointing to me, "know the truth, but we are alone; it is in your power to help me by your silence, or to crush us both by repeating to whomsoever will listen to you those dreadful threats you have used in your passion to your husband, which, even as you utter them, you seem capable of carrying out."

He walked to the door and she made a movement as though she would run after him; but she drew back proudly, and when he was out of the room, followed leisurely.

There was, beyond all question, great wisdom in his advice to her to keep herself hidden. Her manner, even to her father, was aggressive; she had no control over her temper; and as no subject made her more violently passionate than her husband, so it was really imperative that she should not discuss him and his disappearance with strangers, since it was ten to one that her angry warmth prompted her to some observation to furnish fresh scope for gossip and comment. It was indeed scarcely conceivable to me, who thought I knew the truth perfectly, that people were to be found who gave credit to old Mrs. Ransome's horrible accusation. But this was actually the case, and I remember fearing, as I watched the Colonel drive off, that if his endeavors did not result in some practical discovery, public opinion might become strong enough to force the law into a decided attitude, and subject Mrs. Ransome to the merciless ignominy of a judicial investigation.

Unfortunately I had no friends at Copsford, with the exception of the Campions, who, owing to the manner in which I had defended Mrs. Ransome on the occasion of my

visit to Rose Farm, were very reserved in the expression of
their views. The tradesmen whom we dealt with of course
knew me, and were not likely to risk the loss of our custom
by declaring their opinions. However, by putting the
small evidence I myself collected from signs and shakes of
the head and doubting questions with the evidence that I
extracted from the gossip brought to Gardenhurst by the
cook and the housemaid, I was pretty sure that the Colonel
had not overestimated the gravity of the general feeling.
The public dearly loves a mystery; and when, as in this
case, it is a very personal one, it will commonly show itself
partial to the solutions which are most prejudicial to the
characters of those who are associated with the mystery.

Here was a woman of whom exaggerated accounts had
been diffused of the fierceness of her temper. On a certain
night her husband, with whom she was incessantly quarrelling, and of whom her detestation was no secret, mysteriously disappears. On the same night the footman likewise
mysteriously disappears, and with him or them goes plate
to the value of eight or nine hundred pounds. The infer-
ence drawn by the public, pending the arrival of the old
lady upon the scene, is, either that the footman has murdered the master, or that the master, who is notoriously of
unsound mind, has for some utterly unconjecturable reason
helped the footman to rob the house. Both suppositions
are equally probable. But, meanwhile, no steps are taken
by Mrs. Ransome to recover the plate, neither is a single
inquiry made for the missing husband. Her silence adds
piquancy to the mystery, and fills the public mind with
wonderment. Suddenly old Mrs. Ransome comes forward,
and so convinces the chief constable at Copsford that murder has been done that the house at Gardenhurst is searched.
No discovery is made; but the old lady is not the less persuaded that her son has been murdered; and on the testimony of the girl Mary, who swears to having heard Mrs.
Ransome threaten to kill her husband, she applies for a
warrant against her daughter-in-law, which is refused.
Whereupon she dies, and is commiserated as a broken-
hearted mother.

Speaking for myself, I do honestly say that had I been a perfect stranger to the Ransomes and heard the above story, not as I have abbreviated it, but with all the garnishings which gossip and exaggeration had furnished, I should have entertained serious doubts whether, after all, the old lady might not have had very good reason for concluding that her son had been murdered either by or through the wife; nor can I imagine that any consideration of the man's insanity, of the footman's simultaneous disappearance, of the robbery of the plate, of Mr. Ransome's previous erratic habits, would have shaken the suspicions with which I would have viewed Mrs. Ransome's inactivity.

It is well to keep the circumstances of the mystery steadily in view in order to appreciate the very critical position in which Mrs. Ransome was placed.

III

Colonel Kilmain remained in London three days. At the end of that time he returned to Gardenhurst; but of what he had done I obtained no information further than that he had engaged the services of the man who had been recommended to him, and that this man had expressed his wish that the matter might be left solely in his hands. His reasons for desiring to act alone had satisfied the Colonel, and they were no doubt good. I gathered that this man rated his services at a very high sum; and that, in addition to the money that was to be paid for his work, he was to receive a handsome reward from the Colonel if he made any discovery that would exculpate Mrs. Ransome from all participation in the mystery of the double disappearane.

Life at Gardenhurst, from this point, became a dull and monotonous routine. I scarcely knew how the days passed; they were entirely eventless, and slipped imperceptibly away. I speak as they affected me. As to the Colonel, I know that he lived in a state of constant expectation; that the house-bell never rang but that he was on the alert, looking over the banisters of the landing, or thrusting his head out of the dining-room door and listening eagerly; that he rarely left the house longer than an hour at a time, either walking in the grounds or taking short excursions in the country in a direction away from Copsford, and always re-entering with a face of grave expectation, and inquiring of whomsoever he met if any on had called while he was out.

That he did not occupy himself with any pursuit such, I might suppose, as he beguiled the time for him when he formerly lived at Gardenhurst, I am sure. I have some-times seen him endeavoring to fasten his attention on a book, close it abruptly, and either sink into thought or start up and restlessly pace the room.

He was singularly courteous to me—courteous, indeed, to all with whom he came in contact—but he rarely ad-dressed me without bringing the conversation round to the one subject that absorbed his mind; and repeatedly asked me if I knew what they were still saying at Copsford about his daughter. But I never knew, for the reason I have given. Nor, indeed, was it requisite that I should, so far as his curiosity was concerned; for either through some hired agency, or by his own quick powers of observation, he appeared as thoroughly posted in current Copsford gos-sip as if he were visiting at houses all day long.

Meanwhile the emphatic advice which he had given to his daughter to hold her peace and control her temper had been acted on by her with a result which rendered her an-other woman. Her father's conduct, his profound anxiety, his feverish restlessness, and the physical change in him that had been wrought by his troubles, had impressed upon her the gravity of her situation as no words could have done. Then, again, her pride has been roused and wounded by his reproaches and angry injunctions, and she was plainly determined to give him no further reason to reprimand her for the passionate expression of her feelings. She became silent, cold, impassive. Her beauty had a wasted air; but one might easily see by her eyes that the spirit in her was controlled, not quenched; that there was a fever in her heart, though her tongue was still; that memory, bitter at all times, was the more poignant now that it was prohibited the relief of expression.

Her manner to me was kind, but without the cordiality that used to make it grateful. She had no longer any confidences to impart. The load of responsibility had been taken from her by her father; her silence disdained sympathy. She was indeed a changed woman, but—with the stinging sense of shame in her, with bitter remorse to haunt her, with her haughty dissembled love for her father hourly fretted by the sight of his restless anxiety—more miserable than ever she had been while she lived with her husband.

One morning, about three weeks after the Colonel's return from London, Susan came into my room with her eyes red with tears. I asked her what was the matter.

"Why, miss," she said, pulling a letter from her pocket, "I received this just now from father, and he says I mustn't stop here, but go home at once."

"How is that?" I exclaimed.

"He says," she answered, quite sobbing as she spoke, "that the stories which are told of this house make it not proper for me to remain here. He says he don't want to put his opinion in writing, for he knows his place, and other people's business is no affair of his; but a neighbor declares that, if he had a daughter, he wouldn't let her be servant in a house which has got a bad name, and he's quite of that opinion, and I must come home at once."

"We shall be very sorry to lose you," I said, thinking it best to make no further comment, but not a little startled by this very strong illustration of the tenacity and malignancy of the gossip that was afloat.

"It goes very much against me," she cried, "to leave like this. I don't believe a word of the wicked stories that are told. Mrs. Ransome has always treated me well, and it's a pleasure to serve under you; and I know mistress will think me ungrateful and bad-hearted for going away. Yet I daren't disobey father."

"I am sure Mrs. Ransome would not wish you to do so," I answered.

"But what excuse am I to make for going? I mustn't give her the true reason; and unless I tell a falsehood, which I don't want to do, she'll think me heartless."

"If you like," I said, "I will explain the matter to Mrs. Ransome."

The truth was an ugly one to tell; but it seemed to me proper that it should be told, both for the girl's sake and for the Colonel's, who, by this instance, would obtain a new view of the extent and mischief of the current reports.

She thanked me, and begged me to add that she would never have left of her own accord. I asked if the letter contained anything she did not wish me to see. No. She handed it to me, and I found its contents exactly as she had represented them, tolerably well-worded, and very emphatic.

I told her I would return it when I had seen Mrs. Ransome and went up-stairs.

The Colonel and his daughter were together in the dining-room. They had just finished breakfast, and were still at the table when I entered.

"I hardly know, sir," I began, "how to discharge my errand; but I am sure my duty is not to conceal anything from you."

He looked at me inquiringly. Mrs. Ransome clasped her hands firmly on the table. I drew out the letter; the Colonel read it, looked at the address on the envelope, and understood the whole thing at once.

His face was a shade paler, and his voice slightly trembled, as he said:

"Who is the girl's father?"

"He keeps a little shop," I answered, "at the top of High Street, I believe, sir."

Mrs. Ransome looked at the letter, but did not ask to read it.

"Susan," I continued, "came to me in tears, and told me of her father's wish. She has no desire to go, but she does not like to disobey her father, and so I offered to explain the matter to you and Mrs. Ransome. I thought it best that you should know the truth; moreover, it is but justice to an excellent girl that the real cause of her leaving should be explained."

"Phœbe, this concerns your maid—read it," he said.

17

She ran her eyes over the letter; I saw them sparkle.
She looked at me, seemed about to speak, bit her lip, and
flung the letter down.

The Colonel left his chair and paced about the room.

"Does he carry any weight with him, this little tradesman?" he exclaimed, pointing to the letter.

"I should imagine not. I never saw his shop, and I
don't know what he sells. But I gather, from what Susan
has told me, that he is in what is called a small way."

"He is not mixed up with any religious sect here, I
mean? He doesn't preach and preside over meetings, and
that sort of thing?"

"I do not know, sir."

He read the letter again, frowned, thrust it into the envelope, and handed it to me.

"How little it needs to prejudice men's minds!" he exclaimed. "All the memories that cluster about this house
cannot save it from a petty tradesman's suspicions. The
home of a family who for generations have borne the character of, and been honored as, harmless, upright people, innocent in their pleasures, generous in charity, manly and
honest in their dealings with their fellow-men, has ceased
to be a fit place for a servant, forsooth, to live in!"

"Since she is to go, let her go at once," said Mrs. Ransome. "She ought not to be allowed to stop five minutes
in the house."

"She is not to blame, madam. The poor creature is crying at the thoughts of leaving you;" I replied.

"Did you not hear Miss Avory say that before, Phœbe?"
cried the Colonel. "The girl sheds tears to leave you, and
you would thrust her from the house for her attachment."

"Oh, papa, a letter like that makes me hate the whole
world," she rejoined, pushing her chair away from the table.
And then she sprang up and hurried out of the room.

"She *is* to be pitied," said the Colonel, looking at me de-
precatingly. "That letter is a cruel stab."

"The girl will go home and tell the truth," I answered.
"A few emissaries like her to give the lie direct to the
reckless chattering that is going on would do good."

"I suppose time will right us," he exclaimed. "But this ordeal grows so trying that I sometimes doubt if I shall be able to go through it. I would leave Gardenhurst to-morrow and sell the estate, and wash my hands of this unjust, scandalizing neighborhood, did I not fear that our departure would be interpreted as a tacit confession of my daughter's guilt. *How* can people suffer themselves to be prejudiced by reports which have not a grain of evidence to substantiate them? And yet I know that the prejudice is great. Mr. Skerlock keeps me *au courant* of public opinion, and though he tries his best to soften the news he gives me, he has to own that every day which increases the time of Mr. Ransome's absence deepens the curiosity and darkens the suspicions with which people regale each other."

"One would almost think, sir, that you must have enemies at Copsford. Otherwise, how comes this affair, which is really nobody's business but yours and Mrs. Ransome's, to take so prominent a place in people's thoughts and conversation? In London the subject would be forgotten in a day, unless the newsmongers kept it alive. I would give it a month at the very outside to live in a lazy place like Copsford; but I could not imagine it would occupy people's attention longer, unless there were enemies who made it their occupation to keep it perpetually on the *tapis*."

"We *have* enemies, and I know who they are, too—a family with whom Mrs. Ransome was on friendly terms before her marriage. There are three girls, or rather women, highly religious, regular attendants at church, who, I know for a fact, are incessantly talking about Mr. Ransome's disappearance, and compassionating the death of the broken-hearted mother. A single taper will light many lamps. A single tongue is enough to re-illumine a subject as fast as it dies out. These people are the Sneerwell, Backbite, and Crabwell of Copsford. Look at this."

He went to the sideboard, opened a drawer, and took out a newspaper, and handed it to me, with his finger pointing to a particular place in it. The passage was a letter addressed to the editor of the "Copsford Intelligencer," and was signed "Justitia." I forget how it ran, but it was to

the effect that: In May, 18—, a man named Jacobson, liv·
ing with his nephew, was reported missing. Search was
made, and the nephew was as active in the search as the
police, offering, indeed, a reward of five pounds (a large sum
for a poor man) to anybody who should discover his uncle.
The search came to nothing, and the matter passed out of
the public mind, until it was revived by a whisper, originating anywhere, that the nephew had murdered his uncle.
The poor man's house was broken open, but nothing crimi-
nating found. Nevertheless, a warrant was issued, and
he was brought before the magistrates, but discharged for
want of evidence. Three years after the nephew received
a letter from Jacobson, dated from Australia, accounting
for his mysterious departure, and remitting a bank-bill.
By paralleling this case, "Justitia" went on to say, with a
recent local affair of great notoriety, it was manifest there
were two laws—one for the rich, and one for the poor. Had
the individual who figured in the recent local affair been a
poor woman, was it to be doubted that she would have been
haled before the magistrates and examined on the striking
circumstantial evidence which, if rumor was to be credited,
was to be produced? In saying this, the writer wished it
to be understood that he was not actuated by malice. The
individual to whom he referred was personally unknown to
him, and, as proof that he was unbiassed, he heartily wished
her a speedy deliverance from the very curious dilemma in
which she was involved.

"I am surprised that a newspaper should insert such a
letter as that," I exclaimed, restoring the sheet to the drawer
from which the Colonel had taken it. "It is utterly un-
called for. It offers no suggestion. It is of no conceivable use."

"Except to keep the public prejudice alive," he answered;
"and that is what the writer intends."

"Do you know who the author is, sir?"

"Yes: the youngest of the three women I have spoken
of, who used to be friends of my daughter and pretend to
be so still; for she tells me they called here after Mr. Ransome was missing to offer their sympathy and so forth. I

heard the name of the writer from a man who is under a
trifling obligation to me, and who is odd enough to like me
for having obliged him. He had it from the editor of the
paper, who is his crony—one Wilkinson—whom I think I
could reach through the law of libel; but what good would
that do?"

"It is the letter of a despicable coward, sir."

"I do not value it for itself at that," he cried, snapping
his fingers. "Worse than has already been said nobody can
say."

But his manner persuaded me that he did mind it; he was
deeply wounded by it and bitterly distressed.

"All this gossip, all these stabbings in the dark, merely
keep alive my anxiety to receive news from Johnson—I
mean the fellow who is looking for Mr. Ransome. He has
been three weeks at work now, and has not written a line.
But this was understood. He said he would write either to
announce a discovery or to tell me that the adventure was
a hopeless one. You may judge with what misgivings I
await the postman's visits. But I *have* a hope—a hope I
cannot extinguish—that Mr. Ransome will return. Would
to God he would come soon, and end this horrible suspense!
You notice a change in Mrs. Ransome, do you not?"

"Yes, sir."

"She is reserved—at last! She has learned to hold her
tongue. You will do me a service, Miss Avory, by avoiding, as much as you possibly can, all reference to the subject of her husband and the prejudice against her among
the people. A discussion may undo the victory she is gaining over her temper, and make her dangerous to her own
cause again."

I promised to be on my guard, though there was little
need to say so; for, as I have already said, her manner had
greatly changed toward me, and the few conversations we
held together were very prosaic, and almost entirely referred
to the affairs of the house.

I returned to my room, and there found Susan. The atmosphere was haunted by a faint, familiar perfume, which
made me say:

"Has Mrs. Ransome been here?"

"Yes, miss; I have been waiting to tell you. She gave me this."

She pulled a ten-pound note from her pocket.

"She's too good," the poor girl whimpered. "She makes me feel a wretch for leaving her in her trouble. But father's so stern that, if I didn't leave on my own accord, he'd come and fetch me. But, thank God, I've told her that father's reason for taking me away was sinful and false, and I'll tell him so. Mrs. Ransome is a wronged woman; and if I had to go to prison for declaring her innocence, I'd go gladly."

I told her that her father would probably let her return when she had pointed out the injustice of his suspicions and explained, as she well could, the cruel treatment her mistress had received from Mr. Ransome, and the mean, aggressive, malignant character of the old lady. I added that she could serve Mrs. Ransome by disproving the reports she might hear; and I then bade her go to the Colonel and wish him good-by, believing that it would cheer the poor old gentleman to learn what a firm adherent his daughter had in a girl who was infinitely better qualified than the shrewdest outsider to judge of the truth of the rumors that were circulated.

So terminated this incident. It became my business to find another housemaid; and I went to Copsford that day and left word of our want at several shops; not without a misgiving, however, that if the prejudice against Mrs. Ransome were as strong as I might suppose it by the removal of Susan, we might have some difficulty in getting another servant. However, my fear proved groundless; for next day three girls called, one of whom I selected, chiefly on account of her belonging to the factory town that lay beyond the hills, and out of the small-talk that was agitating the Copsford mind.

IV

The autumn passed, and the early month of winter came—
November, laden with gray clouds and chill winds which
stripped the trees of their few remaining leaves.

During all this time no change had occurred in the house.
A shadow was upon the two principal occupants of it which
kept them silent and gloomy and melancholy.

Of the two, the Colonel seemed the greater sufferer. His
anxiety was feverish at times. He had grown so thin that
he resembled a sick man. He slept but little, for often I
would hear him pacing his room at night; and he was usually down of a morning long before the servants had left
their beds. More than four months had elapsed since Mr.
Ransome had been found missing, and not the smallest clue
had been obtained as yet of his whereabouts. Was he dead?
The Colonel once asked me this question, and watched me
with wild anxiety; as if my answer could prove anything.
If he were dead, and proofs of his death could not be procured, Mrs. Ransome's name was virtually banned for life.
Her father might remove her; he might exile himself with
her; but the mystery would live always; suspicion would
become conviction; and her name would be associated in
people's minds with the commission of murder.

The Colonel owned now that he would cheerfully throw
his grounds and house open to the strictest search that could
be instituted. He longed for any proof, negative or positive. The mystery possessed him so entirely that it generated dangerous delusions. The horrible suspicion that his
daughter might be guilty again returned to him. I never
knew what conversations he had with her; but by putting
together the circumstances of her keeping her room a whole
day, and his asking me in the morning, shortly after his
daughter had left the dining-room, many strange questions
about her, I came to the conclusion that the dreadful misgiving which, by his demeanor, had plainly agitated him
for a week past had finally mastered him, and that he had

put her through an examination which could leave her in no doubt as to his thoughts.

For myself, the practical conjectures which I might have hazarded, had I been an eye-witness instead of an actor in these strange events, were disturbed and baffled and forced into over-reaching subtleties by the influences that surrounded me. I tried to strip the facts of all the adventitious garnishings they had been furnished with by gossip, by old Mrs. Ransome's accusations, and, in a special degree, by the disappearance of Maddox, which had complicated the mystery at the very threshold of it. But I could not satisfy myself. Bewildering considerations were perpetually recurring. Where were these two men? How was it that no trace of either of them was to be obtained? The inspector, we had heard, had done his best—that is to say, he had done nothing at all but advertised more capable men of the "want," and they had been seeking Maddox for three months. Other difficulties which encumbered the mystery lay in our inability to assign a motive for Mr. Ransome's prolonged absence; for the attitude his mother had adopted, which was genuine as regarded her belief in her son having been murdered, as more than one witness who sympathized with the Colonel and his daughter testified; and the impossibility of proving that Maddox and his master did not act in concert on that night of their disappearance. The public had evidently hoped to cut the knot by accepting old Mrs. Ransome's statement. But that still left the enigma of the footman's disappearance untouched.

I confess the whole matter was a great puzzle to me. When I had got hold of a thought that seemed extremely likely, it was met by another thought which proved it in the last degree impossible. And though I might try and bare the facts, extrinsic considerations were perpetually coloring them and draping them afresh.

But one morning toward the end of November came very exciting news.

I had risen rather later than usual, owing to a cold I had taken on the previous day, and it was nearly half-past eight before I left my room. On my way down-stairs I had heard the Colonel and his daughter talking rapidly and excitedly, and was quite at a loss to conceive what could have taken him to Mrs. Ransome's bedroom at that early hour.

The morning was a miserable one. Not a gleam of sunshine, and a high piercing wind that splashed the rain, mingled with sleet and hail, against the windows. The grounds, through the glass blurred with wet, looked miserably forlorn; the trees bare, black, and unbending to the gale that swept through them with a noise as of thunder.

I shivered, and hastened to the comfortable fire in my room, and sat brooding over it, sipping a cup of tea, depressed as a cold always depresses one.

In this way twenty minutes passed, and then the housemaid knocked at my door, and said I was wanted. I had been very often wanted since I had been in that house, and very frequently on eventful occasions. I went up-stairs, expecting I know not what news. Father and daughter were together, the Colonel in a great state of excitement—his eyes shining, his face red, walking hastily about the room. Mrs. Ransome was far more collected; quite white, hard in the face as a stone. She played with the food on her plate with a fork; the Colonel's breakfast was untouched; the coffee smoked in the cup, some ham was on a plate—he had helped himself and forgotten to eat.

He passed me hastily, shut the door, and retaining his hold of the handle, exclaimed:

"Mr. Ransome is alive; he has been discovered."

"Is it possible?" I answered, imitating his tone, and speaking in a loud whisper.

"I have Johnson's letter in my pocket. He has been all this time hunting for him. He has found him at last! God be thanked!"

"This is welcome news, sir."

"Doubly welcome, because I had given up all hope. There's a clever dog, this Johnson!" he exclaimed, chuckling and rubbing his hands together. "What patience! what shrewdness! what slow, unerring sagacity he has displayed! Oh, Phœbe! he has saved you! What will the miscreants who have talked about you say now? We will

have him here—we will make a show of Mr. Saville Ransome! We will oblige the scoundrel to show his face, and
prove your innocence! and then——"

Mrs. Ransome lifted her stony face, scarcely the less
beautiful for being passionless, and said:

"Then what?"

He looked at her and then at me, and answered:

"That is an after consideration. We shall have to find
out how mad he is, and act upon our discovery. Could I
have my way, I would flog him every day for a week, and
then kick him into the wide world again. He is a vaga-
bond by nature—I would keep him one!"

"Papa," she said, "I have told you once, I repeat now,
and Miss Avory shall bear me witness, no earthly power
shall ever induce me to live for an hour under the same roof
with him, to look at him, to utter one word to him. He
is no longer my husband. I renounce him before you both;
and may God punish me if by any compulsion, or through
any impulse, I swerve for an instant from my resolution."

The flush in her cheeks faded quickly out, she pushed
her plate from her, clasped her hands, and looked fixedly
downward.

"I would rather see you dead at my feet," he replied,
"than have you own him as your husband. Have no fear;
your separation dates from the day of his disappearance;
and never, while I live, should I suffer you to be reunited.
But you will see him, and pronounce him to be the villain
who has heaped this horrible scandal upon you. That declaration will be your acquittal. Then we will leave this
place, accursed to me by that man, forever. Do you follow
me? Make no foolish vows—suffer no temper to possess
you. Your opposition may ruin us on the very threshold
of our escape from this terrible dilemma. Miss Avory, you
are of my opinion? Mrs. Ransome must not act for herself. She must do as I wish. Is it not so?"

"I am sure Mrs. Ransome will not oppose you, sir," I
answered.

He drew a letter from his pocket, and, without opening
it, said:

"Johnson writes that Mr. Ransome is in lodgings just out of Oxford Street, London. He knows he is the man he wants by the portrait he has of him, by the written description he had from me, by the fact of his having been in that lodging four months. This is good evidence; but more follows. The landlady of the house has been pumped, and her information is to this effect: that her lodger came from the country; that his habits are eccentric—for instance, he keeps within doors all day, and steals forth mysteriously at night; that he has given strict orders to be denied to any caller. He has obviously no pursuit; the landlady is utterly ignorant of the place he comes from, of his former occupation (if he had any), and of his right name—for she has strong reasons for suspecting the name that he goes under, namely, Cleveland, to be false."

"If he is not Mr. Ransome, he ought to be!" I exclaimed. "The description fits him well."

"Yes," he cried triumphantly; "and bear in mind that these are only characteristics which Johnson describes. His face, he says, is that of the man whose portrait he has. By this time to-morrow I shall know certainly. I am to see him to-night."

He looked at the clock and then hastily seated himself and fell to his breakfast, forcing himself to eat and drink.

"Do you mean that he should return with you, sir?"

"Certainly," he answered. "He must come to this house. He must be seen and addressed by several persons— then let him go! my end will have been served."

"But if he should refuse to accompany you?"

Mrs. Ransome looked up at this question.

"I shall find a means of compelling him," answered the Colonel. But all the same, he gazed doubtfully at me, for this consideration evidently had not occurred to him before.

"Johnson would advise you on this matter, sir, and show you how it is to be managed," I said.

"I see two ways of dealing with him. He could be apprehended as a madman at once, or I could threaten him with the madhouse in case of his refusal to accompany me. To judge by your own experience, Miss Avory, and by mine

too, for the matter of that, he is to be easily influenced by
that threat."

"Why must he be brought here?" demanded Mrs. Ransome.

"To prove his mother a liar!" answered the Colonel
passionately. "How shall we bear witness to your innocence if he is not seen by those who believe in your guilt?"

"But if he is proved to be living, no matter by whom,
will not that suffice?" she asked.

"It is far better," I put in, "that he should be recognized
by those who profess to know that he is dead. Out of
Copsford, people are ignorant of this affair; and it would
be a mistake to spread the story of it by bringing in out-
siders to give their evidence who, perhaps, would not convince the people here after all, since it might be reported
that these witnesses were paid by you to give false evidence."

"Quite so," exclaimed the Colonel. "And remember
that our actions need have no reference to any one but the
liars and scandalmongers of Copsford. You have not to
prove your innocence to the law or to the world, but to a
handful of despicable gossips who are to be convinced only
by their eyes." He added emphatically, "I wish you would
see things in their proper light, Phœbe."

"I hate him so," she muttered, "that I abhor the
thoughts of having to confront him."

The Colonel left the table.

"Miss Avory, will you kindly fetch my travelling bag?"

"Shall I send for a fly, sir?"

"No, I will walk. I must post to L—— and catch the
up coach which reaches London at six."

I went to get his bag, and when I returned he was standing in the hall, and Mrs. Ransome was speaking to him from
the dining-room door. She kissed her hand and withdrew.
He took the bag from me and opened the hall door. There
was a drizzling rain, and the high wind made it penetrating.
I again begged permission to send for a fly, but he said he
could not wait; his overcoat was a thick one and would protect him. He lingered a moment, and added:

"There is a great change in my daughter's character. I thought this news would have put her in high spirits. But do you notice how cold and impassive she is? One might think that the discovery of this man involved anybody's reputation but hers."

"She has disciplined herself according to your wishes, sir. Depend upon it, she is not the less sensible of this great good fortune because she bears it with composure."

"Perhaps so," he answered hurriedly. "Good-by, Miss Avory."

He turned up his coat-collar and went into the rain. I was glad to shut the door, for the wind chilled me to the bones, and was perhaps responsible for the quite unnecessary depression that hung about me. Hearty, iron winter, with its vast stretches of snow, and the glorious sunlight scintillating on the ice-coated trees, I love; but this dreary November, this month of sopping rains and earthy smells and cold, unwholesome damps, is a depression and a curse.

The dining-room door was open, and I saw Mrs. Ransome bending over the fire, which roared in flames up the chimney. She saw me as I passed, and called to me.

"Papa will have a cheerless journey," she exclaimed. "What do you think of the letter he received? Do you believe the man has found Mr. Ransome?"

"The description tallies, does it not?"

"I do not greatly value that part about his having been in the lodgings four months, and his stealing out at night, and his name being assumed," she said, chafing her hands quite close to the flames. "I rest my hope on the face answering to the portrait and description. But even there I have doubts. If Mr. Ransome feared pursuit—I assume this as a theory, I don't say he does; he is a madman who defies conjecture—he would disguise himself. In that case, the detective, or whatever he is, would not know him by the description."

"He could not change his face."

"He could shave off his mustache and let his whiskers grow; and then no stranger would be able to identify him with the portrait I gave papa."

"But it is evident," I said, "that he hasn't disguised himself. Besides, we must have confidence in the experience of the man Colonel Kilmain has employed. He would hardly write before he was convinced that the man was Mr. Ransome."

She was silent. The bright flames flashed in her eyes, and so colored her face as to make her complexion brilliant. The attitude she was in finely exhibited the great beauties of her figure. Her rings glittered upon her fingers, and her thick hair looked like ebony in contrast with the ruby glare of the fire.

"Do *you* not think," I asked, "that the man of whom the detective writes is your husband?"

"Do not speak of Mr. Ransome as my husband, Miss Avory," she answered quickly. "You heard what I said just now before papa. He is less to me than the smallest fragment of those ashes there. I abhor the sound of his name. Not the least curse that this wretch has visited on me is my being obliged by the force of circumstances to think and speak of him constantly. When you name him, call him what you please—anything but my husband."

She spoke with great emphasis, but without passion. The experience she was living through was so far beneficial to her that it had taught her to subdue her temper. Time was when the remonstrance she had just spoken would have been delivered with flashing eyes and a face of anger.

She continued in a moment or two:

"You asked me if I think this man whom papa has gone to see is Mr. Ransome. I answer, no."

I looked at her with surprise.

"I told papa my opinion when he read me the letter. The impression is instinctive—what else?" She glanced at me. "And of course he was angry, because his heart is in this discovery—our reputation, our honor, and my future involved in it; and he believes the man is found. I do not. I believe the man is dead."

She ceased, looking intently at the fire. Finding me silent, she fixed her eyes on me with a curious smile, and said:

"Why don't you ask me why I think he is dead? Are you ever troubled by the same suspicion of me that haunts papa?—a suspicion that turned me into stone when I first understood it, but to which I have accustomed myself; because I reason that, if one can doubt me, why not all—my own father, and you, who, were you a relative, could not know me more intimately than you do?"

The scornful smile again played over her mouth.

"Mrs. Ransome," I said, "why do you put such a question to me? I have told your father that I believe in your innocence as I believe in my own. I should be mad indeed if I doubted you."

"Why?" she asked, very quietly. "Take the trouble to recall what you know. Then assume my guilt, and see if you cannot establish it. Shall I help you?"

I made no reply.

"On the night of Mr. Ransome's disappearance," she continued, "you heard noises, did you not?—the turning of the handle of a door, the sound of a footstep on the landing; is it not so? I told you that I myself had heard Mr. Ransome enter his bedroom. Let us call the hour eleven. He was found missing, let us say, at eight o'clock next morning—not before. From eleven till eight is nine hours. In that long time a greater bungler than one who was impelled by a hate no words can express would have finished the task completely, disturbed the room to suggest a robbery, and obliterated every sign that might lead to the discovery of murder."

I stared at her with astonishment.

"You have thought of all this—confess, Miss Avory!" she exclaimed, with a laugh. "And I'll tell you something more that has troubled you—where I could have hidden the body. Oh!" she cried, clenching her small hand; "but for this pastime of thinking how I *could* have killed him, I should go mad over the horrible monotony of our one speculation—where is he?"

"Pray remember your father's injunction," I said, while she laughed again at my startled face; "consider the consequences if you should be overheard."

"What would you have me talk about? May I not vary
at the theme from my diversion? You are a very cautious
body, I know—quite Scotch in your slow approaches to a
thought. Suppose the suspicion that has occurred to my
father should have occurred to you?"

"It never has."

"May I not be allowed to sport with it?"

"But the sport is full of danger," I replied, scarcely
knowing whether her trouble had not unhinged her mind.

"Well then," she replied, preserving her ironical tone
and sarcastic smile, "let us go back to what we were saying. I wanted to know why you did not ask me my reason
for supposing Mr. Ransome dead?"

"Since you wish it, I will ask you now."

"How I could frighten you if I pleased! If I were an
actress now, to scowl and mutter and wave my hand and
cry, "No matter!" and exhibit other alarming suspicions
of guilt after the stereotyped fashion. But I must descend
to prose; so forgive me for disappointing the uncomfortable
fancies I have raised by saying that I think Mr. Ransome
dead merely because he stops so long away."

She threw her head back and laughed hysterically. The
note in her laughter made me understand her mental condition. It was now plain that the excitement with which
the letter her father had received had filled her had been
rendered dangerous by suppression; and the internal irritation to which its concealment had subjected her nerves was
now beginning to tell. My surprise left me; but not to appear to change the subject too abruptly, I said:

"We must hope that he is not dead."

"We must hope that he is. Why should such a man
live?" she exclaimed with gathering excitement.

"For yours and Colonel Kilmain's sake," I replied, "it
is essentially necessary that he should be discovered."

"Ay, and then let him die," she cried out, with a loud
peal of laughter.

A moment after she was in hysterics. I had locked the
door, and was holding her down upon the sofa in less time
than I could have counted twenty. I would not call for as-

aistance lest, in her attack, she should repeat some of the wild things she had been saying. It was well I took the precaution. For a time she was positively delirious, seemed to think her husband present, and tore at the sleeve of her dress, and held up her arm, and bade him look at his finger-marks, and then shrieked out that she would have his life. Her struggles were so great that she threw me down, but I was up again in a moment, sitting on her, and pinning her to the sofa with all my strength. Extraordinary fancies possessed her. At one moment she cried out that there was a hearse at the door, and then exhorted me to order the coffin out of the room. Did I not see it? Look, there it was on the table! Afterward a skeleton menaced her from the window. She writhed, and screamed, and shuddered, beating the air with her tossing arms, and changing her screams into wild peals of laughter, which subsided after a while into sobs, and then the fit gradually passed away.

Meanwhile, somebody outside had been hammering at the door with a persistency perfectly maddening. But not until Mrs. Ransome was exhausted did I choose to pay attention to the sound, and, suddenly looking out, I found the cook and the housemaid, ghastly pale, and evidently laboring under some horrible impression.

"For God's sake, what is it, miss?" they cried.

I answered that Mrs. Ransome had been attacked with hysterics, and bade the housemaid get me some water and a glass. They saw into the room, and therefore knew that I spoke the truth. Off they ran, and one brought a glass and another a jug, which I took, and shut the door in their faces.

Hysterics are not very alarming in our sex. The fit passed from Mrs. Ransome with her sobs, leaving her a little shaken, but not paler than she was before. I hung about her for a time, forcing what cheerful subjects I could think of upon her mind, stirring the fire so as to keep it merrily roaring, and doing my utmost to save her from a relapse.

She did not recur to what she had said before the fit took her. To speak the truth, I don't believe she knew what

18

she had said. When she looked out of the window and saw
the drizzling rain and gleaming grounds, she spoke of her
father's journey; but there was no nearer reference than
that in her conversation to the subject that had made
her ill.

It was very fortunate for my peace of mind that she *had*
fallen into hysterics. Had she remained cool, I must certainly have taken her remarks seriously; and it is not at all
improbable but that the suspicions which she pretended to
think I possessed would have been excited in me. Even
as it was, her ironical, hysterical badinage had put thoughts
into my head which would never have entered without any
help. For instance, when I would recall her father's suspicion of her, I speculated on the evidence there might be
against her to justify his misgivings, and never found any.
But, thanks to her own mocking suggestions, I could understand now that it was possible to imagine her guilty without grossly violating probability. What were her own
words? That there were nine hours, from the time of Mr.
Ransome's entering his bedroom to the time when it was
discovered that he had not occupied his bed, in which to
put an end to his life and remove all traces of the deed. I
had never thought of that before. I was sorry to have to
think of it now. The coquetting with such a theory was a
ghastly amusement. I could only be thankful, both for her
own and her father's sake, that she had made *me* only the
butt of her tragical humors.

V

I might hope now that the mystery which had puzzled
everybody for the last five months was about to be solved,
and all the trouble and suspicion it had brought melt into
thin air.

It was not to be supposed that the man employed by Colonel Kilmain, after promising to write only in the event of
utter failure or complete success, would, after four months
of patient inquiry, during which he would in all probability
have met with several men sufficiently like Mr. Ransome to

put him on his guard against being duped by a passable resemblance, commit himself to such a deliberate assurance as would take the Colonel post-haste to London, without good and sufficient reason.

We at Gardenhurst had nothing to do but await the issue of the adventure. That the man living in lodgings out of Oxford Street, London, was Mr. Ransome was one thing; that Colonel Kilmain could induce Mr. Ransome to accompany him to Gardenhurst was another thing. In this last arrangement I anticipated a very serious hitch would take place; and how the Colonel would manage I could not guess.

So that day passed, and the next, and a third, and the Colonel neither wrote nor returned.

Meanwhile Mrs. Ransome had resumed her reserve. She was, to all appearance, as lifeless, cold, and indifferent as if her father's quest were of less concern to her than to me. I could not comprehend this disposition, which was not to be accounted for by assigning it to the belief of her husband's death which she had expressed. Unless she positively knew that he was dead—and of course I was perfectly sure she did not—she ought, in all reason, to have found some cause of excitement, of anxiety, of curiosity, of hope, in the issue which any near day was to expose. She appeared to me to be governed by a sense of unendurable wrong, which turned her into stone, dried up all of the sources of passion and feeling, and left her a mere image, barely directed by mechanical instincts. If this were the true cause of her dead and icy behavior, it was, beyond all question, in a large measure owing to the suspicion her father had entertained against her. The prejudice and the hostile accusations of strangers and acquaintances had heated her to passion and scorn; but her father's doubt would break her down, transmute her nature into rock, and fill her with that sense of utter loneliness which forces all feeling, passion, and emotion inward, and makes the soul heedless of her own interests, and of all the influences and movements which surround her.

The fourth day since the Colonel's departure came and went. Had the detective mistaken the man he had sum-

moned the Colonel to see? Surely Mrs. Ransome would receive a letter next morning. I confess I awaited news with
profound eagerness and curiosity. But the fifth morning
came and brought no letter.

That was a wintry day, I remember: bleak and dry, with
spaces of snow stretched among the hills and a steel-colored
sky. The fires burned fiercely, and in the passages of the
house one's breath rose like steam. The birds made black
knots among the bare branches; and sounds from the town—
the ringing of bells, the cries of men, the rattling of
wheels—came thin and clear through the air up to the
heights where Gardenhurst stood.

The morning passed. I saw Mrs. Ransome, but she made
no comment on her father's silence; and ardent as my own
curiosity was, I had not the courage to thrust my conjectures
upon her frigid reserve.

At three o'clock in the afternoon I was in my bedroom,
when I heard the sounds of carriage-wheels rolling over the
iron ground of the avenue. I threw open the door and went
out on to the landing and listened. The hall bell pealed
and I hurried down-stairs. My idea was that the Colonel
had returned with Mr. Ransome, and my curiosity was so
superior to all other considerations that I would not have
missed being in the hall to receive the runaway, to see
whether he was changed, to hear what he would say, for a
purse full of money. This may seem improper; but I am
quite willing to admit that in a large number of points I was
not a jot better than I should be.

I was in the hall as soon as the housemaid, and I stood
by her side as she opened the door. In came the Colonel,
wrapped in his overcoat, his throat muffled up and his hat
drawn down to his ears. A closed fly stood at the door, and
the horse smoked like newly kindled leaves.

"Where is Mrs. Ransome?" the Colonel exclaimed, paus-
ing a moment before passing through the anteroom. Yet
he was too impatient even to wait for an answer, for he ran
through the room, and the door blew to behind him with a
bang.

‾ ‾ ‾   ‾ ‾ ‾ ‾ ‾ ‾ ‾ ‾ but it was empty. The driver, en-

veloped in a number of capes, pulled out a pipe and a tinder-
box and began to smoke.

"Are you to wait?" I asked him.

He replied that that was his orders.

I closed the door and followed the housemaid down-stairs.

A whole half-hour passed, during which no sound save
the movements of the servants in the kitchen broke the silence that reigned in the house.   Whatever the conversation
was about up-stairs, it was manifestly carried on in very low
voices.   I sat over the fire, listening and wondering what
had brought the Colonel home in such a violent hurry, and
what he had been doing during the last five days, and
whether, by keeping the carriage waiting, he meant to return to London.

At the expiration of the half-hour I heard the Colonel
calling my name from the top of the stairs, and, hastening
from my room, I found him standing in the hall, muffled up
just as he had emerged from the fly.

He beckoned me into the library and shut the door.   He
did not remove his hat, nor did he pull his muffler below
his mouth; the consequence of which was his voice was
smothered and I had to listen intently to catch what he
said.

"Mr. Ransome is found.   We have him at last.   You
will be glad to hear this."

"Sincerely glad, sir," I answered, impressed by the
eager, frightened expression in his eyes, and by the singular
paleness of his face; which signs I attributed to the excitement under which he was laboring.

"I must return at once, for I have to be in London to-
night," he continued, hurrying out his words.   "I would
not bring him to Copsford before apprising my daughter of
the discovery and telling her my plans.   He declares he will
not live with her.   But he has consented to come to this
house for an hour in order to meet such gentlemen as I may
choose to invite and let them see that he is living.   His
stipulation is that on the termination of this interview he is
at liberty to withdraw; and he has exacted a promise from
me neither to follow nor in any way to molest him."

"That is all that you require, sir!" I exclaimed, to the full as excited by the news as he was.

"That's all. I have threatened him with the madhouse should he refuse to accede to my wishes. I told him that my daughter is suspected of having murdered him, and that he alone can clear her of the horrible suspicion."

"But are you not afraid that he will make off while you are here?"

"No; he is watched. I know my man, and do not trust his promises. I must make haste; I hope to return to-morrow."

He waved his hand, hurried out of the library, and before I could reach the hall door the carriage had driven way.

His haste was extremely agitating and flurrying, and though, perhaps, it could not exaggerate the importance of the news he brought, it wonderfully helped to impress its consequence and value upon my mind.

I went to the dining-room, partly because I wanted to hear what Mrs. Ransome had to say, and partly because I believed she would expect me to come to her. I knocked, opened the door, looked in, and found the room empty. The drawing-room was also empty. I tried her bedroom, and there discovered her, with the door locked. She called out that she was lying down, and wished to be alone. So I returned down-stairs.

There was nothing more reasonable than that she should be too much upset for a time by the news her father had brought her to be able to converse. The arrangement agreed on between her husband and the Colonel, though manifestly the most suitable and politic one that could have been entered upon, was not the less extraordinary, and the bare consideration of it would be very trying to her. If I had gathered the Colonel's meaning aright, Mr. Ransome was to meet several gentlemen from Copsford, and having satisfied them that his wife was an innocent woman, quit her forever. This was very well, and as it should be, and what, no doubt, she wanted; but to a woman possessed of her pride the antidote was almost as bad as the bane. The meeting of persons at her house would be the publishing of her

misery; it would be known that her husband refused to live
with her; and ugly constructions would in consequence be
placed on her temper and character. So that she would
only escape one prejudice to become the victim of another.

As these considerations occurred to me, I wondered
whether the Colonel's wisest policy, after all, would not
have been long ago to remove his daughter from Copsford,
and leave the truth to be unfolded by time. There could
be no doubt that Mrs. Ransome's presence in the neighborhood had perpetuated the story, and supplied an incessant
provocation to gossip. But then the Colonel's view was
that his daughter's departure would corroborate suspicion.
Again, the idea of his daughter being followed by suspicion
was unendurable to him; and so sensitive a man would
never have ceased to reproach himself for allowing gossip
to frighten him and his daughter away before he had made
every effort to vindicate her from the infamous charge which
old Mrs. Ransome, dying, had bequeathed to the people of
Copsford.

I had not had time, during our brief exchange of words
in the library, to ask the Colonel if Mr. Ransome had spoken
of Maddox. In all probability, as I had over and over
again surmised, the man had acted without the knowledge
of his master, and had, by accident, hit on the night on
which Mr. Ransome had decamped to commit the robbery.

The Colonel had no doubt spoken of this to his daughter;
and I waited with lively feelings of curiosity for an opportunity to converse with her.

My impatience was not long taxed. Scarcely an hour
had passed since the Colonel had left the house, when I
heard a footstep on the kitchen stair, and Mrs. Ransome
came into my room.

She rarely visited this part of the house now, and I
might be sure, by her coming, that her purpose was to talk
to me about Mr. Ransome.

She closed the door with a little shiver, and complained
of the cold, hugging a shawl over her shoulders about her,
and taking a seat close to the fire. I looked at her face attentively, attracted by an expression that rendered her

beauty almost unfamiliar. I could no more describe it in
words than paint it in colors. A bitter hardness, that set
the mouth as firm as stone, was its abiding characteristic.
But neither resolution nor severity was all that it suggested;
fear was there, suppressed and beaten down, indeed, but
leaving traces of its presence in every glance, in every movement of the lineaments; and there was a submissiveness
about her, too, which had been heretofore utterly foreign to
her haughty bearing.

She spoke of the cold, and was then silent, with her eyes
on the fire. After an interval, she asked if it were I who
had knocked at her door an hour ago? I answered yes.
She was again silent, and her silence puzzled me. If she
did not wish to speak about her husband, why had she
sought me? But it was difficult to understand why she
should not wish to speak of him. Here was a misery, that
had engrossed her for many months, solved at last. In a
few hours the suspicion that had weighed like a nightmare
upon her would be removed. Should not such a removal
fill her with exultation, and so charge her heart with
thoughts and hopes that she would be wild to utter them?

Her silence was so unaccountable and oppressive that I
broke it at last by floundering headlong into the matter
which occupied my mind.

"This is a happy termination of all your troubles, madam.
I am as truly glad to hear that Mr. Ransome is found as if
my own character were involved in the discovery."

She looked up, and said quickly:

"Oh, you know, then, that the man papa went to see is
Mr. Ransome?"

"Yes. Colonel Kilmain hurriedly gave me the news
before he left."

"What did he tell you?"

"That he had found Mr. Ransome, and compelled him by
threats to come and testify to his being alive, by meeting
certain gentlemen whom your father will invite here for the
purpose."

"Was that all?"

"There was no time to say more."

She clasped her hands over her knees, and stared fixedly into the fire.

"Is Mr. Ransome aware of his mother's death?" I asked.

"Oh yes; papa told him, of course," she answered, without looking at me.

"He was fond of his mother. I should think the news would be a great blow to him."

"He would rather have heard of my death, no doubt."

"Was anything said about Maddox, do you know, madam?"

"Oh, Mr. Ransome knows nothing about the footman," she replied, following up my question so rapidly that she almost took the words out of my mouth.

"Then my theory was right, after all!" I exclaimed. "Maddox stole the plate on his own account. I always believed him guilty on the evidence of the book I found in his bedroom."

"Not always. You once agreed with me that he might have acted under Mr. Ransome's instructions."

"Why, yes, madam; at the beginning I did. But that was a long time ago; and in those early days of the mystery we were all too puzzled to be able to think at all."

"You must understand," she said, "that we have only Mr. Ransome's word that Maddox was not concerned with him. Mr. Ransome is as great a liar as his mother, and I should refuse to take his assurance."

She said this warmly, but quickly controlled herself, and looked at me with a smile that accorded ill with the acrimony of her words.

"Has Mr. Ransome explained his object for running away?" I inquired, sensible of and struck by the bitterness of her manner, which was inconsistent with the subject we were discussing, and which was the more apparent for the coating of feeling and interest which she tried to hide it under.

"He is mad!" she exclaimed, with a shrug. "You must find your explanation in that."

"Mad, indeed!" I responded. "Imagine his stopping four months in an out-of-the-way London lodging! What

answer has he to the charge of striving to ruin you by pretending that he was murdered?"

"Miserable coward!" she cried, clenching both hands
spasmodically: "he has no answer.   He is a devil, who
does evil for evil's sake."

"I suppose Colonel Kilmain had great difficulty in obtaining an interview with him?"

"Oh, very great, no doubt. But, Miss Avory," she exclaimed, turning smartly upon me, "you must remember
that my father was in a great hurry, and had no time to relate the whole story to me.   You ask me a great number of
questions, to many of which I can only imagine answers."

I colored up as I said:

"I must apologize for my curiosity.   The subject has occupied our attention for so long a time, that I cannot prevent myself from taking a great interest in it."

"Oh!" she exclaimed, forcing a smile, but looking nevertheless toward the door, as though nothing but a sense of
duty kept her in the room.   "I fully appreciate your sympathy, and gladly tell you all I know.   Mr. Ransome, I
believe, is to return with papa to-morrow, and will stay at
Copsford, I fancy—but of this I am not sure—for a few
hours: long enough to enable him to be present at the meeting which is to take place in this house.   He then leaves
me, and we shall see each other no more.   But now I am
telling you what you know."

I remained silent, not wishing to challenge another reproof.

"I would part with ten years of my life," she continued,
"for Mr. Ransome to give proofs of his being alive by any
other means than that of meeting people in this house.   Of
all the humiliating positions that man has put me in since I
first met him, this will be the worst.   For, do you know
that papa will insist upon his stating his reasons for leaving me; and what will be said when he declares he will not
live with me? when he may utter falsehood after falsehood
to win the sympathy that cowards are never able to get on
without?"

"It is indeed a very hard alternative," I answered; "but

I see no better alternative. Your father wishes to prove the scandalmongers liars; and he is wise in making the proofs thorough—in obtaining men whose testimony will be indisputable to see and speak to this man whom the people think has been murdered."

She made no answer to this; and presently left her chair and took a turn or two about the room. She twitched at her shawl, and exclaimed:

"I am chilled to the bones. There is no fire in my bedroom, and the window-glass is varnished with frost."

"Let me get you a cup of tea, madam."

"No, thank you."

She looked at me steadily, then averted her eyes, and said:

"Mr. Ransome, I believe, does not admit that his leaving me was part of a plot which his mother was to carry out. But there is no doubt that this was his motive."

"You have always thought so," I answered.

"Yes; and papa agrees with me now, and so have you agreed with me sometimes."

"At all events, the theory explains the extraordinary accusation that old Mrs. Ransome made against you."

"You may be sure I am right. And how is such villainy to be met but with deceit? I mean," she added hurriedly, looking at me in a vague way, "when you have a madman to deal with you are privileged to use the best stratagem that occurs to you to render him harmless."

"Unquestionably," I answered, thinking that she referred to the mode in which her father had trapped Mr. Ransome and obliged him to meet witnesses at Gardenhurst.

Her manner changed; she laid her hand on the door, and said, with a smile:

"There is nothing more to be said on the subject at present. We must wait."

"Yes, madam. Please God in a day or two your troubles will be ended, and then I hope Colonel Kilmain will take you away for a change of scene. Your health has been undermined by your anxiety."

"We shall see," she answered; smiled again, and went
out. But before she closed the door I heard her sigh
heavily.

VI

The Colonel did not return next day. The day following was Thursday. At noon I walked to Copsford to make
some purchases, and on my way home met Mrs. Campion.
I at once told her that Mr. Ransome was found, and was
expected to arrive at Gardenhurst with the Colonel every
hour; at which she looked thunderstruck, and exclaimed,
again and again, "Well, I never!"

"So you see," I remarked, "that you have all been
cruelly wronging Mrs. Ransome."

"Yes, indeed. And I feel as if I would rather have bit-
ten my tongue off than said an ill-natured word of her.
But I never believed what was reported. No, I give you
my word I didn't, Miss Avory. What I really expected
was, that she had drove her husband, by her temper, into
running away and committing suicide, or something of that
sort. As to murdering him," she tossed her hands and
shook her head.

"The gossips will have something else to talk about
now," said I.

"Well," she cried, "you have given me a start! Mr.
Ransome found after all this time! What in the name of
goodness has the man been doing with himself?"

"Keeping company with cats," I answered, laughing.
"Living in London lodgings, lying close all day, and creeping forth like a rat at night. If the busybodies here had
only taken the trouble to remember that this miserable individual is *mad*, a vast deal of mischief would have been
saved, and the trouble that has half broken Mrs. Ransome's
heart averted."

"Oh dear!" she cried, "I am as much to blame as anybody; for though I never believed half the things that were
said, I've consented to them by listening without contradicting. How angry Mrs. Parsons will be! All along

she's been saying that Mrs. Ransome killed her husband, and that the law isn't equal. There'll be some jokes at her expense, I warrant. There are others too as confident as confident i' the truth of the story, who won't relish being proved false."

"I quite believe you. We are all so kind and charitable that there's not a man or a woman among us but will take Mrs. Ransome's innocence as a heavy personal disappointment. I must be getting home. Good-by, Mrs. Campion. Remember me to your husband."

The air was nipping, and I walked quickly. The bleak hills made the landscape desolate. On the summits of many of them the snow lay thick and the trees resembled black skeletons upon the white ground. The road was resonant, the hedges looked hard as bayonets, and the wind froze the ploughed lumps of soil in the fields into rocks. When I was close to Gardenhurst a fly, drawn by a single horse, came down the hill and drew up opposite the gateway. From it issued the Colonel, who gave some instructions to the driver. The fly then drove off, going up the hill.

I advanced quickly, and the Colonel, hearing footsteps behind him, halted.

"Oh, is it you, Miss Avory?" he exclaimed. "I saw you just now, but did not recognize you. I have come from Peterham. Mr. Ransome is there. We left by the night-coach from London and arrived this morning at ten. Does my daughter expect me?"

"Yes, sir. She thought you would return yesterday."

"I could not, for reasons I will explain to her. Mr. Ransome refused to go to Copsford. He is stubborn—wretchedly stubborn—as all mad people are. And I dare not be too exacting lest he should defy me by turning tail again."

He was going to knock, but I asked him to step round to the garden entrance where the door might be opened from without. He laughed, and said that he must be losing his memory not to think of this, and walked down the side path hastily. He was muffled up to the throat, just as I had before seen him; his manner was jerky and feverish; he showed no signs of weariness in his movements, though I should have thought, considering the repeated journeys he had taken, that he would by this time be utterly fagged out.

His daughter saw him from the dining-room window, and came out to meet him. They entered the room together, and I went up-stairs to remove my bonnet. When, after ten minutes or thereabouts, I descended, the dining-room door stood open, and the Colonel, hearing my footsteps, called to me. I went in and found them seated before the fire. The Colonel had unmuffled himself, and was warming his hands, red with the cold, by holding them close to the blaze. He requested me to shut the door, and pulled a chair close to the fire, making way himself, and begging me to draw near. However, my self-respect would not permit me to encroach in this manner; so, feigning not to hear, I took a seat at a proper distance and prepared myself to attend to what he should say.

"We desire to have no secrets from you, Miss Avory," he began, assuming a smile which curiously recalled the expression Mrs. Ransome's face had worn two days before when she came to my room after her father had left the house. "You have been in some degree an actor in this strange affair throughout, and deserve our united thanks for the resolute manner in which you have championed our interests. It is only just that I should acquaint you, not only with my actions, but with my intentions."

"I can assure you, sir," I replied, "that I feel an interest very superior to mere curiosity in this affair, and will only be too glad to do anything I can to bring Mrs. Ransome's troubles to a speedy termination."

She turned her head and thanked me with a smile.

"I have put down," he said, first chafing his hands and then drawing forth a pocket-book, "the names of four gentlemen whom I mean to invite here this evening to meet Mr. Ransome. When I have lunched I shall write the letters myself, and must ask you to do me the favor to deliver them at their respective addresses. More than this: you will greatly oblige me by personally seeing these gentlemen, and learning from their own lips whether they can attend or not. The fly that brought me here will return at two o'clock, and by four your round of visits will have been completed."

"Your letters, I suppose, sir, will explain your wishes; and my simple business is to hear whether it is convenient to them to keep the appointment you make."

"That is all. If one or two of them only can come, I must invite others. I consider, in the interests of my daughter, who has been cruelly prejudiced by the false statements of Mr. Ransome's mother, that we cannot do with less than with four credible witnesses—men of position in the town, whose word is unimpeachable."

He turned the leaves of the pocket-book, and read aloud:

"Mr. Skerlock, Dane Villa, High Street; Mr. Ledbury, Homersham House, Queen's Road; Sir Anthony Lauder, The Vale; the Reverend Henry Hastings, 9 Albion Square. The first three are magistrates; the fourth, being a clergyman, will make of course, a highly respectable witness."

"Should any of these gentlemen be out when I call, am I to wait?"

"You must use your judgment, Miss Avory. I would rather have these gentlemen than any others I know. But you must not wait too long; the appointment is for eight o'clock to-night. I must know certainly by five if these gentlemen can attend."

"They may think the notice rather short, sir," I suggested.

"I cannot help that. I have a madman to deal with, and must conform to *him*. He refuses to show himself at Copsford for fear of being hooted. He stipulates to come to and leave this house under cover of night; to remain here only for such a length of time as shall enable the witnesses to see and address him, and then to leave, having already imposed a binding obligation on me not to follow, or have him followed, nor take any measures to ascertain where he goes after he quits Gardenhurst."

He glanced hurriedly at his daughter as he spoke. She did not remove her eyes from the fire. He added, with a strange, nervous smile playing over his face, not only exaggerating his haggard looks, but expressing the most profound uneasiness:

" It is not necessary to explain to *you* his motive for insisting on these conditions."

" Miss Avory herself once threatened him with the madhouse," said Mrs. Ransome, without looking around.

" It is fortunate that he is to be influenced by that threat," I exclaimed, " or he might decline to show himself."

" Oh, he would decline," cried the Colonel quickly. " He held out for some days; but I terrified him at last."

" Did you say he is at Peterham, sir?" I asked.

" Yes; he is not known there."

" Have you left him in charge of anybody?"

He answered me with a faint but a genuine smile, which made me look at him curiously.

" Suppose he should take it into his head to run away, sir?"

" While I am here, you mean? He'll not do that. He knows I would have him hunted down. He has been seen by too many persons to escape me."

He now pulled out a slip of paper scrawled over in pencil; he adjusted his glasses; and while I watched him I thought over that odd smile of his, and wondered what there had been in my question to amuse him.

" This is the draught of the letter, Phœbe, I mean to send by Miss Avory," he said.

I rose.

" Pray keep your seat," he exclaimed, looking at me over his glasses. " I scratched these headings as I came from Peterham. I think they will do."

He read: " Dear Sir,—A dreadful suspicion, the nature of which I need not enter upon, having my daughter for its object, has been, and still is, current among the inhabitants of Copsford. In order to disprove the false accusations preferred against my child by the late Mrs. Ransome, I have had diligent inquiries made for Mr. Ransome, and have been so fortunate as to find him. My own assurance of this fact might not satisfy the scruples of those who have made it their business to give currency to the atrocious report to which I have referred; nor, under the circumstances, should I consider my own word sufficiently emphatic to substantially vindicate my daughter. I have, therefore, to beg that you will do me the honor to attend at my house this evening, at eight o'clock, in order to meet Mr. Ransome, and bear witness in the interests both of humanity and justice to the groundlessness of the scandal that has deeply affected my daughter's mind, and injured her health. Believe me, etc."

The reading of this letter was made so much to resemble a piece of acting by the absent way in which Mrs. Ransome listened to it, that a suspicion, to which I could give no words, entered my head. It took my thoughts away, and I neglected to make any comment on the conclusion of the letter. Looking up, I met the Colonel's eyes fixed on my face; but in a second he turned to his daughter and said:

"Will that letter do, Phœbe?"

"Very well, I think, papa."

"How does it strike you, Miss Avory?" he asked, with a smile utterly unlike the brief glimpse of honest amusement I had caught before.

"It is an invitation they are pretty sure to accept, sir."

"Then it will answer the end it is written for."

The housemaid came in to lay the cloth for lunch, and I left the room, receiving from the Colonel a very politely worded injunction to hold myself in readiness for the arrival of the fly.

Dinner awaited me in my room, and I sat down to it at once, and never seasoned a meal with deeper cogitation. I was very much puzzled. There had been signs and looks, and an over-shrouding air which gave to the conversation that had just terminated a thoroughly perplexing unsatisfactoriness. What made Mrs. Ransome so listless? What made the Colonel so nervous and forced in his manner? I had expected in both of them a very different reception from this of the fortunate termination of the inquiries for

19

Mr. Ransome. A genuine satisfaction, I should have thought, was bound to prevail over the repugnance to the ordeal which Mrs. Ransome had yet to pass through. The suspicion that had long lain upon her was a heavy pressure, from the relief of which the spirits would rise and inspire a glad behavior.

Yet everything was so straightforward that my inquisitive doubts could find nothing to lay hold of. That Mr. Ransome was found was certain, if on no better evidence than the letters I was shortly to deliver. I might have known what to suspect had the discovery of the man been based on no better proof than mere assertion. Everything was so probable as to defy misgiving. So trifling a matter as Mr. Ransome's objection to go to Copsford lest he should be hooted—a fear perfectly consistent with his insanity, his cowardice, and his sense of the wrong he had done his wife— was a corroborative detail as cogent as strong evidence could be.

I finished my dinner, and went up-stairs to dress myself. When I descended, the fly was at the door, and the Colonel waited for me in the anteroom, with the four letters in his hands.

"You will lose no time in delivering these letters, and receiving answers, Miss Avory."

"I will be as quick as I possibly can, sir."

"Thank you. You had better take the houses in the order in which I have placed the letters. They follow regularly, and the flyman can make one road of them."

"Very well, sir."

He opened the hall door and escorted me, bareheaded, to the fly. He saved me the trouble of directing the driver by giving him a list of the addresses, waved his hand, and off I started, mechanically running my fingers over the letters, and reading the names upon them.

The driver of the fly was a Peterham man, but he knew his road thoroughly. I should here mention that Peterham was a small town about four miles from Gardenhurst, on the London road.

The first house we stopped at was The Vale, Sir Anthony

Lauder's residence: a big building situated in a valley separated from Copsford by a hill. The house abutted on the highway, and was screened by trees growing in a row behind a wall liberally garnished with iron spikes. I got out of the fly, rang the bell, and asked for Sir Anthony. He was at home. I was shown into a large, bleak room, with some smouldering coals in the grate, and an austere and portentous parrot in an iron cage on a table. The parrot and I stared at each other for ten minutes, and then the bird called out in a loud voice, "Here he comes!"— which was perfectly true, for the door opened, and in came Sir Anthony Lauder. He was a small, spare man, with a richly oiled brown wig, and a cast in the eye. He bowed, and gesticulated with his hand, but seemed too cold to sit down. I handed him the letter that bore his address; whereupon he, with very great elaboration of manner, drew forth and put on a pair of gold-mounted spectacles, looking at me the while, and attentively scanning my dress, evidently being under the impression that I had called for money.

He read the letter through, and cried, "God bless me!" but perhaps imagining that there was a lack of magisterial dignity in the exclamation, he looked grave, reflected, and then said:

"You will please inform Colonel Kilmain that I shall have much pleasure in acceding to his request."

That was all I had to hear; and, making my bow I quitted the house and drove to Mr. Ledbury's residence. This was close to The Vale. Mr. Ledbury was not at home, but he was sure to return in three-quarters of an hour. So leaving word that my business was very pressing, and that I would return at half-past three, I drove to Mr. Skerlock's house, which he was in the act of leaving when I arrived there. I told him who I was, and gave him the letter. He led me into a snug little study, where a fire roared up the chimney, and where the furniture was so homely and pleasant that it was as agreeable and satisfactory an illustration of the old gentleman's character as his kindly face. The walls were gay with summer pictures,

and the bookcases laden with volumes which touched the
air with the dry aroma of calf and morocco.

Mr. Skerlock read the letter twice—I suppose the Colonel had made a less formal epistle of it to him—and then,
folding it up and putting it in his pocket, took a pinch of
snuff, and exclaimed:

"I always said the man was a rascal. So he is found at
last! And the poor Colonel wants some of us to verify the
villain, that his daughter may be cleared? Of course I will
attend; and I only wish he had asked me to present myself
with a horsewhip. I would give a trifle for the privilege
of flogging the rascal who had subjected a beautiful and innocent woman to a monstrous and unnatural suspicion."

I thanked him, and said that I knew the Colonel was
very grateful for the interest he had taken in his daughter
throughout this strange affair. I added, that had Mrs.
Ransome only acted on his (Mr. Skerlock's) advice, she
would have spared herself much of the humiliating scandal
that had followed the accusations of her husband's mother.

"Yes," he answered; "she should have let the law take
its course with regard to the robbery. She did herself an
injury in refusing to instruct the inspector. She knows
now, I suppose, that the footman *did* steal the plate; and
that Mr. Ransome was ignorant of the robbery?"

"I believe so," I replied. "But doubtless Colonel Kilmain will tell you the whole story. I have other visits to
make, sir, and must not delay them."

He led me to the fly by the hand—an old-fashioned piece
of courtesy, but a very graceful one—and, as the Colonel
had done, stood bareheaded in the cold, bowing to me as
the horse trotted off.

I now went to Mr. Hastings's house, in Albion Square,
where I was kept waiting in the passage while the servant
took the letter up-stairs. The reverend gentleman, a thin,
pale young man, came down presently, looking rather
scared; and taking it for granted that I knew what the
letter was about, stammered that this was scarcely a matter in which he cared to be mixed up; that he was fervently
rejoiced to learn that the wanderer had been recovered; but

that he almost wished the Colonel would depute some shrewder person than himself to undertake this delicate duty of verification.

"It is the Colonel's wish," I answered, "to substantiate the report of this discovery (which, of course, will go the rounds) by the testimony of a clergyman. He will, I am sure, be greatly disappointed if you decline to meet Mr. Ransome."

He read the letter over again, and after humming and hawing awhile, said:

"The Colonel speaks of my bearing witness in the interests both of humanity and justice. I must not close my eyes to that view; and you may therefore tell him that I will be at his house at the appointed hour."

Congratulating myself on this result, I re-entered the fly, and was driven back to Mr. Ledbury's house, where I waited twenty minutes before he came in. This gentleman was of the stern order of mortals, highly important in his manner, a very rigorous and unbending administrator of the laws of the country (as the magistrate's clerk found them), much disliked by everybody, and under the happy impression that he was universally venerated and beloved.

He looked at me very attentively after he had read the letter, and asked me who I was. I told him.

"Are you acquainted," he said, "with the nature of this communication?"

I replied that I was.

"Oh! and why am I wanted to identify a man who may identify himself by paying a flyman and getting himself driven through the town?"

I answered that I thought the letter he had in his hand answered that question; and added that three gentlemen (I mentioned their names) had consented to attend at Gardenhurst.

"Oh, Sir Anthony is to be there, is he?" exclaimed Mr. Ledbury. "And Mr. Skerlock? Indeed! Well, ma'am, the town shall not say that I have failed in the duty I owe it, as one of its magistrates. You may present my compliments to Colonel Kilmain, and inform him that I shall call

at his house at eight o'clock this evening. Mr. Ledbury's
compliments, ma'am; and you may add, if you like, that
my attendance at that hour will cause me great personal
inconvenience, but that, as a magistrate, I am always ready
to sacrifice all social and commercial considerations to my
public duties."

I left the house, glad that my unpleasant mission was
over, and particularly glad to get away from this highly
important and intensely disagreeable public servant. All
four errands had proved successful; and now that they
were accomplished, and I was journeying homeward, I
began to wonder whether, after all, the "meeting of verification"—as I was disposed to call it—which the Colonel
had commissioned me to bring about, was the wisest thing
he could have done. No doubt the evidence of these four
men would utterly put an end to the suspicion that hung
over Mrs. Ransome; but would it kill the prejudice?
Would it not be thought a violent remedy? Would not
people say that the Colonel should have considered his word
enough; that his extreme efforts to vindicate his daughter,
in the absence of any better proofs of her guilt than mere
popular gossip, were derogatory to his dignity as a gentleman—and so forth?

I had considered his policy sound at the first blush; but
now, when I reflected that the missing man was found, I
was strongly disposed to believe that the Colonel's most
dignified course would have been (secure as he knew his
daughter's reputation now to be) to leave the scandalmongers to find out their own falsehoods, and to commit to time
the task of bringing about the revulsion of feeling which
invariably takes an exaggerated form when the public themselves find out their mistakes. He might then be sure of
the sympathy he now sought for his daughter. But to extort a confession of error from people was not the way to
go to work if he wished to maintain the dignity of his child.

These reflections occupied me during my return to Gardenhurst. The Colonel had evidently been waiting for me;
for, on the fly stopping, he himself opened the door, and
eagerly asked me what answers I brought.

"All four will be here, sir, at the hour you named."

"Then you have done your work well, Miss Avory; and I am heartily obliged to you," he said. "Don't let me keep you standing here. It is bitterly cold. Come into the dining-room. My daughter is as anxious as I am to hear what these gentlemen said."

He led the way; but Mrs. Ransome was not in the room. He did not notice her absence; and as though he had utterly forgotten his remark about her anxiety, began to ply me with questions.

First of all, what did Sir Anthony say? And after I had told him, then what did Mr. Ledbury say? And afterward he must hear of the reception of his letter by Mr. Hastings. And finally, what did Mr. Skerlock say?

He listened with an air of keen anxiety to the account I gave him of my four visits, interrupting me with numerous suggestions: such as, Did Sir Anthony question me about Maddox? Did Mr. Ledbury appear at all doubting after reading the letter? Was I sure that bashfulness or nervousness *only* was the reason for Mr. Hastings' disinclination to attend the meeting, and not a dislike of Mrs. Ransome or a distrust of his (the Colonel's) object?

By many of these questions he pre-supposed on my part a very wonderful capacity for reading secret thoughts. I answered him as well as I could; but even after the story of my visits had been told and told again, he was still holding on, so to speak, to the skirts of it, begging me once more to describe Sir Anthony's manner when he read the letter, and to try to remember if Mr. Ledbury had said anything more than what I had repeated, and looking eagerly at me as he spoke, and almost oppressing me with his nervous and feverish anxiety.

Presently he said:

"This is a painful ordeal for my poor girl to go through. I don't think I shall allow her to be present. She ought never to see her husband again; and least of all, under such circumstances as these, when the man means to inform the witnesses that he refuses to live with his wife."

"I don't think Mrs. Ransome ought to be present, sir."

"So I say. But if I seem to hesitate, it is because I believe that all considerations should be sacrificed to the end
I have in view—that of clearing her name. The question
is, would her presence give this meeting a more authentic
character?"

"I don't see how it could, sir. The gentlemen you have
invited will be able to satisfy themselves. Mrs. Ransome's
being by and looking on will not make her husband more
her husband than he is."

"You think so? Put yourself in the place of one of the
witnesses. Would you feel better satisfied if Mrs. Ransome were in the room?"

"I don't quite understand, sir," I answered, remarking
that he hesitated to give full expression to his thoughts.

"I ask you to imagine yourself a witness; and I wish to
know what course I can adopt so as best to convince you
that the reports which have been circulated are utterly
false."

"You produce the man who is reported to have been
murdered. What better proof of Mrs. Ransome's innocence could I wish, sir?"

"And Mrs. Ransome's presence in the room would not
add weight to your conclusions?"

"Not in the least. My ears and eyes would not deceive
me."

He drew a deep breath, and exclaimed, "That decides
me. I am glad to be able to spare my daughter this trial."
He added, after a short silence, "The meeting will take
place in the drawing-room. Some refreshments will be
served to the gentlemen when Mr. Ransome is gone. I
wish for an excuse to detain them in order to hear what
they may have to say."

VII

The afternoon passed. It was the season when the night
falls early. At five o'clock I was sewing in my room by
lamplight. Outside there was a high wind and a bleak
gray sky; for an hour the snow had fallen heavily; but

that was past, and what glimpse of the grounds I could catch showed them lying white and spectral in the gloom.

The dinner went up-stairs at the usual hour, but was soon despatched, and some time before seven the dessert was removed. The cook, who had received very indefinite intelligence of what was going forward from the housemaid, came and asked me if it were true that Mr. Ransome was coming to the house that night. I told her it was true. Was it possible, she wanted to know, that Mrs. Ransome was going to live with that wretch of a man again, after his deserting her, and making people think that she had murdered him? I replied that he was coming merely to show himself to a few persons, and that he was not likely to be in the house above half an hour.

"Well to be sure!" she exclaimed. "What a singular idea! After seeing his wife he means to go away again?"

"Yes, for good."

"Oh dear!" she cried. "I wish I was Mrs. Ransome, just for five minutes! Wouldn't I give him something as 'ud make him remember me to his dying day!"

"Why, would you scratch him?" I asked, laughing.

"Ah, that I would!" she answered. "I'd give him a dose as would make him swear doctor's physic were nothing to it. An idle, good-for-nothing lout! to run away from his wife, and to bring the voice of scandal upon her, and then to turn up and coolly call to say he wasn't comfortable, and didn't mean to live with her again! I'd give it him if I was his wife! What time is he coming here?"

"At eight."

"Do you think it 'ud gratify missis if I was to stand behind the door and give him a push as he goes out?" she asked, gazing at me earnestly.

"That wouldn't do at all."

"You think not? I'm the woman to do it, I tell yer, miss. Let the word be spoke, and I'd knock his hat off."

I assured her that her mistress stood in no need of such demonstrative sympathy, and got rid of her by saying that I was too nervous to talk; which was true enough.

Indeed, it was drawing near the hour when the visitors

were to arrive; and, to say nothing of the fact that this
was the culminating point of a mystery that had perplexed
us for months past, I had fears that some sort of disagreeable and painful scene must take place before the meeting
concluded.

It once entered my mind to wonder why the Colonel did
not ask me to join the other witnesses; but I reflected that
my testimony might not be held as impartial, and my presence therefore would be useless.   All the same, I would
have given a good deal for the privilege of being in the
room.   In any case, the scene was bound to be a curious
one.   Moreover, I had a longing to hear what Mr. Ransome
would say.   One thing was certain: those who were assembled would see that he was mad.   No one but a madman
would, in his place, enter the house.   It became a question
whether the Colonel was acting humanely, now that he had
caught Mr. Ransome, in letting him go again.   A man who
could act as this madman had acted stood, in sober earnest,
in very great need of control.   But it was impossible for
me to conceive the many reasons, outside the essential
reason with which I was acquainted, which the Colonel
might have in choosing the course he was adopting.

It was now ten minutes to eight.   The night outside was
quite black.   I went up-stairs, and, seeing the drawing-
room door open, peeped in.   The room was empty.   A
small lamp stood on the table, and there was a shade over
it, which threw the upper part of the room and the circum-
ference of the walls, half-way down from the ceiling, into
gloom.   I wondered if the meeting was to take place in
that light.   If so, such of the spectators as were short-
sighted would have a hard job to see each other's faces.

No sound came from the room opposite; but I heard the
creak of boots pacing the carpet restlessly.   I noticed now,
what I had not noticed before, that the hall-lamp burned
dimly.   Thinking this should be remedied, I drew a hall-
chair under it, and stood up to see if the wick had been
trimmed.   The sound of the chair dragged along the floor
brought the Colonel out.

"What are you doing, Miss Avory?" he exclaimed.

"I am looking to this lamp, sir, which burns badly."

"It may want more oil," he said, and stood watching me a moment or two; and then withdrew. But he put out his head again, saying, "Let Sarah answer the door when the bell rings."

"Yes, sir."

I turned the wick up, and the lamp burned brightly; which done, I went down-stairs.

It was three minutes to eight by my clock when the hall bell rang. I called to Sarah, who hurried to the door. Wondering if this were Mr. Ransome, I listened at the foot of the staircase, hoping to hear his voice. There was the tread of footsteps, and I heard the Colonel say, strongly and loudly, "This way, if you please," and they walked toward the drawing-room. Sarah came down-stairs and whispered, "It's Mr. Ransome."

"Are you sure?" I exclaimed, my heart beating in the absurdest way.

"Yes, miss; he gave me his name; but master came out and took him to the drawing-room."

"Is he changed?" I asked; but remembering that the girl had never seen him, I said, "How does he look?"

"Why, he's very handsome; and has a black mustache and a high forehead like a poet. I don't know what color his eyes are; they look black; but the light in the hall is so bad that I couldn't see him well."

"Why, I just turned the wick up," I said. "There's oil enough to burn all night. Go and turn it up again. The other gentlemen who are coming won't be able to find their way."

She was running off when the bell pealed again; and scarcely was the visitor admitted when the bell rang a third time; and by a few minutes after eight the four invited gentlemen were assembled in the drawing-room. Every time the housemaid came down-stairs, the cook questioned her eagerly; and I will own to leaving my door open expressly that I might hear what the girl said. By this means I learned that Sir Anthony and Mr. Ledbury had come together; and that the last to arrive was Mr. Has-

tings, who hung back when the door was opened and looked
as if he would have liked to run away.

Up-stairs all was quite silent. Mrs. Ransome had gone
to her bedroom, so the housemaid had told me, where a fire
had been lighted an hour or two before. I concluded that
it was hardly possible Mr. Ransome would remain any
length of time, and I was mastered by an irresistible curiosity to see him—and not only him, but the whole formal
scene. How was this to be done? I had no fear that the
Colonel would be displeased by my curiosity; on the contrary, I was sure he would think it extremely reasonable,
and invite me himself to see Mr. Ransome if it could be
managed without my appearing among the gentlemen.

A thought struck me. It was twenty chances to one if
the curtains to the windows which looked on to the terrace
were drawn. I might without being seen obtain a good
view of the interior of the room from behind one of the pillars; and scarcely had the idea presented itself when I was
creeping softly up-stairs.

The safest mode of gaining the grounds was by the house
door facing the avenue. After the warmth of my room the
hall struck bitterly cold. It would never do to enter the
raw night air without being well protected; so I stole up-
stairs for my thick waterproof cloak, noticing, as I passed,
the dimness of the hall-lamp and wondering for what reason
the flame was kept so low.

Enveloped in my cloak, the well-lined hood of which was
over my head, I returned swiftly and on tiptoe to the hall,
reached the house door, and adjusting the latch to prevent
it from locking me out, plunged up to my ankles into the
snow which had been driven by the wind in heaps around
the walls. Overhead it was pitch-dark; but the reflection
of the snow served to guide my steps. The wind roared
dismally among the trees, and I was so much dismayed by
the sound of it, and the piercing cold and the intense gloom,
that I was within an ace of returning. But my ardent
curiosity prevailed; and walking as swiftly as I might,
sometimes stumbling against a bush from which the wind
had shaken the snow, and which rose black and invisible in

"FACING THESE MEN, HIS BACK TO THE FIRE, AND HIS HEAD THROWN
DEFIANTLY BACKWARD, STOOD MR. RANSOME."—Page 301.

my path, and sometimes tripping over the box, I passed around the house and reached the terrace.

The curtains in the windows fronting the grounds were drawn; the damask that draped the dining-room windows shone warm and red with the quivering fireplay behind; but the velvet curtains of the drawing-room effectually obscured every ray of light. Just as I had anticipated, however, the curtains of the window overlooking the terrace were not drawn. There was a clear space of glass between each. I drew behind one of the pillars and looked into the room.

The light shed by the lamp was feeble; but some one would seem to have just stirred the fire; for the flames streamed brightly and produced the strangest effects of dark shadows and red brilliance in the room and on those assembled there. The four guests sat in a group on the right-hand side of the table; their faces were toward the fire and the light of the lamp shone upon them. The Colonel stood by the side of Sir Anthony Lauder, with his arms folded on his breast, his head lowered, his brows contracted. Exactly facing these men, his back to the fire, and his head thrown defiantly backward, stood Mr. Ransome. One hand was thrust into his trousers pocket, the other negligently played with his watch-chain. His attitude was perfectly easy; but owing to his head being in the gloom which the shade over the lamp threw upon the upper portion of the room, it was impossible for me to clearly discern his face. I looked at him very attentively. So far as I could make out, the six months had wrought no change in him. But there was something, not only in his attitude, but in the resolute gaze which he fixed on Mr. Skerlock, who was at that moment addressing him, which impressed me in a very peculiar manner. Owing to the distance at which I had posted myself from the window I could not hear a word that was spoken within; there was nothing, then, to withdraw my attention from the central figure. The longer I looked the more confused and odd became the feelings which the sight of him aroused in me. That I was actually beholding Mr. Ransome I never doubted; all the signs by which I might know him were there—the mustache growing low on the upper lip; the black eyes; the high forehead; the unparted hair; the long jawbones; the slim figure. And yet, had the conviction possessed me that this man was not Mr. Ransome, I believe that my emotions would not have been other than they were. His imperturbable air startled me. That, at least, was a new characteristic. My memory brought him before me as dubious, nervous, shrinking, with convulsive movements of hands and feet, with sudden upliftings of the brows, with quick, elusive glances. He had acquired a new kind of courage certainly to enable him to support with an ease that any man might have envied the steadfast and hostile regard that was fixed upon him.

Mr. Skerlock was growing excited, and the murmur of his voice reached me through the closed windows. Sir Anthony nodded portentously, and from time to time Mr. Ledbury whispered Mr. Hastings, who sat with his hands twisted over his thin knee.

By this time I was nearly frozen; moreover, I feared that Mr. Ransome might leave the room at any moment, and so cause the hall door to be shut, which would prevent me from entering the house without ringing the bell—a notion I did not relish, because, though I fully intended to tell Colonel Kilmain that I had taken a peep through the window at Mr. Ransome, I disliked the idea of the servant who admitted me guessing that I had been spying.

I was about to turn away, when I was suddenly brought to a dead stand by a movement at the end of the terrace, where the alcove was. My eyes were now used to the darkness, and turning them in the direction of the sound, I perceived the outline of a man standing close against the wall.

I was so horribly frightened that my exclamation of "Who's there?" was scarcely better than a gasp.

"It's me, miss," said a man's voice, which I did not recognize; and a figure stalked out, touching his cap. "I'm Poole, miss," he continued. "I'm up to no harm; I only wanted to see Mr. Ransome, as everybody said was murdered."

"Oh!" I exclaimed; and that was all. In another moment I was gliding round the house, with my heart beating from the recent shock, as though I had barely escaped some dreadful danger. I pushed open the hall door, and closed it softly, then hastily removing my cloak I threw it over my arm, and went down-stairs.

I was just in time; another minute and I must have met Mr. Ransome at the door, for hardly was I in my room when I heard Colonel Kilmain's voice, and the footsteps of two persons passing to the door by which I had entered. Shortly after this the Colonel returned. He walked quickly, and the hum of voices, that had flowed into the hall, was abruptly silenced as the Colonel closed the drawing-room door after him.

The bell rang, and some refreshments, in the shape of spirits, wine, cake, etc., were taken up-stairs. The voices came loud and eager through the door as the housemaid passed into the room. I strained my ears to catch what was said, being very curious to know if there was any dis-agreement among them respecting the identity of Mr. Ran-some; but not a word was distinct.

I calculated that, altogether, Mr. Ransome had not re-mained longer than fifteen minutes in the house.

By this time my pulse was beating quietly enough. The fright that the man Poole had given me was passed; and I regretted now that I had been too cowardly to ask him what he meant by lurking about the drawing-room windows at eight o'clock at night, when he was supposed to leave off work at dusk—that was, about four o'clock. However, the rencontre was scarcely worth making a mystery of. A little reflection found me quite willing to believe his state-ment, that he was there merely to see Mr. Ransome. I had been there for the same purpose, and what was true of me should be true of him.

At nine o'clock either Mr. Ledbury's or Sir Anthony's carriage drove up. As all four gentlemen were going the same road, here was a good opportunity for such of them as would have to walk the distance to get a ride home. They all left the drawing-room at once; and I heard the Colonel thank them for their attendance.

"Your appeal was in good taste, and highly reasonable," a voice exclaimed. To which another replied, "I fancy I could tame his obstinacy were the leisure given me." The Colonel cried, "Hush! gentlemen; the kitchen is under you!"

They were some time putting on their coats, and then they all passed out of the hall to the door, where the carriage had drawn up.

In a few moments the Colonel returned; he hesitated a while in the hall, and then called my name softly. Had my door been closed, I should not have heard him. I found him standing near the drawing-room door. He was pressing his handkerchief to his head, and though his face was deadly pale, a triumphant smile hovered about his mouth.

"Will you go and tell Mrs. Ransome I am alone, Miss Avory?"

I knocked at her bedroom door. She leaned with her elbow upon the toilet-table. The room was lighted only by the fire, which had burned into a red core, and threw out a red glow. Her face was reflected in the looking-glass, and both the reality and the counterfeit were like ghostly countenances staring at each other. I gave her the Colonel's message, and she instantly started up, and came to the door. I followed her down-stairs, neither of us speaking a word; and I was making for the kitchen staircase, when the Colonel called to me.

When I entered the drawing-room he shut the door, and placed the lamp on the mantelpiece. Mrs. Ransome glanced at me, and I caught her make a slight impatient gesture to her father, evidently objecting to my presence. He took no notice. I could not very well take a hint of this kind, or I should have left the room. She went close to the fire with a shiver, and seated herself on a low chair, with her eyes on her father.

All this scarcely took a minute; then the Colonel, leaning with his back against the mantelpiece, said:

"Phœbe, the gentlemen are perfectly satisfied. Mr. Skerlock wished me to send for you that he might tell you, in the name of those assembled, how deeply they deplored the anxiety that has been caused you by your mother-in-law's accusation. But I would not allow you to be called. Mr. Ledbury applauded my reasons, and left it to me to express their sympathy."

"I should not have gone had I been called," said Mrs. Ransome.

"No, of course not; because you are determined not to meet your husband again, and you have a good reason for being resolute," he exclaimed, speaking *at* me, though he addressed his daughter. "But that was not my motive. I considered your dignity and your feelings."

She was silent.

This silence struck me as very curious. It was thoroughly to be expected that she would ply her father with questions, and show herself excited in a high degree by the strange scene that had just been concluded. Did my presence act as a restraint? I certainly could not understand why the Colonel should want a stranger like me in the room. Much, surely, he had to tell his daughter which he would not speak before me.

"Mr. Ransome behaved well, I must do him that justice," he said. "He was cool and collected, with no hint of madness in one of his looks or remarks. When he was gone, Mr. Hastings wondered how people could think him mad; but Mr. Skerlock answered that madmen were not always foaming at the mouth; the most dangerous among them are those who hide their madness under a perfect disguise of sanity, because then they always throw you off your guard."

Mrs. Ransome still kept silence. He fixed his eyes on me after he had spoken, which obliged me to answer:

"That's no doubt true, sir."

"He stood here," he went on, planting himself in the middle of the hearthrug, "and we were seated where you are, Miss Avory. There was an embarrassing silence when we were all assembled and I had closed the door. I broke it by thanking the gentlemen for their attendance, and by explaining my reasons for inviting them to this house. I
20

then pointed to Mr. Ransome, and said, 'There stands the
man, gentlemen, who has been reported murdered, and
whose death has been attributed by false and malicious
tongues to my daughter. The evidence of your own eyes
will now enable you to convict the originator of this report,
either as a wilful and cruel liar, or as having been mad at
the time of harboring the suspicion to which she gave
tongue.' Mr. Skerlock at once said, 'I did not require to
see Mr. Ransome to know that your daughter was an injured and guiltless lady. I believe I shall convey the sen-
timents of my companions when I express our deep concern
that the voice of scandal should have placed you and yours
in this painful position.' Upon this Mr. Ransome said,
'Colonel Kilmain has explained my motive for coming here.
My domestic affairs make no portion of the business of this
meeting. I must merely inform you that I left my wife
because I was not happy with her, and that nothing but a
wish that justice should be done her could have induced me
to enter this house again. I believe,' he said, addressing
me, 'that you have no further need of my presence.' I
would have conducted him out of the house there and then;
but Mr. Hastings took it into his head to offer him a short
lecture on his duty as a husband. And then Mr. Skerlock
asked permission to speak, and told him that if he had one
spark of honor left in his composition, he would not leave
Copsford until he had convincingly proved to the people
that they had committed an atrocious act of injustice in
crediting his mother's accusation against his wife. Sir Anthony declared that it was one of the cruellest wrongs that
had ever come under his notice; and Mr. Ledbury assured
us, in a loud, emphatic voice, that far smaller sins than his
had been visited with very heavy punishments. The moment they were silent, Mr. Ransome bowed and walked out
of the room."

Though it was supposed that he was addressing his
daughter, the whole of this story was delivered point-blank
to me. I listened with great attention, but could not rid
myself of a haunting sense that there was something strange
and startling hidden behind all this, and that, let the secret

be what it would, it was known to Mrs. Ransome. Her undissembled indifference was thoroughly bewildering. She asked no questions; she never raised her eyes; she hardly appeared to pay attention to what her father said. Nor was *his* manner a whit more satisfactory. His story had flowed glibly, indeed; but there was something forced and unreal in his voice—something constrained and difficult in his bearing—something that irresistibly persuaded me that in what he was saying and doing he was not true to himself. But no conceivable reason why this should be entered my head. Every instinct in me felt the mystery; yet my judgment, in defiance of intuition, obliged me to witness the whole affair as real, plain, and straightforward.

I could see that his daughter's lifeless manner made him uneasy, for he glanced at her repeatedly and impatiently; but she would not look up.

A perfect silence followed the conclusion of his narrative, and he fell back in his former place against the mantelpiece. Presently I said:

"I saw Mr. Ransome, sir, and, considering the peculiar position he was placed in, it struck me that his bearing (I did not hear him speak) was very different from what I should have expected it to be seven months ago."

When I said this, Mrs. Ransome looked up sharply, and stared at me.

"Saw him?" exclaimed the Colonel, in a low voice. "Where? You were not in this room."

"I saw him from that window," I answered, pointing. They both turned their heads quickly in the direction. "I was curious to see if he was at all changed."

Mrs. Ransome watched me with a frown.

"When was that? How long were you there? I did not see you," said the Colonel, speaking quickly, and with an air of suppressed excitement.

"I did not wish to be seen, sir. I stood behind one of the pillars."

It was impossible for me to assume that I had done wrong, and so I offered no defence. They both looked at me intently, but with different expressions. There was dark anger in Mrs. Ransome's face; in the Colonel's an alarm that made his forced smile painful.

"What took you to the window, Miss Avory?" demanded Mrs. Ransome imperiously. "Your presence was not wanted, or my father would have invited you to join the others."

"Miss Avory had a perfect right to look at Mr. Ransome if she chose," exclaimed the Colonel, rebuking his daughter with a wave of the hand.

"The interest I have taken in this affair throughout is the only excuse I can offer," I replied. "Had I thought the action would have incurred your displeasure, I would not have committed it."

"Miss Avory, there is not the least need to apologize," said the Colonel. "Of course you were right to look at the man. Why did I bring him here but that he might be seen? I wish the servants had joined you. The greater the number of witnesses the better."

"I was not alone, sir. There was another spectator."

"Who?" he demanded, the smile leaving his face in a flash.

"The under-gardener, Poole."

"Poole! at such an hour!"

"He was hiding when I saw him. I was too frightened, not knowing who he was in the dark, to stop and question him."

He walked to the window, opened it, and called "Poole!" He stared into the blackness, came back, seized the lamp, and went into the terrace. The cold air rushing through the open window drove Mrs. Ransome closer to the fire. She hugged herself, and shuddered.

"I don't suppose he is there now, sir," I called out.

"I don't see him," he answered, re-entering the room, and closing the window. "Of all creatures, what should Poole do in the terrace at such an hour? He leaves the grounds at four, doesn't he?"

"I believe so. I suppose he was attracted by the same motive that drew me from my warm room into the snow— curiosity. Indeed he admitted as much."

"No doubt!" he exclaimed, with a loud, violent laugh. "So that makes six witnesses instead of four. Better if the number were sixty. Phœbe, why do you look so sulky?"

"I am not sulky, papa," she answered, with a faint smile, that quickly vanished when she turned her eyes down again.

"You found Mr. Ransome changed, you say, Miss Avory?" He dropped his head on one side to catch my answer.

"There was a composure in his manner which seemed to me unlike what I can remember of him."

"You said, I think, that you did not catch his voice?"

"No, sir."

"Then you can scarcely assume any change; or how are you to know that the manner and attitude he adopted were not meant to correspond with his language?"

"I don't think he spoke during the time I watched him."

"Papa, you have said he was defiant," exclaimed Mrs. Ransome impatiently.

"He was defiant. When he stated his intention of never again returning to this house, he looked boldly at us, as if he suspected his assertion would provoke indignation. You might have seen him at that moment, Miss Avory."

"Very likely, sir."

"But still," he continued, half turning away from me while he chafed his hands before the fire, "there is a change for the better in the man's bearing. He is not the nervous, jerky, furtive being he used to be. I noticed this in London. He looks one steadily in the face, and speaks temperately. Perhaps his madness is leaving him, or," he added, looking at me over his shoulder with a smile, "the cunning of madness has increased, and he adopts this col‧ lected manner that he may defy me to prove him mad should I ever take it into my head to lock him up in a lunatic asylum."

"I am very glad it is all over, sir," I exclaimed, rising; for it was nearly ten o'clock, and I had several things to do before going to bed.

"Yes," he answered, looking at me strangely, and passing his hand over his forehead; "but it has been a bad
business—a wretched, miserable business from the beginning."

"For me, papa," said Mrs. Ransome.

"And for me!" he cried, with a sudden passion; "and
even for her," pointing to me, "and every member of this
household. Has it not been thought that that wretched
man has been murdered here—in this very house? All
who live here have had their share of the suspicion that
has hung like a cloud over the place, depend upon it.
What would I not give to find Maddox?"

"Happily, sir," I said, "there is no mystery about him.
The discovery of Mr. Ransome reduces the footman to a
mere robber."

He glanced at me, and then breathed quickly, like one
who hastily catches himself up in the act of speaking.
Finding that he remained silent, I moved toward the door,
lingering a moment or two in case either of them had more
to say, and then left the room.

So now, then, the mystery was ended; and from this
night Mrs. Ransome was freed from the horrible suspicion
that had been fastened upon her more than half a year ago.

But *was* the mystery ended? There was that in me
which assured me it was only just begun; and the strange
fancy became a haunting conviction, in spite of every reason
I could think of to prove it absurd.

I quitted the drawing-room possessed with a peculiar
feeling of disappointment; this I could account for. I had
certainly expected to find both the Colonel and Mrs. Ransome—and especially the latter—much more greatly excited
than they had shown themselves. When I considered the
nature of the accusation that had been disproved, the sense
of security and triumph that must inspire both father and
daughter in knowing that the detestable and honorable lie
which had been started by old Mrs. Ransome was forced
back in the throats of those who had repeated and believed
it, I was amazed to reflect upon the forced, unsatisfactory,
and uneasy air of the Colonel, indicative of anything but

gladness, and the incomprehensible listlessness and reserve of his daughter. But a few days ago both of them would have cheerfully surrendered ten years of their lives to have been able to lay their hands upon Mr. Ransome; and now he was found, and now men of credit and honor had beheld him, and would, of their own accord, spread the news, and eagerly vindicate Mrs. Ransome's character; and yet they had both struck me as being as little satisfied with the sequel of this extraordinary affair as if the missing man had never been discovered.

I was greatly puzzled. That there was something wrong in all this, something hidden, something mysterious, I was as sure as that I breathed. Three foundations I had for this notion: the behavior of the Colonel; the indifference of Mrs. Ransome; the anxiety the Colonel had exhibited in his manner to me, in his having summoned me to the drawing-room, and thus placing me on the same level with his daughter as an interested party in the business. There was something more than courtesy in this: there was design in it that had no reference to politeness.

And there was even a fourth matter that somehow served to complicate my private bewilderment: I mean the presence of the under-gardener, Poole, in the terrace. I fancied I had explained this satisfactorily when I assumed, on his own declaration, that he had been drawn there by curiosity. But when I thought over it, I could not bring myself to believe that mere curiosity only had tempted a man, after a day's work, to leave his fireside, plunge into the snow, and hang about the terrace, with the risk of being discharged should he be caught.

Was he in any way concerned in Mr. Ransome's disappearance or recovery? This seemed as absurd as the numberless other questions I was now incessantly putting to myself. One thing, at all events, I can safely aver: that when I went to bed that night my mind was in a greater state of mystification than ever it had been throughout the whole period of Mr. Ransome's disappearance, dating from the moment when I had first discovered his absence, up to this time of his being proved alive.

VIII

I come now to what I always recall as the strangest portion of the story I am relating; but before I enter upon it,
I must first prepare the way by a brief account of the events
of the fortnight that preceded the incident I refer to.

I had very confidently expected, now that Mrs. Ransome's life had been purified from the suspicion that darkened
it, that the Colonel would shut up his house and take his
daughter away; and considering the nature of the troubles
they had escaped, I was pretty sure, when once they were
away, that they would never return.

But I very soon discovered that it was not the Colonel's
intention to leave Gardenhurst.   Indeed, he indirectly implied as much, but expressed no reason for abandoning the
idea he had on several occasions vehemently threatened to
carry out.   I found, however, nothing particularly un-
reasonable in his remaining in his old home.   In one sense
he and his daughter could scarcely have lived a more retired life had they banished themselves to some Continental
solitude.   On selfish grounds I was glad that they kept
where they were: my duties were light, my salary liberal,
and in spite of the change that had come over Mrs. Ransome since the time when her mother-in-law had first excited suspicion against her, I was more comfortable at
Gardenhurst than ever I had been in any former situation,
and could scarcely doubt that any change which befell me
must be for the worse.

Among other things which did not strike me so forcibly
then as they did later on, when I was able to piece them
into a whole and gather their import fully, was an alteration
in the Colonel's manner to me, quite distinct enough to make
itself felt, though by no means so obtrusive as to occasion
speculation.   There was less cordiality and more elaboration in his politeness.   The ease that had made his courtesy especially grateful and in no sense embarrassing was
missing; his behavior was formal and anxious.   If ever I
had occasion to wait upon him, he thanked me for my
services as he might an equal.   When we met on the stairs

or in the hall, he made way for me studiedly and had always a gravely courteous remark to offer. There was even, at times, a diffidence in his accost. But on the subject of Mr. Ransome he was silent. Often as we would speak together—of the house, of his daughter's health, of the servants, of my duties, of any such matters—not once during the interval this part of the story is now occupying did the smallest reference to his son-in-law escape him.

I coupled this strange silence with the various odd fancies that possessed me, and made them by the union more bewildering yet. There was no reason that I could imagine why he should cease to honor me with the confidence he had never before withheld. It was beyond question that his mind was very full of the subject. His daughter's relations with her husband were as unsatisfactory as they could well be. Mr. Ransome could return at any moment and insist upon living in the house if it so pleased him. No law as yet had sundered them. She was still as absolutely his wife as ever she had been; but their union was now hampered by the most delicate and distressing conditions. The Colonel was bound to feel her position keenly. The freedom with which he had heretofore spoken to me on matters equally confidential with this made it natural to suppose that he would sometimes express his thoughts about her to me. But the topic never formed any feature of our conversations. And further, if the discovery of Mr. Ransome had promised to restore peace of mind to the Colonel, the hope so raised was disappointed; for his care and anxiety were assuredly greater now than ever they had been; and his difficult assumption of a placid exterior only served to exaggerate the emotions it was designed to conceal.

Of Mrs. Ransome I saw but little. The housemaid usually brought me her instructions; and all her migrations were from the bedroom to the dining-room. But the little I *did* see showed me a woman cold, stony, and sullen—lifeless in her abnormal inactivity, unsmiling, silent, inattentive even to the meaning of her own remarks. The change was scarcely credible. The blood seemed to have turned to ice in her veins; the light was quenched in her eyes; her hands were so thin and white that thinner and whiter they would not be when they were composed in her coffin. Reading appeared her only occupation; but if I might judge by the little I beheld, I would declare that I never found her with a book in her hand of which she could have told me the name.

If the spirit of her mother-in-law had felt its revenge balked by the discovery of Mr. Ransome, it might now hold itself satisfied. Here was but the pale, nerveless shadow of a woman melancholy as death where had been a beautiful, imperious creature, so graceful as to gladden the eye with the lightest movement of her handsome shape, so spirited and radiant, even with the burden of a brutal husband upon her, as to create an atmosphere of light and music around her by the movement of her eyes and by the sound of her voice.

What effect the discovery of Mr. Ransome had had upon the popular prejudice against the wife I never could learn from the Colonel. The weather was very inclement, and in that fortnight I don't think I went to Copsford more than twice, and on neither occasion did I glean any particulars as to what the people were saying of the Ransomes. However, the cook knew a good number of persons in the town, and the housemaid also had her friends; and from one and the other of them I picked up scraps of information which showed me that the town was very talkative about her innocence, and that Mr. Ransome was generally considered a brute.

However, I did not take much interest in what the neighbors thought, and hoped that the reason of the Colonel's silence was contempt of public opinion now that his daughter's name was cleansed. I could form some idea of the general feeling by a letter that appeared in the local paper which was published every Saturday; this letter was printed in the number issued on the same week in which the meeting had been held at Gardenhurst. One of the tradesmen brought the paper to the house and lent it to the cook. The letter was aimed at "Justitia," the writer of the communication to which the Colonel had called my attention some

time before. It was scornful, but not particularly witty.
It spoke of the wrong that had been done to an innocent
lady; it praised the father's manly efforts to vindicate his
child from the diabolical accusations of a certain elderly and
undoubtedly mad lady lately deceased; and it exhorted the
people of Copsford to be a little more cautious for the future
in harboring suspicions on the testimony of insane persons,
and wound up by congratulating the magistrates on the judgment and spirit they had shown in refusing to allow a guiltless lady to be arraigned before them.   The editor made this
letter the text of a leading article, in which he bullied the
inspector for his bovine zeal, and asked, with many notes
of interrogation and exclamation, " what man can consider
himself safe in a country where such outrages are sanctioned
by the law?"

These were straws that showed which way the wind was
blowing.   No doubt the Colonel and his daughter read the
article and the letter, but they did not advert to them in my
presence.

And yet in this fortnight only two persons called at the
house—Mr. Hastings and Mr. Skerlock.   Mr. Hastings
merely left his card; Mr. Skerlock called twice, the first
time with his wife.

I knew little of what went on up-stairs; what the Colonel
did and talked about; what Mrs. Ransome thought.   I had
been quietly and courteously shut out from the sphere of
those interests in which I had taken part, and was now the
complete housekeeper, with nothing to attend to but my
duties.   But I was not allowed to feel this as a slight.   Indeed, this gentle exclusion was reasonable and proper; for
now the trouble was over, the memory was a bitter one; and
its disposal left them no excuse to raise me again to the
flattering level I had held while the matter was mysterious,
and the trouble of it heavy and harassing.

Exactly a fortnight had elapsed since the meeting between
Mr. Ransome and the witnesses had been held.   Winter
had set in with great severity.   There was no snow, but the
earth had been frozen into black iron by the bitter north

wind. A leaden sky had prevailed for some days, giving an indescribable aspect of forlornness to the naked trees and the dead, leafless desolation of the country round. The birds moped upon the skeleton branches, and the wind plained about the house like the voice of a grieving spirit. The freezing air penetrated to the bones; but for days I had not quitted the house. The want of exercise had caused me to toss wakefully on my bed; and, having an hour to spare, I enveloped myself in my thick cloak and warm gloves, and went for a walk in the grounds.

The hills stood livid and austere upon the land, and in the valleys there was the gloom almost of twilight. Here and there upon the rugged fields lay patches of snow—remnants of the fall that many days before had blanched the country for miles around. The grass crackled crisply under my feet, as if each blade were an icicle.

I turned off to the right and walked toward the kitchen gardens, intending to take the whole circuit of the grounds. This was practicable, owing to the path which ran close alongside the hedges, and which the gardeners kept pretty free of the nettles and brambles and weeds that grew on the bankside.

I caught site of Poole, digging, some distance off. He turned his head, cased in a hairy cap, to look at me; then planted his spade afresh and put his foot upon it. My thoughts went back to that night when I had encountered him in the terrace. I eyed him curiously; for in some instinctive manner, which I could not in the smallest degree understand or account for, I associated him with the long disappearance of Mr. Ransome.

I walked on briskly, going down the hill. How bleak and bitter was the wind! but my rapid pace circulated my blood, and I enjoyed the exhilarating, wholesome warmth of quick exercise. Some crows, looking larger than hens, frightened by my footsteps, rose from behind the hedge, and startled me with their abrupt and noisy soaring.

I reached the bottom of the grounds and pursued the path that led directly to the trees. Their dark straight trunks, close against each other, looked the ribs of many wrecked

"THERE'S A DEAD MAN YONDER! I TOORNED UP HIS FACE WITH MY SPADE."—
Page 317.

ships; high among their topmost boughs the rooks' nests
swung tattered and black. Under 'them the shadows lay
dark and heavy and repellent; one strip of sunshine would
have made the scene exquisitely picturesque, for the fibrous
outlines were full of grace, and there would have been softness and color in the gloom had there been the broken illumination of sunlight to contrast it with. But the lead-colored sky made the aspect of the trees ghastly, and the wind
awoke weird sounds among them.

I was turning to the left to take a cut across the grounds,
when I heard the sounds of footsteps trampling and crunching the dead leaves, and a man came running out from
among the trees. He was the upper-gardener, named Walters, an elderly man who had worked on the estate, so he
had told me, all his life. His face was now deadly pale,
his eyes were wide open, and he wore an expression of intense horror and fear. As he ran, his head struck against
a bough which tore his cap off; he did not stop to recover
it, but was hastening onward, when he caught sight of me;
on which he stopped, motioning with one hand, and wiping
his forehead with his sleeve, unable to speak.

Astounded by his extraordinary behavior, I went up to
him and asked him what was the matter. He tried to
speak, but his tongue clove to the roof of his mouth, and
after gasping out some utterly inaudible sentences, he
pointed to the trees, and clasped his hands over his breast,
breathing heavily.

I strained my eyes in the direction he indicated, but could
see nothing to account for his terror. Not until I had repeated my question thrice, and given him time to collect
himself, could he answer me; and then the first words he
faltered out were:

"There's a dead man yonder! I toorned up his face with
my spade. It was a sight to strike me blind!"

"A dead man?" I exclaimed, involuntarily falling some
paces away.

"Ay! he lies there agin the hedge. I first unearthed his
hair, an' I pulled at it, not knowing what it wur, and the
head come oop out o' the soil wi' the jerk."

In an ecstasy of disgust he rubbed his hands madly together, and then wrung the fingers that had touched the
corpse.

I thought he must be under a delusion; and seeing the
other gardener in the distance, leaning on his spade and
watching us, I called and beckoned to him; whereupon he
came running toward us.

"Oh, Jim!" groaned the old man, pointing, "there's a
dead man yonder! My God, he's a sight to strike me daft!
I was diggin' out a plot o' grass to trim the corner o' the
lawn with, where it's wore down, meaning to fetch it from
oonder the trees where it wouldna' be missed, when I dug
up a man's hair, an' as I hope to go to Hiven, I didn't know
what it wur, and took an' pulled it, an' the face came out!
—don't go near it!—it's an awful sight! Christ forgive
me! had I known what it was, I wouldna' ha' meddled wi'
it for the king's money!"

The under-gardener was as white as a sheet. He stammered out something; and then crying, "I'll not go anear
it! I can't bear the sight o' such things," walked some
paces away, and stood staring at the spot the other man had
indicated.

The idea suddenly seized me that this dead man was Mr.
Ransome. God knows what put the thought into my head,
and made me grasp it as a conviction in the face of the conclusive evidence I had received but a fortnight ago that Mr.
Ransome was living.

My mind disconnected the man I had seen from the man
who lay dead beneath the trees at once.

My eagerness to confirm my suspicion rose paramount to
all other considerations. I felt my heart turn sick at my
own audacity; nevertheless I said to Walters:

"Show me the place where the man lies."

"No, miss! don't ask me. I can't look at it agin! an'
it's no sight for you, or any man or woman."

"Are you afraid of a dead man?" I exclaimed.

He shuddered, but made no answer.

"Will you accompany me?" I called to Poole.

He looked at me sullenly, and replied, "What do you

want to see it for? Don't you hear what Walters says,
that it's no fit sight for any one?"

"Suppose it should be Mr. Ransome?" I said, thinking
aloud, and scarcely conscious of the import of the conjecture.

"Ah, indeed!" exclaimed Poole, looking up and shaking
off his sullen manner. "It may be master; and I'll tell
you if it is the moment I see him. I don't mind going
with you, miss. You'll come along with us, Joe?"

"No! haven't I told yer?" cried the other, violently
starting backward. "Go an' look at it if you will. One
sight o' such a thing's enough for me."

"Run to the house, then," I exclaimed, "and tell Colonel
Kilmain what you have seen. There's your cap on the
ground yonder."

He picked it up, fixed it with a trembling hand on his
head, and walked off quickly.

"This way he said it was, didn't he?" said Poole, walking toward the trees. But when he was in their shadow he
stopped.

I also stopped. My curiosity was fast losing its audacity,
though I was still so eager to know if this dead man were
Mr. Ransome that to set my mind at rest there were few
things I would not have dared.

"Did you ever see a dead man?" whispered Poole, turning a face of ashy paleness toward me. There was something about the man a great deal more intimidating than the
idea of beholding a corpse.

"I will wait for Colonel Kilmain," I said; and returned
to the open grounds. He came after me, and leaned against
a tree.

"I'll wait, too," said he; "I'll not see it alone. It's
given Walters a turn, an' it may serve me worse."

He was silent for some moments, and presently said:

"I wouldn't mind wagering a pound against a shillin' that
it's Mr. Ransome."

I looked at him steadily, and asked what made him think
that.

"Missis," he said, withdrawing from the tree, and bending forward, "you were watching along with me that night in the terrace—do you remember?"

"What then?"

"You saw Mr. Ransome, did you?"

"Yes."

"Are you sure it was master? Could you swear that the person who stood with his back to the fire, and his face dark with the cover over the lamp, was the same gentleman as left yon house getting on now for eight months ago?"

I stared at him with mingled astonishment and fear; for he was putting into words, and clearly defining to myself, the vague and elusive suspicion that had haunted me for the last fortnight.

"Did not you think that man Mr. Ransome?" I asked.

He cast his eyes down, and, pointing with his thumb over his shoulder, exclaimed:

"If he don't lie there, I'm willin' to lose a pound agin any man's shillin'."

"But," I replied, "even if he is dead there, that should not prove he was not in the drawing-room the other night."

"Supposing he *was* in the drawing-room," he exclaimed. "It'll soon be found out. . . . Ah! here they come."

I looked up the grounds and saw the Colonel approaching us rapidly, followed by the gardener. He was in his dressing-gown, and walked, or almost ran, in a breathless manner. He showed no surprise on seeing me, but called out when he was yet some distance off, "What is all this about?" In a few moments he was at my side.

"Walters says there is a dead body lying under the trees, sir."

"Have you seen it?" he asked me.

"No, sir."

"Have you courage to see it?"

No; my courage was gone.

"Show me where it lies," he said, addressing Walters.

"I'll show you the place, sir; I can't go near it," replied the old man, wiping his face with a red pocket-handkerchief.

"Was it Mr. Ransome, Joe?" inquired Poole.

The Colonel turned with a flash upon him.

"What makes you ask that?" he demanded furiously.

"Have you seen the body?"

"No, your honor."

"Then what the devil do you mean by saying it is Mr. Ransome?"

"I asked Joe if it was, sir."

The Colonel looked as if he could have struck him, then walked under the trees, calling to Walters to follow.

Poole strode sulkily off to where he had been at work, and in a few moments was digging with an air of unconcern.

When the others were some distance under the trees, the gardener stopped and pointed. The Colonel pushed forward and disappeared. The gardener remained where he had halted, looking in my direction. After a lapse of five minutes the Colonel returned; the gloom among the trees was too heavy to enable me to see his face until he was close to me—it was ghastly! He brushed past without appearing to see me; but when he was yards away, he turned and called my name. I went after him.

"Well for you," he exclaimed, "that you have not beheld that sight. It is awful!"

I shuddered with the horror that came over me, and asked if there were really a dead man there?

"Really!" he gasped. "Oh, shocking! shocking! He might have lain there for years. His face is gone—the head only is exposed—the rest of the body is under the earth."

He pressed his hands to his eyes and groaned.

"Who is it, sir? Surely not Mr. Ransome!" I stammered.

"Did you not hear the answer I made to that simpleton yonder?" he cried fiercely. "Mr. Ransome was at that house a fortnight ago—you know he was! The body under the trees has been where it lies for months—I will swear it! If you think it is Mr. Ransome, go and look at it and tell me if the decay of a fortnight will make such a picture as you may there see!"

21

We rapidly neared the house. I was silent, marking furtively the efforts he made to subdue himself. On cross-ing the lawn he stopped.

"That body must be some stranger's," he exclaimed, "who was trespassing on these grounds, and died suddenly or was killed there. He lies close to the hedge that divides the estate from the fields."

"But Walters says he was buried when he found him."

"By time. The wind has blown the soil over him and the grass has sprung up around him, and so he seems to have been buried. What a horrible discovery! the worst that could have occurred! What am I to do now? I must send to the police, I suppose."

"The body cannot be left where it is."

"You had better go—no, I'll go myself. . . . This will revive all the old detestable suspicion which I had hoped was laid forever. I'll be foremost now. They shall not say I tried to conceal this discovery. Who can he be? Who can he be?"

He muttered this question several times, with his eyes fixed vacantly on my face, then wheeled round and hurried into the house.

Neither of the servants knew of the discovery yet, and I was resolved not to be the first to give them the news. Life appeared to be a strange dream just then, wherein the act-ing was confused, and from which I could wrest no specific meaning. I hid myself in my room and tried to collect my thoughts. What was the import of the horrible thing that had been found? I thought of what Poole had said, and how his assertion that the man he had seen in the drawing-room was not Mr. Ransome had given life and shape to my own suspicions. And then I wondered if the dead man were Mr. Ransome. If so, and the Colonel's conjecture as to the time the body had been dead were true, then assuredly had he been lying there ever since he was missed—an over-whelming thought. Then what would appear? That he had committed suicide? This theory I could not entertain. Had he meant to kill himself, he would have done so in his bedroom. Besides, the body was found under the earth;

and I could not conceive that the winds of seven or eight months, nor of as many years indeed, could heap and plant a grave over the dead. Had he been killed? By whom? By Maddox? Or—and the pulses of my heart seemed arrested by the thought—was this discovery going to confirm old Mrs. Ransome's accusation?

But my speculations galloped too fast. Was it Mr. Ransome who had been present in the drawing-room a fortnight before? Let me say it was, and then it was manifest, on the Colonel's testimony, that he who lay under the trees was not Mr. Ransome. Let me say it was not; and I involved myself in a maze from which there was absolutely no exit; because it was taxing my imagination utterly beyond its strength to conceive that any man could be found so like Mr. Ransome in person, manners, and voice, and possessing withal the minute personal knowledge that was necessary to the completeness of the impersonation, as to deceive the Colonel and the four gentlemen who confronted him and persuade them that he was the missing man.

I did not hear the Colonel leave the house; but presently my ear caught the gruff tones of a man speaking in the kitchen, and in a few moments the door of my room was thrown open, and the cook rushed in to tell me that a corpse had been found in the grounds, and that the gardener was in the kitchen telling them about it. I answered that I was aware of the fact, having been in the grounds at the time of the discovery; whereas, scared by my coolness, she bolted out, that she might not miss any portion of Walter's narrative. By-and-by I heard a pair of feet travelling nimbly upstairs. I had no doubt they belonged to the housemaid, who was gone with the news to Mrs. Ransome; and this was the case, for after a short interval she returned with an order for me to attend mistress in the dining-room.

"What is this about a dead body having been found?" Mrs. Ransome exclaimed, when she saw me.

I told her what I knew.

"Where is my father?"

"He has gone, I believe, to inform the police of this discovery."

"Is it known who the dead man is?" she asked, com
pressing her lips the moment she had spoken and render·
ing them bloodless.

"No, madam; but I dare say they will find out soon."

"Can it be Mr. Ransome?" she cried. "Where is the
gardener? He saw him. Did he describe the face?"

"The face is decayed."

"Can it be Mr. Ransome?" she repeated. "If so, then
he has been murdered by Maddox."

I did not catch the true signification of this remark at the
moment, and had she continued speaking, I might have
passed it by without notice. But the sudden flush that
came into her face and then left it blanched beyond the
power of words to describe; the quick, agonized movement
of her lips; the recoil of her whole figure; the half-reel, the
lowered head, the eyes full of torment, flashed its import
upon me.

I dared not speak—I dared not look at her. In that
breathless interval she succeeded in mastering herself. She
made a movement, and I glanced at her. Her hands were
clenched, but she held herself erect, and in a low voice said:

"I am so in the habit of associating his first disappearance with Maddox that I can never think of him—even
now—without forgetting that he has been to this house,
and is known to be alive. You can understand this."

I answered something at random. She strode across to
me and put her hand on my arm. I felt the pressure of
her grasp long after she had removed her fingers.

"In God's name look at me!" she exclaimed, in a voice
like a moan. "You forget what habit does—what the habit
of thinking for months and months of one thing only—of
one wretched and abhorred thing only—does! I said that
if the dead body in the grounds is Mr. Ransome, he was
murdered by Maddox. I forgot that Mr. Ransome is living. Do you understand me? Why will you not look at
me and answer?"

"I am looking at you, madam. The only answer I can
make to you is, that I pray, with all my heart and strength,
that the dead man is not Mr. Ransome."

She let fall my arm, and turned away.

"It is my destiny!" she exclaimed, keeping her back upon me, "that I should be perpetually saying or doing things to misrepresent myself. But I am not to blame. There is no one who speaks to me but is determined to interpret every look and syllable of mine to my prejudice. My dead mother-in-law," she added, with a low, bitter laugh, "gave me a bad name, and, like the dog of the proverb, I may as well be hanged."

I could find no answer to make to this; but it struck me sorrowfully, and as a remark not very far from the truth.

We neither of us spoke for some moments, and then she confronted me, and inquired if I knew how long her father would be.

"Perhaps an hour," I said.

"What will be done with the body?" she wanted to know.

I answered that there would be an inquest held upon it; and that, in all probability, every member of her household would have to appear as a witness.

"For what purpose?" she demanded, looking at me searchingly.

"I am little acquainted with these matters," I replied; "but I know that it is always customary for a coroner's jury to assemble when a dead body has been found, in order to learn how he came by his death."

"But if the face is not distinguishable, how will they know who he is?"

"They will probably find some clue in his dress."

"Will they bring him to this house?" she exclaimed, with a shudder.

"I dare say they will, madam. The town-hall, or a tavern near the scene of the discovery, is generally chosen for such inquiries. But we are a good distance from Copsford, and they are not likely to carry the body along the main road."

"Will they examine me, do you think?"

"It is impossible that I should know."

"Don't they expose the body at an inquest, and make the people who give evidence look at it?"

"Yes."

She seated herself hastily, and leaned backward.

"I wish papa had taken me away before this discovery had been made," she exclaimed faintly. "Suppose they bring the body to this house! How horrible to feel that such a thing is under one's roof! how horrible to remember that such a thing has tainted the atmosphere in which one lives!"

"Oh, madam," I replied, "do not let us think of the poor dead creature in that way. God knows how he may have died. It is dreadful to imagine him lying all alone under those dark, silent trees, uncoffined, with never a prayer from living heart to God for him. If he is a stranger, what mourners may he not have left! I am ashamed to think that I was afraid to look at him. Whom can he now harm? The strongest and wisest of us shall be as he is in a very little while; and we are so much more akin to him now that he is dead and corrupted than ever we could be were he living, that I blush for my humanity when I remember that I shrunk from the thought of going near him."

She shuddered again, and clapped her hands over her face.

An hour after the Colonel had quitted the house, he returned with the inspector and two other men, who came along the avenue bearing a stretcher, which they set down before the door. The housemaid, looking like a ghost, came to tell me they wanted a sheet. I took one from the clothes press, and went up-stairs with it.

The Colonel and the inspector stood by the stretcher, and the former looked so ill that, for the life of me, I could not help saying to him:

"I hope, sir, it is not necessary that you should again see the body."

"Why not?" he exclaimed loudly, reproving my sympathy with a violent frown.

The reproof made me feel that I had acted with great impertinence; and I faltered out:

"I beg your pardon, sir; I thought you looked wearied."

"What do you mean, Miss Avory? For God's sake be

intelligible!" he cried, staring at me; while the inspector stared at both.

Almost confounded by the quite unexpected effect of my remark, which had been uttered out of my full sympathy for him, I explained that he had himself told me the body was a horrible sight; and I feared that by looking on while it was dug up he would be subjecting himself to too heavy a trial.

"Really you are very kind to take so much interest in me," he exclaimed, with an angry sarcastic laugh, which brought the blood burning to my cheeks. "Why the sight of the body should affect me more than anybody else you shall take another opportunity to explain. Is that the sheet? Throw it on the stretcher. Mr. Inspector, are we ready? The gardener will find us a spade."

The party moved off. I closed the door, overwhelmed with shame. My tongue had undoubtedly betrayed me into an indiscretion; but still I thought he had acted with great unkindness in refusing to understand the obvious and sole motive I had in addressing him.

I presently got the better of my offended sensitiveness, and seeing the dining-room deserted, went in and watched the party walking down the grounds. The Colonel marched in front, with the inspector, whose head moved slowly from side to side as he took in the prospect, first on his left hand and then on his right. Presently they hailed Walters, who came to them. An altercation, which found the gardener very obstinate, appeared to take place; which resulted in Poole being called. It was soon apparent to me that both men refused to disinter the body. One of the bearers of the stretcher cut the matter short by snatching the spade Poole carried out of his hands, and then the four disappeared behind the brow of the hill, leaving the two gardeners staring after them.

For a long while I held my post at the window. The fire in the grate crackled and spurted, and in the silence that reigned throughout the house I could hear the wind sullenly roaring among the leafless branches in the avenue. The scene was no less desolate now than it had been all the morning. The same lead-colored sky hung like a near pall over the hills, and all around the horizon, not concealing the view, but making it infinitely sad and bleak, was a chilly, crawling mist.

My fancy was fascinated by the horror that lay under the distant trees, and set to work to image the thing as it would be seen when the soil that hid it was dug away, and the body exposed to view. Again and again I asked myself if this dead man could be Mr. Ransome, and if he had died there, or been murdered, and if killed, who was his murderer. And though the body should not prove to be Mr. Ransome, could I continue to believe that the man who had come to the house a fortnight before was he? Imagination was quickened by the tragic circumstance of the time, and I found myself reasoning from premises that had not before occurred to me. Thus I remember that the lamp had burned dimly in the hall on that night Mr. Ransome was expected, and that the room in which the meeting had been held had been rendered so gloomy, that it was with difficulty I had distinguished the lineaments of the man who confronted the gentlemen. But when I recalled the impression his face had made on me, I was again infinitely puzzled: for beyond all questions, in size, shape, eyes, in every point I could recall, he who had stood with his back to the fire was Mr. Ransome.

I was recalled from these reflections by the sight of the party returning. The inspector walked in advance; behind him followed the men, bearing the stretcher now covered with a sheet; by the side of the stretcher was the Colonel.

I crouched back from the window. If ever I had boasted my courage, I felt its worthlessness then. I trembled from head to foot. My pen cannot describe the picture as I beheld it; the ghastliness of the white sheet contrasted with the sombre sky overhead; the bending figures of those who bore the stretcher; in the distance, the two gardeners, close together, watching.

Were they going to bring the body to the house? Surely. When they were yet some distance off, they halted, and the

Colonel came forward quickly. I waited in the hall to receive his orders. He threw open the door violently and entered, stopped abruptly, pressing his hand over his heart,
and then in a hollow voice requested me to get him some
brandy. I flew to the sideboard and returned with a bottle
and a wineglass; he filled the glass full and emptied it, half
filled it again and swallowed the draught, and handed me
the bottle.

"The body is to be taken to the spare bedroom."

"Who is it, sir?"

"Mr. Ransome, the inspector thinks. Is my daughter in
her bedroom?"

"I believe so."

"See that her door is closed. Off with you!"

I slunk away stunned. Mrs. Ransome's bedroom door
was shut. I hurried below and was met by the cook.

"Are they bringing it here?" she whispered.

"Yes," I replied. "Hush! where is Sarah?"

"Here," answered the girl, coming out of the kitchen.

"Do not go up-stairs either of you," I exclaimed.

"Tell me, only tell me, miss, I am dying to know;"
burst out the cook; "is it Mr. Ransome?

I refused to answer her, and motioning her back, went to
my room and shut the door.

When the agitation into which I had been thrown by what
the Colonel had told me was in some measure passed, my
curiosity again came to the front, and I opened the door to
hear what was going on upstairs. All was quiet. I concluded that the Colonel was with his daughter in her bedroom, and was debating whether there was any need for me
to remain in the basement, when footsteps sounded in the
hall—a heavy, creaking, professional tramp—and the inspector came to the head of the kitchen stairs and looked
down. I shrunk away, having no wish to undergo a cross-
examination. He presently began to march up and down
the hall.

I passed the next two hours in my room, incessantly pondering over the extraordinary fatality of this discovery and
wearying myself with conjectures as to how it would all end.

I could not understand the Colonel's meaning by the answer
he had made to my question about the dead man; for if the
inspector knew the body was Mr. Ransome's, the Colonel
should know it too; yet his answer had implied that he did
not know. Perhaps he had not dared look at the corpse,
and so got his information about it at second-hand.

It was now long past the lunch hour, and the cook wanted
to receive orders. There seemed a kind of mockery in the
thought of taking food under such circumstances; but nature had to be supported somehow or other; and I considered it my duty to go up-stairs and ask Mrs. Ransome for
instructions.

I crept softly, for the presence of the dead seemed to impose a strange need of stealthiness and silence. The dining-room door was ajar, and through the opening I saw a
constable sitting close to the door. So then the inspector
had been relieved; but I had not heard the constable come
to the house.

He followed me with his eyes, his duty being to prevent
any one from leaving the house.

The drawing-room door was shut; I thought Mrs. Ransome might be there, and peeped in. I was surprised to
find the Colonel alone, seated in an arm-chair with his arms
folded. I was hastily withdrawing when he pronounced
my name, and on my looking in again, desired me to enter
and shut the door. I apologized for my intrusion and explained that I was seeking Mrs. Ransome.

"Don't go near her," he exclaimed. "She must be left
alone. What do you want?"

I spoke of the lunch.

"For whom? not for us. Neither of us could taste food.
Sit down for a moment, Miss Avory. I was sorry to speak
to you so rudely this morning. I perfectly appreciated your
kindness in desiring me not to witness the disinterment of
the body. I felt ill, and no doubt looked so. But all the
same your advice was unwise, because the inspector is full
of suspicion, and he would not have scrupled to form any
monstrous conclusion on the mere idea, suggested by you,
that I was afraid to look at the dead man."

"I am very sorry, sir. I understand the reason of your anger now. I should have taken this view."

"We will say no more about it; the discovery of the body is an awful calamity. I have a conviction that it is not Mr. Ransome; still, it may prove so."

"But what makes the inspector think it is, sir?"

"The body is dressed in Mr. Ransome's coat."

I started and exclaimed, "Whom else, then, can it be?"

"They would not give me time to examine the body closely," he said, pressing his hands convulsively together, and looking downward with a most piteous expression. "'It was for the jury to decide, not for me,' the inspector kept on saying; and they laid the body on the stretcher, and covered it up; and there is a man there—pointing toward the door—who will not let me enter the room in which it lies."

"But how should the inspector know that the body has Mr. Ransome's coat on?" I asked.

"There are some letters in one of the pockets. The man wouldn't show them to me. We crammed them back, and then the body was laid on the stretcher, and covered. All that he said was, 'This is Mr. Ransome.'"

"Did you not say, sir, that the body appeared to have been lying where it was found for many months?"

"Yes; it has mouldered away into a ghastlier thing than the mind can conceive," he answered.

"Then, sir, you can be sure it was not Mr. Ransome, for he was here a fortnight ago."

He started, looked up, and clenched his hand.

"That is my reason," he cried out hoarsely, "for saying this dead man is not Mr. Ransome. The body would be fresh—must be fresh, if it were he! This man has been lying there months and months—there is no face left—he is a skeleton in clothes—an awful sight!"

The blood rushed into his head, and the veins grew knotted about his temples; never was countenance more tragical than his while he continued staring at me, and the blood darkened his skin, and drops of moisture gathered upon his forehead.

I dared not hazard any more questions. I asked him if

he would let me bring him some refreshment. He shook his head violently, and waved his hand without speaking. Before I reached the door he cried out to me not to go near his daughter; she was not to be spoken to—she must be left alone.

I left the room, bewildering my mind with the new and conflicting information he had communicated.

A little after two o'clock a coffin was brought to the house —three men carried it—and an old woman came with it; and they all went into the bedroom where the corpse was. After they had been there some minutes, the old woman came down-stairs for some hot water. I was in the kitchen when she entered, and shrank from her as from something evil. Indeed, she was ugly enough to have sat for the portrait of the hag who turns over the contents of the trunk in the last plate of the wonderful " Rake's Progress." She did not speak a word. She took a jug from the dresser, put it under the cock of the boiler, and stood working her jaws as she watched the steam. When the jug was full she raised it and tottered out of the kitchen. I heard her scraping her way up-stairs and along the hall, and then the bedroom door was shut. Not more than half an hour was occupied by these people to prepare the body for the inquest. When their task was accomplished they glided out of the house noiselessly.

As if these circumstances, crowding upon each other's heels, were not exciting enough, a new and extravagant detail was communicated by the presence of a crowd of persons in the avenue. Ill news, it is said, flies apace; and it was very certain it had not lagged in this instance.

I first caught sight of the people from the window of my own room. There were a good many children in the crowd, a number of men, and several women, some of them with babies in their arms. They were very orderly, and stood staring intently at the house. The coffin had probably attracted them, or maybe the report had spread that a dead body had been found at Gardenhurst; and guessing the mission of the coffin-bearers, a crowd had followed to the gates, from where, finding no portion of the proceedings were to be seen from the road, they had gradual y pushed their way into the grounds.

I was very indignant at the sight of these intruders, and was about to run up-stairs, when, to my great satisfaction, I saw the inspector, followed by a couple of constables, propelling his way by the officer-like process of planting his elbows in the chests of those nearest at hand; and in a very few minutes the avenue was deserted.

The inspector now returned with one of the constables, having perhaps, left the other to guard the gates; and when Sarah came down-stairs, after having admitted him, she told me he had ordered her to leave the door open, as the coroner and jury were expected to arrive in a few minutes.

I hoped that Mrs. Ransome had not seen the crowd. There was something peculiarly degrading in *their* presence. I wondered that she chose to be alone. Guilty or innocent, her full heart would surely need the solace of utterance. If innocent, how terrible must be the sense of the dreadful humiliation that had been brought upon her and her father! If guilty, what must be her thoughts, knowing that she was standing on the very brink of discovery. My sympathy was so strong that I was about to go to her, in defiance of her father's injunction; but the resolution was driven out of my mind by a sudden disturbance up-stairs, caused by the arrival of some of the jury. They were conducted into the library, where they were kept waiting for the others, who shortly arrived. I then heard them all go up-stairs.

I was ignorant of the meaning of their movements, and listened to their footsteps curiously. Presently the two gardeners came into the kitchen through the back door, followed by a constable, who stepped up to me and asued me my name. On my replying, he exclaimed, "Oh, you are to give evidence. You are not to go up-stairs, please, until you are called."

"I suppose I may go into my room?" I said.

"That there?"

"Yes."

"Anybody in it?"

"No."

" Yes, you can stop there."

Saying which he re-entered the kitchen.

I had now to wait for about half an hour, during which some of the other witnesses were examined; and then I was told to go up-stairs by the constable. The inspector received me without speaking, and mounted to the bedroom, motioning me to follow. I made strong efforts to control myself, but my agitation was very great, and my nerves, as I entered the bedroom, threatened to give way.

The scene into which I was admitted was one that might have fairly oppressed a stouter heart than mine. The window-blinds were drawn up, and the coffin, supported on chairs, had been placed close to the window to receive the light. The sheet that had covered the body was thrown negligently over the foot of the coffin, which was of a pale yellow. I halted when I saw this dreadful object and a sudden faintness came over me. To my surprise the inspector, dropping his dictatorial tone, approached me and said very kindly, " You are only required to take one look. It's necessary for the evidence you'll be called on to give. The others have viewed it. You must take heart—there's nothing to hurt you."

I stared at the coffin, shuddering violently, but at the same time laying the utmost control upon myself, because I knew it was absolutely necessary that I should look at the body. I now observed that the lid of the coffin framed a long piece of glass. The inspector took my hand, quite gently, for which I felt immeasurably grateful to him, and I walked with all the boldness I could summon to the side of the coffin and looked through the glass.

For some moments I could see nothing, for my head swam and the glass seemed dark; then the outline beneath defined itself and I saw—but what I saw I will not describe. The memory haunts me to this hour, and often makes a portion of my dreams.

"Take particular notice of what you see," said the inspector; " that'll help you to tell the jury what you think."

I did so, being now able to discern the ghastly and shape-

less contents of the coffin clearly enough; and then sick,
cold, and horror-stricken, I backed away and walked with
faltering movements to the door.

I was detained, however, by the inspector, who took a
coat, which I had not perceived, from the side of the coffin,
and asked me to inspect it. I draw near and looked at it
attentively. The cloth was green, in portions mouldy, and
stained by the damp of the earth. I could not pretend to
say of what material the coat was made; in shape it was
loose, with pockets at the side and a breast pocket, from
which the inspector drew three papers and desired me to
look at them. The first of these papers was a receipt from
a harness-maker at Copsford, made out to Mr. Ransome;
the second was a letter from old Mrs. Ransome, dated from
Guildford; the third was a portion of a letter, but whether
in his own writing or not I could not say. But very few
of the words were decipherable owing to the humidity having caused the ink to run. The harness-maker's receipt,
however, was in good preservation, and the words "To —
Ransome, Esq.," written on a ruled line at the head of the
bill, were very distinct.

I breathed freely when I was out of that room. The inspector told me to stop in the hall; but I had not waited
above twenty seconds when the cook came out of the dining-
room, yellow with fear, and made for the kitchen staircase
with surprising agility.

The inspector now desired me to enter the dining-room;
I did so, and found myself in the presence of a number of
men, two of whom were familiar to me as our baker and
chemist. I was in the temper to be easily frightened; but
happily the coroner, one Dr. Sheldon, was, without exception, the most amiable-looking old gentleman I ever saw.
His glance met mine so kindly that I was at once reassured,
and felt as collected as perhaps under the circumstances it
was necessary I should feel.

I recall the scene distinctly; but recollect only the leading questions which were put to me. There was one little
man, with a very snappish manner and a very sour face
who frequently interrupted the coroner's examination itu.

irrelevant questions, which he delivered with an air of great
knowingness, and then dropped his head on one side, with
an artful smile at his companions, to catch my answer. The
rest were very grave and attentive, and obviously considered
the coroner a great man.

Were I to relate even what I can remember of the examination I underwent, the record would extend to a great
many pages. An abridgment of my answers would present
the substance of the evidence I gave in this form:

That my name was Caroline Avory and that I was housekeeper; and that I had been in my present situation since
June. Had viewed the body and was sure it was not Mr.
Ransome's; because the hair on the head of the body was
brown, and Mr. Ransome's hair was very black. Could not
identify the body with any person I ever had seen, owing
to the face being decayed out of all resemblance to anything
human. Could not say whether the coat was Mr. Ransome's or not. Remembered seeing him wear a coat cut in
that fashion. Had seen the papers found in the pocket of
the coat, but could not imagine how they had come there.
Was quite positive the body was not Mr. Ransome's for two
reasons: first, that its decomposed state proved it to have
been dead for many weeks, whereas Mr. Ransome was alive
and at his house a fortnight before; secondly, neither the
hair, nor, so far as the outline could be distinguished, the
shape of the head, was that of Mr. Ransome. Could swear
that all Mr. Ransome's linen was marked with his initials,
S. R. Knew that he was mad and of very eccentric habits,
but had never heard that he was subject to fits. Had heard
footsteps outside the house on the night Mr. Ransome was
missed; was sure that some one had been walking in the
grounds. Could not tell whether the body was the footman's; believed it more likely to be the footman's than Mr.
Ransome's; but considered if it were the footman's it could
be identified.

And so on: evidence that conveyed no further illumination than my profound conviction that the body was not Mr.
Ransome's. Two of the jury tried hard to shake me on this
point; but my persuasion was too firm for them. It was

enough that the body had brown hair. To suppose that black hair would turn brown after death was absurd; and unless this could be supposed, then most assuredly the dead man was not Mr. Ransome. The coroner took up one of the jury on this and silenced him. I then left the room.

Shortly afterward the jury withdrew to the library to consider their verdict. When I got down-stairs I found the under-gardener and the cook hotly arguing. Poole was very quiet and determined. As I passed the door the cook cried out to me to come and say if I believed the body lying up-stairs was master's.

"No," I replied; "who says it is?"

"I say it is, an' I'll swear it," rejoined Poole.

"You must be as blind as a mole," exclaimed Walters, "not to know the difference between brown hair and black."

"I don't care nothing for that," retorted the other. · "It's brown now, aut it was black once."

"That's nonsense," I said. "The coroner himself will tell you so. By such assumptions you may prove the dead man anybody."

"Besides," cried the cook, "the inspector himself told me that the body must have been lying under the trees for months an' months to be in that state; and have you lost your memory not to know that Mr. Ransome was alive an' hearty this day a fortnight ago?"

"Alive an' hearty, yes!" sneered Poole, with a glance at me. "Did yer see him?"

"You did, and so did I!" I exclaimed.

"Ah, and so we did. And pray was you satisfied that he *was* Mr. Ransome?" he demanded very impudently.

The cook and the gardener stared, and the first said, "Why, what's come to yer, man? Would you fly in the face of the gentlemen as saw him wi' their own eyes and was satisfied?"

"Saw him!" said the man contemptuously; "I reckon they saw as much of me. Why was the light turned down, and the shadder thrown over his face, I should like to know?"

22

"Have you spoken to the Colonel of these doubts of yours?" I asked him.

"No, I haven't," he answered fiercely; "but I don't fear his knowing of them."

"Then you had better do so. If you don't, I will."

"So you may, and be d—d to you!" he cried. "I'm not afraid of you nor the Colonel either, nor e'er a one in this house. What I told the jury I'll stick to: that the man up-stairs is Mr. Ransome!"

And with a brutal laugh the fellow walked out of the kitchen.

There was something far more puzzling than irritating in this man's reckless boldness. What made him assume as a *fact* the notion that had flashed across my mind only as a suspicion, and a suspicion so dangerous and alarming that I summarily rejected it as often as it recurred to me?

Walters was beginning to comment on his mate's rude and violent behavior, when the cook interrupted him by crying, "Hark!" The jury were leaving the library and turning to the dining-room with their verdict.

I went out of the kitchen, greatly excited, and mounted the staircase half-way, fearing to advance and listening with strained attention. In a short time the jury left the dining-room and filled the hall. There was a great buzz among them while they adjusted their hats. I ascended to the top of the stairs, determined to know what the verdict was; but was at once reassured by the sight of the Colonel, who was conversing with the coroner, and whose face, white and thin and sickly looking, wore a smile.

I said to a tall, beetle-browed man, "Will you tell me the verdict?"

"Why, ma'am, that the man is dead; but who he is, and how he came by his death, there is no evidence to show."

I thanked him, and slipped away out of the hall.

This, then, was the end of it! And how would the public receive the verdict? The dead man was most unquestionably *not* Mr. Ransome. The jury had obviously found that out by better evidence than any I could have given them. But if he was not Mr. Ransome, how came he with

Mr. Ransome's coat on, and with letters belonging to Mr. Ransome on him? And what made Poole so positive that he *was* Mr. Ransome? I had before, involuntarily, and on no better evidence than the casual meeting him on the terrace, suspected Poole of having played some part in the mystery which had puzzled Copsford, and those who knew what Copsford never could know, ever since the day of Mr. Ransome's disappearance; but his behavior in the kitchen— his dogged declaration that the dead man was Mr. Ransome, his equally dogged declaration that the man who had been brought to the house by the Colonel was not Mr. Ransome—all decided me in regarding him as capable of explaining the whole of the mystery away, if he chose to tell what he knew. At all events, I resolved to have a talk with the Colonel about him.

By half-past three the house was deserted, and not very long afterward a hearse drove up, and some men came in and carried the coffin away. The gloom seemed to lift with the departure of that ghastly burden; but I was sure that the room in which it had been deposited would never be entered again by those to whom the house belonged, and that it furnished an association which, during the remainder of the time the Colonel and Mrs. Ransome stayed at Gardenhurst, would make their home insupportable and odious to them.

IX

The afternoon wore away, and a little before six o'clock the Colonel sent for me. The night had fallen densely, with a high wind that whirled the snowflakes in the air, and sometimes brought smart discharges of hail against the windows.

He was in the dining-room.

"I have been with my daughter all the afternoon. She has been very ill. They made her look at the body, which was cruel. It was an unfit sight for a woman to behold. And after she had given her evidence, she went to her bedroom and fainted, and there she lay on the floor, unconscious, for an hour."

"Oh, sir, I wish I had known it!" I explained. "You told me not to go near her."

"She is better now. You can take a cup of tea presently to her. What a day this has been!"

"Thank God it has ended, and ended well, sir!"

"Did you see the body?"

"Yes."

"It was a shocking sight," he said, with a shudder.

"I cannot understand why they should have tried to identify it with Mr. Ransome, sir. The coroner, as a doctor, must have known that the poor man, whoever he is, has been dead many weeks; and were they not all aware that Mr. Ransome was here a fortnight ago?"

I faltered as I asked this question. He took me up quickly.

"Of course they were aware; and that helped them to their verdict. A doctor named Mason examined the body wehn it was up-stairs, and gave medical evidence."

"What evidence, sir?"

"Why, that he could find no marks of violence. For my part, I don't think he had the stomach to examine the loathsome thing. I believe he stared at it through the glass, and pronounced upon what he saw. The face had mouldered away, and I should imagine that without a minute inspection it would be impossible to detect signs of violence on that part of the head amid such corruption. Did they show you the coat?"

"Yes, sir."

"Was it Mr. Ransome's?"

"I could not possibly say."

"How came the letters there?"

"That is a mystery."

"Ay, more bewildering than anything that has yet occurred. The trousers and waistcoat were of coarse material, and did not match the coat. There was no mark on the linen. The boots had rotted and broken open. He might have been a year lying where he was found."

"Was he not buried, sir, when found?"

"He was close to the surface. Whether his grave was dug for him or not I cannot imagine. Had he borne signs of violence, then they would have said that his grave had been dug."

"Did it occur to anybody to suggest that he was Mad-dox?" I said.

He started, looked at me earnestly, and said:

"The footman! I never thought of that. Why should it not be Maddox? The existence of the letters belonging to Mr. Ransome might then be explained."

"Easily, sir; by supposing that the letters were stolen from his master's bedroom."

"But for what purpose?"

"I cannot guess."

"But nothing *but* the letters were found in the man's pocket. You remember the footman—I never saw him: stay—I forget. I saw him when I came to Gardenhurst from Boulogne; but I have no recollection of his face and appearance. Did the dead man resemble him in any particular?"

"In none that I can recall, sir. Yet whom *could* such a thing resemble?"

"Was Maddox's hair brown?"

"It was dark; but you must remember, sir, that I had not been here long when he was missed, and during that time I saw but very little of him—not enough to leave a distinct impression of him upon my mind, as I discover now, when I endeavor to recollect his face."

"This is a curious conjecture of yours, though," he exclaimed. "Suppose the dead man should be Maddox?"

I was silent. He looked at me inquiringly.

"I am striving to recall him," I said. "Maddox was of a middle height, with a somewhat similar cast of face to Mr. Ransome's—I mean, the jawbones were long and the face thin. The dead man—I could see nothing of him!" I exclaimed, shuddering at the hideous recollection.

"Let us imagine the dead man Maddox," he said, taking a chair, and motioning me to be seated. "How came he where he was found? Did he die there, or was he killed?

But he would not be dressed like that, would he? I know
what his livery would be.   What was his undress?"
  "He always worked in the morning in a sleeved waist-
coat and black cloth trousers.   If he had to answer the
door he would slip on his coat belonging to his livery."
  "The body was not dressed in black cloth?"
  "No, sir."
  He was a long while silent, and then repeated:
  "Suppose the man *should* be Maddox?"
  "The body is certainly not Mr. Ransome."
  "No; that is past doubt.   The letters prove nothing;
they make a mystery, but they prove nothing."
  "It might have been surmised that this man was Mad-
dox; that Mr. Ransome had killed him, and was hiding
himself for fear of the consequences."
  "Why may not the surmise be entertained now?" he de-
manded eagerly.
  "Because Mr. Ransome was here a fortnight ago, sir."
  "Ah, to be sure," he replied, drawing back and clasping
his hands firmly.   "The chain is so confused that I am apt
to overlook some of the links."
  I took care not to let him see that I noticed his confusion.
  "Your under-gardener, Poole," I said, "declares positively that the dead man is Mr. Ransome."
  "Yes; he was the only one of the witnesses who stated
that.   He is a blockhead, and acquitted himself like one
during the examination.   He showed a curious animus
against us by implying that Mr. Ransome had been murdered, and that the body up-stairs was his.   He knew, of
course, that that had been the current suspicion for a good
many months.   I shall discharge him by and by, but I
must not be in a hurry; it would not answer my purpose
for people to say the man was discharged for suggesting
that Mr. Ransome had been murdered."
  "He may be a blockhead, sir, but he is a very dangerous
one.   He does not scruple to declare it as his opinion, that
the man who came to this house a fortnight ago was not
Mr. Ransome."

"He says that!" he exclaimed, knitting his brows. "Did he give his reasons for having this notion?"

"No, sir."

"You found him peering from the terrace into the drawing-room that night?"

"Yes."

He got up, went to the window, and stood there for some moments, his face concealed from me. Presently he turned and said:

"You supply me with a good reason for discharging him. He *is* dangerous. That notion of his would be a very compromising rumor to start, wouldn't it? After this discovery and inquest too! . . . Your suggestion about Maddox has put a thought into my head; but I am not sure that I shall act upon it. The inquest is over, the body will be buried. I shall require a little reflection before I resolve to disturb these ashes again, and fix attention upon a new inquiry. And now, Miss Avory, will you be so kind as to take my daughter a cup of tea, and see how she is?"

This was the most unsatisfactory conversation I had ever had with him. Whatever his views were, he had not conveyed them. That he believed the dead man to be Maddox, or that he believed him Mr. Ransome; that he believed Mr. Ransome dead, or that he believed him alive; that he believed the man whom the detective Johnson had found to be Mr. Ransome, or that he believed him to be somebody else—was as little to be guessed by me from his manner, as the name of the body was to be guessed from the inquest that had been held upon it.

What, then, was this mystery? for a mystery there was, dark and complex, known to the Colonel and his daughter, and to them alone. Had Poole any share in it? He had worked for some years on the estate; he had, to the best of my knowledge, always been well-treated by Mrs. Ransome; it was impossible, therefore, to suppose that the evidence he had given, or rather the assertions he had made, were dictated by ill-feeling toward his employers. Surely I might almost be justified in supposing that he had a particular reason either for knowing Mr. Ransome to be dead, or for wishing him dead, by his declaring that the discovered body was Mr. Ransome's. He might, indeed, have been deceived by a fancied resemblance; he might even believe that the humidity of the earth, which had rotted and colored the clothes into an indistinguishable texture, would likewise transform the hair from black into brown. But certainly his obstinacy would yield to the conjoint testimony of the other witnesses, who, every one of us, had positively affirmed that the corpse was not Mr. Ransome's.

His tenacity, however, persuaded me that he was sincere in his belief that the man who had come to the house a fortnight before was not Mr. Ransome. The most ignorant person could not have beheld the condition of the corpse without being quite satisfied that it had been dead for months. To assert, then, that this body was Mr. Ransome's was tantamount to saying that Mr. Ransome had been dead for many months.

These thoughts occupied my mind while I prepared the tea which I was to carry to Mrs. Ransome; and when the tray was prepared, I took it up-stairs.

I knocked timidly, not being sure that my visit would be welcome. Mrs. Ransome's voice bade me enter. I found her lying in her dressing-gown upon the sofa, which had been wheeled close to the fire. A pair of candles were alight on the mantelpiece. The atmosphere of the room was almost disagreeable with the mingled perfumes of toilet-vinegar and other scents. She looked pale and exhausted, and her heavy white arm, bare to the elbow, hung languidly down over the side of the sofa.

I told her that her father had requested me to bring her some tea. She thanked me without turning her head, but did not ask me to sit. I could tell by her few words of thanks that she had not the strength to converse, and was looking about her to see in what way I could make her more comfortable before quitting the room, when she asked me in a low tone if I had been examined by the jury.

I replied that I had.

"Did they make you look into the coffin?" she asked.

"Yes," I answered.

"Will you ever forget what you saw? While I live that horrible sight will haunt me. Why did they force me to look at it?"

"There were no other means of identifying him. All the witnesses had to look. We were thus enabled positively to declare that the dead man was not Mr. Ransome."

"Suppose he had turned out to be Mr. Ransome, what would have been done?" she inquired, rousing herself a little.

"Such a discovery would have been very unfortunate and menacing, after the suspicions which have been bandied about."

"People, of course, would have said that he had been murdered, and that his mother was in the right when she accused me of the crime."

"No doubt something of the kind would have been said."

"And what would they have done to me?"

"Nothing. What proofs would they have to go upon?"

"Will the matter end now?" she demanded, with a small feverish impatience quickening her physical lassitude.

"No doubt. The jury are satisfied that the dead man is a stranger. How he came where he was found, and how he managed to have letters belonging to Mr. Ransome on him, are problems which may never be solved. The face was decayed beyond all possibility of recognition, and the worst that can now be said is, that the body of a man was found at Gardenhurst, under what the newspapers call suspicious circumstances."

"The letter from Mrs. Ransome was dated last April, papa told me. The harness-maker's bill is two years old."

"Indeed! I forgot to ask Colonel Kilmain about the dates of these papers. I *cannot* imagine how this unknown man came by them."

"Could not they tell whether he had been murdered or not?"

"It seems they could find no signs to indicate a violent death. Suppose he was murdered. A single blow might have killed him. That blow need not necessarily leave

such a mark as would be distinguishable amid the decay of
the body.   In the absence of such sign, I don't see what
other conclusion the jury could have arrived at than the
plain verdict they recorded."

"Who could he have been?" she inquired.   "How came
he at Gardenhurst?   Was he a friend of Mr. Ransome?
But even that would not account for his having papers of
Mr. Ransome upon him."

"I asked Colonel Kilmain if he thought the body was
Maddox's."

She started forward, and exclaimed, with a deep-drawn
breath:

"It may have been Maddox!"

"The hair was brown.   Maddox's hair was brown, was
it not, madam?"

"It was dark, certainly," she answered, looking at me
eagerly.

"Unfortunately," I continued, "the hair was the only
recognizable sign the body presented.   There was literally
nothing else that would help to prove the theory that this
man was Maddox.   Nothing was found in his pockets but
those letters of Mr. Ransome.   Whoever the man was, it
was pretty certain that if he was not murdered he was
robbed.   One cannot conceive that a man would be wandering about with nothing in his pockets but letters belonging
to another man, of no use to him."

"But is *nothing* to be said in favor of your conjecture
that he was Maddox?" she said, sinking back and resuming
her listless manner.   "Let it be one or the other of them;
master or man—it would not matter.   One of them, dead,
might explain the disappearance of the other."

"You mean the original disappearance?"

"Yes, of course," she answered quickly.

"We know, on Mr. Ransome's confession, that he knew
nothing of Maddox and the robbery of the plate."

"I told you that myself."

"Yes, madam, you did."

"But are we bound to believe what Mr. Ransome says?
Make me believe that the dead man who we have seen to

day is Maddox, and you will convince me that he was murdered by Mr. Ransome."

"I should hesitate to take that view, even supposing we
knew this body to be the footman's. Had we not full
proof that Mr. Ransome was living a fortnight ago there
would be much more probability in the conjecture that the
body was his, and that he had been murdered by Maddox."
She sipped her tea languidly, and said, "Mr. Ransome
had not brown hair."

I was anxious to drop the subject, for I found myself
getting into a labyrinth, and dreaded lest I should make
some remark, inadvertently, to lead her to suspect that I
questioned the identity of the man who had been brought
to the house by her father. On this account I said nothing
to her about Poole. There were many reasons why I
should not appear to possess such a suspicion. I had
largely shared her own and her father's confidence, and
could not, consistently with the gratitude I felt toward
them both for many acts of kindness, imply my belief of
their being guilty of an extravagant imposition, the main-
tenance of which made falsehood a compulsory condition of
their actions and speech. Again, in the event of my suspicion proving right, I had to consider the great provocation the Colonel had received to practise this imposition, in
the overwhelming accusation old Mrs. Ransome had brought
against his daughter, and in the sinister scandal that had
been circulated to her dishonor in Copsford. But chiefly I
had to consider that my suspicion might be quite unwarrantable; and certainly, when I came to examine the foundation
on which it rested, I could refer it to no better origin than
the assertion of Poole (who could not know more of the
truth than I), and to one or two slips I had noticed in the
Colonel's and his daughter's conversation with me.

She continued harping for some time on my theory, that
the dead man might be Maddox; and then she told me the
questions which had been put to her by the coroner, and
how she had fainted when she reached her bedroom. At
this juncture her father entered the room, which gave me
an opportunity to slip away.

I little guessed, as I went down-stairs, how very close we all were to the solution of one portion of the mystery, of which these pages tell the story. Fateful as the day had proved, the strangest of the events which belonged to it had yet to happen.

On reaching the basement, I heard the sound of a male voice in the kitchen, and there found the upper-gardener, Walters.

"Good evening, mum," said he. "I thought I'd just step this way, to larn if there was anything fresh."

The kitchen was very warm, and looked very comfortable. A bright red fire glowed in the grate, and shone in the well-polished crockery and glasses upon the dresser. Through the window one might see the snowflakes falling, gleaming white in the light as they dropped softly past the black glass. At the end of the table sat the housemaid, sewing, the picture of a smart English servant. The cook confronted the gardener, her red, fat arms upon the table, her attitude and face alive with the curiosity and awe the events of the day had inspired in her soul. The gardener looked rather shiny with the snow that had melted upon his shoulders. He was partaking of some tea and bread and butter, which the hospitable cook had been good enough to set before him. Very homely and honest was the aspect of his old brown face, freed of the stains and damp of his day's labor by a plentiful application of soap. The scene was so cozy that I was tempted to draw one of the wooden chairs from the wall.

"I hope the mistress ain't none the worse for what's happened," exclaimed Walters.

"The sight of the body made her ill," I answered.

"An awful sight!" said the cook. "Sarah and me sleep together to-night. I wouldn't lie alone not if I was to be boiled alive for refusin'."

"You should ha' see it as I did," exclaimed Walters. "Close agin the hedge the grass is pretty short and fine. I took my spade and planned out a good-sized sod, ready for lifting. Then I dug my spade in, and heaved up; but the tool slipped, as though I had struck glass, and brings

up some stuff along wi't which I fell on my knees to look
at, for I reckoned it wur a new kind of plant, and was
puzzled by it. I did think it uncommon like hair too; an'
when my nose were close again it I noticed that the mould
had a queer look—a kind o' crumbly look—though it was
hard enough with the frost. I gave a kind o' pull at the
hair, not knowin' it to be such, and the soil gives way like
pie-crust, and out came the man's head; an' I think it
drove me daft for a while, for I stood looking at it a bit
quite silly."

"I should have run away! I should have thought I had
opened a hole for the devil to come through!" said the cook
in a faint voice.

"What 'ud ha' been the good of running away?" replied
Walters. "Had he looked like a dead man I'd ha' felt no
fear, no more than if I wur looking at you. It wur the
suddenness of the head jumping up out o' the mould, and
the ugly, mangled face as came out along with it, as turned
me sick and silly."

"All of us here," said I, "saw the body in the coffin; did
any of you trace a likeness to anybody you knew in it?"

"There wur nothing to see—nothing like a man, I mean,"
replied the gardener.

"Do you remember Maddox?"

"I remember him, rather," cried the cook.

"Did it strike you that the dead man might be Maddox?"

"No," answered the cook breathlessly. "Is he Maddox?"

"I am sure I don't know," I replied. "Maddox had
brown hair, and so had the body."

"I don't think Maddox's hair was brown, mum," said
the gardener. "It was darker than brown—it was very
near black."

"You're wrong," exclaimed the cook; "it was lighter
than brown; it was more the color of your hair, Miss
Avory."

"I say it was very near black," persisted the gardener.
"Cast your thoughts back, missis, an' you'll agree with
me."

"If he is Maddox," said I, "he'll not owe his identifica

tion to us. But the matter is of no consequence, for the jury have disposed of it as far as it can be disposed of.'

"They made me look at the corpse," said the housemaid, "when they found out I had opened the door to Mr. Ransome that night he came here. I didn't notice the hair was brown."

"What color wur it, then?" asked the gardener.

"More the color of my hair," she replied; her hair was a light auburn.

The old man pish'd, and drank his tea.

I began to appreciate the difficulties lawyers complain of in trying to obtain evidence. Here were four of us, all professing to know exactly what we were talking about, flatly contradicting one another. I changed the subject by asking Walters when his daughter was going to be married to Poole.

"Oh, it's off," he answered. "She an' him quarrelled some time ago. His temper don't please her."

"She has acted wisely in my opinion," said I. "There's something wrong about him, and I should very much like to find out what it is. What made him so impertinent to me to-day?"

"Something's come over him lately that's often puzzled me myself," replied Walters. "He used to work well when he first came here; but he's grown very careless and skulking, and I'm constantly at him for neglecting his work and doing things wrong. He talks of goin' away—leavin' the country. The sooner the better—that's what I says."

"Fancy his declaring that wasn't Mr. Ransome who came here the other day," exclaimed the cook. "Is he in his right mind, I wonder?"

"One would think, to hear him talk," said I, "that he knew more about Mr. Ransome than he chose to tell. His declaring that the dead man was Mr. Ransome, in defiance of his own eyes—for he was in the terrace that night peeping at the gentlemen in the drawing-room through the window—seems very suspicious to me."

"If the dead man had been Mr. Ransome," cried the cook warmly, "it would be as likely as not that Poole had murdered him!"

"Hush!" said Walters, "you mustn't talk like that!"

"Did he ever speak to you about Mr. Ransome?" I asked the old man.

"Well, yes; more nor I cared to hear. When them suspicions about Mrs. Ransome first got about, he was always knocking off work to come an' have a yarn about the master. But I wouldn't have nothin' to say to him. It wur no business of his or mine."

"What did he say?"

"Why, that his notion was, Mr. Ransome *was* murdered, an' that the murder 'ud one day be brought to light."

"How should he know, if he didn't do it hisself?" demanded the cook.

"His idea was," continued the old man, taking up his cap and looking toward the door, "that Maddox had played off on the master's madness, an' got him out o' the house, and then killed him. And then he'd say, 'If that ain't true, Joe, who knows if the old lady warn't in the right?' This 'ud make me angry, and I rather believe as the cause of that quarrel 'tween him an' my gal was my sayin' that he wur no man for strivin' to ruin the character of the mistress as paid him, an' had always been kind to him."

Saying this, he got up, emptied his tea-cup, wished us good-night, and walked out of the kitchen.

I stopped in the kitchen for the rest of the evening, preferring the company of the servants and the cheerful fire to the solitude of my room, where I very well knew the spectre of memory—the face I had looked at through the glass in the coffin—awaited me. The housemaid told me that the Colonel was with his daughter in her bedroom. They were talking over their future plans, no doubt; and, among other matters, I might now conclude that I was not likely to be housekeeper at Gardenhurst much longer. Mrs. Ransome must utterly abhor the place by this time. Even I, who found a comfortable home in it, was growing very weary of its monotony. The estate itself was a little Paradise; but places are made pleasant not by pleasant sights, but by pleasant associations. The house had been gloomy enough while Mr. Ransome inhabited it. The suspicions

his disappearance engendered had made it a very dark and
melancholy home indeed.   It scarcely needed the discovery
of the dead body, and the abundant gossip that would be
excited by it, to make Gardenhurst intolerable to its
possessors.

The cook and I talked over the probability of both of us,
before long, being in search of new situations; and then we
passed in review all that had happened since I had been in
the house, and conjectured, as best we could, Poole's motives in protesting that Mr. Ransome had been murdered;
and then, by an easy transition, we got upon the subject of
the inquest, and which set us talking of murders in general,
while the housemaid entertained us with an account of the
murder of a factory apprentice in the city she came from,
which was so ghastly (related as it was with demure unc-
tion, and much secret enjoyment of the perspiration it engendered), that I heartily sympathized with the cook's
terrors, and looked forward with some apprehension to my
usually lonesome job of locking up the house for the night.

When Sarah had taken up the hot water and glasses at
ten o'clock, she told us that Mrs. Ransome was in the dining-room with her father.   Hearing this, I thought it my
duty to go and inquire how she was.   So I went up-stairs.
Certainly Mrs. Ransome looked very ill.   The hollows
under her eyes were quite livid, and contrasted painfully
and disagreeably with the ashy paleness of the rest of her
face.   She was wrapped in a dressing-gown, and sat on a
low chair before the fire; while her father, looking fagged
to death and very nearly as ill as she, leaned back in an
armchair opposite her, his hands folded on his breast, and
his face full of deep and painful reflection.

I asked Mrs. Ransome if there was anything I could do
for her before she went to bed.

"No, thank you; there is nothing, Miss Avory."

"I persuaded Mrs. Ransome to come down-stairs," said
the Colonel.   "She has been in her bedroom nearly all
day."

"I think Mrs. Ransome wants a change from this house
altogether, sir," I exclaimed, impressed more and more, the

longer I looked at her, by her forlorn, weakly, and broken hearted aspect.

"She shall have a change before long, depend upon it," he answered, with sudden energy. "And the change shall be a permanent one, too."

"I am afraid you have eaten nothing to-day, madam."

"Very little; but I shall feel better to-morrow, I hope," she replied. "I am going to bed in a few minutes. Will you tell Sarah to see to the fire in my room?"

I attended to her request myself, and after I had heaped some coals on the grate, could not forbear gazing around the large and handsome apartment, and reflecting on the many strange events that had taken place since I first peeped into this room on my arrival at Gardenhurst. I recalled that night when, from the bedroom overhead, I had heard the handle of a door turned, the tread of a footstep in the garden, the creak of the staircase on the landing. I recalled my astonishment on discovering next morning that both Mr. Ransome and the footman were missing. I recalled the long and tedious interval of suspense that had followed that discovery, and the supposed final solution of the mystery in the visit of Mr. Ransome to Gardenhurst. Who was that man? Was he indeed Mr. Ransome? If so, how came my doubts of him? What grounds had Poole for his positive declaration that this man was not Mr. Ransome? And who was the dead man who had been unearthed from his resting-place under the trees?

As I asked myself these questions, as I reviewed the whole of the conflicting circumstances as they occurred to my mind, I felt that the mystery was darker than ever it had been before; that the very details which might seem to explain away the most puzzling portions of the enigma had, in reality only more hopelessly complicated it. If the man that had been produced by the Colonel *were* Mr. Ransome, where was he now? How was it, that amid the numerous conversations I had with the Colonel and his daughter during the fortnight, no reference to his whereabouts—no comment upon his extraordinary and final leave-taking—no conjecture as to his intentions—had ever escaped either of

23

them? And where was Maddox that he was not to be found? The detection of the footman should have seemed an easier task than the detection of his master; for, in robbing the house, he had carried away many tokens of his guilt, through any of which the police might trace him.

A footstep startled me from the reverie into which I had fallen. I left the room, and met Mrs. Ransome coming up-stairs, followed by her father. They wished me good-night as they passed, and I observed that as Mrs. Ransome turned the bend of the staircase, she threw a startled glance at the door of the room in which the body had been lodged. The mere existence of that room was now a horror in the house. The Colonel called to me when I was in the hall:

"Miss Avory, I shall not come down-stairs again. You can send the servants to bed, and lock up."

"Very well, sir," I replied.

I heard him go with his daughter into her bedroom. He was clearly very anxious about her.

Had I not secretly shared in the cook's fears, I should no doubt have found them comical enough. She was decidedly annoyed to hear that the Colonel had told me to send the servants to bed, declaring that in her last place the servants never went to bed before eleven; that for her part she didn't feel at all sleepy; that six hours' sleep was long enough for anybody in health; all which meant that she was afraid to go up-stairs. Grumbling, and starting at the shadows thrown by her candle, and peering earnestly ahead of her, she passed out of the kitchen followed by Sarah, who nearly trod her down in her anxiety to keep close. Their footsteps died away, and I was left alone.

I was not so in love with the silence and loneliness of the lower part of the house at that moment as to care to loiter; accordingly, I lighted my candle, and locked up the basement, after raking out the fire in my room. This done, I went up-stairs and bolted the hall-doors, and went into the dining-room to see to the fastenings of the windows. I was so used to this last duty of my every day's work that I went about it quite mechanically. I directed my steps to the drawing-room, meaning to extinguish the hall-lamp as

I went up-stairs. The small flame of my candle barely pierced the gloom of the large room, darkened yet by its sombre drapery, the velvet curtains, the dark walnut furniture, the chocolate-colored carpet. The atmosphere was raw and nipping. Colder it could scarcely have been had all the windows been wide open. My impression was that one of the windows *was* open.

I placed the candle on the table, and walked to the window facing the door. That was fastened; so was the next. I went to the others facing the terrace.

Through them—not a window in the house had shutters—I saw the grounds stretching pale beyond the pillars of the terrace—a blank surface of snow gathering depth even as I watched from the flakes which thickened the air. The snow aided by the moon, whose light was not to be eclipsed though her orb was hidden, made a species of twilight in which even objects some distance off were visible. The near bushes, whitened atop, their under-branches blackly marked upon the snow, resembled human beings; nor was it difficult, by keeping the eye fixed on them, to imagine that they moved.

I had halted a moment before the first window overlooking the terrace. I now passed to the second. But scarcely had I looked through it, when I shrieked and recoiled. Staring in through it, in a crouching posture, so as to see into the room through the curtains, which were festooned off at the point where his eyes were, was the figure of a man. I could not distinguish his face; the candle was too far off to reflect its light upon him; nothing but his outline, sharply defined against the snow, which formed the background, was perceptible.

I stood for a moment rooted to the floor, my mouth dry, my heart beating wildly, my whole body struck motionless by the sudden terror caused me by this unexpected apparition. In that moment the figure motioned with his hand; the gesture acted upon me like a shock of galvanism. Swiftly as my legs could carry me I fled from the room, and bounded up the stairs.

I knocked furiously at the Colonel's bedroom door, but

elicited no answer; but in a moment or two Mrs. Ransome's bedroom door was opened, and the Colonel came out. Within I saw Mrs. Ransome seated before the fire.

"What is the matter, Miss Avory?" asked the Colonel.

"There is a man on the terrace, sir," I answered, breathlessly. "He is looking through the drawing-room window."

"Where is your candle?"

"I left it burning in the drawing-room."

He hurried down-stairs. I followed him, taking courage from his presence, and eager to show him where the man had been, in case he should be gone. I heard Mrs. Ransome call to me, but would not stay to answer her. My belief was that the man was Poole. The Colonel had snatched a stick from the hat-stand, and had passed through the drawing-room when I entered; he was in the act of opening the terrace window.

"Be on your guard, sir," I cried; "there may be more than one."

"Let there be a dozen," he answered, "some of them shall find me tough enough, I promise. Bring the candle this way."

As he spoke he threw open the window and stepped out, grasping his stick with both hands. The bitter night air streamed in and sent shudder after shudder through me. The Colonel stood full in the window, a foot beyond it, looking steadily to the right; and I heard him say:

"What are you doing there?"

A voice answered. I did not catch the words, but the tone thrilled through me as though a voice had spoken from the grave.

The stick fell from the Colonel's hand; he threw up his arms in a wild and unaccountable gesture.

"At last!" he cried. In another instant he had thrust forth his hands and whirled, with the strength of a giant, the man into the room. He had him by the collar; he retained his hold for several moments, then let go. The man's arms hung idly by his side. The Colonel fell back a step, and they looked at each other without speaking.

Fifteen days before, dating from that very night, the

man I now looked at was supposed to have been at Gardenhurst. Fifteen days before this man had been young-look-
ing, well-dressed, fresh and spruce as any careful buck of
the age.

In a fortnight what had he become?

A ragged-faced, bearded, dishevelled madman, with eyes
bloodshot, wild and famished; with features nipped and
pinched and bloodless; with a gaze aimless and wandering,
but sinister. Could a fortnight work such a change? This
man I knew—knew him as I knew the man before whom
he stood stirless in all but his eyes. This was the man
who, many months ago, had left the house, whom some
thought dead, whom some thought murdered—him, and no
other, as surely as he who had confronted the four gentlemen in this very room fifteen days before was *not* Mr.
Ransome!

What a sight!—how piteous!—how broken!—how un-
speakably changed!

He was kept at bay by the Colonel's eyes; but if ever
madness, desperate and hunted, restrained for the moment, but waiting its opportunity, was embodied, it stood
there.

The Colonel's self-possession was extraordinary; the
passion that had burned in him on his discovering who this
intruder was, had given way before the tragically wretched
aspect the man presented. There would, indeed, have been
something unworthy in anger in the presence of such a
creature as this; whom, when the first shock of amazement
had passed from me, I could not behold without compassion. To all appearance frozen by the cold, he yet seemed
insensible to the sufferings it must have caused him. His
clothes were thin, and scarcely fitted to protect the body
from the chill even of a spring night. They were, moreover, soiled and worn and travel-stained. His beard was
short and curly, but obviously the growth of many weeks.
His hair was long and (he had removed his hat when the
Colonel had released him, and there was something indescribably touching in this purely mechanical act of courtesy) fell in tangled curls about his forehead. He never

looked either at the Colonel or me, but glanced round the room, and frequently in the direction of the door.

The silence was broken by the Colonel. He had been looking at him fixedly, and now said:

" What do you want here at this hour?"

" I have come to see my wife," he replied, and as he made this answer he looked at me momentarily and smiled.

" You choose a strange hour to return to her. You have been more than half a year away. Where have you been all this time?"

The Colonel asked these questions quite calmly. But he looked at the man as he would look at a hound who might fly at his throat if he averted his eye.

" I will tell my wife where I have been and why I left her. Let me see her."

" You cannot see her now. To-morrow, perhaps. Where do you come from? are you stopping at Copsford?"

" I am stopping nowhere. I have my fancies, and I go where they lead me." He looked downward with a smile and added, " Am I not well-dressed enough to see my wife? If not, let me go to my room. I have clothes there."

He addressed himself to me; that is, with his face turned in my direction, but with his eyes on the floor. " And I can shave also, and wash myself. I can shave by candle-light. She'll know me then."

The Colonel glanced at me. He was obviously, for the moment, at a loss to know how to act. The flame of the candle I held was waved to and fro by the draught from the open window. He noticed this rather than the bitter cold of the night air, and desired me to close the window. I put the candle down and turned to obey his order. Mr. Ransome took the candle in his hand.

" I know where my room is and where my wife sleeps," he said, with a strange mixture of courtesy and cunning in his manner. " Do not trouble to accompany me."

He made a step toward the door. The Colonel seized his arm and took the candle from him.

" I have told you that you cannot see your wife to-night,"

he said; "if you are in want of a lodging I will accompany you to Copsford and obtain one for you."

The man stood stock-still, looking irresolutely and with the expression I well remembered from the door to the ground, over and over again.

"I have my sleeping-places and can find them without help," he said, after a short pause. "I have come to see my wife. You cannot prevent me from seeing her, sir. She is lawfully my wife, and I claim the right to see her."

He raised his voice, and there were symptoms of irritation in his subdued but rapid gestures. I noticed that he put his hand to his breast and kept it there a moment.

The perfectly sane manner in which he spoke threw the Colonel off his guard.

"You dare not say that you have the right to see your wife. You deserted her many months ago, and by so doing have forfeited your claims as a husband. You have brought misery and shame upon her and me! Coward!—beware! do not anger me. I have many wrongs to avenge—do not force me to recur to them at this moment."

His eyes shone, he clenched his fist, and advanced a step as though awaiting or provoking an excuse to strike. I trembled from head to foot. His passion seemed to transform him into a figure of iron. I transferred my gaze to the nerveless, attenuated madman, and felt that let him give but a sign and I should witness him prostrate and bleeding on the ground.

The wretched creature's hand again sought his breast, and he glanced toward the door.

It opened at that moment—opened wide—and Mrs. Ransome stood on the threshold. I heard the madman shriek; I saw him spring toward her. The Colonel was after him like a flash of light; a pistol-shot rang through the room; and while the echoes of the report still reverberated, both men were on the ground locked in a deadly struggle.

I stood for a moment transfixed, and then rushed forward. Mrs. Ransome kept her place in the doorway. In the gloom I could not for a moment or two tell which man was undermost; but when I had approached close I beheld the Colonel kneeling on Mr. Ransome's breast, both hands upon his throat. The madman's face was livid with strangulation; there was foam upon his lips, white and thick; his arms beat the floor; his eyes were upturned and showed the whites with horrid effect against the dusky skin in which they were set.

"You will kill him!" I shrieked, and looked imploringly at Mrs. Ransome; but she resembled a grand image of stone motionlessly gazing down upon the shocking spectacle.

"You will kill him, sir!" I shrieked again; and in my agony and misery I could have thrown myself upon the men and plucked those remorseless fingers from the choking throat.

"Fetch me a rope—quick!" cried the Colonel; never shifting his attitude, swaying only to the movements of the tortured body he was strangling.

There was a box-cord in the pantry. I had seen it there that morning. I rushed into the hall, groped my way down-stairs, felt for and found the cord, and returned with it.

The madman lay still enough. I thought he was dead. The Colonel let go his hold of the wretch's throat to take the line. But no sooner had he raised his hands than Mr. Ransome gave a twist, dislodged the Colonel, gained his feet, and rushed toward his wife. She fled to her father with a wild and pealing cry, eluding by a hair's breadth the outstretched hands of the madman. In a moment he was down again, felled by a blow that brought him to the earth like a log; and with marvellous rapidity and presence of mind the Colonel was winding the cord round and round him.

He stood up when his task was done, breathless and panting. Mrs. Ransome cowered near him.

"Are you hurt?" he asked her, gasping out his words.

"No," she answered.

"Miss Avory, I dare not leave this man. You must go to Copsford, and procure help."

"Yes, sir;" and I was preparing to leave the room when

"WHEN I HAD APPROACHED CLOSE I BEHELD THE COLONEL KNEELING ON MR.
RANSOME'S BREAST."—Page 360.

the madman began to plunge. His efforts to liberate himself from his bonds were frightful to witness. He kept his
eyes on his wife, and wrestled madly with his arms, sometimes getting on to his knees, and then falling backward or
forward as the case might be, cursing and blaspheming,
and plunging amid such cries as might fitly issue from the
lips of the damned. He was raving mad now, and with
his discolored face and flaming eyes formed a picture the
awfulness of which I cannot believe was ever paralleled.

"Away with you, Miss Avory!" cried the Colonel. "If
you are afraid to go alone, waken the other servants, and
make them accompany you."

"I am not afraid to go alone, sir."

And as I made this answer, I hastened out of the room.
In less than five minutes I was equipped in cloak and bonnet, and toiling through the deep snow.

I was not above a dozen yards away from the house,
when I was brought to a stand by the sound of a second
pistol-shot, instantly followed by a scream. My momentary belief was that the man had actually accomplished the
object which manifestly had brought him to the house, by
shooting his wife. Faint with fear and horror I staggered
back to the house. The door of course was closed. I rang
furiously, waited, rang again and yet again. Had my ears
deceived me? Was the shot I had heard but the echo ringing in my head of the first shot that had been fired in the
drawing-room?

Hark! footsteps came quickly along the passage; the
door was opened.

"Who is that?" demanded the voice of the Colonel.

"I, sir. Has Mrs. Ransome been shot?"

"No. Come this way—see for yourself."

The passage and anteroom were in pitch darkness. I
groped my way after him, and gained the hall, where the
lamp burned brilliantly, and followed into the drawing-
room.

I saw what had happened quickly enough. Mr. Ransome had succeeded in liberating his right arm from the
rope in which the Colonel had bound him; twisted along

the floor to where the pistol with which he had aimed at
his wife had fallen, and shot himself with it. He lay on his
left side, stone dead, with a dark spot over the right temple.

Mrs. Ransome was in a swoon, upon the floor, with the
two pale and horrified servants whom the pistol-shots had
brought from their beds, busy about her. One of them had
brought a candle, and this helped the illumination of the
candle I had myself left in the drawing-room. But both of
them together shed but a very imperfect light, and the
strange and shocking tragedy seemed to borrow not a little
of its ghastliness from the gloom that lowered sullenly in
the large room.

"He had shot himself," said the Colonel to me in a whisper, "before I could raise my hand. He was bellowing one
moment, and then he was still; and I went to my daughter,
meaning to conduct her past him out of the room. But
scarcely had I turned my back, when the shot was fired.
My daughter screamed, and fainted. I thought he had
killed her. I rushed back, and saw that he had shot himself. Look at him. He still holds the pistol, do you see?
It is double-barrelled—observe that! There is no doubt
that he meant to kill her first, and then himself."

"Is he dead, sir?" I asked, trembling violently.

"Dead? Ay! would you wish it otherwise? You need
not linger. Go and ring the inspector up, and tell him
what has happened. The end has come, indeed! You told
me you were not afraid to walk alone—are you? Both
those women shall accompany you if you wish."

He was almost wild with excitement, and gasped out his
words in the strangest manner.

"I will go, sir, at once."

"I dare not leave the body, for fear that it should be
disturbed," he continued, walking with me to the door.
"His attitude as he lies dead there proves suicide. That
hand of his clutching the pistol bears witness to the doer of
this deed. Do you understand me? Murder has been
talked of for a long while. He must not be touched. Let
the inspector find him as he is. The villain is his own
witness now. Lose no time, Miss Avory."

part five

THE COLONEL'S STORY
(*Concluded.*)

I

I TAKE up the thread of the story at the point where Miss Avory begins her second instalment—namely, on the day on which I quitted Gardenhurst for London, in obedience to the letter of the detective, Johnson, whose positive declaration that he had found Mr. Ransome left me in no doubt of the success of his quest.

That letter had found me hopeless. Over and over again I had patiently pondered every chance that was in the least likely to occur to remove from my daughter's character the stain that Mrs. Ransome's accusation had left upon it. I had advertised in the then most popular prints, offering a large reward for the discovery of the man whose description I gave. I had set to work one Mathewson, the same who had given me information respecting the writer of the letter signed "Justitia," to make patient and diligent inquiry, not only in Copsford, but throughout the neighborhood, after the two missing men. I had offered, through the inspector, a reward to any of the constables under him who should bring me information regarding either Mr. Ransome or Maddox.

In vain. My advertisements were unanswered. My Copsford emissary could obtain no clue of any kind, though he questioned the country-people far and wide. The inspector never had any news to give me. And, worse than all, my London man, Johnson, in whom I had lodged all my hopes, remained silent.

My depression at times was overwhelming. In a sense

I became a monomaniac. My mind refused to admit any
other thought but the one question—How was this mystery
to be solved? My imagination grew intolerably morbid.
Miserable misgivings possessed me, the darkest of which
was a suspicion of my daughter. I own that there were
times when it seemed to me *likely* that she knew what had
become of her husband. What could her resolute denials
prove? Her protestations of innocence were inflamed with
passion, and increased my fears. Her fierce allusions to
her husband terrified me, as the delirium of guilt rendered
callous by hate and rage. There was another consideration
that staggered me—the haughty and contemptuous intrepid-
ity with which she had at first encountered my suspicions.
I never thought of referring this attitude to the indignation
and pride of conscious innocence.

I could scarcely credit my senses when I received Johnson's letter. But the summons to London was peremptory,
and, as you have read, I lost no time in obeying it.

The day was a detestable one, wet, windy, and depress-
ing to the last degree. At Copsford I hired a post-chaise,
which took me to L—— at a gallop, and I was just in time
to catch the up-coach. I remember that journey as clearly
as I remember anything; the wet and hazy landscape, the
damp, silent passengers, the deserted streets of the town
through which we passed, the gloomy and humid coffee-
room in which we dined, our entry into London, with the
yellow lights shining through the fog.

It was half-past seven. Johnson, who had calculated
the hour at which the coach would arrive, had appointed to
meet me at a coffee-house in the Strand. A church clock
was striking eight when the fly that had brought me from
Southwark set me down at the house.

Johnson waited for me in a private room behind the bar.
He was a thin, undersized man, with a pale, inflexible face,
iron-gray eyebrows, small whiskers, and a steady, resolute
manner. He had for many years followed the queer profession of hunting down people and hunting up evidence,
and had been recommended to me by the Copsford solicitor
as singularly keen, patient, and sagacious.

"Good-evening, sir," said he. "You have had a cold ride to London. Never remember this month so wintry before."

"I had given up all hope of ever hearing from you," I replied.

He smiled, dropped his mouth on one side, and suggested that something hot would do me good after my journey. He also suggested that something hot would do him good after his waiting. His taste led him to boiling hot rum and lemon-peel. Our wants having been supplied, he routed the fire into a blaze, took a chair on one side of it, and without more ado related his story. That story he conveyed with very remarkable brevity, by the simple means of omitting half the words another man would have used, and by relating only the actual facts of it.

It was to this effect:

Unknown to me, he had begun his inquiries by stopping at Copsford for two days. By this sojourn he gained nothing. So he set to work to beat the neighborhood. A man answering to Mr. Ransome's description had been seen to pass along the road leading to Sandwell a few days before; he followed, called at every inn and tavern in the place, but obtained no tidings. He travelled to the next town, and there procured information that led him further north. He had, he believed, lighted on the track of Mr. Ransome, and the one or two stories he told me of his manner of making inquiries astounded me by the cunning and cleverness they illustrated.

Step by step he traced the man through half-a-dozen towns and villages, and finally landed himself at Guildford, having in his progress made the circuit of two counties.

It only remained for him to find out the house in which Mr. Ransome had put up. But this took him a whole day. The house was a mean tavern, up a back street. But the discovery was made a day too late. The landlord positively declared that the gentleman who, he said, had called himself a Guildford man, though he had never seen him before, and who, in his opinion, was mad, had left that morning for London, having slept one night in his house.

I had explained to Johnson the nature of the suspicions that were entertained against Phœbe; and he would therefore have known, by communicating the news that Mr. Ransome was alive, that those suspicions must fall dead. But he was too slow and careful a man to report on hearsay evidence only. He could never imagine that it would have infinitely relieved *my* misgivings of Phœbe to learn that Mr. Ransome was living, for the reason that he had no notion that I questioned my daughter's innocence. I had informed him that there was no chance of obtaining my daughter's acquittal at the hands of public opinion until Mr. Ransome was found and produced; and so, until Mr. Ransome *was* found, he saw no end to be gained by writing to me.

At the booking-office of the coach he substantiated the landlord's information by the testimony of the book-keeper, who stated that the man described had started for London by the coach that morning.

There was nothing to do then but follow Mr. Ransome to London. He admitted that the quest took the aspect of a difficult and chance affair, now that it was to be pushed in a metropolis in which the hiding-places were as numerous as the population.

Many weeks passed of which he offered no account. He might wish me to suppose that he had been vigilant and active all this time; and doubtless he was, as the sequel showed.

He was walking up Oxford Street one night, when there passed him a man whom he instantly turned and followed. The light of a street lamp had disclosed a face which seemed to correspond in every particular with the description he had received of Mr. Ransome. The man went as far as the Tottenham Court Road, where he entered a chop-house, and supped. He then came out, walked up Oxford Street, and turned into Berners Street. When halfway advanced along the street, he stopped before a house and admitted himself with a latch-key.

Johnson watched this man for several days and nights running. He discovered that he never emerged in the daytime; that his regular hour for sallying forth was about half-past ten at night; and that his object for so sallying forth was for no more sinister purpose than to obtain some supper and some exercise.

Such habits, coupled with the striking resemblance of the man to Mr. Ransome, would naturally confirm Johnson in his theory that his long search was ended at last. But he was too cautious to form conclusions by what he saw only, He boldly presented himself at the house, and had an interview with the landlady, whom he easily pledged to secrecy, by representing that her lodger was a man of fortune, who had run away from his friends, and, that, if she would help him to restore the gentleman, who was eccentric, to his home, she might depend upon receiving a reward. By this means he learned that the lodger had been four months in the house; that he went under the name of Cleveland; that she was positive that was not his real name; that he was singular in his habits; that she could not tell where he came from; and she finally ended by informing Johnson that, from what he had told her, she had not the least doubt her lodger was the person he was in search of.

Such was Johnson's story, the whole of which was conveyed in about ten minutes, in brief, dry monosyllables, while he sipped his rum and water and aired his legs at the fire.

"And now, what is to be done?" I asked.

"You must see him."

"Certainly. At his lodgings?"

"No; he'll sup to-night in Tottenham Court Road. He has three cook-shops, and he takes 'em in turns. We'll go there, and you shall have a look at him through the glass door, when the time comes."

"What time?"

"Eleven o'clock."

I was in the humor to witness nothing inconsistent with the part I deemed this madman capable of playing in any piece of personal information about him that Johnson could tell me of. That he should sup furtively at low cook-shops was in nowise more surprising than that he should run away from his home, and hide himself in London and elsewhere, for no other reason than because he was mad.

The long time Johnson and I had to wait before the hour for repairing to Tottenham Court Road arrived could not be more fitly employed than by our ordering and eating a supper. I was in a high state of excitement, and was perfectly satisfied by the answers Johnson made to my numberless inquiries that the man he had discovered was Mr. Ransome. He was equally confident, and in great spirits, which he expressed by a fixed and cunning smile, and numerous winks and odd, ironical ejaculations.

The coffee-house in which we supped was a very respectable house, and since I was in it, I thought I might as well sleep there as anywhere else. I therefore ordered a bedroom to be got ready, and a fire lighted; and having made this arrangement for passing the night, prepared to accompany Johnson to Tottenham Court Road.

He had watched his man long enough to count with security upon the regularity of his habits; but of course, he told me, he could not guarantee that the man would be at the chop-house at eleven, or at any other hour that night. We must take our chance; under any circumstances he could certainly procure me a view of the man next day.

The night was a cheerless one, raw and foggy, slushy under foot, thick and black overhead. The flyman chose those intricate and grimy streets which lie between Holborn and the Strand; and in some of them the only signs of life and light visible came from the public-house, where, as we rattled past, I might catch a glimpse of a white-faced, hungry-looking crowd, assembled round the bar, and a woman or two outside in the street waiting, and presently overtake a drunken man reeling to his home.

It was ten minutes to eleven when we alighted at the corner of Tottenham Court Road. I told the driver to wait, and went with Johnson up the street. On the right, a few minutes' walk from the corner, was a little chop-house—low pitched, with a couple of shelves in its window, upon which were displayed to the best advantage such eatables as the proprietor might think would best attract customers. The glass entrance-door was closed. Johnson stepped up to it, and looked through, came back to me, and said, "He's not there yet."

I pulled my shawl well about my mouth and ears, and with Johnson at my side, twice took the turn of the pavement, from where the fly stood to the chop-house. I had plenty of patience, and was ready to wait as long as Johnson should think necessary.

We were returning, with our faces directed up the pavement, when a man passed us, walking quickly, going the same way with ourselves.

Johnson pulled my sleeve.

"There he is," he exclaimed.

I stepped out briskly; but before I could get near enough to enable me to see his face he turned into the chop-house.

"Go to the door, sir, and look at him," said Johnson.

I went close to the glass, and peered through it; while Johnson remained outside. The man stood at the counter, waiting to address the shopman, who was attending to an old man at a side table. The interior of the shop was well lighted, and I waited with indescribable anxiety for the man to turn his head. He was dressed in a thick topcoat, dark trousers, and a low-crowned, broad-brimmed hat, fashionable at the time for country wear, and such as I had myself seen on Mr. Ransome at Gardenhurst.

During some moments he kept his face turned away, so that I could only see the back of his head; but he presently looked round, with an impatient gesture, and I saw Mr. Ransome, as I remembered him at Broadstairs, cleanly shaved, long-jawed, the mustache long on the upper lip, the eyes black!

In the conviction that possessed me that this was the man, I could have rushed forward and seized him, so fierce was the sudden passion the sight of him excited in me. Johnson unconsciously restrained me by a whisper.

"Is he the man you want?"

"Yes," I answered, so agitated that I could scarcely articulate.

24

"You are quite sure, sir?"

I looked at the man again.

He kept his hat on. I wished that he would remove it. Beyond all possibility of delusion the resemblance was too startling for me to conceive it an accident. There was in-deed something wanting in the attitude, something wanting in the movements of the body—for he was now speaking to the shopman—which would have dissatisfied me there and then but for the overwhelming impression produced by the face. It was long since I had seen Mr. Ransome. I had to date my recollection of him virtually from my acquaint-ance with him at Broadstairs; for my visit to Gardenhurst when he was there had been short, and my impressions confused by my anxiety and the discomforts of my brief stay.

"If I could hear him speak," I whispered, "I should be more satisfied."

"Impossible now, sir," replied Johnson. "If he should see you, it's ten to one if, on going to his lodgings to-mor-row, we shouldn't find him bolted. Come away if you please. I'll tell you my plans as we go along."

I walked with him to the fly, and we started for the Strand. His plans were simple enough. He would call for me at ten o'clock next morning and accompany me to Berners Street. The landlady, on my telling her that her lodger was the man I sought, would take me to him, heed-less of the injunction he had given her to admit no one who asked to see him. This had been arranged between her and Johnson. It was best that I should have my interview with Mr. Ransome alone. Johnson would remain down-stairs. I should have to use my own judgment in dealing with the man; but if he refused to show himself at Cops-ford, I must then take measures to obtain conclusive testi-mony to his being alive.

I bade Johnson good-night at the door of the coffee-house, and he walked away toward Charing Cross. Wearied by my journey and the excitement of the day, I called for a candle and went to bed; but not to sleep for a long while after I had extinguished the light. The windows of my bedroom overlooked the Strand, and the incessant clattering of the vehicles passing to and fro over the stones, until my ears got used to the noise, kept sleep banished as effectually as if a drummer had been stationed in the room. I heard the unfamiliar chimes of the church-clocks striking about me, and the murmur of voices in the room, overhead and next door. Moreover my bedroom was small, stuffy, and oppressively furnished with curtains which loaded the bed, and loaded the windows, and made breathing a matter of calculation and labor.

But I should have fared no better, as respected rest, had I occupied my room at Gardenhurst. The one question that engrossed me was—was the man I had seen Mr. Ransome? Had I dared to own the truth to myself, I should have answered in the negative. It had been Mr. Ransome's face—his height—his figure; but with something missing: a subtle something my memory was powerless to define, though it felt the want.

But my doubt of his identity would involve too overwhelming a disappointment, too heavy a shock to the hopes on whose fulfilment I had counted with reckless and determined confidence, to suffer me to admit it. I reasoned that in the time during which the man had been absent from his home he had changed; he might be less mad; the eccentric life upon which he had voluntarily entered might have modified by conditions of its own, which I could not guess, the characteristics of movement, of glance, of attitude, which I seemed to remember in my daughter's husband, and which I had missed in the man Johnson had taken me to see. In the months which had elapsed since I had last beheld him, his insanity might have sobered and wrought the subtle change which baffled and frightened me. I ought to have managed somehow to hear his voice. Johnson should have suffered me to linger a little while longer at the door to observe if he removed his hat. Had I been permitted to obtain more evidence of the man's identity by a longer observation of him, I should have been spared the miserable and tormenting hours of suspense which found me sleepless even after the dawn had brightened on the window-blinds.

I was up and dressed by nine and had finished breakfast when Johnson arrived. The streets were still full of fog, amid which hung the sun, a copper-colored ball. My morning's reflections had deepened my misgivings that the man we were about to visit was not the man I wanted; but I did not express my fears to Johnson.

"We'll stop at the corner of the street," he said, as we entered a fly. "If we drove up to the door the sound of the wheels might make him look out of the window. He mustn't see you. Stand well in the door when you've knocked."

"Am I to ask for Mr. Cleveland?"

"Yes, and give your name. The landlady'll know who you are then."

We alighted at the corner of Berners Street and dismissed the fly. When we had walked a short distance, Johnson said, "Yonder's the house. Go and knock boldly, and keep well to the door."

I did as he bade me, while he walked leisurely forward, looking across the street away from the house that his face might not be seen. He returned when the door was opened.

"I wish to see Mr. Cleveland," I said to the woman, whom I judged, and soon discovered, to be the landlady. "My name is Colonel Kilmain."

She looked hard at me, caught sight of Johnson, smiled, and asked me to walk in.

Johnson followed me into the hall.

"Is he up?" he asked.

"Yes, having breakfast," answered the woman.

"Better walk up at once, sir," said Johnson, interrupting me as I was about to ask the landlady some questions. "I'll stop here. Just direct the gentleman, missis."

Although I had formed no plan of action, I followed the woman up-stairs, having very little doubt that, if the man turned out to be Mr. Ransome, I should soon find out what to do. We went up three flights of stairs, and the landlady, halting on the landing, pointed to the door on the right, and said in a whisper:

"You had best walk straight in, sir; for if he should

"FOR A MOMENT OR TWO I STOOD MOTIONLESS, PERSUADED THAT MY
DAUGHTER'S HUSBAND WAS BEFORE ME."—Page 373.

guess who you are, he might turn the key, and then there'd be no chance of getting at him at all."

Saying which, she went down-stairs, while I walked to the door, beat an apologetic rap with my knuckles, and entered quickly.

I found myself in a bedroom. Up in a corner stood a gloomy fourposter, and near the door was a chimney, with a small fire burning in the grate and a little kettle singing on the fire. A round table had been pushed to the window, and on it was an apology for a white tablecloth, furnished with a plate, a cup, a loaf of bread, an egg, and a teapot.

At this table was seated the gentleman whom I had viewed through the glass door of the chop-house, breakfasting, in his shirt-sleeves, unshaved, collarless, and with his unbrushed hair so exact a counterpart of Mr. Ransome's that for a moment or two I stood motionless, persuaded that my daughter's husband was before me.

He looked at me with profound astonishment, turning slowly in his chair, and letting fall the knife with which he was about to help himself to a slice of bread. Then jumping up, he exclaimed:

"Who the deuce are you, sir? and what do you want in my bedroom?"

His voice disillusioned me in a second. Had he undergone a bodily transformation, I should not more certainly have known that he was not the man I wanted.

Perhaps in some small measure I had anticipated the disappointment; but the blow was not the less prostrating. I felt myself turn deadly pale, I breathed with difficulty, and put my hand against the wall to steady myself.

He continued staring at me with unfeigned amazement. If he thought me mad, nothing could have been more just than his supposition.

"I apologize for this intrusion," I stammered. "I have been misled. This is a dreadful mistake."

"Have you come to see *me?*" he asked, taking me in from top to toe and eying me very suspiciously.

"No," I answered; "not you, but a man whom you closely resemble, named Ransome."

"My name is Cleveland," he exclaimed quickly. "I gave orders to the landlady of this house not to admit anybody who asked for me."

"The whole thing," I replied, recovering a little of my composure, "is a mistake. I was so confident that you were Mr. Ransome that I did not scruple to intrude upon you. I beg, sir, that you will accept my most humble apology."

"Oh, no need to say that," he exclaimed, softening as if by magic. "I see that you are disappointed and distressed. Pray sit and rest yourself."

I was about to decline to intrude upon him an instant longer, when, struck anew by his startling resemblance to Mr. Ransome, an extraordinary thought entered my mind. It came upon me like an electric shock, terrifying me by its audacity, and yet fascinating me too by its extreme practicability. I remained rooted to the ground while I watched him hurriedly slip on a collar and his coat; and then, breaking away from the spell in which my idea had bound me, I pulled a chair forward and seated myself.

He had now made himself presentable and resumed his seat.

"You have no need to make any apologies," he said, after keeping his eyes fixed on me for some time in expectation of being addressed; "and there is no necessity to explain unless you want to do so. I see that this is a mistake; though it's a rather curious one, isn't it?"

"So curious," I replied, "that I should not feel justified in quitting this room until I had satisfied you that I am the victim of an extraordinary error and a most bitter disappointment. Can you spare me ten minutes? Or, if you should wish to be alone, will you allow me to call upon you in the course of the day at any hour you may name?"

"You don't trespass," he answered; "I was just finishing my breakfast. Will you have a cup of tea?"

I thanked him, and he poured some tea into a cup, which he took from the mantelshelf. His manner was wonderfully cool and easy. When silent, his resemblance to Mr. Ransome was extraordinary; but when he spoke, his voice

and the expressions which entered his face modified the
likeness. The essential difference between the two men
lay in the eyes. This man's were black, but clear; but
Mr. Ransome's were dusky, not brilliant, and the irids
tinged the whites.

I was about to begin my story when I recollected that
Johnson waited below. It was manifest that, if the plan
I was now fully resolved to submit to Mr. Cleveland (as I
must henceforth call him) was to be carried out, Johnson
must not guess that we had mistaken the man. I therefore
explained that I had left a companion in the hall, whom I
did not wish to keep waiting, and with an apology for quitting the room, I hastened down-stairs, taking care to leave
my hat behind me, that he might know I should return.
When I reached the second landing, I leaned over the banisters and called to Johnson, who was seated on a hall chair,
sucking the top of his stick.

He looked up.

"It's all right," I said; "you need not stop. Call at the
coffee-house to-night at nine."

"Right you are, sir," he answered, nodded coolly, walked
to the hall door and let himself out. Of course, if I was
satisfied, he was. He had, he considered, done the work
for which I had hired him, and had nothing more to do but
take his money.

I returned to the bedroom, repeating my apology for having left it, and begging Mr. Cleveland to have a little
patience, as I would presently explain to him who this man
was I had dismissed. The feeling that Johnson was out of
the house, somehow, increased my courage. I carefully shut
the door, and drawing a chair close to the table, began my
story without further word of preface. There was little
that I either softened or omitted. Every moment was con-
firming my resolution to use this man as an instrument for
freeing my daughter from the suspicion of having murdered
her husband; and I plainly perceived that my initial step
must be to closely and faithfully relate every particular
connected with Mr. Ransome's mysterious disappearance.

"And now, sir," I said, bringing my story to an end,

"you understand the reason of this intrusion upon you, and the bitter disappointment the discovery that you are not the man the detective has been searching for causes me."

"Perfectly. I wish I were the man, for my own sake. Do you smoke? I can offer you some tobacco."

"Thank you, I have some cigars; will you take one?"

I handed him my case; he extracted a cigar and lighted it.

"Am I so very like Mr. Ransome?" he asked, stretching himself backward, and looking at me with a smile.

"So like that I could have sworn you were he when I saw you last night."

"But all the same, I can't think much of your detective's sharpness for bringing you up from the country before making sure that I was somebody else."

"You must remember," I answered, "that every inquiry he made appeared to corroborate the strong evidence of the likeness. You have been here four months."

"Yes, that's true."

"Your habits are--well, I must call them singular. You keep indoors all day—pray pardon me; I wish to show you the reasons for the detective being deceived."

"No offence," he exclaimed coolly; "but how the deuce do you know that I have been here four months, and that I stop indoors all day?"

"Johnson got his information from the landlady—acting, you will understand, under the impression that you were Mr. Ransome."

"Ah! and what else did my landlady say?"

I should have been going too far to have asserted that the landlady had hinted his name was assumed. There was no direct proof of that; moreover, his affairs could no longer be objects of my curiosity now. So I replied that what I had told him was, I believed, the chief information Johnson had obtained from the landlady.

He smoked unconcernedly for some moments, and then, glancing at me, exclaimed:

"Mr. Johnson might have got me into a mess. You have been very candid, and no harm can be done if I follow your example. My own story is not quite so tragical as Mr. Ransome's—indeed, I am afraid it is dreadfully vulgar and commonplace. I am in hiding from my creditors."

He laughed, and added, "What a good cigar this is! Smoking such tobacco recalls old times."

"Are your debts heavy?"

"Pretty heavy. I would rather be here than in the Fleet. I'll tell you a secret; I am waiting for a chance to get abroad."

"I am going to ask you some questions, not out of curiosity, but for a motive I will presently explain. My difficulty is heavier than yours. We can help each other. If you will extricate me, I will extricate you. You speak of getting abroad. Where do you wish to go?"

"America."

"Have you no friends in this country who will help you?"

"I have tired the governor out," he replied, flipping his cigar-ash over the carpet. "I dare not even write to him, for he has sworn in the last letter he sent to give my address to my creditors if I apply to him for money again."

"What money do you require to carry you abroad?"

"I could do with two hundred. I have written twice to a screw of an uncle, and got a letter this morning from him enclosing ten pounds. What's the use of ten pounds? I can't begin life on that. And if the bailiffs nab me, I'm done for; there's not a relative but would rather see me dead in jail than advance the money I owe to get me out."

"I'll give you two hundred pounds if you will do what I want."

He looked at me steadily a moment, sucked his cigar, expelled a thick cloud, and asked—"What?"

"If you'll personate Mr. Ransome for half an hour."

He whistled, laughed, looked grave, and said:

"What's the part, sir?—a ghost's?"

"I am perfectly serious," I answered, relieved by the levity with which he received the remark. I had expected a very different answer. "My daughter's character is at stake; a monstrous falsehood was started by her mother-in-law and credited by heaps of persons living in our neighborhood. I must deal with this lie by another lie; but a lie more honest, for it has for its object the vindication of an innocent and cruelly wronged woman—my only child! Will you help me?"

"I cannot answer off-hand," he replied, growing nervous on a sudden. "I want the money, but I don't know whether I can earn it in this way. Do you mean to say that people who knew Mr. Ransome will believe I am he?"

"I will take care they do not find out their mistake."

"But what good will half an hour's acting do?"

I threw down my cigar, and rose in my agitation.

"I have not yet formed any plans," I responded, pacing the room. "The scheme I have suggested only occurred to me when I saw you just now. Will you let me call upon you at this hour to-morrow? I shall then have matured the plan, and will lay it before you complete."

"It is a perilous undertaking, isn't it?" he asked, taking the little kettle from the hob, where it was shooting a long volume of steam into the room.

"What peril there is," I answered, "is not likely to reach you. You can, if you choose, make arrangements to be on your way to America the day following your visit to Copsford."

"But won't somebody see with half an eye that I am *not* Mr. Ransome?" he exclaimed, stretching his legs before the fire, with a coat-tail over each arm.

"His mother is dead. My daughter will be in the secret. The very audacity of the scheme will diminish the likelihood of detection; and I'll take care that you are seen only by those who are not so familiar with Mr. Ransome as to distinguish the difference between you."

"What are you going to do with the servants?"

"They shall not see you."

"You want me to go to Copsford, is it?"

"That will require consideration. I can only see dimly as yet how the thing is to be done; but it *is* to be done. Will this hour to-morrow suit you?"

"Yes, very well."

"You must not," I exclaimed earnestly, "suffer yourself to be prejudiced against this undertaking until the matured scheme is placed before you."

"Look here," he answered, "if I should consent to do what you want, you must pledge me your word not to grow inquisitive about me, and try to find out my name, and where I came from, and who I am, and all that."

"I promise you, on my honor," I replied, perceiving now that the landlady was right, and that Cleveland was *not* his name.

"I want the money you offer, and don't mind lending you a hand to get your daughter out of her scrape. But just as we were strangers to each other an hour ago, so we must be strangers to each other the moment the business is over; I go my way, and you go yours. Is that understood?" It was the one condition of the scheme I could have most wished to insist upon.

"Perfectly. I should have stipulated for this myself, had I not feared that you might misconstrue my object."

"Very well, sir. Then I shall expect you here to-morrow morning at this hour."

In a few minutes I was walking briskly in the direction of the Strand.

II

Johnson called at the coffee-house that night as I had directed him. The heaviest obligation of my scheme was the necessity it placed me under to tell falsehoods. But the obligation was a condition of the scheme, and not to be obviated.

I informed him that I had to call on "Mr. Ransome" next morning; that I had represented the critical position in which his mysterious disappearance had placed my daughter; and that I had no doubt he would keep the promise he had made me to accompany me to Copsford.

Johnson highly relished this satisfactory conclusion of his labors, and very naturally began to ask me some questions, which grew so embarrassing, that to end them I pulled out my check-book and wrote him a draft, under cover of which I was enabled to get rid of him, without his conceiving his dismissal sudden or odd. Before he left me, he said that, if Mr. Ransome gave me any trouble, I was to let him know, and he would undertake to oblige him to present himself at Copsford.

I slept but little that night; but the result of my long meditation was to supply me with a very perfect plan for carrying out my stratagem.

At the appointed hour next morning I repaired, with a composed face, but a very agitated mind, to Berners Street, and was admitted by the landlady, who dropped a curtsey on seeing me.

As she was conducting me up-stairs, she stopped to ask me if her lodger was the gentleman I wanted. I held up my finger very seriously, and shook my head; from such vague signs she could draw any meaning that pleased her.

"I'm not to be forgotten, sir, Mr. Johnson said, if the lodger *is* the gentleman," she remarked.

"I'll remember you," I replied. And I may as well say here that I kept my promise; for after I returned to Gardenhurst, I sent her ten pounds, which I considered was about as much as her services were worth.

Mr. Cleveland was fully dressed, and waited for me. I was greatly struck by his singular likeness to Mr. Ransome, which was more defined now that he was trimly habited. He bowed politely, and placed a chair for me near the little grate; then threw himself into his easy-chair, and asked me if I had matured my scheme.

"Fully," I replied, and inquired how it struck him now that he had had time to reflect over it.

He wanted to hear my plans before he answered that question.

The manner in which he said this fully persuaded me that he would consent, and merely dallied that he might make me believe he had scruples. Encouraged by this belief, I unfolded my plans, which were as follows:

I was quite certain that, although Mr. Ransome had lived two years at Gardenhurst, he was little known to the Copsford people. For his habits were wayward: he was repeatedly absent from his home; in his walks he chose the country, and seldom the frequented paths of it.

It was my intention, I said, to summon three or four witnesses to the house, men of position, whose word would be held conclusive. I had noted down four names, two of whom I knew were acquainted with Mr. Ransome, though it was impossible they could be so familiar with him that they should be able to detect an impostor in Mr. Cleveland. Curiosity, strengthened by the appeal I would make, would bring the other two to the house; and they were bound to assume the truth from the assurance of their colleagues.

The two gentlemen who knew Mr. Ransome were Mr. Skerlock and Mr. Hastings. The others, who, if they knew him at all, could only know him by sight, were Mr. Ledbury and Sir Anthony Lauder. If two out of the four attended the meeting, I should be satisfied; but I should be better satisfied to have them all.

I proposed that Mr. Cleveland should accompany me to Peterham, where his very name would be unknown; for he might run a risk should he stop at Copsford. The interview should take place in the evening, and I would take care so to regulate the light in the room that his face should be imperfectly beheld. This would require judgment on his part, but the ruse was practicable, and might be so adroitly managed as to escape the attention of the witnesses, who, having no suspicion of the plot, would find nothing to attract them in such minor details.

I told him that the only person of whom I stood in the least fear was Miss Avory, the housekeeper—that was, if she should see him; but of this there was little danger, for I would take care that he was admitted by the housemaid, who had come to the house some time after Mr. Ransome had left it, and therefore, did not know him; and that on the termination of the interview, which need not be protracted beyond a quarter of an hour at the very outside, I would myself conduct him to the hall door.

For the matter of the interview, it was imperative that he should say as little as he could. This I might manage

by putting questions to him which would imply his intentions to the audience, while they would involve him in
monosyllabic replies only. For instance, I would ask him
if his reason for leaving the house was because he was unhappy with his wife? And I would then demand if he
still adhered to his resolution not to live with her again?
Questions of this kind would convey the substance of the
motives which I wished our auditors to believe had impelled
Mr. Ransome to quit his home, without obliging him (Mr.
Cleveland) to enter into any explanations himself. I submitted that the audacity of the scheme would insure its
success; that my name stood so high that the witnesses
would never dream I could lend myself to a scheme which
people who had no sympathy with the extraordinary end
for which I was working would call dishonorable; and I
wound up by appealing to his humanity to assist me in
cleansing my daughter's name of the cruel and unjust stain
that rested upon it.

There was no need for this appeal. I had seen in his
face that his mind was made up before I had finished telling him my plans. But that final sentence of mine was a
lucky stroke, for it enabled him to waive the money profit
of the undertaking as a quite outside consideration, and to
profess himself willing to help me because I had touched
his feelings. This was ridiculous; but I swallowed the
absurdity with a grave face, thanked him cordially for his
acquiescence, and said that I would put notes to the value
of two hundred pounds in his hand when I conducted him
out of the house after the interview.

Though the plot was ripe and my agent willing, I deemed
it advisable to wait a day or two in London before returning to Gardenhurst, conceiving that a greater air of truth
would attach to the undertaking if I afterward stated that
the reason of my stay in London was the difficulty I met
with in prevailing upon "Mr. Ransome" to accompany me
to his home. There was a perpetual reference in my
thoughts to Miss Avory, whose sagacity I had learned to
respect. I was, indeed, so afraid that she would discover
the imposition that all manner of schemes for obviating

this risk entered my head. Sometimes I made up my mind to discharge her; but abandoned the intention when I considered its heartlessness, and recalled the obligations Phœbe was under to her. Then I thought of sending her away on a holiday; but feared the conclusions she would draw when she afterward learned that I had brought Mr. Ransome to the house in her absence. Then I thought of taking her into my confidence, and leaving it to her to acquit or condemn me for my guilty efforts on behalf of my child; but the notion of such candor alarmed me. In truth, my fortitude was great enough to carry me through the commission of a wrong, but was not yet equal to the task of confessing it.

I therefore adhered to my original arrangement of so contriving the interview that none but those who were invited as witnesses should see the representative of the missing man.

Before I could take Mr. Cleveland to Peterham, it was necessary that I should see Phœbe. I would gladly have been spared the ordeal of obtaining my child's connivance at a discreditable plot. This, indeed, was the hardest trial of all—harder even than the pitiful and humbling necessity my scheme forced upon me of speaking falsehoods and acting the liar's part.

On the fourth day, dating from my departure from home, I returned to Gardenhurst.

I had been with Mr. Cleveland every day, had had long conversations with him, had instructed him to the utmost heights of my memory in the character he was to enact; but found, by his not choosing to understand my motive for lingering in London, that he was impatient to get through the play and obtain the reward.

I considered this a useful state of mind, which must not be toyed with; and therefore, to lose no time, ordered the fly that carried me from Copsford to wait at Gardenhurst, that I might be able to catch the coach and be in London again that night.

The cause of my having to repeat these wearisome journeys was Mr. Cleveland's steadfast refusal to quit his hid ing-place until I had gained my daughter's consent to the scheme.

That consent was yet to be gained.

Miss Avory received me at the door. I hurried past her, and found my daughter in the drawing-room. The fly was waiting; it gave me an excuse for despatch, and I lost no time in telling her my scheme. She was thunderstruck, terrified, indignant, by turns; if the scheme were discovered, would not (she wanted to know) her guilt appear conclusive on the mere evidence of the stratagem I employed to clear her? I replied that, if I had the smallest fear that the scheme *would* be discovered, I would not attempt it. I represented to her that either her husband was dead, or hiding in some distant country, and that there was little or no chance of her ever hearing of him again; that unless he could be proved to have been alive after his disappearance from the house, her guilt would remain a permanent assumption in the minds of those who believed old Mrs. Ransome's accusation; that if this suspicion were not effectually removed, by any means, base or honorable, her position would grow more critical as time progressed; for the murmurs of the gossips were not to be silenced. The attention of the law might be directed to her, and any day might witness her arrest on no better evidence than the persistent suspicion of the neighbors—a suspicion the durability of which might cause even humane and upright men to regard the disappearance of her husband as significant and worthy of inquiry.

In spite of these arguments, which perfectly expressed the reasons that moved me to this undertaking, she remained obstinately opposed to the scheme, until my anger was aroused, and I swore that, if she refused to help herself by helping me, I would leave the house and never see her again.

This threat, which I was quite in the temper to carry out, frightened her into submission. I thereupon hurriedly acquainted her with the arrangements I had made to bring about the interview, exhorted her to be on her guard against Miss Avory's inquisitiveness and left the house, after hav·

ing addressed the few words to Miss Avory in the library
which she has mentioned in her narrative.

This confession need not go much further.   The story of
the scheme has already been related.   I merely undertook
in this place to show how it originated and the manner in
which I carried it through.

The account I gave to Miss Avory of the meeting in the
drawing-room, shortly after the gentlemen had left the
house, was accurate enough.   But no words will express
what I felt when I stood in that room with the four gentlemen ranged on one side of the table gazing at the impostor,
whose nonchalance filled me with alarm.   Had I guessed
that we had a secret witness in Miss Avory, I believe I
should have lost all control over myself, so convinced
should I have been that her keen eyes would master the
truth at once.

Just as I had anticipated, the success of the scheme was
owing to its audacity.

Mr. Skerlock and Mr. Hastings had seen Mr. Ransome;
the other two might probably have never set eyes on him.
But their ignorance of the real man was a consideration that
I took care should not occur to them.   Mr. Ransome had
been reported murdered; to disprove the report he had come
to Gardenhurst.   Witnesses were invited to behold him.
They came to see Mr. Ransome.   It was impossible they
should conceive that any other man but Mr. Ransome was
likely to be introduced to them.   It was their honest persuasion that Mr. Ransome stood before them.   They left
the house, to a man, satisfied.

This was, I dare say, a trick which would have been impracticable to any man who stood less high than myself in
the general esteem.   The stratagem cost me my honor; but
I was content to make the sacrifice; for my honor was of
little worth to me while my daughter lay under the darkest
of suspicions.

Mr. Cleveland did not act his part well.   But he had acted
it ten times worse than he did, no doubt of his identity
would have been excited.   He remained a quarter of an
hour in the room; and the moment Mr. Ledbury, who had

25

been pompously inveighing against his cruelty, was silent,
he bowed and walked out.   I followed him, and as I opened
the hall door, slipped the bank-notes I had promised into
his hand.

"Take my warmest thanks for what you have done," I
whispered.

"All right," he replied.   "Keep your promise;" by
which he meant the promise I had made him not to inquire
into his past.   He left the house, and I have never heard
of him from that day to this.

I lingered until I heard the fly that waited for him drive
off.   I then rejoined the others.

The worst of the ordeal was over.   I had both the nerve
and the spirit now to act my part well.   Mr. Skerlock came
up and congratulated me on the resolution I had shown in
bringing the man to the house.   My remedy, he said, in
summoning witnesses might be considered by some an extreme measure.   But in his opinion I was perfectly justified
in doing what I had done.

"It is idle to deny," he exclaimed, addressing the others,
"that public opinion has been excited against Mrs. Ransome
by her mother-in-law's accusation.   It is true that Mrs.
Ransome has not been formally charged with the commission of the deed which public prejudice has placed to her
account.   But a sensitive mind will find but little difference
between the humiliation of a legal inquiry and the humiliation of gossip.   It behooved Colonel Kilmain to spare no
efforts to prove his daughter an innocent woman.   I rejoice
in the triumph of his efforts and congratulate him on his
successful vindication of his child."

Sir Anthony spoke to the same effect; and then Mr. Hastings made a speech in which he exhorted me to direct my efforts toward a reconciliation between the husband and wife.

To this I replied that I had done all I meant to do; and
shuffled out of that embarrassing view of the question by
begging the gentlemen to help themselves to wine.

There was a bitter irony in all this, which I felt more
acutely when I was alone and recalled the scene and the
conversation.

Yet I might have hoped that, when they were out of the house, some degree of tranquillity, some sense of security would have returned to me. But scarcely was the hall door closed upon them when I thought of Miss Avory. I dreaded meeting her infinitely more than I had dreaded the interview between Mr. Cleveland and the witnesses. When, after I had called her to join my daughter and me in the drawing-room, she had spoken of having seen "Mr. Ransome" through the window, my dismay was so profound that, but for the ready relief I obtained from the excuse she gave me to run to the window to see if Poole were there, my agitation must then and there have betrayed me.

And yet in a few days the mystery was to be cleared up. Had Johnson but delayed writing to me for those few days, I should have been spared the deception I practised, which, abundantly as I can excuse its commission, I can never recur to without pain and remorse. The sense of the wrong my daughter and I had jointly perpetrated estranged us. A deeper gloom gathered over both of us; for while, on my part, no effort could crush out of my heart the detestable suspicion of her, which sickened my waking thoughts and poisoned my dreams at night, so, on her side, the thoughts of the barbarous injustice that had been done her was rendered more poignant yet by the remembrance that she had connived at a deception to vindicate the innocence which should never have been doubted.

Other sources of anxiety contributed to make my life at this period a burden. I instinctively felt that Miss Avory's suspicions were excited; that, though she could find no reason for challenging the identity of the man I had brought to the house, she was full of distrust. The necessity of seeming to her other than I was, of conversing as though Mr. Ransome's discovery were an accomplished fact, was an odious and unbearable trial to me.

Again, I was haunted by the fear that Mr. Cleveland might betray me. At the onset I had felt satisfied that my secret would be safe with him; but my confidence was diminished by my nervousness, and by the consideration that he was poor, that he was unscrupulous (as I might judge by

the readiness with which he had fallen into my scheme)
and that he might threaten me with exposure if I refused
to buy his silence.

Existence became intolerable. My scheme had, indeed,
succeeded so far as my daughter's character was concerned;
but I was soon taught that, though her innocence was established, the evil repute that had so long hung about her name
still lingered, and would take a long, long while to become
extinct. With the exception of Mr. and Mrs. Skerlock and
Mr. Hastings, no one called on us. There was only one
remedy for this state of things—to quit the country. I
abhorred the name of Copsford. Gardenhurst had grown
hateful to us both as the scene of miseries which memory
would find ineffaceable. If I delayed carrying out my resolution, it was because I doubted the wisdom of abrupt departure. Life seemed so full of contingencies that I knew
not what to-morrow might bring forth. The discovery of
Maddox, for instance, might expose the whole of my conspiracy; and if that exposure happened, and Mr. Ransome
remained unfound, the public would assuredly leap to the
conclusion that my daughter was actually guilty of her husband's death, that I was aware of the fact, and that I had
adopted the extraordinary measure of introducing an impostor to the house in the hope of effectually averting
suspicion.

Such was the state of affairs when the dead body was
found under the trees at the foot of the estate. Many years
have passed since that time, but the horror with which the
news of the discovery affected me is as fresh in my memory
now as if the event had taken place yesterday. My belief
was that the body was Mr. Ransome's. I plunged into the
trees alone, for the gardeners had not the courage to follow
me; but the spectacle that met my gaze was too loathsome
for me to examine. Not until the body was in the coffin
was I enabled to take note of the details of its ghastliness;
and then I was satisfied that it was not Mr. Ransome. Yet
how came the letters belonging to Mr. Ransome in the
pocket of the coat on the body? The jury's finding was
worthless as respected the solution of this new mystery.

But as to the verdict itself, I had anticipated it on the mere strength of the evidence of Mr. Ransome's hair being black and the hair of the body being brown. Miss Avory spoke to me afterward of Poole; how he had sworn that the dead man was Mr. Ransome; how he had declared that the man I had brought to the house was an impostor. I can scarcely recall the impression this information made on me, for the final event followed so rapidly that my memory grows confused in trying to separate the actions and emotions of that bewildering day. But one conviction seized and never left me—that in some way Poole was connected with the mystery that had perplexed and overwhelmed us since the long gone-by fateful month of July.

How Mr. Ransome came to the house on the night following the day on which the inquest was held, and how he died, you have read; the truth is perfectly told in Miss Avory's statement. It was not the ending I could have chosen for the unhappy man; but being done, it was not to be wished undone. It terminated for him a life that would have been worse than a hundred deaths; while it dismissed his wife from an abhorred companionship, and liberated her from a servitude so unbearable that the mere story of it does not convey one fraction of its real anguish.

Had any of the gentlemen whom I had invited to bear witness to the existence of Mr. Cleveland as Mr. Ransome attended the inquest (which, as in the former case, was held at Gardenhurst, owing to the distance at which it was situated from Copsford), it was almost certain that the trick I had practised on them would have been discovered. The dead man, with his sunken, wasted face, his beard, his wild, neglected hair, bore but little resemblance to the man I had introduced; nor was it possible that the change could have been accounted for by the brief time that had elapsed since he was supposed to have come to the house, smooth-cheeked, healthy-looking, trimly attired, decorous in manner and aspect. But the jury knew of this only on hearsay. The witnesses comprising my daughter, myself, Miss Avory, the cook, and the upper-gardener, Walters, all swore to his being Mr. Ransome. The jury were satisfied; people who were not present and did not therefore see the corpse, were equally satisfied; and the funeral, which took place three days afterward, found and left everybody, with three exceptions, perfectly persuaded that the Mr. Ransome whom the four gentlemen had seen and the Mr. Ransome upon whom the inquest had been held were one and the same person.

The three exceptions were my daughter and myself, of course, and Miss Avory. She had guessed 'the truth the moment she set eyes on the real man. The doubts which had long haunted her scarcely needed this confirmation of their accuracy. ·

I consulted with my daughter, and asked her if Miss Avory should be taken into our confidence. We were about to leave Gardenhurst forever. My daughter could hardly find a better, a more faithful, and a more sympathetic companion than her housekeeper, who had proved herself in every respect superior to her position, and who was well qualified to be raised to a higher and more congenial footing.

My conversation with Phœbe resulted in my having a long interview with Miss Avory, to whom I imparted the whole story of my plot. She listened without surprise, without interruption, without demonstration of *any* kind, and when I had ended, said:

"Had I been in your place, I should have done the same thing, sir. We know the accusation to be false *now;* but Mrs. Ransome always knew it to be false."

I told her that she was the only person, unless I excepted Mr. Ransome's personator, who knew of the scheme; and I added that my reason for taking her into my confidence was to prepare the way for offering her the post of companion to my daughter. She was overjoyed by the proposal, and accepted it at once; and it was in this way that she came to reside with us.

I sold Gardenhurst, and quitted it for Tours, at which place we resided for some years after leaving England. There was only one person in Copsford to whom I bade farewell—Mr. Skerlock, whose kindness to my daughter and myself throughout our trying experience I could never forget.

The sale of the estate, however, detained me unwillingly

for some time longer than I wished; and I tried to put the
delay to some use by inquiring where Mr. Ransome had concealed himself during the long months he had been absent
from his home.   But my efforts proved fruitless.   I never
succeded in obtaining any information respecting him, in
discovering a single creature who had met him.

My conclusions, however, in which Miss Avory concurred,
were probably near the truth.   I supposed that he had left
the house in a fit of madness, impelled by his horror of the
threat Miss Avory had implied, and by his serious persuasion that she would contrive to have her threat executed.
The words he had made use of to her proved his belief that,
up to the moment of his conversation with the housekeeper
in the drawing-room, that day when his mother was in the
house, his secret, or, in other words, his madness, was unsuspected.   There was nothing for it, then, but to suppose
that the fear which Miss Avory's professed discovery had
inspired, added to his horror of being confined in an asylum,
had driven him from the house, and kept him a wanderer
during the long space of time that separated his disappearance from his return.   Whether he was actually the man
whom Johnson had followed to Guildford and there lost
sight of it was impossible to guess.   But it was past all
question that the object of his return to Gardenhurst was
to shoot his wife.

On this part of the mystery I can throw no further light;
nor is it possible to state, on more authoritative grounds
than conjecture, that his mother was really sincere in believing that he had been murdered.

And Maddox? and the dead man whom we had found in
Gardenhurst, with letters on him belonging to Mr. Ransome?

Some years had to elapse before this perplexity was
unriddled.

Poole had left Gardenhurst a few days before the return
of Mr. Ransome.   He was away from his work one day,
and next morning Walters told me that he had met him,
and that he had said he didn't mean to do any more work
for Colonel Kilmain.

I was too much harassed and troubled at the time to think
much of this; but I was pleased that the man had dismissed
himself from my service, as I had resolved to get rid of him,
but hardly knew how to do so without implying that his
discharge was owing to his assertion that the man I had
brought to the house was an impostor.

After Mr. Ransome's death and funeral I often thought
of Maddox, and of the dead body we had found, and of the
probable share that Poole had in the mystery; but his absence frustrated my curiosity, and my stay in England being
enforced for a few weeks, I was unwilling to rake up the
ashes of the past by making any other inquiries than those
I was secretly prosecuting with respect to Mr. Ransome's
actions and hiding-places during his disappearcance.

Four years after I had left Gardenhurst I came to London on business for a week. I stopped at a hotel at the
West End, and was one morning reading a newspaper, when
my attention was attracted by some closely printed matter,
headed "Confession of Murder!" I looked down the col-
umn, and saw the name—James Poole.

I began to read.

The confession was to this effect:

A man name James Poole had called at the police office
at Copsford, and asked permission to make a statement.
He said that five years ago he was employed as under-gardener on the estate formerly belonging to Colonel Kilmain,
called Gardenhurst. The name of the footman in the service of the family was Maddox. One day Maddox proposed
that they should rob the house. A quantity of valuable
plate was kept in a safe in the housekeeper's room; he had
taken the impression of the lock in wax, and sent it to a
chum of his in London, who had forwarded him a key made
from the impression. He wanted assistance to carry off the
plate, secrete it, and dispose of it by degrees. Poole lived
in a small cottage away from the town, which offered a good
hiding-place for the booty, and Poole could send small par-
cels of it from time to time to Maddox, in London, who
would convert the silver into money.

Poole consented, and a night for the robbery was fixed

upon. On that night Mr. Ransome left the house. By what Maddox afterward told Poole, who waited for him in the avenue, it appeared that the footman, on quitting his bedroom, was alarmed by hearing some one moving on the landing beneath. He looked over the banister, and saw a figure glide out of Mr. Ransome's bedroom and go downstairs. After waiting a short time, he descended, and peeped into Mr. Ransome's bedroom, the door of which was open, and there found a candle burning. There was nobody in the room. He listened, and heard footsteps outside the house hurrying toward the avenue. Poole believed that Maddox robbed his master's room during this interval, he having afterward heard that the drawers had been ransacked. The dressing-case, of which there had been some talk, he knew nothing about. That, he dared say, Mr. Ransome took away with him. After a long time Maddox came out of the house through the drawing-room window, which he said he had found open, and met Poole, who told him that Mr. Ransome had just gone through the avenue, creeping along in a strange way. Maddox answered, with a laugh, that if he came back, he'd miss a coat, for he had taken the liberty of putting on one of the coats he had found hanging behind the door, so that if his description should be given, he would not be known by his clothes. Fearing that Mr. Ransome might be lingering at the gates, Poole proposed that they should bear the sack containing the plate to the trees, and make for the cottage by the way of the fields. He had armed himself with a bludgeon in case of being met or followed; he declared that the temptation to kill Maddox did not enter his mind until they were among the trees; and the devil whispered that one blow would make him master of the booty in the sack; and, in a moment, he struck his companion with all his strength across the face, between the eyes, with the bludgeon, and the man fell backward with a groan, and expired. Poole left him where he lay, and hoisting the sack on his shoulders, made for his cottage, where he hid the sack, and, taking a spade, returned and buried Maddox, after emptying his pockets, under the trees, near the hedge, where he was found. He did not feel his crime then, nor for a long while afterward. He worked as usual on the estate for fear that, if he left it, he should be suspected of having had a hand in the double disappearance which was puzzling everybody. He further stated that his object in swearing that the body when found was Mr. Ransome's, was that people might believe the missing master had been murdered by Maddox. For the last two years he had been haunted by his crime night and day, and was now a doomed man and forced to confess his guilt. If they doubted his story, let them pull up the flooring of the cottage where he had lived, and there they'd find the sack of plate. The report added that the cottage had been searched, and the sack containing the plate discovered.

That was all.

I had come to England for a week only; but I had to stop a month. For next day I went down to Copsford, identified my daughter's property, and was bound over to give evidence at the forthcoming assizes. The trial was purely formal. The prisoner pleaded guilty and had declined counsel's aid. The duty of judge and jury was therefore not very arduous; the one returned a verdict, the other passed sentence, and the man was hanged.

Since that time I have often been tempted to commit this story to paper; but have invariably been deterred by considerations having reference wholly to my daughter. Those considerations are no longer paramount; the wrong I committed I may now expiate by public confession. Some few, I doubt not, may yet be living who will not be displeased at an opportunity of reading the true history of the strange affair that took place many years ago, which excited much interest at the time, and was long afterward remembered as the Copsford Mystery.

THE END.

Lightning Source UK Ltd.
Milton Keynes UK
UKOW04f1939120215

246203UK00001B/29/P